About

Mary Brendan was alw[...] romance, especially th[...] writes gritty sagas und[...] was born in north Lond[...] and is now back closer to her roots and her adult sons in a village in Hertfordshire. When time permits, she relaxes by browsing junk shops, or by researching family history.

Regency Scandals

Regency Scandal:

The Road to Ruin

MARY BRENDAN

MILLS & BOON

First Published in Great Britain 2021
by Mills & Boon, an imprint of HarperCollins*Publishers* Ltd,
1 London Bridge Street, London, SE1 9GF

www.harpercollins.co.uk

HarperCollins*Publishers*
1st Floor, Watermarque Building,
Ringsend Road, Dublin 4, Ireland

THE ROAD TO RUIN © 2021 Harlequin Books S.A.

Tarnished, Tempted and Tamed © 2015 Mary Brendan
The Rake's Ruined Lady © 2014 Mary Brendan

ISBN 978-0-263-29915-1

MIX
Paper from
responsible sources
FSC™ C007454

Printed and bound in Spain
by CPI, Barcelona

TARNISHED, TEMPTED AND TAMED

Chapter One

'So, you are happy to be travelling all alone, then, Miss Chapman?'

'I am, ma'am,' the young lady answered through lightly gritted teeth. She had been asked the same question, in the same scandalised tone, about five minutes previously. Even before then two other women, and a gentleman, had made similar enquiries, couched in a slightly different way. Each interrogator had in turn professed a concern for her welfare rather than an interest in her business. In the close confines of the mail coach Fiona Chapman could not escape the ladies' judgemental eyes or the fact that they were whispering about her behind their gloved fingers. Only the middle-aged farmer had not returned to the subject of her lack of a companion after his initial remark.

A triumphant blast of the driver's horn proclaimed the rattling contraption to be approaching a watering hole. Miss Chapman's fellow passengers stirred excitedly at the prospect of stretching their legs and having some refreshment. A few minutes later, from under the brim of her chip-straw bonnet, she watched them all alighting. The farmer, who had introduced himself and his wife as the Jacksons, had sat opposite Fiona, accidentally banging his tweedy knees against hers every time the coach leapt a rut. Now he kindly held out a hand, helping her to alight onto the cobbles of the Fallow Buck public house. Fiona gave him a rather wistful smile because he reminded her of her late papa with his wispy salt-and-pepper hair and rotund girth straining his waistcoat buttons. But Anthony Chapman had been older, Fiona guessed, than this fellow. Her father had died of a heart attack a few years ago at the age of fifty-two and the sad occasion had been the catalyst to Fiona making this journey.

'Don't be paying heed to my wife, miss.' Mr Jackson patted Fiona's hand before letting it go. 'She's a worrier and not only on her own account. We've two daughters, you see, so know a bit about what girls get up to.' He slid Fiona a startled look. 'Not that I think you're up to anything, my dear Miss Chapman,' he burst out. 'Oh, no… I wasn't suggesting…or prying…'

'I understand.' Fiona gave him a kind smile, taking pity on his blushing confusion. Of course he thought she was up to something…just as the ladies did. And they were right to be suspicious; well-bred young ladies did not as a rule travel unaccompanied on public transport.

'Our two girls have settled down with their husbands. Good fellows, both of them, and Dora and Louise have each got a brood round their ankles.' He gave Fiona an expectant smile, perhaps hoping to hear that such a blissful ending might be on the cards for her before it was too late.

Fiona knew that it was clear to all but a blind man

that she was not in the first flush of youth and remaining on the shelf was thus a possibility. She'd no claim to beauty, either, and looked what she was: a spinster in her mid-twenties, with a pleasant rather than a pretty face and hair a disappointing shade of muddy blonde. She spoke in an educated way and that together with her neat attire proclaimed her to be not poor, but not rich, either, holding a status somewhere in between the two.

Mr Jackson poked an elbow in Fiona's direction, offering to escort her into the tavern. While they had been conversing his wife and the Beresford sisters had gone ahead and disappeared inside the open doorway. 'Mrs Jackson is alarmed in case any harm is done you, you see. And I have to admit I share my good lady's worries.'

'I'm sure I shall arrive in Dartmouth in one piece,' Fiona returned with a smile that concealed the fact she wasn't as confident as she sounded. She had left London in good spirits despite her mother begging her not to act so rashly. But the further west she journeyed the stronger grew her doubts over the wisdom of her impetuous decision to take up gainful employment in a strange and remote place.

She'd read about Devon and Cornwall in books and studied pictures of wild seas crashing against rugged coastlines. She'd seen images of country folk dressed in plain coarse clothes and shod in clogs. It was all a far cry from the sophistication of the capital city in which she'd been reared. But then Fiona had never really been part of that life, either, preferring to read or paint than attend society parties with her mother and sister. She'd been sure she was ready for a change, even before change had been forced upon her by her papa's demise and Cecil Ratcliff's arrival.

'You're an innocent, my dear, not used to country ways, I'll warrant,' Peter Jackson broke in on Fiona's deep thoughts. 'There are nasty individuals about these parts who'd rob blind a lady…or worse…' he mumbled. 'So you be on your guard every minute. Before we go our separate ways we'll give you our direction just in case you might be in need of assistance. If your *business* doesn't go the way you want you might need a friend…'

Fiona knew the man was keen to know what her *business* was, but she'd no intention of elaborating. She'd been reared to guard her tongue and her privacy in case the *ton*'s gossips concocted something out of an innocent remark. The fact that her destination was the home of a widower was sure to set tongues wagging; she'd thought carefully about it herself before accepting the post of governess to two motherless children at Herbert Lodge.

'Thank you for you kind advice, sir, I will remember it,' Fiona promised, while holding on to her bonnet as a stiff breeze lifted it away from her crown.

Mr Jackson had introduced himself and his wife to Fiona earlier, when they had set out from the staging post in Dawlish. He'd told the assembled company that he and his dear lady were returning home having attended the nuptials of a niece. Miss Beresford and her sister Ruth had also boarded the coach at Dawlish but were due to alight first. Fiona and the Jacksons were travelling further on into Devon.

On entering the tavern Fiona and Mr Jackson found the trio of ladies already ensconced in comfy chairs around the blazing logs and the landlord dancing attendance upon them.

'Now you must come and sit with us close by the fire, Miss Chapman,' Mrs Jackson called from her cosy position, waggling her fingers to draw Fiona's attention.

'The coffee is very good in here…or I could recommend a hot toddy to warm you up?' Peter Jackson suggested, solicitously drawing closer an armchair for Fiona to sit in. 'We stop here quite often, don't we, Betty, and find the fare very acceptable. I had a beef and oyster pie on the last occasion and very tasty it was, too.'

Mrs Jackson sanctioned her husband's review by nodding vigorously. 'I'd take the rum, Miss Chapman,' she gave her verdict on the beverages. 'I'm having a nip. The way that wind is howling down the chimney the afternoon is sure to turn colder.'

The younger Miss Beresford slid forward on the worn hide of her armchair to whisper to Fiona, 'Pardon me, but are you absconding to elope?'

'No! Indeed, no…' Fiona choked on a half-laugh, glancing urgently about to see if anybody had overheard. Only a serving girl was behind, clearing tables of used glasses, and she seemed more interested in gazing through the window and flirting with the stable hand out in the yard. 'Do I give the impression that I might be a runaway bride?' Fiona whispered.

'I just thought it would be exciting if you were… What an adventure that would be.' Ruth Beresford gave a giggle that sounded odd coming from a woman who seemed at least thirty years old.

'The Duke of Thornley's daughter is getting married.' Mrs Jackson had caught the gist of the young ladies' conversation and thought she'd take up the challenge of prising some information from Miss Chapman. 'His Grace is rumoured to be generous and will doubtless treat his estate workers to a feast during the celebrations.'

'Let's hope he serves pheasant, then,' Mr Jackson said drily. 'The Thornley estate is overrun with the creatures—they're a blasted nuisance, squawking and wandering on to the roads,' he explained when Fiona looked mystified.

'A society wedding!' Ruth Beresford breathed, and gave Fiona a wink as though they shared a confidence.

'I shall see if our host has a pie kept warm,' Mr Jackson said, changing the subject. He could tell that Miss Chapman was becoming increasingly embarrassed at Ruth's hints she might be eloping. A similar thought about Fiona's lone journey had run through Peter Jackson's mind, but he would never have aired it. 'Would you like to eat something?' Peter asked his wife while traversing the room to the bar.

'Oh, yes, indeed,' Mrs Jackson said.

'I fancy a beef sandwich if the landlord can rustle up such a thing,' Ruth Beresford told her elder sister. 'Might I have my coins?' Valerie Beresford delved into a pocket and drew forth a little pouch she'd been keeping safe.

Fiona was also feeling hungry. She put her reticule on her lap and opened the strings to find some money. The thought of a beef sandwich, with horseradish, was making her mouth water. She decided to add her order to her companions and take up Mrs Jackson's idea of a rum toddy to wash it down and keep the chill at bay. Now out of the coach and relaxing with her travelling companions, she felt her misgivings about her new life fading away. Everything would be fine as long as she kept her mettle…

'What in damnation are you doing here?' The gentleman's harsh demand suggested an imminent display of anger, but he remained lounging at ease in his chair. A slight hardening in his handsome features was all that attested to his annoyance.

Oh, but he was furious… Becky Peake knew that very well. He hadn't shouted at her, although she knew she deserved it. His voice had been stone cold and so were those eyes that resembled chips of charcoal.

'Don't be cross with me, Luke,' she begged. The landlord of the tavern had shown her to the back room and Becky now skipped over the threshold, closing the door behind her. 'I don't want to be left behind in town when you're so far away.' Approaching his chair, she attempted to perch provocatively on his lap.

But he got up from the table with a muttered oath and walked away.

Becky, always pragmatic, looked at the appetising plate of food he'd abandoned. 'I'm famished…might I tuck in if you've finished?'

He flicked a hand. 'Help yourself.'

Becky untied her bonnet strings, allowing her dark curls to bounce to her shoulders. Loosening the cloak fastened at her throat, she settled down to enjoy the cold meats, springy aromatic bread and cheese piled on to the plate. Suddenly aware that her lover was gazing thoughtfully at her, Becky used the snowy napkin to dab her pout. 'What is it?' She dimpled. 'Do you forgive me? You look as though you do…'

'Well, that depends,' he said with a fractional smile.

'You always overlook my peccadilloes when I'm attentive to you.' Becky sounded confident and got up to sashay towards him, then coil her arms about his strong neck.

'Your impertinence is not a peccadillo and I won't forget it, sweet, but now you're here perhaps there's a way you could make up for it.'

Becky unhooked a few more of her cloak fastenings and shrugged out of the garment. Beneath it she wore a flimsy lemon gown that clung to her curvaceous figure. 'I'll do whatever you say…' she purred suggestively.

'Good…' he growled, removing her arms from about his neck. 'Let me put a proposition to you…'

Chapter Two

'I'm not set against your plan, Your Grace. I simply think that it is too soon to implement it.'

'Pray, why is that?' Alfred Morland, Duke of Thornley, was not used to being gainsaid, especially by persons of vastly inferior rank. But this was no ordinary man. Major Wolfson was a veteran of the Peninsular Wars and had a catalogue of commendations attesting to his military expertise and bravery. The Duke of Wellington, a mutual acquaintance, had recommended the major's services when Thornley outlined his predicament. Since His Grace was in great need of somebody possessing Wolfson's qualities, he was repressing his temper as best he could while glaring at the tall figure standing opposite. He was a fine figure of a man, Thornley inwardly sniffed, and he could believe Wellington's boast that no sane fellow would cross his former aide-de-camp without good cause and serious consideration. But having invested much time and thought in this intrigue the Duke of Thornley very badly wanted to see action as soon as possible.

Since Napoleon had been defeated, Major Wolfson had been hiring out his talents; not that he needed the money—Wellington had let on that the fellow had banked an inheritance from his late grandfather that would make Croesus envious. Apparently, Luke Wolfson liked the life of a soldier and had no interest in settling down as a country squire in Essex. Such a thrill seeker had seemed a prime candidate to carry out the mission, but Thornley could see that the fellow was not at all impressed with his brainchild to outwit a local villain.

Luke took a hearty swallow of the brandy the duke had given him when feeling affable, then placed the glass on the mantel. 'There is a risk to a young woman's life which surely makes rigorous checks imperative before the point of no return.'

'I have engaged you, sir, in the hope that you will deal with any dangers facing the doxy. If you find the task onerous or beyond your capabilities, you have only to say and I will employ another mercenary.'

'In which case you will certainly need to delay while you find someone willing to take on the job and infiltrate the Collins gang.' Luke's lips slanted in a subtle smile as the older man brooded on those salient points, like a bulldog chewing a wasp.

'The woman is being paid handsomely for her trouble…as are you,' His Grace sourly reminded.

'Indeed, and I have promised Miss Peake she will be back in town by next week spending her earnings. I would not want to be arranging her funeral instead.'

'Well, tell the chit she might have a bonus if she agrees to expeditiously get this over with.' Thornley gave the major a dour glance. 'No doubt you expect a

similar favour even though you have already negotiated a princely sum for yourself.'

Luke gave an easy shrug. 'If you want to offer an inducement to accelerate matters, I will, of course, accept
it. But the risks remain the same and I would urge you
to think carefully before pelting headlong into this. If
Collins smells a rat, you might gain nothing and tempt
the gang to persecute you and your daughter. Her welfare is paramount, is it not?'

'It is!' Wolfson's last remark had touched a nerve.
The Duke of Thornley adored his daughter. He knew
she got bored in Devon confined to the house. But
Thornley was loath to let her out much, even with her
maid, to enjoy the local markets and emporiums because of the gang of ruffians infesting the area. 'If the
blackguard smells a rat it will be because Wellington has overdone your praises. I'm paying you to ensure that Collins suspects nothing.' His Grace thumped
down his brandy glass on the desktop, shoving himself to his feet. 'You forget yourself, sirrah, to be lec-
turing me!'

'I was under the impression you would welcome
such advice,' Luke said mildly. 'In fact, I thought you
summoned me here for that very reason.' Their combatant gazes tangled, but Luke could see the duke was
not going to back down and admit his mistake. 'Jeremiah Collins kidnapped, then returned a young dandy
to his family on payment of a hefty ransom some six
months ago.' Luke shot the duke a glance and saw him
redden. 'You knew about that…got your inspiration
from it, I take it.'

'Of course I knew,' His Grace blustered, smarting
under the mild accusation of stealing an idea from the

very person he wanted to see strung up. 'My friend, Squire Smalley, sits at Devizes. The matter had been hushed up to prevent local folk panicking, but obviously not well enough if *you* managed to find out about it.'

A half-smile tilted Luke's moulded mouth. 'Like you, sir, I have friends in high places,' he said quietly.

'Around these parts…and in London, too, for that matter… *I* am high places.' The arrogant statement had barely quit the Duke of Thornley's lips before he regretted it, but Wolfson had too much to say for himself and needed slapping down. 'You are either with me, Major, or against me. Let me know which.'

'My apologies—it seems we are at odds over this. I couldn't in all conscience proceed knowing I've no faith in the scheme as it stands. I've not gathered enough intelligence to safeguard Miss Peake. And in truth I'd sooner not get any woman involved in such peril.' Luke gave a small bow. 'I will have my lawyer return to you the deposit you've paid and deem the contract void. I'll bid you good evening.'

Luke cursed beneath his breath as he strode for the door without a backward glance. He was willing to forgo his fee; he'd not liked the sound of the job from the start and had only agreed to travel to Devon and discuss it with Thornley as a favour to the Iron Duke.

A mission where a knife might be slipped between one's ribs was par for the course in Luke's line of work, but Becky was unlikely to have encountered anything more perilous than an admirer lying in wait for her on an unlit path at Vauxhall Gardens. Luke preferred working alone. He'd discovered a woman accomplice was needed only after he'd turned up in Devon and

Thornley had described explicit details of his plan. Still Luke had bitten back a refusal to get involved out of deference to his old army commander. Over many years the Duke of Wellington had not only been a colleague, but a good friend to Luke, despite the disparity in their ages and status.

Within an hour of concluding his first meeting with Alfred Morland, Luke had contemplated returning to Thornley Heights to express his regrets to the duke and bow out. Then his mistress had unexpectedly shown up, having pursued him to Devon. He'd been both enraged and astonished at Becky's audacity, but had realised that with her love of money and excitement Becky would jump at the chance to get involved in an intrigue. The complication of finding a woman to employ, willing to risk abduction by a gang of smugglers, had been removed; Luke had realised he'd find no better candidate.

Becky was a competent actress; in fact, had she stayed in London rather than tracking him a hundred miles, she would have been treading the boards in Haymarket as Desdemona. Thankfully, Luke had no further need to be anxious whether his mistress would measure up to the job of impersonating a duke's daughter. He wished he'd never mentioned anything about it to her as she'd boasted from the start that she'd make him a fine accomplice. She'd be disappointed to be sent back to town earlier than expected. But sent back she certainly would be now, because her following him had been the final straw as far as Luke was concerned.

As Luke proceeded rapidly towards the huge oaken doors set at the end of a quiet marble hallway the butler materialised to hand him his coat. Before he could quit the house a young woman called his name, causing him to pivot about.

Lady Joan Morland hastened down the last few stairs, causing the ancient manservant to raise a disapproving eyebrow at his master's eldest child.

'Has Papa persuaded you to get our scheme quickly over with?' Joan whispered once at Luke's side. Joan knew her father would be annoyed to find her apprehending his business associate to grill him for information. But as the business concerned her Joan was of the opinion she was entitled to know about it.

'No…he has not,' Luke replied after a moment's consideration. 'We've failed to agree on some matters so somebody else will take over my role if your father decides to carry on with the plan.' He bowed and proceeded to the door.

Joan looked crestfallen to hear the news and trotted after Luke. 'That's a shame—that odious man is becoming a terrible nuisance. He has beaten up two of our estate workers because they informed against him supplying a dreadful batch of brandy that was so strong it killed people. Now everybody is too scared to even mention his name in the village. But we are not! He'll not browbeat us into putting up with his rampage.'

'Has Collins ever seen you?' Luke asked.

Joan shook her head. 'Not as far as I'm aware. I don't go out much… Papa doesn't like it. But I'm not frightened of such as Collins! I've told Papa he won't keep me indoors, hiding away.' Joan sighed. 'Really I'd like to move back to London where it's gay and there's lots to do.'

Luke allowed a slight smile. She might be young—
still a teenager, her father had told him—but she had
pluck.

'Collins's luck will run out. I imagine the authorities must be closing in on him and will apprehend him
quite soon.'

'People in these parts have been saying that for
over a year and still he carries on as he pleases.' Joan
dismissed the notion of an early arrest. 'A Lieutenant
Brown of the coast blockade was found clubbed in a
lane, close to death,' Joan said. 'I think we all know who
is responsible for that! And even more kegs of brandy
have washed ashore this week…so my maid told me…'

Luke gave an answering grimace that conveyed he
wasn't happy to hear the news, but wasn't surprised by
it. 'I have to be going now,' he said, bowing politely
and giving the young woman a smile.

Lady Joan was trying to prick his conscience and
tempt him to again become embroiled in her father's
harebrained plot to lure Collins into the open so he
might be caught. But in Luke's opinion the duke, being
self-opinionated and arrogant, was underestimating
the wily intelligence of his foe. Collins was no fool
and Luke knew he and the Duke of Thornley would
never see eye to eye on how to go about things. Without full control, but with the responsibility of the mission's outcome squarely on his shoulders, Luke couldn't
carry on. Besides he had pressing matters elsewhere
to deal with.

He wasn't looking forward to his meeting with Drew
Rockleigh. But the matter that was threatening their
friendship had to be dealt with before he returned to
the metropolis.

Chapter Three

'Are we travelling back to London later today?'

'You are…' Luke said with a smile. Turning to the mirror above the fireplace in the inn's private parlour, he began deftly folding his neckcloth while meeting Becky's gaze in the glass.

'It's too bad of the duke to cancel this escapade.' Becky bit into her toast with an irritated little sigh. 'He should allow me my fee. I want a new hat.' Becky watched Luke's broad back as he shrugged into his tailcoat.

'He didn't cancel it. I did. And I'll give you some spending cash, sweet, don't worry.' He wasn't the only mercenary in the room, Luke realised, suppressing laughter in his throat. But he preferred mistresses who were content with sensual satisfaction plus a generous allowance that allowed them to shop freely, without demanding more of his time and freedom than he was prepared to give. Unfortunately, Becky had been pushing the boundaries of her role. Their last few visits to the opera had seen her becoming tediously jealous, watching his movements around other women. He knew it was time to end their relationship and would do so when he returned to town. He blamed himself, in part, for her stalking him. He'd told her his destination, if nothing else about what business was taking him to the West Country. But he'd never imagined that she'd have the outrageous cheek to come and check up on him.

'Will you return to Eaton Square soon?' Becky knew Luke was still reining in his anger over her unexpected appearance, so sounded quite meek.

She had never set foot inside Luke's Mayfair mansion. As his mistress she'd never be invited to do so and to pay an impromptu visit would be tantamount to professional suicide. No distinguished fellow would pursue a liaison with a courtesan who proved to be an embarrassment to him and his family. Of course, Becky was aware that Luke had few living relatives to upset. He was an only child and his paternal grandfather had outlived both of his parents, but that was the extent of Becky's knowledge of her lover's history. And she knew better than to chivvy for more details of his past.

Becky liked a challenge and had boasted to her friends that she could hook the 'soldier of fortune' as he was nicknamed. And she had. He'd taken her under his protection and set her up in Marylebone almost five months ago. She'd no wish to see their affair come to an end. Luke Wolfson's rakish reputation and his gypsy-dark good looks were irresistible to Becky. But she was a seasoned paramour and recognised the signs of a man preparing to bed hop. She'd noticed him responding to a flirtatious redhead at Vauxhall in that quietly amused way of his. But Becky wasn't

too bothered about her, or any *demi-rep* who had a
yen for Luke Wolfson. It was another, serious, rival
who had her rattled.

'The London Season will soon be underway...'
Becky tried another tack to discover Luke's plans as
he'd grimaced his indecision in answer to her earlier
question.

'What of it?' Luke asked, turning from the mirror.

'Will you stay permanently in town for the Season?'
Luke had a vast acreage in Essex. Becky guessed he
had a *chère amie* in the countryside to keep him company on his long absences from her bed. But a fat-
ankled milkmaid didn't bother her, either.

'Perhaps... Why do you ask?'

'Harriet Ponting has arrived in town with her
mother.'

'And?' Luke's expression remained impassive as he
straightened his shirt cuffs.

'Oh, you know what's expected of you!' Becky
cried, covering her pretty features with her palms.
'Her mama has been spreading rumours for ages that
you are ready to pay court again to her eldest daughter.'

'Is that right?' Luke murmured distantly, with an
expression that Becky, peeking behind her fingers at
him, recognised. He was letting her know that any
marriage plans he had were none of her concern and
he was displeased that she'd raised the topic.

'I'm going to settle the shot... Pack your things,
sweet, we're leaving...'

Becky watched him exit the room, a sulky twist to
her lips. In her opinion it *was* her concern. She might
not be genteel, like Harriet, but she had plenty to offer

a gentleman as his wife. Becky wanted to join the number of other ambitious courtesans who had dragged themselves up by their bootstraps to marry rich and influential men and bear them legitimate heirs. Harriet Ponting had already turned Luke down once and didn't deserve another chance at being Luke's wife, Becky thought.

'Oh, it's too much to bear!'

'Now, now, calm yourself, my dear,' Peter Jackson soothed his wife. He drew her closer to him beneath the tree so they might get some better shelter from the driving rain.

Fiona had huddled with the Beresford sisters beneath the dripping skeleton of another oak, but as a loud clap of thunder sounded she glanced up warily, through rain-clumped lashes, at groaning overhead branches.

'Perhaps we might be safer out in the open,' Fiona said, pulling the hood of her cloak further forward to protect her face.

'But we will look like drowned rats,' Ruth and Valerie Beresford chorused, shrinking back to the bole of the tree.

'Better that than get struck by lightning,' Fiona pointed out.

She suddenly made a dash towards the coach, which was tilting precariously to one side. The driver and groom were making a valiant attempt to repair the broken front axle, while hampered by the violent elements. The storm had seemed to spring up from nowhere just as they hit a particularly isolated stretch of road. Toby Williams put down his hammer as Fiona

stopped by his side. Wearily the coach driver pushed
to his feet and patted at the nearest horse, murmuring
comfortingly to the sodden beast. The team had bowed
their heads beneath an onslaught that was sending riv-
ulets of water dripping down their flanks and manes.

'It's no use, miss, I'll have to return to the Fallow
Buck and get help. It's beyond my skill to get this accursed thing again up and running.' The driver indicated his young apprentice. 'Bert here will stay by
you all. He can take my blunderbuss for protection.
I think you will all be safe enough in the coach—it's
stuck firm in the mud so shouldn't tip over. You can't
remain out in the open or you'll catch your deaths—'

'Do you think Bert might need the blunderbuss?'
Fiona interrupted, suppressing her alarm. The lad had
not looked too happy on hearing he was about to be
abandoned by his senior and put in charge of protecting the coach's drenched, vexed passengers. Never
had Fiona felt quite so out of her depth amongst these
country folk and the eerie alien environment they in-
habited. She'd only rarely in her life travelled outside
London and its bustling, clamorous streets. Then it
had been to stay with friends who lived in a quaint
cottage in a Hertfordshire village. She wondered if
in these parts ferocious animals living in the woods
might prey on them, so asked the driver though fearful of his answer.

'Well…you never know, better to be safe than sorry,'
Toby Williams prevaricated. He knew very well that
any predatory vermin were human, not animal. The
Collins gang infested the area from Kent to Cornwall,
all along the coast. That group of marauding criminals would think it their lucky day if they stumbled

across a party of defenceless people. Jeremiah Collins would relieve them all of their valuables, and the ladies of their virtue, if what Toby had heard about the vile blackguard was accurate.

What really worried Toby though was that his apprentice, Bert, might be relieved of his life. The lad was only eighteen, but already had a wife and child relying on him. Collins was suspected of murdering a Revenue Man in Rye, but he was a wily individual and had been on the run, keeping one step ahead of the law for more than a year.

It was said that Jem Collins felt he had nothing to lose. He knew the noose awaited him and so was on a spree to create havoc and rake in as much profit as he could before judgement day came, as it must in the end.

'I'll tell the others to return to the coach,' Fiona spluttered through the icy rain pounding her face. As she bolted back towards the copse it ran through her mind that the little group would be bitterly disappointed—as was she—to hear the vehicle couldn't be repaired so they could get quickly under way.

'Shall we keep our spirits up by playing a game? We could sing a song?' Fiona suggested in desperation as the weather outside continued to batter and shake the coach. Despite the drumming of the rain on the roof Fiona could hear Valerie Beresford snuffling in one corner of the vehicle. In the other, Mrs Jackson was crying with more abandon while her husband patted alternately at her hands and her shoulders to try to quieten her.

'Well…this is an adventure…' Ruth Beresford said and gave Fiona a nervous grin.

'Indeed…and one I'd sooner not have experienced.'
Fiona sighed wryly. She was determined to keep buoyant. She was the youngest woman in the party so should
be the strongest, mentally and physically, she'd reasoned. She lifted a corner of the leather blind at the
window and peered at poor Bert marching forlornly to
and fro, the blunderbuss up in readiness to be aimed. It
was getting dark and Fiona feared that before too long
nightfall would overcome them, hampering their rescue team and also throwing her companions further
into the doldrums.

'How much longer will that wretched man be?' Mrs
Jackson wailed. 'I'm frozen stiff and will catch my
death of a cold.'

'Hush, my dear, I'm sure Toby is doing his best. He
will be back before you know it.' Mr Jackson again
rubbed his wife's sleeve in comfort. When he turned
a glance on Fiona his expression showed his deep concern. His wife *was* likely to take a chill from the soak-
ing, as she regularly suffered from such ailments, but
it was the vulnerability of their predicament that was
frightening the life out of the farmer.

Beneath his breath he was castigating himself for
not bringing along a weapon of his own. But he'd taken
this route in the past and was aware that Toby Williams
always kept a couple of loaded guns on the vehicle as
protection for himself and his passengers. An hour or
more ago, Toby had unharnessed the youngest horse
and taken his pistol with him as his own protection on
his gallop back to the Fallow Buck. So now they had
just a young apprentice and a single weapon to protect them all.

'A rider is coming!' Bert had whipped open the

coach door to yell that news over the cacophony of wind and rain.

'Close it before we are awash in here, you stupid boy,' Mrs Jackson screeched, beating away a torrent of raindrops with her hands.

Mr Jackson had grown pale at the news of a stranger approaching, but said manfully, 'Let me sit at the front, by the door.' He surged forward, pushing his wife's quivering figure behind him. 'Hold up that gun, young man,' he ordered Bert. 'I take it you're familiar with how to use it and reload it if the need arises?'

Bert wobbled his head in agreement, looking terrified.

'How many riders?' Mr Jackson croaked. He realised it might be Toby Williams returning, but doubted it was; insufficient time had passed for their driver to have reached the Fallow Buck, let alone return with help.

'Just the one, I think, and I only glimpsed him in the distance, through the trees.' Bert swung about at the unmistakable thud of hooves. The lad had sensed that the farmer shared his fears about what might be about to happen: with a whistle, the approaching stranger might bring the rest of his gang swarming out of the undergrowth once he realised how vulnerable they were. Or it could be a lone highwayman, who'd chanced upon them…

Luke slowed to a trot and cursed beneath his breath on seeing the calamity before him. He was only a short distance from his destination and for a split second felt tempted to ride on towards it. He was cold, wet and hungry, but he knew he could not leave the wretches stranded. The least he could do was offer to fetch help, while hoping to hear that it was already being summoned. A horse was missing from the harness and he guessed one of the coachmen had ridden off on it. The young fellow with the blunderbuss looked trigger happy so Luke supposed he ought to quickly declare himself friend rather than foe. But he understood why these folk would be nervous of strangers; since Thornley's daughter had told him of smuggled spirits coming ashore, he'd heard from other sources, too, that the Collins gang were busy.

At the window of the coach he could see a round male face and a woman's pop-eyed stare beaming cross the fellow's shoulder. Dismounting, Luke gave a friendly salute, then tethered his stallion to a low branch and squelched through mud to the far side of the lopsided carriage to assess its damage.

As soon as the rain had started hammering down, he'd rued his decision to travel, but he'd set out in fine weather that afternoon, travelling west, with the intention of visiting Drew Rockleigh who had a hunting lodge in the neighbourhood. He'd visited the place before, then under far more pleasant circumstances than drew him there now. But if a fight between the two men were unavoidable, then Luke would as soon get it over with than it hung over them both like the sword of Damocles.

He squatted, saw the axle was in two pieces and stood up almost immediately. It would be quicker and simpler to get another coach out to rescue these unfortunates than try to repair the sorry contraption. He sensed he was under close scrutiny and through a blur of water dripping off the brim of his hat saw a woman's indistinct features.

'Where were you heading?' A hand swiped the worst of the wet from his face as he walked closer and got a better view of her. She was younger than he was by some years, although not as youthful as Becky, and her severe expression made her look plainer than she probably was.

'Dartmouth…' Fiona knew to be careful with her answers. They didn't yet know anything about this fellow to be able to trust him. Mr Jackson's instinctive alarm at knowing a stranger was in their midst had made Fiona suspect the area was populated with criminals. 'Where were *you* heading?' she countered, blinking to get a better look at him. When she did focus properly on his lean, rain-sleek visage her breath caught in her throat. He was the most disturbingly handsome man she'd ever seen.

'Lowerton…a village a few miles distant,' Luke explained hoping to put her at ease. One of her hands was holding the open window ledge and he could see the tension in her grip.

'Has somebody gone to fetch help?' Luke angled his head and included the others in the coach in his request for information.

'Our driver has and is expected back at any moment. Would you introduce yourself, please, sir?' Mr Jackson insisted, peering across Fiona's shoulder at him.

'My apologies… Luke Wolfson…at your service…'

'I am Peter Jackson, and this is my wife and these two ladies are the Misses Beresford, and the lady nearest to you is…'

'Miss Fiona Chapman,' Fiona quietly introduced herself as Mrs Jackson's coughing drowned out her husband's voice.

Fiona was feeling more relaxed than she had moments ago. Mr Wolfson had spoken just a few sentences, yet there was something about his tall, imposing presence that now seemed reassuring rather than threatening. He spoke in a calm, cultured way and was dressed in expensive clothes, so would indeed be an odd highwayman—although she'd heard that wily miscreants sometimes garbed themselves in stolen finery to mislead their victims as to their true characters.

She sensed that her fellow travellers were becoming equally glad that Mr Wolfson had happened by. Another man—especially one of Luke Wolfson's age and muscular stature—could only be of help, if he stayed around. Fiona wondered if he might soon bid them farewell now he knew help was on its way.

Bert had trotted around the coach to stand by the newcomer's side and gaze at him deferentially, the blunderbuss pointing at the ground.

'Are you cold?' Luke had seen Fiona huddle into her cloak and pull the hood forward over a bonnet.

'Very cold, sir. We all left the coach earlier so the driver might better attempt to mend it…alas, to no avail.' She gave a small shake of the head. 'Toby Williams has given up on it and returned to the Fallow Buck for a wright with better tools. The trees gave us little shelter from the storm and we all got drenched through.'

'I'd say this one's beyond quick repair and out of action for a while. Your driver should bring out a fresh vehicle.'

A groan of dismay from Mrs Jackson met Luke's bad news about their transport. Fiona nodded acceptance of his verdict, she'd come to a similar conclusion herself.

'I hope that Toby will return very soon.' She glanced in concern at Mrs Jackson as the woman again started to cough.

'I'll light a fire—you could gather around it and dry your clothes while you wait for your man to show up.' Luke frowned at the nearby copse as though assessing its suitability as a shelter.

'Fire?' Peter Jackson left off thumping his wife's back to bark an incredulous laugh. 'I'd like to think he might manage it, but I doubt it somehow.' He gazed at Luke's retreating figure. 'He'll not find a stick of dry kindling about anywhere.'

'It's good of him to try,' Fiona murmured, also watching Mr Wolfson's impressively broad back.

Twenty minutes later the farmer was eating his words. The driving rain had slowed to a drizzle and meekly Mr Jackson followed the ladies towards the trees where a welcoming blaze could be seen. In a clearing, further into the wood than the little party had previously ventured, a fire was steadily taking hold, protected by a tent of evergreen branches that Luke had propped over the flames. Intermittently there was a hissing sound as raindrops slithered through ivy on to glowing embers.

'I should get out of these wet things—I will be laid up for weeks, I know I will,' Betty Jackson grumbled through chattering teeth.

'Stand close to the fire, my dear, to keep warm.' Mr

Jackson took off his greatcoat and used it to shield his wife from view as she shed her sodden outer layers. The Beresford sisters took up position on the opposite side and performed similar tasks for one another, Ruth giggling the while.

Fiona moved away to allow them some privacy while they juggled their coats and shawls and attempted to pat dry their damp bodices. She held out her hands to the flames, but now being a distance from the fire she gained scant benefit from it.

'You're soaked, too—take off your cloak and wear my coat while it dries.'

Startled by the mild command, Fiona stuttered, 'Thank you…umm…for the…kind offer, sir. But it would hardly be fair—it is still drizzling and your shirt will get wet.' She gave Luke a fleeting smile, averting her gaze as his dark eyes bored into her. She turned up her face to the heavens, shivering as a chill mist bathed her complexion. 'I will take this off, though,' she added lightly, removing her bonnet and giving it a thorough shake by the brim to remove rain that had settled in the straw.

Her heart had begun to pound at an alarming rate and confusingly she was uncertain whether she wished he would go away. Yet he'd been unfailingly polite and helpful. Without turning to check if it was so, she was sure their Good Samaritan was still watching her while he removed the long leather riding coat he wore.

'Here…take it… I'm used to braving the elements,' Luke said firmly, settling the garment around Fiona's shoulders before walking off.

With no time to properly protest Fiona pressed together her lips and held on to the garment by its lapels. It trailed on the ground, so long was it, and she tried to hoist it up a bit to prevent the hem collecting mud. The leather held a scent redolent of her dear papa's study. Once the room had been crammed with cracked hide sofas and cigar smoke, but all had been removed and sold since Cecil Ratcliff had married her mother.

Jerking her mind to the present, Fiona quickly slipped out of her soaked cloak and, with Mr Wolfson's replacement garment about her narrow shoulders, she gave her own a good shake to dislodge water from the woollen surface.

The two gentlemen and young Bert were hanging the ladies' outerwear on sticks they'd rammed into the ground about the perimeter of the fire, creating a humid atmosphere as steam rose from the clothes.

Luke returned to Fiona and took her cloak to hang it up.

'I'm famished,' Valerie Beresford moaned, fiddling with the pins in her straggling hair. 'I hope that Mr Williams will bring us back some food.'

'He will,' the absent fellow's nephew assured the company. 'He'll turn up with every possible thing to make you comfortable.'

'A refund on the fare would make *me* easy,' Mr Jackson snorted. 'The contraption could not have been roadworthy to sustain such damage. I took a look at that pothole that overset us. It was not so great an impediment for a vehicle in good order. Highway robbery indeed! These coach companies charge a ransom for inferior transport.'

Mrs Jackson joined her husband in carping about the cost of their tickets and Valerie Beresford added to the debate, making poor Bert sidle off into the shadows, looking chagrined.

Having found a low tree stump that might serve as a seat, Fiona dusted a pool of moisture from it with a gloved palm, then sat down with a sigh to wait for Toby to return.

Chapter Four

'Whereabouts in Dartmouth are you headed, Miss Chapman?'

Having stretched Fiona's cloak over two staves to aid its drying, Luke had strolled closer to her to ask his question.

After a slight hesitation Fiona told him. She realised there was no reason not to. Mr Wolfson didn't seem a person given to gossiping. Besides, they would never meet one another again after today so it was unlikely that any confidence she bestowed would be of note to him. Even were it to be repeated, who would care— apart from a few people dear to her—that Fiona Chapman, spinster, had left home, so unpleasant had her life become, to take up employment as a governess.

She had heard her chosen profession could be quite wretched and lonely. A governess was not quite a servant, yet neither was she a member of her charges' family. Her position fell somewhere in between, and she risked being resented by her inferiors and despised by an employer who'd deem her presence an irritating necessity. And the children might be horrors, too…but

Fiona was confident she was a capable, resilient sort, content with her own company if no other were to be had.

'Are you travelling on business or pleasure?' Luke asked, turning Mrs Jackson's coat so the lining faced towards the fire.

'Business…' Realising she was staring, Fiona dragged her gaze from where his linen shirt, dampened by drizzle, clung to the muscled contours of his ribs. The buttons at the throat were undone and his swarthy skin gave him a dangerously foreign air. Yet he was a refined Englishman, of that she was sure, although he'd disclosed nothing about himself.

Luke turned to glance at her with an elevated eyebrow, wordlessly requesting more information about her plans.

Again Fiona was tempted to tell him and that was odd for she was normally an extremely private person. In one way she found this gentleman's virility daunting, yet his confident, capable manner was soothing too. The dark, romantic atmosphere of flame-daubed shrubbery and the sound and scent of spitting kindling was having a peculiar effect on her, she realised. She felt enchanted, bound to this good-looking stranger's side, and willing to confess her life's secrets until he chose to draw a halt to their conversation.

'I'm on my way to take up a position as a children's governess,' Fiona said.

'You're brave, then, as well as…foolish…' At the last moment Luke had substituted something truthful yet unflattering for the compliment that had almost rolled off his tongue. He'd astonished himself by being uncharacteristically familiar with a genteel woman he barely knew. Fiona Chapman wasn't beautiful… She wasn't even conventionally pretty despite the sweet halo of fawn curls fluffing about her heart-shaped face as the glow of the fire dried her off. Earlier, when her hair had been sleek with rain Luke had thought her a brunette and her features, though small and regular, were nothing much out of the ordinary. Yet something about her was undeniably attractive to him…and he'd almost told her so.

The spell had been broken; Fiona shot to her feet from her makeshift stool, wondering if he was being sarcastic. She was sure he'd been on the point of calling her beautiful and she knew she was nothing of the sort. Fiona came to the depressing conclusion that Mr Wolfson, despite his worthy practical skills, had a shallow side and it was hardly the time or place for insincere flattery.

'Foolish?' she echoed coolly, hoping to convey she wasn't impressed and wasn't playing his game. 'Pray, why do you think that of me, sir, when we barely know one another?' No doubt he believed she'd be better served seeking a husband to care for than children to tutor.

'You're travelling alone, aren't you?'

'I am,' Fiona crisply owned up.

'Then I'll amend what I said and call you *extremely* foolish. These are dangerous roads stalked by violent criminals, as I'm sure your coachman or Mr Jackson must have told you by now.'

'Even could I afford her, how might a lady's maid protect me from such as highwaymen?' Fiona snapped. 'A female dependant would be a burden, not a comfort, to me for I would fret constantly for her safety as well as my own.' Fiona spun away, ready to march off after her parting shot. She'd taken just two steps when hard fingers clamped on her wrist, arresting her.

'And who will you burden with your safety, Miss Chapman? A middle-aged coachman, or a youth unable to handle a gun correctly? A farmer who has his wife to attend to? Me...?'

Fiona twisted her arm free, glaring at him with tawny eyes that held a feral spark. 'I expect no one to look after me, sir. Least of all you. I can care for myself.'

'Can you indeed?'

The murmured words held a soft mockery that brought high spots of angry colour to Fiona's cheek-bones. 'Yes...I can,' she vowed sturdily.

He gave a slow nod, accepting what she'd said, but Fiona knew he was still laughing at her even if he had dipped his head to prevent her seeing the expression beneath his long black lashes.

'Are you going to castigate the Beresford ladies for travelling without a servant?' Fiona demanded. 'Or is it just me you wish to condemn as a nuisance for having the temerity to do so?'

'Just you...'

'And why is that?'

'You are younger and more comely than the other ladies, as I'm sure you're aware. If your coach were held up, you would draw the attention of felons who might want to take more than just material valuables from the women they rob.'

That took the wind out of Fiona's sails and put a deeper blush in her cheeks. She swallowed, said hoarsely, 'You seem to know a worrying amount about it, Mr Wolfson.'

Luke's mouth quirked. 'Over the years I've learned lots of things.'

'I'm sure…and have you now learned not to stop and help stranded travellers, lest they irritate you?'

'I confess I was tempted to keep going.'

Fiona found that admission rather shocking, given that he'd helped enormously, keeping them safe and sound by lighting a fire and drying their clothes. 'It's good to know that your conscience got the better of you in the end, sir,' she said faintly.

Fiona backed off a step, then swung about. A moment later she realised she still had on his coat. Whipping it from her shoulders, she handed it over with a stilted 'Thank you, I've no further need of it.'

This time he let her go and Fiona walked swiftly to where the others were congregated, discussing animatedly how long Toby had been away and when they might expect his return. It was obvious to Fiona that Mr and Mrs Jackson had worked themselves up into quite a tizzy about the calamity, blaming the coachman for all their ills.

As though in answer to Mrs Jackson's prayer—chanted between coughing fits—the sound of hooves and rattling wheels was heard.

Bert leapt up from where he'd been squatting by the fireside. He picked up the blunderbuss and looked fearfully in Luke's direction for a signal as to how to proceed.

Luke had already removed a pair of duck-foot pistols from his saddlebag and his fists were curled about the weapons in the pockets of the leather coat he'd donned.

A moment later Bert was grinning and rushing

towards the road as he recognised his uncle's voice booming out his name.

'I'll bid you farewell now your driver is back,' Luke interjected when there was a break in the frantic conversation batting between Toby Williams and an irate Peter Jackson.

'Our gratitude goes with you, sir,' Peter announced. 'You've done us all a great service.' He held out his hand and vigorously pumped Luke's fingers. 'This fellow has been a godsend in your absence,' he told Toby Williams accusingly.

'I take it you'll overnight at the Fallow Buck?' Luke addressed the remark to the driver.

Toby Williams gave a nod, ignoring the glare he got from Mr Jackson. 'I must thank you, too, for your assistance, Mr Wolfson.' He held out his hand.

Having shaken it Luke bowed to the Beresford sisters, who fluttered about him and offered him their fingers to hold. Mrs Jackson went so far as to give him a motherly pat on the cheek to display her appreciation.

Then he turned to Fiona. 'Miss Chapman...' He gave a slight bow and received a dip of the head in return.

'I hope you reach your destination safely,' he said quietly.

'And I return you that wish, sir,' Fiona replied.

'The name of the family who has employed you is...?'

Fiona no longer felt swayed to tell him anything about herself. She answered him with a concise farewell and a frosty smile before following her fellow travellers towards their replacement vehicle.

But she was acutely aware of every sound behind as

a horse snickered on being mounted. When the slow clop of hooves told her he was negotiating a path away from them through the woods she felt a peculiar lump form in her throat. It was nothing more than anxiety over the loss of him guarding them, she told herself crossly.

Once the luggage and the spare horses had been transferred to the new coach, a confab began with the driver.

'In my opinion it's best that we return to the Fallow Buck,' Toby Williams argued with Peter Jackson, who'd said he wanted none of it. 'It's a treacherous night. After all that rain the road will have washed away and it's not a good idea to travel in the dark in any case, what with villains about.' He'd lowered his voice for the last bit so as not to alarm the ladies.

'And I say we carry on,' Peter Jackson declared. 'We have lost enough time already and my wife needs to be home in her own bed. She's caught a devil of a cold and might need a physician.'

'Yes… I…might…' Mrs Jackson stressed.

'I want to get home, too!' Valerie Beresford wailed. 'I wish Mr Wolfson had stayed and ridden alongside us. I felt safe in his company. Will you not fetch him back, sir?' She tugged on Toby's sleeve.

'I think he turned south,' Bert piped up helpfully.

'Never mind him. He's gone,' Toby said shortly, miffed that a passing stranger had thrown his own role as saviour into the shade. 'We should rest the night at the inn and leave the horses we've no need of. Then start off fresh in the morning in good light and better weather.'

'Mr Williams has a valid point,' Fiona ventured an

opinion. 'We do not want to end up sliding into a ditch in the dark and again be stranded out in the open.'

'We will not be so lucky next time to be saved by such as Mr Wolfson,' Ruth interjected, wringing her hands. She seemed to have given up on craving an adventure and looked as heartsick as her older sister following their misfortune.

'I say we hurry up in getting home!' Mr Jackson loudly insisted as his wife obligingly started to hack and slap herself on the chest. 'The Pig and Whistle is not so far in front of us and we can leave there the nags we don't need.' He pulled out his watch. 'At a strong pace we might reach the inn by half past midnight and will lose no time at all in ending this infernal journey.'

'Very well…be it on your own heads.' With no more ado Toby climbed angrily on to his perch, signalling for his nephew to join him.

Fiona awoke about a mile into their renewed journey, feeling unrefreshed and rubbing her gritty eyes. Although she'd been wretchedly uncomfortable, squashed in the corner of the seat, she'd managed to doze fitfully. Ruth Beresford was snoring beside her, her head drooping on Fiona's shoulder. Rather than wake her and ask her to shift along a bit to give her more room, Fiona chose to put up with her cramped position. The mood in the coach as they'd set off had not been happy and Fiona would sooner suffer sore muscles than more moaning.

At first, her companions had agitatedly watched passing scenery to spot lurking dangers until, one by one, they'd settled back into the squabs. Mr Jackson had been last to succumb to the rocking of the coach and to close his eyes. They were making steady progress towards the Pig and Whistle. Fiona was glad, even if none of the others seemed to have been, that Toby Williams was sensibly taking a slow and easy pace along the perilous road, slick with mud.

When they'd started out Peter had loudly commented that Toby Williams was deliberately dawdling to annoy them all. He had hammered on the roof of the coach in protest. Thankfully, the driver had ignored the command to increase speed and they continued to go along at a sedate pace.

Pinned against the window as she was, Fiona had little choice but to gaze into the darkness dappled by the flickering coach lamps. Patches of vegetation loomed into shape, adopting a yellow gloss before returning to an inky outline as the vehicle lumbered past. Fiona shivered, unable to stop imagining that behind the dense bushes unfriendly eyes were watching them.

For all her proud boast to Luke Wolfson that she could look after herself, Fiona knew she couldn't. She was a fish out of water in this rural environment and wished as dearly as did the others that Mr Wolfson had accompanied them on this dark and lonely road. For some reason that she refused to attribute to simple conceit, she sensed that had she asked him to stay with them, he would have agreed to do so. But they'd parted coolly and now he would be miles distant and close to his destination if not already arrived at it.

He'd said he was going to Lowerton, but she doubted he was a local and lived permanently in a Devon village. Fiona imagined he was, like her, from London and wondered if she'd ever passed Luke Wolfson on a city street. Perhaps, without realising it, she might have bumped into him while out shopping, or when socialising with her sister and their friends at the pleasure gardens. She pondered for a moment on the likelihood, but doubted a meeting had occurred; she would have noticed him even if he'd overlooked her.

And he would have done so. Her younger sister Verity had always drawn the gentlemen's attention and their friends, Elise and Beatrice Dewey, were both blonde beauties, now married to eminent millionaires.

Fiona had been the oldest of their group, but when all the others settled down she had never felt miffed that, being plain-faced, she'd been passed over. Until now. The thought of Luke Wolfson flirting with her sister or her friends irked her and she knew it was ridiculous to feel that way. How could she possibly be jealous of something that hadn't occurred and concerned a gentleman she scarcely knew?

Irritated with the direction of her thoughts, Fiona sighed beneath her breath. She squeezed shut her eyes, hoping to block Mr Wolfson's rugged features and husky baritone from her mind. On opening them again a gasp of shock abraded her throat. She quickly blinked and craned her neck, but the shadowy silhouette she'd glimpsed was lost to her as the coach rumbled on. She tensed, wondering whether to alert Mr Jackson or the driver to what she thought she'd seen, but then if she were mistaken, and there was nothing out there but a deer, she'd just cause more bad feeling. But…it might have been Luke Wolfson who'd felt conscience bound, as he had once before, to help them on their way, her inner voice argued.

Before Fiona could find a solution to her dilemma

the coach juddered as the driver reined in and the silence of a moment ago was shattered by shouts from within and without the vehicle.

Peter Jackson fell almost into Ruth Beresford's lap while his wife, who'd been resting on his shoulder, rolled sideways on to the empty seat. Only Fiona, primed to something afoot, had not tipped from her perch at the abrupt halt.

The sound of a gunshot brought in its wake an eerie silence. Then there was another bang and Mr Jackson flung open the coach door and leapt out, flailing his arms for balance.

The sight that met their eyes was shocking enough to make Valerie Beresford swoon against her sister's breast and Mrs Jackson squeak in fright before shouting for her husband.

Only Fiona and Ruth remained quiet, although Fiona imagined that Ruth Beresford was as terrified as she was at the sight of the grinning felon pointing a weapon at them.

She knew he was smiling from the crinkling about his eyes; the lower half of his face was concealed behind a neckerchief.

'Out you come, then, ladies, let's take a look at you,' the ruffian jovially ordered in a voice muffled by cotton.

'You will not lay a finger on these ladies!' Peter Jackson roared, shaking a fist at the fellow, although visibly perspiring in fear.

Once disembarked, Fiona could see that the highwayman was not alone; his associate was astride a horse a yard or two away. His features were also partially concealed, nevertheless he seemed vaguely familiar to her. And then her eyes fell on a sight that made her groan in dismay. Toby Williams had been unusually quiet following the hold up because he was occupied tending his wounded nephew. Young Bert was lying on the ground and his uncle was crouching beside his still figure, trying to staunch his bleeding.

Ignoring the highwayman's demand that she stay where she was, Fiona spontaneously rushed to help the invalid if she could.

'Is he badly hurt?' she breathed, watching as Toby tried to dry Bert's wound with a handkerchief. But as fast as the fellow turned the wad to find a clean spot, it again became scarlet with blood.

Crouching close to the floor to protect her modesty, Fiona lifted her skirt a few inches and ripped a length of lawn from her petticoat hem. She handed it to Toby who gave her a grateful smile and proceeded to fold it into a thick compress.

'I told Bert to lay down the blunderbuss as soon as I saw 'em flanking us.' Toby shot a baleful glance over a shoulder at the robbers. 'I knew we was done for and no use making it worse than need be,' he added plaintively. 'But the dunderhead loosed off a shot in a panic. Bert never could hit a barn door—now what am I to tell his mother about all this?'

'He will be all right…I'm sure.' Fiona whispered, hoping that Bert, if conscious, would not be depressed by a doubtful inflection in her voice. The boy had his eyes closed and his deathly pale complexion was dreadfully worrying. As his uncle stuffed the linen inside Bert's bloodstained shirt, binding his injury, Fiona tore again at her petticoat to provide a fresh bandage should it be needed.

'You…come here!' the older highwayman barked at Fiona.

Fiona glanced over a shoulder to see that the younger man had dismounted and joined his comrade on foot. They were both levelling pistols, swinging them threateningly between their victims.

The youth suddenly whispered something in his senior's ear and Fiona had an uneasy suspicion that what was said concerned her as two pairs of eyes narrowed on her.

'Come here, you defiant wench!'

The felon strode to Fiona, jerking her upright by the elbow. He propelled her towards the youth who stared at her over the top of his mask.

'That's her, right enough,' the lad said. He turned to whisper in his cohort's ear, 'Running off to be wed.'

'Leave her be, or you'll have me to answer to,' Peter Jackson bellowed. He beckoned frantically to Fiona to come to him, but his efforts to protect her were rewarded with a clubbing from the villainous youth's pistol butt.

Mrs Jackson dropped to her knees beside her prone husband, her wail rending the night air, while the two Beresford ladies began whimpering behind their fingers.

'Let me go!' Fiona wrenched her arm to and fro, attempting to liberate it from a painful grip. 'What is it you want? Money? Here, take it.' With her free hand she pulled from her pocket a pouch containing her coins.

That gesture brought a chortling sound from behind a neckerchief. 'Why, thank you…' the older highwayman said sarcastically, jingling the little bag of money in front of his colleague's face. 'Not enough in there,

I'll warrant, to keep us happy.' But despite his contempt for Fiona's worldly goods, he pocketed it before making a lunge for her. 'Whereas you, my dear, are treasure to somebody I know.' Grabbing her behind the knees, he swung her up and over his shoulder.

Chapter Five

If he'd not been a military man Luke might have mistaken the muffled boom of the blunderbuss for the bark of a deer. As it was he reined in sharp with an oath exploding between his teeth. Another bullet was let loose far in the distance and this time he recognised the retort of a pistol.

The stallion had also heard the sounds and, attuned to his master's need for speed at such signals, required little prodding in turning and flying back the way they'd come over black, muddy fields.

When thirty minutes later Luke reined in his mount its flanks were foamy with sweat. He approached the road cautiously, then, slipping from the saddle, covered the last hundred yards on foot, guided by the stationary coach lamps. Immediately he feared the worst as he heard the sound of groaning and women weeping being carried on the still night air.

His fingers tightened on the duck-foot pistols and his jaw clenched as he glimpsed through the undergrowth the spectacle before him. Having ascertained that the thieves had left the vicinity, he loped onwards, calling out to announce his presence in case a bullet was fired at him.

The Misses Beresford were the first to spot Luke. They scrambled from the coach where they'd been sheltering and rushed to cling to his arms, garbling a version of events.

Peter Jackson was sitting on the ground, a hand pressed to a crust of blood on the back of his head. His wife continued dabbing frantically at his throbbing brow with a rain-dampened hanky and howled curses at the vile cowards who'd caused this mayhem.

But it was the unmoving boy sprawled on the mud with his uncle fussing over him who drew Luke's concerned gaze, but only momentarily. He suddenly realised that the person he most wanted to see was absent. Freeing himself from the spinsters' clutches, he strode to the coach and looked inside.

'Where's Miss Chapman?' Luke demanded, a surge of furious emotion suddenly overtaking him.

'They've taken her.' Peter Jackson shook his head, tears rolling down his face. 'I couldn't stop them, sir—they knocked me down when I tried to…'

'Who was it?' Luke snapped, coming closer, restraining an urge to grab the man's lapels to hurry his answer.

Peter raised his eyes to a flinty black stare. 'There were two of them. They wore masks, but I'm sure that Collins is behind it. The evil blackguard!'

Luke spun towards the driver; Williams was, after all, in charge of his customers' safety, yet he'd offered no explanation or apology for Miss Chapman's kidnap. But the man was distraught and Luke bit back the ferocious accusation he'd been about to let fly.

'I think he's dying,' Toby gurgled, patting Bert's face with increasing strength in an attempt to bring the youth round.

'Get in the coach…all of you…apart from you!' he ordered Toby. 'Help me lift the lad—we'll lay him on a seat and the others will have to squash together on the opposite side. Come, quickly now!' he snapped at Toby in the hope of penetrating the man's shock and galvanising him into action. 'The Pig and Whistle is a few miles away and you can get help for your nephew there. Pray to God we're in time for him…'

The ladies tottered aboard the coach once more, followed by Mr Jackson. Luke and Toby gently lifted the invalid, then settled Bert on the worn upholstery. Although Toby winced on hearing the lad moaning, Luke was gladdened by the sound.

'He has not fallen too far into unconsciousness,' he reassured the driver. Pulling Toby away from fussing over the boy, he slammed shut the door. Once up on the driver's perch Luke took the reins firmly; he didn't want Toby Williams turning them over in a ditch in his agitated state.

'Should you not tie your horse to the back of the coach, Mr Wolfson?' Toby attempted to calm himself and be of assistance.

'No need to worry about him—Star will follow.' Following his concise reply about his finely trained stallion, Luke set the team to a trot. They'd soon cleared the woods and he put the horses to a faster pace, his eyes narrowed and straining to see through the darkness for hazardous obstacles littering the terrain in order to avoid them in good time.

But as much as he was occupied by the job at hand

an image of a woman with fawn hair and golden eyes was in his mind, too. Luke knew that if Collins had harmed a hair on Fiona Chapman's head the dragoons on the smuggler's trail wouldn't be needed after today; Luke would find the lawless bastard and kill him himself.

Fiona felt scarcely able to breathe with a silencing gag wedged between her lips. As she'd been carried off she'd kicked, scratched and yelled so much that the two men had reined in after a short gallop to secure her hands and ankles together. They'd called her foul names while roughly curbing her thrashing. Then, when satisfied they'd quietened her, they'd carelessly flung her across the horse's back in a way that knocked the breath from her body and made her feel faint.

Now her head was hanging low, banging against the animal's belly and she could feel a heavy hand pressing down into the centre of her back to keep her from sliding off the beast. A hammering at her temples was making them ache abominably, but instead of feeling frightened she felt enraged, and instead of self-pity she inwardly berated herself for not putting up a greater fight and making good her escape.

She was incensed to be suffering such treatment. No man had ever raised a punishing hand to her, not even her father when she deserved chastisement. When Cecil Ratcliff's attempts to manhandle her had grown beyond bearing she'd hit him across the face with her silver-backed brush, then packed her belongings shortly afterwards.

But she realised others had suffered, too, at the hands of these ruffians. Young Bert might have perished and Mr Jackson was certain to have sustained concussion at the very least. Fiona felt tears prickle her eyes, not just because of her own uncertain fate, but because of that of her fellow travellers.

The junior highwayman had stolen the spare horses, tethering them behind his own mount, and the drumming of a dozen or more hooves was increasing the pounding in Fiona's skull. Just as she thought she could stand no more of the interminable journey, and of struggling for breath while blocking out her aches and pains, the horse was slowed to a trot.

Moments later they were at a standstill and her captor dismounted, pulling her down so she collapsed to her knees at his feet. Her hair, wound neatly at her nape that morning, had escaped all its pins and Fiona could feel its heavy weight on her shoulders and straggling around her face. She remained still, listening, sensing that others were around. She heard muffled male voices, then boots on gravel. A moment later she was hoisted up by an arm and the blindfold and gag were removed.

By a filtering moonlight Fiona saw that a rather thin, nondescript fellow was gazing at her and that they were standing within the grounds of a graveyard. The bulky outline of a church, its spire soaring against a navy-blue sky, was outlined on a mound some yards away. Closer to her were scattered headstones and box-like tombs topped with eerie sculptures. She suppressed a shiver, not wanting these vile rogues to know that they, or her surroundings, intimidated her.

'Jeremiah Collins, at your service, my lady.' He raised a hand, taking a thick fawn tress between calloused thumb and forefinger. 'Would I be right in

thinking you are the Duke of Thornley's daughter?'
He cocked his head, inspecting her.

'No, you would not, you buffoon,' Fiona snapped,
slapping his hand away from her hair.

Jeremiah chuckled. 'She's the spirit of a highborn
lass right enough, Fred...but I'm not sure. The major
said the jaunt had been cancelled.' He turned to the
senior of the two felons who he'd addressed as Fred.
'She's plain as a pikestaff and older than I expected. I
think you've brought me a pig in a poke, not a ransom.'

Fred Ruff was embarrassed by his boss's criticism.
He ripped down his neckerchief so he might speak
more clearly, uncaring of Fiona seeing his face now. If
Collins were right and he'd taken a worthless woman,
then she'd need to be disposed of. In that case it would
be immaterial whether his victim could recognise him
again. 'Mayhap the major's been playing with us so
he might keep all the money in his own pocket,' Fred
blustered, but shot his youthful accomplice a baleful
look. Sam Dickens had convinced him they were on
to something big and that Jem Collins would praise
them to the skies for using their initiative and abduct-
ing the chit.

'That's her!' Sam also removed his disguise while
wagging a finger in emphasis. He knew he was in trouble if he'd led Fred up the garden path. 'Megan told me
they was talking about the estate and the old duke's
pheasants and a society wedding feast. They said about
this one eloping...whispering they was like it was a big
secret, Megan said.'

'We were! But the Thornley wedding plans are nothing to do with me personally!' Fiona interjected in exasperation. She glowered at the youth. *Now* she knew

where she'd seen him before: he was the stable hand who'd been flirting with the serving girl at the Fallow Buck. 'My name is Miss Chapman and I've journeyed from London.' She realised that the dolts had confused her with a duke's daughter, living locally, and abducted the wrong person. She felt like shouting a laugh. Sooner or later they'd realise their mistake and if her stepfather were approached to pay up for her release the miser would pay them not a penny piece. And her mother had nothing left now of value to offer.

Collins turned towards Fiona, rubbing his chin thoughtfully with thumb and forefinger. 'You might be right, Fred, about the major trying to cut us out of the deal. He might want to pin the deed on us, but keep all the spoils. If that's what he's about, then the fellow will be close by and mad as hell that we've got to this little lady before him.' He circled Fiona, looking her up and down. 'Perhaps you aren't as bad looking as I first thought.' He cocked his head. 'You're Quality, no disguising that, even dressed in these plain things.' He fingered her woollen cloak. 'But then you'd want to look unexceptional, wouldn't you, my dear? Drawing attention to yourself would be a mistake till you'd got your lover's protection.'

'Perhaps her swain would stump up a ransom for her, too,' Sam suggested brightly. 'We could play 'em one off against t'other.'

'He's poor as a church mouse, according to the major's report, that's why she's eloping—because her father won't hear of the match.'

'But maybe we can't trust *his* word!' Sam exclaimed.

'You're all talking rot!' Fiona shouted in frustration. 'And you might as well let me on my way, for I'm expected elsewhere to take up a position in service. The authorities will be on your tails by now. My travelling companions will have reported this outrage.'

'She's no domestic, I'll stake my life on it! She's lying!' Sam triumphantly declared.

'I'm a governess and I'll be missed by my employer. He'll send a search party if I don't turn up,' Fiona warned.

Jeremiah Collins again raised a hand to touch her, but Fiona stepped out of his reach, glaring at him. He looked quite inoffensive with his wispy fair hair and wiry frame. But she sensed that behind his pale eyes lurked a vicious and devious mind and she wanted to be quickly out of his clutches.

'I think you're a crafty wench, accustomed to lying,' Collins said slowly. 'If you're Thornley's spawn, you'll have been deceiving your papa for some time, gallivanting with a ne'er-do-well to escape being married off to an old roué.' He clucked his tongue. 'His Grace won't be popular if he tries to pass off spoiled goods to his new son-in-law, even though the fellow can match him for years. Thornley will pay handsomely to get you back and keep quiet this escapade.'

A glimmer of revulsion flitted across Fiona's features at the idea of a young woman being forcibly married off to an aged lecher. As for the poor young lady being compromised following her abduction by highwaymen… Fiona realised that fate now applied to *her*. If it ever got out that she'd been in the company of three brutes—and of course it would because many people knew of it—then she would be thoroughly ruined.

Collins had noticed her distressed reaction and smiled with nasty satisfaction. 'Come…come… I have sympathy for your plight, my lady, but I've money to make and pleasure to take before I swing on Gallows Hill.' He strode to his comrades to mutter beneath his breath, 'I think she could be Thornley's brat, but if she's speaking the truth, and is Miss Chapman, we've got ourselves a millstone round our necks. There's only one thing to do with such: cut 'em loose and cast 'em in the sea so they sink.'

'Shall we scout around the local hostelries for the major? If he's still in the neighbourhood, that'll tell us what we need to know,' Fred Ruff hissed.

'If Wolfson's still in the vicinity then we won't need to go looking for him, he'll find us,' Collins answered with a sly grin. From the two meetings he'd had with Major Wolfson, Collins had gauged he was not a man to cross. But then Jem Collins could match any man alive for ruthlessness. Nevertheless, he was regretting agreeing to do business with him.

By straining her ears Fiona could just catch snippets of their conversation. She heard the name Wolfson and a hand squeezed at her heart. 'Are you talking about Luke Wolfson?' she burst out.

Three pairs of eyes were swung in her direction.

'What do you know of the major?' Collins demanded.

'Nothing… I've just heard his name before,' Fiona murmured, feeling as though she'd taken a blow to the stomach.

So, *the major* they were talking about and Luke Wolfson were one and the same. *He* was the fellow these thugs thought had crossed them in a deal they'd struck to kidnap the Duke of Thornley's daughter. But when Wolfson had come across their broken coach he'd had the intelligence to deduce that Fiona Chapman was who she said she was. No doubt he'd gone after the *real* prize…wherever the poor wretch might be.

Now she realised why he'd paid her such attention: Luke Wolfson hadn't been flirting with her, he'd been assessing her and, unlike these fools, had come up with the correct answer. She supposed it had been rather good of him to warn her about the hazards for a young woman travelling alone! He was preparing her for villains such as himself who preyed on female victims.

Suddenly Fiona felt very alone and frightened. From the moment these thugs had hauled her away from her travelling party she'd harboured a tiny hope that Mr Wolfson would somehow discover what had happened to her and ride to save her from these savages. But he was no better than them and he'd provide no service she'd welcome! Of that, Fiona was certain.

From the age of sixteen, when she'd left her home in the countryside to make her fortune, Becky Peake had regularly used payment in kind for things she wanted but couldn't afford. But rolling in hay with a yokel for a ride on his cart was a new low for her. She felt ashamed of herself and wished she'd not spent all the cash Luke had given her on a fancy hat and a night of gambling at the Red Lion at Exeter. Then she might have had the wherewithal to hire a tired nag, or a two-wheeled gig, to follow her lover without resorting to soliciting.

Luke had paid for Becky's coach fare back to London but, on impulse, she'd disembarked before the vehicle had travelled east far enough to cross the county line. Her need to stay close to her lover, lest he replace her with somebody else, was lately always on her mind.

Becky doubted that she would ever love Luke Wolfson in that selfless way her mother had adored her father, but she did know that she craved his company. Major Wolfson was the most attractive and exciting man Becky had ever known; she wanted to be permanently in his life, sharing his adventures and his riches. She fantasised that they would have a brood of beautiful children and then, if the fire in her blood was quenched by the passing of the years, she'd settle into a comfortable life in Essex as lady of the manor with five handsome sons about her silk skirts, and her husband providing her with every little luxury that her heart desired.

'Take you on a foo more miles if yer like.' A gap-toothed fellow shattered Becky's delightful daydream with his coarse country brogue.

'Here will do very well, thank you,' Becky replied in her crispest tone. She continued tying her garters and ignored the farmer grinning at her while he buttoned his trousers. She brushed down her dress and stood up, picking bits of straw from her bonnet.

A moment later Becky was at the barn door and peeking through a crack. Nobody seemed to be around so she slipped out and sashayed off towards the village square, tying her new hat in place as she went. She was hoping that Luke would still be lodging at the same inn; she knew he'd planned to see a chum before heading home. He'd not told her any more about it, no doubt chary of her turning up unannounced at the fellow's home. Becky knew she might have been tempted to do so, too, in her obsession with Luke. But she was sure he'd again put up at the King and Tinker on his way back so she headed in that direction to wait for his return.

'How is he, sir?'

Luke had been saddling up in the stable yard of the Pig and Whistle when he spied the doctor exiting the hostelry. He had quickly intercepted the physician, keen to know how young Bert fared now he'd been ensconced in one of the inn's bedrooms.

'I've dosed the patient with a sleeping draught to aid his recovery.' The doctor gave a grim shake of the head. 'His wound is clean now and luckily the bullet passed through. Bert Williams is young and strong, but he's bled a lot.' He sighed pessimistically in conclusion, then climbed aboard his trap and flicked the reins over the pony's back.

Luke was about to swing into the saddle when he saw Mr Jackson and Toby Williams coming towards him at quite a pace. He hesitated and patted the flanks of the replacement beast he'd hired. Star was limping a little after his punishing ride and Luke didn't want to risk a lame horse hampering him in his search for Fiona Chapman.

'What are we to do about…you know…?' Mr Jackson blurted in a whispering hiss. 'My lady wife and I cannot in all conscience proceed on our way and just ignore the fact that Miss Chapman has been kidnapped by those beasts.'

'I know, sir, but I've asked you to give me a day or so to find her,' Luke replied in an equally muted tone. 'You and I both know that an unmarried young woman's future would be blighted for ever by such a tale becoming common knowledge. And it will, if the authorities are alerted to her abduction. Better I try to get her back and help her to reach her destination. Then she might pick up her life where it left off before this disaster befell her.'

'But the poor lass is bound to be in hysterics and will give the game away herself,' Peter Jackson argued.

'She put up quite a fight, as I recall,' Toby Williams pointed out, sounding in awe of the young woman's pluck.

Luke gave a wry smile; he recalled very well his chat with Fiona Chapman and he sided with Toby's opinion: she was no pushover and he doubted that any lasting harm would be done…as long as he reached her in time. He knew how Collins's mind worked: he was a businessman above all else and if he thought he could turn a profit from Fiona Chapman he'd try to sell her back to her family. To do that successfully, he'd need to return her intact. What was puzzling Luke was the reason he'd taken her in the first place. The other travellers hadn't had any valuables stolen and he found it hard to believe that Collins would think Fiona's ransom might turn a tidy sum. From her appearance, and her need to seek employment, her family connections were modest, Luke reckoned. And if Collins sought simply to use her for his own amusement… Luke's jaw clenched and he suddenly mounted the horse.

'Blight the poor lass's life, good 'n' proper, it would,' Toby stated bluntly. He was feeling better now his nephew was abed and sleeping soundly. 'My young niece was led astray by an older fellow…married her, though, he did…albeit with a gun at his back.'

'I don't think it's seduction or a wife Collins is after,' Luke said drily. 'Give me a day or two and I will return with Miss Chapman, God willing.'

Chapter Six

Fiona knew she had only one chance at escaping her dank stone-cold cell that reeked of mildew. If she failed to make her getaway the Collins gang would thereafter guard her like hawks. Also, they might kill her for making the attempt, thinking her too much trouble to contend with. Eventually her captors would realise she was who she said she was and they'd want to quickly rid themselves of her.

She was thankful they had not yet discovered that she had little monetary value. Nevertheless Fiona didn't relish the idea of being stuck with this motley crew for weeks while they tried to negotiate a price for her return with her stepfather. They'd certainly dispose of her rather than drag her along while trying to outrun their pursuers. Cecil Ratcliff would enlist the help of the authorities rather than part with any cash to have her discreetly returned. Her mother might weep and protest about the cost to her daughter's reputation should the disaster be broadcast, but Ratcliff wouldn't care about that.

Fiona shifted position on the straw pallet on which

she was perched. It had served as a very uncomfortable mattress last night, not least because she feared beetles were also using it as a bed. She had sprung up at one point when the night was at its blackest, having sensed a creature on her arm. Fidgeting to and fro, she studied the bed for movement, wondering if she'd been bitten by bugs.

Her hands had again been tied, but her feet were free and the gag left off, no doubt because her screams would go unheard in this isolated spot. After her capture yesterday she had been dragged, kicking, into the derelict church and down into the crypt to be locked in. But she could hear the gang members coming and going. Fiona's greatest fear was that her gaolers might all be shot and killed by the dragoons without giving her location, leaving her to starve to death in her grisly prison. Fiona knew she'd sooner perish quickly than endure that fate and it renewed her determination to flee for her life at the first opportunity.

She started on hearing footsteps on the stairs, then the key struck the lock and she knew Sam was bringing her supper. He would untie her hands so she might eat, as he had earlier, when bringing her a lump of greasy pork she'd been unable to stomach. But he'd not been so squeamish; when he'd returned to again fasten her wrists, he'd gobbled up the meat before leaving her alone.

The youth sauntered into the room and put down a plate of bread and cheese on the rickety stool below the window. The single-square pane was set high up and looked far too small for Fiona to slip through, even had she managed to reach it to break the glass. Earlier, she'd used the three-legged seat to stand on to test whether it would be possible to wriggle out into the graveyard. It had proved a fruitless exercise; the tempting glimmer of light had remained beyond her stretching fingertips.

Awkwardly Fiona pushed to her feet by using her clubbed fists. The muscles in her legs were horribly stiff and unobtrusively she tried to ease them by flexing them beneath her skirts. In a moment, if luck were with her, she must run as fast as she could.

Alarmed, Fiona saw the youth turn towards the door without approaching her. 'What about my hands?' she burst out. 'I cannot eat like this.'

Sam turned back, looking churlish. His master was above stairs and had told him to take no chances with the sly minx. 'You can if you're careful...see...' Sam mimed having his wrists tethered in front of him and picked up a crust, taking it to his lips.

'Please... I cannot... I have pins and needles because the twine is too tight.' Fiona raised her arms. 'See how white my hands have become.'

Sam tutted impatiently, then, after a moment of pursed-lipped consideration, his conscience got the better of him and he drew a knife from a pocket.

'Thank you, Sam,' Fiona said in a shaky voice. 'You're kind...not like the other two...'

'Don't try to sweet-talk me.' Sam spat. 'I can be as tough as me pals. Don't go thinking different.'

Fiona nodded to humour him. 'I can see you're a strapping lad. Megan is your sweetheart, then?' She held out her wrists for the binding to be cut, hoping that if she kept him talking she might eventually win him over and make him see how stupidly he was acting. Then he might not only free her hands, but assist her in escaping. He looked to be no more than seventeen, yet he was risking a premature and degrading end on the gallows by associating with Collins.

'Ain't telling you nothing, so keep quiet.' Sam slashed the rope.

'Megan will be distraught if you're sentenced to hang,' Fiona persisted.

'I said keep quiet!' Sam snarled and raised the knife to touch her throat.

Fiona sadly realised he might be young, but he seemed as steeped in evil as his older colleagues. She stole a glance at the oil lamp on the floor. If she could just get him to turn his back for a moment she'd swing the stool at his head and dart outside. She didn't want to hurt him, but then she feared that Sam Dickens would have no qualms about hurting her…perhaps fatally…

'Would you light the lamp for me? It's getting dark.' Fiona indicated the brass implement on the cold stone floor opposite the stool.

Sam muttered in irritation, but drew forth a tinder-box from a pocket and crouched down. Silently Fiona lunged for the stool, sending the plate of bread and cheese flying as she swung the wood with all her might at his bowed head.

Sam grunted and toppled forward, but beyond that Fiona didn't tarry to see what damage she might have done to him. She flew out of the door and up the narrow winding stairs, holding her skirts high to prevent them tripping her up. She could hear Sam groaning a vile curse after her, but Fiona plunged on, the thud of blood in her ears making her deaf to any more of his abuse.

She cried out in despair as she felt a hand manacle her arm, dragging her up the final steps. Throwing back her head, she gazed in shock at the swarthy features of Luke Wolfson. But a glimmer of hope that he'd come to rescue her was soon quashed.

'If this is the best you can do, Jem, I'm astonished you're still at liberty. Can your men not even keep a woman under lock and key?'

Luke pushed Fiona in front of him, but she sensed that his callous fingers held a secret tenderness.

'She's a spirited lass…these high-born women are bred to it.' Collins was seated on the end of a pew and swigging from a bottle. Outwardly he appeared little bothered by his captive's attempt at escape. Inwardly he was seething at Sam Dickens's incompetence and the fact that this man had witnessed it. Jem was proud of his reputation as a ruthless villain and resented being shown up in such a way. 'She's been too spoiled by her doting papa, I'll warrant. Though I imagine the duke might take a lash to her back when next he sees her.' Jeremiah wiped his mouth with a hand. 'This brandy is not as good as the last lot we took off the Frenchies.'

'She's not Thornley's daughter, I've told you that,' Luke said mildly. 'Lady Joan is not yet turned twenty and this one is probably half a decade older.'

'I'm almost persuaded to believe you…' Collins's tone hinted that he believed the opposite were true. 'She says she knows of you.'

'She does, but not as well as I'd like to know her,' Luke said with deliberate lust roughening his voice. 'We met on the road when the carriage she was travelling in came a cropper.' Luke tilted up Fiona's chin with a dark finger. 'She's Fiona Chapman and on her way to be a governess.'

Fiona jerked her face away, but not before she'd

given him a ferocious glare from amber eyes bright
with despising. Accusations were circling her mind, but
much as she was tempted to spout her opinion of Luke
Wolfson's vile character she sensed it best to appear
subdued and focus on her escape. She'd not yet given
up on renewing her attempt to flee these criminals.

'You'd tame her, would you?' Jeremiah Collins
snorted a laugh, having seen Fiona's defiance. He
stroked his chin in that thoughtful way he had. The
major had given the same name as the woman had herself, so Jem knew that Ruff and Dickens had brought
him a hapless impostor. But it seemed she interested
Wolfson or why would he bother coming after her?
Miss Chapman might yet turn him a profit, Collins
realised.

'If you're right, Major, and she's a governess,' he
purred, 'of what use is she to you?' Collins got up
and sauntered closer to the couple. 'She's no beauty
and thin with it. I heard you've brought a pretty little
ladybird with you to warm your bed at the King and
Tinker.' He gave Fiona an insultingly thorough look.
'She has a certain buttoned-up charm, but I can't see
a rake like you falling for it.'

'I like *unbuttoning* prim spinsters,' Luke murmured,
tightening his grip on Fiona who'd spontaneously stiffened on hearing Collins's description and Luke's lewd
response. 'The sport's in the chase and the conquest,
not in bedding jades.'

'Where's that vicious bitch!' Sam had crawled on
his hands and knees up the stairs and now staggered to
his feet, blood dripping from his skull on to his shirt.

Instinctively Fiona shrank back against Luke as
the youth's lips were flattened against his teeth and

he lunged at her. Luke immediately floored Sam with one easy punch.

'Come, have we a deal?' Luke sounded impatient. 'You might as well let me take her. The people she travelled with have reported the incident and you'll have abduction and rape added to your crimes.'

'And so will you, by the sound of things, Major,' Collins returned smoothly.

'No woman's accused me of force and neither will this one when I've finished with her.'

Collins burst out laughing. 'Take her, then, before I do. You've given me a hankering for Miss Chapman with such rousing talk.' He leered at Fiona and wound a long loose tress about his hand, then gave it a possessive tug.

'Leave her be, she's mine,' Luke said, deceptively mildly.

Fiona sensed the atmosphere between the men change and held her breath, wondering if they were about to fight over her. But Jem slowly withdrew his fist and her hair spiralled to her shoulder in a soft ringlet he'd formed.

'When you've done with her, Wolfson, let me know and perhaps I'll buy her back…at a reduced price, of course…' He gave Sam a punishing kick as he passed his sprawled body. 'What of the Thornley business?'

Luke shrugged. 'I think her father's got her under lock and key until he walks her down the aisle. I'll take a bottle of that brandy off you, too. Put it on my bill.'

'Fred will get it for you,' Collins said. 'Are you staying in these parts?'

'Who knows?' Luke replied. 'I go where the money takes me.'

'A man after my own heart.' Collins chortled.

'And where are you headed?' Luke asked.

Collins shrugged. 'To the beach to collect some kegs, then, like you, Wolfson, I'll be following my next fortune.'

Luke smiled but he knew, as did his adversary, that neither of them trusted the other and thus would not disclose a single word about their plans. Suspicion was as thick as smoke in the air. Luke drew from his pocket some cash and tossed the notes on to the pew, keen to get going before Collins's mood changed.

'That should cover everything.' He pushed Fiona in front of him towards the exit.

'Boss says you want one of these.' Fred Ruff had been busy packing barrels of contraband spirits into a freshly dug grave atop a grassy knoll. Some of the liquor had been diluted and decanted into bottles, ready to be supped by the gang. The brandy in the kegs was so strong that it could kill a man if drunk neat. Instances had been recorded of poor wretches, ignorant of the danger, made mad or suffering a painful death from imbibing smuggled brandy straight from the barrel.

The bottle that Fred handed over hadn't been diluted, on orders from Collins, and he turned away, grinning, as Luke stuffed the poison into his saddlebag.

Unceremoniously, Luke girdled Fiona's slender waist with ten firm fingers and swung her up to sit sideways on his horse. Immediately he mounted behind her before she'd time to spring down.

Luke set the chestnut to a trot, weaving between graves till he neared the lychgate, a controlling arm about Fiona's middle. He dipped his head to hers in a way that might have seemed amorous to his audience.

But though his lips hovered inches from her small ear his instruction was not sweetly voiced.

'Be still! I've come to get you, not hurt you, you silly chit!' he growled.

Fiona bristled at that. Silly, indeed, she thought, to have ever imagined it had been a boon to have this fellow cross her path! She tensed in his arms as a thumb on her ribs shifted leisurely to and fro, perhaps involuntarily, perhaps in a crafty caress. She knew it would be easy to succumb to his warm strong body and nestle into him. And, as he'd boasted just a short while ago, Luke Wolfson considered himself a master of seduction. Fiona craved somebody to trust and help her out of this dreadful mess, and he'd seemed sincere earlier when protecting the coach passengers. But then she'd not been alone with him and as vulnerable as she was now! Other people had been present and so had loaded weapons ready to be used to see off marauding strangers.

Luke Wolfson and Jeremiah Collins were colleagues, she reminded herself. With her own ears she'd heard them discussing their business deals. They'd plotted to kidnap a duke's daughter and she knew if *the major*, as Collins had named Wolfson, were ready to risk the consequences of mistreating a powerful aristocrat's child, he'd have no qualms about ill using her before discarding her.

Once out of the graveyard Luke urged the horse to speed up along the lane, but still Fiona sat rigidly on the animal, arching her spine to put space between their torsos.

'You'll fall off like that.'

His mild amusement put her teeth on edge, but she

refused to comment or tussle with him when he suddenly jerked her back against his chest. She knew he was quite aware of her intention to escape him at the first opportunity. So she would need to seem compliant, even resigned to her fate if she were to outwit him. Luke kicked the animal to a faster pace and it leapt forward, causing a rush of chilly air to spike Fiona's cheeks. She turned her face into his coat to protect it from the chafing cold. *Jump and run* was the phrase pounding in her head in time with the beat of four hooves. She'd sooner take her chances alone than in the company of this rogue. The main roads were dotted with cottages and taverns and Fiona was confident she'd stumble across a place where she might seek help from decent people.

Luke could feel the tremor in her. He knew he should pull up and do his best to reassure her that his intentions were honourable. But it wouldn't be easy quickly convincing her he wasn't in league with Collins after what she'd heard. And he didn't have the time for a lengthy explanation about his work for the Duke of Thornley. Luke knew that presently his priority must be to get as far away from the smugglers' base as possible.

The gang consisted of more men than those currently congregated at the church that served as a temporary camp and contraband store. Jeremiah could call on a dozen or more fellows to boost his gang's numbers, if need be. Luke wouldn't put it past the treacherous devil to renege on the deal they'd just made. Collins might send men after them to snatch back Fiona, then God help her…

The horse responded to his renewed prodding, but it wasn't an Arabian like Star and lacked a thoroughbred's agility and pace. He knew he couldn't rely on a tired farm animal to outrun any pursuit.

After a mile Luke turned abruptly off the highway and headed into undergrowth. If Collins did intend to double-cross him he'd send men along the main routes. Luke knew he didn't have enough ammunition in the duck-foots to hold off a sustained attack so would need to rely on evasion rather than aggression to get them to safety.

Fiona chewed her lower lip, her heart pounding. There was no reason why he should divert from the beaten track if his intentions were to help her rather than himself. She knew the further into the woods he took her the more nefarious must be his intentions and the more difficult it would be for her to find her way back. She could twist about and demand he tell her what he was about...or she could act unsuspecting, then catch him by surprise with a distraction that would allow her to spring down and flee.

His arm had loosened about her, but she had previously felt the muscle beneath his sleeve and knew it would tighten like a vice the moment he sensed her pull away.

With an inner prayer, and feeling guilty for doing it, Fiona kicked backwards into the horse's flank. The beast reared and, as she suspected, Luke's instinct was to control the animal rather than her.

Beating at his face and chest with her fists, she managed to wriggle and squirm to the ground. She ended, with a thud, on her knees and, though winded, was soon on her feet again. Ignoring his harsh command to halt, she bolted, her skirts held high as she leapt over scratching brambles and undergrowth. She stumbled between dense dark bushes, carrying on swerving to and fro till her burning lungs felt they might burst and she could go no further. Clutching at the gigantic bole of a tree, she looked up and glimpsed through whispering leaves a silver disc strung with cloud. She listened, straining her ears for sounds of pursuit, but could hear nothing but the raucous rasp of breath in her throat.

After waiting what seemed like an hour, but was probably less than fifteen minutes, she slowly slid her back down the tree trunk till she was squatting close to the ground. She pulled her cloak tighter about her and settled her chin down low into its woollen folds.

She wondered if he'd gone off and left her, thinking her not worth pursuing. Luke Wolfson had a woman ensconced at the inn, so Collins had said. Despite his boast about liking a chase, Fiona reckoned the major would take his pleasure with the waiting jade rather than exert himself further. Fiona let out a quiet sigh, settling her back against the rough bark of the tree. She'd no chance of finding her way back to the road in the dark so she'd need to wait till morning before making a move.

Chapter Seven

'Right… I've let you sleep for ten minutes, now it's time to go…'

A rough hand shaking her shoulder brought Fiona awake with a start. Her head jerked away from her clasped hands, pillowing her cheek on the forest floor. A second later she realised her nightmare had become reality, but her scream had barely quit her throat when cut off by five hard fingers.

Luke had sat beside Fiona, curled up on her uncomfortable mould bed, for more than half an hour. He'd watched her small features twitch and her brow crumple as she dreamed of something unpleasant…him, he'd guessed. Still, he'd not the heart to wake her till the nightmare worsened and she'd moaned in a way that reminded him of Becky in the throes of passion. So he'd sprung up, knowing it was time to leave.

He could easily have outrun Fiona and captured her within a few minutes but he'd not wanted to lose their transport. The untrained nag would probably have bolted had he let go of it. Without a horse—even one such as the aged chestnut mare—they'd be yet more vulnerable to Collins's malice. Stupid as the thought was, Luke was beginning to wish he'd brought Star along, lame or not. But that stallion had been with him for two years and served him faithfully. He'd no wish to see a fine beast that suited him perfectly, irrevocably damaged...whereas this shrew was testing his patience to the limit and he was sorely tempted to go and leave Fiona Chapman to her own devices.

Dragging Fiona to her feet and ducking her small fist, he snaked an arm about her waist, tugging her spine back against him to avoid being kicked on the shins again.

'For pity's sake!' Luke snarled in exasperation, knowing that to quieten her he'd need to get rough. He thrust her fighting form away with such force that she collapsed to the musky earth. He followed her down, barring her escape by pinning her torso on the dirt with one arm braced across her bosom. His hand went to her face, steadying its wild movement so her eyes, still heavy with sleep, were level with his.

'Shall I take you back to Collins?'

That dreadful threat brought an instant response. Fiona gave a quick shake of the head, terrified that he might be mean enough to do such a thing. She'd fallen into such a deep, troubled slumber that she'd not heard him approach and couldn't yet force her wits to function properly. But she was alert enough to know she still didn't trust him. She was conscious, too, of the familiar scent of his riding coat and the long muscled body imprisoning hers. Her lips parted as though she'd say something, but the words jumbled into chaos in her mind.

'Do you want my help to carry on to Dartmouth so you might take up your employment?'

Fiona blinked, wondering why he would offer to do that. It was certainly the better of the two options so she nodded slowly, humouring him. By the filtering moonlight she saw his eyes drop to her parted mouth and quickly pressed together her lips, looking away.

'Well, Miss Chapman,' Luke said huskily, 'let us go then before Collins's men turn up. I've an inkling they might and they've nothing good in store for either of us.'

Fiona allowed him to take her elbow and haul her to her feet. He released her and went to the horse tethered to a branch. She darted a scouting glance about, teetering on her toes and unwittingly betraying her intention.

'Please don't,' Luke said, barely sending her a glance. 'I'll catch you and tie you up because you're becoming tiresome…'

'I'm becoming tiresome!' Fiona echoed in an outraged whisper, abruptly finding her voice. The muzz in her head had cleared and she marched towards him, but he continued seeing to the horse rather than paying attention to her. 'I've been abducted, gagged and bound, fed disgusting scraps and threatened with… with vile abuse…'

'You can't blame me for any of that,' Luke drawled.

'If my memory serves, I think I can, sir!' Fiona fumed, incensed by his nonchalance.

He turned and looked at her through the patchy, silvery light. 'You're questioning my seductive skills?'

Fiona moistened her lips. She sensed…hoped…he was being humorous, but was in no mood for levity.

'I'm questioning everything about you, Mr Wolfson,' she retorted hoarsely.

'And with good cause, but I've no time to explain any of it right now. I didn't have to come and get you, you know. I've business to see to and could have let the authorities take on the job of searching for you.'

'Why didn't you, then?' Fiona demanded, hoping to corner him into admitting his guilt and association with the gang.

'I had an idea where they'd taken you and that things might turn extremely unpleasant for you, my dear. The dragoons have been after Collins for more than a year—still he's at large because they've failed to catch up with him. By the time they found you, you'd have been dead…or wishing you were…' Luke gazed at her. 'Collins wanted a profit from snatching you, even after he'd accepted it was a case of mistaken identity. He'd not have harmed you until he'd approached your family for a ransom and been unsuccessful. I'm guessing that as you're seeking employment, your parents are not financially well off.'

'How astute of you,' Fiona breathed, then felt foolish for resorting to sarcasm. He'd only pointed out a glaring truth. 'And why would you feel responsible for rescuing me, Mr Wolfson?'

'I'm damned if I know,' Luke muttered.

'And how is it that you knew where to find me?'

'That's one of the questions I've no time to answer right now.'

'But I'd like an answer, please. As you've correctly guessed, there's no reward on my head. If you think because you seem a well-bred ruffian you stand a better chance than Collins of prising cash from my stepfather, I can assure you, you won't. I'm no use to you, you know,' Fiona taunted.

'I wouldn't say that…' Luke returned softly, a dangerous glint in his eyes letting her know she insulted him again at her peril.

For a moment Fiona felt unable to avoid his black diamond gaze. She knew what *use* he'd hinted at and was glad that the dusk hid the blush warming her cheeks. Suddenly she sensed how very alone and lost she was. Canopies of branches overhead swayed, giving tantalising glimpses of the open sky, but all around thickets hemmed her in. She was completely at this stranger's mercy.

'You're a boost to my eternal salvation, my dear,' Luke muttered on a short laugh that shattered the tension between them.

Fiona was not fooled by his self-mockery or the intention behind it; he'd let her know that he'd sooner keep her docile, but if she challenged him he also held the power and the means of retaliation, should he choose to exercise those.

Abruptly he lifted her on to the mare, not with swift mastery as he had before but with a touch more gallantry. 'Now…as I hold all the cards, don't argue, just do as I say and all will be well,' he growled. 'If you want something to occupy that busy tongue of yours you might pray to the Almighty that the gang are too busy collecting kegs on Dawlish Beach to come after us.'

'I'm back at Dawlish?' Fiona forgot in her despair to leap off the other side of the horse. She'd lost two whole days' travelling if she were now again at that staging post.

'You were taken some distance…' Luke mounted in a lithe movement, then turned the horse's head and they picked a path through the shadowy forest towards the road. Just a clop of hooves and chirruping night-time noises broke the eerie silence until a fox shrieked close by, making Fiona almost jump from her skin. Again she felt that small movement against her ribs as his thumb brushed slowly to and fro in reassurance. She felt in such a state of confusion that she had difficulty making sense of her predicament or deciding how to act. Trying to escape again, so soon after the last failed attempt, seemed idiotic. Memories of the home she had left behind collided with thoughts of the uncertain life she was going to. The fate of those she'd travelled with, and her own safety, were also vying for her concentration. Yet…her greatest concern was about her captor. She wanted to believe him honest and sincere, with her best interests at heart, despite everything indicating that the opposite were true. Nothing made sense, and the more Fiona picked at the different strands of information in her mind, the more her hopes that Luke Wolfson was a decent fellow unravelled.

She had quit her home in London because her life had become unbearable. Now she felt she had jumped straight from the frying pan into the fire. Yet, regret was absent; she didn't trust Luke Wolfson and he frightened her, but, oddly, the idea that she might never have met him seemed worse.

Maude Ratcliff bitterly regretted marrying for the second time. She had dearly loved her first husband and missed him more every day now that she had a spouse she feared and despised.

Had Anthony not succumbed to a heart attack she'd still have a comfortable life and her eldest daughter living with her. Now Maude felt quite alone in the world. Losing Fiona's company was a torment. And it was all her own fault for being a stupid woman flattered by a younger man's lies.

Verity, Maude's second child, had been married for several years and had two delightful babies and another on the way. Writing to Langdon Place in Shropshire and worrying her daughter and son-in-law was not an option for consideration as far as Maude was concerned. She would have to try and solve the crisis alone. And, of course, she could only do that if she had some cash of her own to back her plans to abscond from the man making her life a misery.

With a glance over a shoulder Maude took out her jewellery box from where she'd hidden it in a blanket ottoman. She knew that Cecil had gone out, yet sometimes he returned quietly and she was constantly alert to him creeping up behind her to spy on her. Lifting the lid of the casket, she sifted through the pieces for something to sell. Her husband had already taken to the pawnbroker all the fine gemstones. But he'd overlooked these insignificant items and thereafter Maude had kept them out of sight. She was hoping he'd forgotten about them, but doubted he had. Despite their great sentimental value, she'd sooner part with the trinkets and have the cash herself than let him appropriate the proceeds of the gold and silver her beloved Anthony had lavished on her. She fingered a small locket, the best piece, wondering if its value would provide enough gambling chips to give her a chance of winning a hundred pounds or so with which she might disappear.

When Anthony had been alive they'd often played
piquet and he had praised her skill in the game. The
locket was gold, studded with turquoise chips, and had
been an anniversary gift when she was a woman of
about Fiona's age. But by her mid-twenties, Maude
had two daughters, although she'd never borne more
children. It was a great sadness to her that Anthony
had never had the son he'd wanted.

If she had had a boy all would be well, she told herself. She would be able to confide in her son and he
would protect her from the avaricious monster who'd
sneaked into her life by deception.

Attuned to every sound, Maude hastily dropped the
locket and closed the lid of the box, shoving it out of
sight. She must assume the role of devoted wife even
if in reality she'd sooner stick a knife in Cecil's back.
Maude knew the only way she'd ever get free of him
was to play him at his own fraudulent game.

'Ah, there you are, my dear…'

Cecil Ratcliff was a fellow of thirty-five, so in his
prime, and a decade younger than Maude. He had an
average height and build and regular features although
his brown hair was already thinning. He was nothing out of the ordinary. But he thought he was, and by
some peculiar quirk he'd managed to persuade several
women he was, too. Then, when he'd got them hooked
and within his power, they discovered he was nothing
but a selfish parasite.

At the moment he was posed against the door frame,
gazing at his wife with mild blue eyes. 'Should you not
be downstairs arranging dinner, Maude?'

'Rose knows what to cook. I spoke to her earlier.'
Maude got up from the dressing table, and to conceal

the quiver in her hands she clasped them behind her back. She hated herself for feeling too intimidated to order him away from her. Her daughter was gone now and couldn't be harmed, but Maude knew the man she'd married still had her to punish. 'We have some mutton left…and a caper sauce to go with it…'

Cecil tutted, coming further into the room. 'You know I have no liking for such scraps. A joint of beef and perhaps a duck is always more to my taste.' He took one of Maude's cheeks in thumb and forefinger and pinched in a way that seemed playful. 'You'd prefer that, too, wouldn't you, dear?'

'The butcher's bill must be paid before he'll deliver…' Maude began, her hands gripping tighter behind her back as she eased her face from between his bony fingers.

'Bumptious fellow.' Cecil flicked the small pearl ear-clips she wore, then, raising both hands, tugged them together from her lobes. 'Very well, if the upstart wants something, we'll give him these and have a fine feast on the proceeds.' Pocketing the jewellery, he sauntered from the room.

Maude watched him, her eyes brimming with tears and loathing. She knew very well that her earrings would buy her husband a night of carousing, not a dinner for them both. But the loss of her possessions she could tolerate. The loss of Fiona was harder to endure. And how her daughter must hate her for bringing such as Cecil Ratcliff into their lives.

'I like Mr Wolfson and I really think we should persuade him to come back and help us, Papa.'

'I shall determine what to do!' The Duke of Thornley shot his daughter a stern look over the top of his newspaper, but he never remained cross with her for long.

After his wife had died he had gained great comfort from his eldest child's companionship. Joan had only just made her debut at sixteen and a half when her mother expired after a long illness. The duke had wanted Joan to make her come out when older but his beloved wife had desired seeing Joan launched into society, so he had relented. They both knew the time left to them, as a family, was short. Then on the twelfth of August that year—the Glorious Twelfth—with dreadful irony, the duchess had been buried quietly, as had been her wish, in the small graveyard surrounding the chapel on the Thornley estate.

So Joan had been propelled into adulthood before Alfred Thornley would have liked. But the girl had always been mature for her age, although she had an adventurous side better suited to her having been born a boy.

The duke yearned it might have been so. His wife had left him with a son and heir, but at seven years old the boy was too young to be of interest to him and was mostly away at school. Thornley sighed; Joan was right: if he were to do what he saw as his paternalistic duty as largest and wealthiest landowner in Devon, and rid the county of the Collins gang, he'd need assistance from the likes of Wolfson. But the mercenary was no longer at the King and Tinker. His Grace had sent a servant to the inn and the message from the landlord, relayed back to him, had been that Luke Wolfson had travelled west towards Lowerton. But the major had left his doxy still ensconced there, reassuring Thornley that the fellow would return to collect her before heading to London. When Wolfson did show up the duke knew he'd have to eat humble pie if he were to gain the man's attention. The major had always been impeccably polite, but Alfred sensed he didn't suffer fools gladly. He knew he'd been idiotic, allowing pride to make him deaf to the mercenary's advice.

'We cannot keep up the pretence of planning a wedding with a fictitious groom for ever, Papa.' Joan had been buttering her breakfast toast while pointing out a salient point. 'We must strike soon or the opportunity to tempt the reprobate into the open will be lost. The longer it drags on the more likely it will be that Collins might spot the ruse.' She sipped her tea, gazing fixedly at her father to hurry his response. When none came she continued, 'Mr Wolfson might still be lodging at the inn. We should send one of the boys to give him an invitation to dine this evening.'

'He's gone off to his friend's hunting lodge at Lowerton and from there is heading back to the city. The landlord has sent word of it. I doubt Wolfson will be back.' His Grace thought it best not to mention to his dear child that the fellow *would* pass through again… just to collect his concubine.

'Well, we could send word to the hunting lodge; Lowerton is not so far—'

'We will not!' the duke interrupted tetchily before adding in a conciliatory tone, 'I've told you that I have arranged to dine with Squire Smalley this evening.'

'Oh…I forgot…' Joan said meekly; her father had indeed informed her earlier in the week that he was visiting the widower. She always received an invitation too, but found an excuse to stay at home. She had no wish to listen to two fellows reminiscing about their late wives, while drinking themselves silly. Joan brightened. 'Lowerton is a sleepy village; there cannot be more than one hunting lodge in the vicinity...'

'Mmmm...' His Grace mumbled, looking up as the butler entered with the post on a silver tray.

Alfred glanced at the parchments, tutting as he recognised the heavy black script of a fellow magistrate on one of them. There was no need to open the missive to know its content. It would again be complaints about the smugglers stirring unrest among commonly law-abiding folk. Thornley knew he was likely to hear similar concerns from his friend Smalley when they dined later on. Folding his newspaper, he pushed away his untasted plate of kedgeree, feeling irritated.

Again he admitted to himself—if not to her—that his daughter had spoken sense when mentioning the matter ought be attended to before it was too late. Having intentionally leaked the news that he'd set up a match between Joan and a non-existent rich friend, due to return from overseas, it seemed daft not to proceed quickly. The duke had been criticised behind his back for forcing Joan to wed a middle-aged man against her will. But generating juicy gossip that might reach the ears of the gang had been the intention from the outset. To outsiders, father and daughter were at loggerheads because the girl had settled on marrying a secret lover. In order to preserve the scheme's authenticity most of the servants also believed it to be true; just the housekeeper and butler and a few close friends—sworn to secrecy—knew the truth. So deceit had crept into Thornley Heights and His Grace didn't like that one bit. But his daughter—proving her daredevil nature—

had been all for the scheme from the start. She still was, hence her constant badgering to get Wolfson to put it into action.

Thornley picked up his post from the tablecloth, pushing back his chair. 'I must attend to business, my dear.'

Joan watched her father depart without mentioning Wolfson's name again. From experience she knew that her father was best left to stew on matters if he were not to become extremely stubborn. But time was not on their side.

Having finished her breakfast, Joan returned to her chamber and gazed out across verdant parkland while her mind bubbled with activity. Her father wouldn't hear of her getting personally involved in the plot. If any harm were to befall her it would be the end of his sanity, he'd declared. So, after a sulk, Joan had agreed to a stand-in. She wondered who Wolfson had chosen to play her part in the drama. Was the young woman the same age and dark-haired, like her? Her impostor must be a brave soul to undertake the grave risk. When local gentry visited her father Joan had overheard them all discussing the increasing savagery of the gang. The evil reprobates took their work very seriously and would kill or maim to get, and keep, their riches. Recently there had been a report that the smugglers had turned on some of their own: two known criminals had been found with slit throats, no doubt executed for a betrayal.

Joan wrapped her arms about herself. But the thrill shivering through her was not simply caused by unpleasant thoughts; she wondered what it would be like if she truly *did* have a secret lover to elope with. But there was nobody she'd yet met that she fancied in that way. Even Wolfson, handsome as he was, didn't make her heart *really* flutter…but she did trust him to do the deed and get her father a victory against the gang.

Joan turned from the window with a thoughtful smile. Lowerton was not *so* far away. And her father was out this evening. She could reach the village, deliver her plea to the major, and be back before morning. Her father always returned from his friend Smalley's, sunk in his cups, and staggered straight to bed. So he would not even know she'd been out…

Chapter Eight

Fiona's head had fallen against Luke's shoulder as the chestnut cantered through tall meadow grass with dawn breaking at their backs. Surfacing from her doze, she heard the mare whinnying a protest and realised their mount was being forced to speed up and veer to the left.

Blinking open her eyes, she saw they were exchanging mild brightness for cool shade. Once behind a tall screen of hawthorn Luke pulled the horse about to face the way they'd come. He murmured to the exhausted beast, then leant forward, fondling the animal's nose to quieten its snorting.

'What's happened?' Fiona started to ask, conscious of his cheek shaving her complexion. She'd only previously seen him through dusk and drizzle and flickering lamplight. Angling back her head, she looked at him now in pale daylight and with a solemn intensity that she didn't understand. But it seemed he did and her avid interest amused him.

Oh, he knew he was good looking, Fiona thought sourly, and no doubt believed she'd be putty in his hands should he choose to lay them on her. Well, the conceited devil would find that she'd have no difficulty in resisting him! 'Why have we stopped?' she demanded, squinting into the bottle-green depths of the copse.

'Because they'll catch up with us soon.'

'We're being followed?' Fiona forgot about seeming aloof and stared at him in alarm.

'They've been behind for some miles, but are now closing on us fast. This poor nag can't outrun them so best let them pass. If we keep giving them the slip, they'll tire of the game and head back to lucrative business in Dawlish.'

'We must quickly find an inn and seek shelter in case they don't give up!' Fiona blurted, eyes widening in apprehension.

'In these parts you never know what help to expect,' Luke returned ruefully. 'Some people don't take kindly to interfering strangers. They like buying cheap goods from smugglers. Not everybody is against the gang.'

That information came as a great shock to Fiona. She knew nothing of rural codes. Her attempt to escape had been thwarted, but it hadn't once occurred to her she might have been foiled, not by Luke Wolfson or the Collins gang, but by country folk who'd betray her for the price of a barrel of brandy.

'We'll carry on to the King and Tinker and make plans there for your onward journey.' One of his fingers was placed against her mouth, silencing her immediate protest at the delay, before it was pointed at the road.

Fiona heard the drumming of hooves before watching, from behind their leafy camouflage, two horses thunder past.

'It's Sam Dickens and Fred Ruff!' She was fully alert now and had identified her two kidnappers with no trouble, her eyes remaining fixed on their figures until they were just dark specks in the distance. 'They intend to steal me back from you and try to ransom me.' Fiona couldn't control the wobble in her voice, but she refused to display any other sign of fright.

'They won't succeed, trust me.' Cupping her sharp chin in his hand, he turned her head towards him. 'Trust me…' he ordered huskily. 'I swear I won't harm you, or ransom you.'

As their gazes merged, Fiona noticed that his eyes were sepia brown and fringed with long child-like lashes. It would be easy to feel overwhelmed by his masculine charm, she realised. But unanswered questions about him were still cramming her mind and she was determined to have at least one puzzle solved before they set on their way.

'How did you discover I'd been abducted? You were long gone when our coach was held up by those two.' She nodded at the horizon over which the smugglers had disappeared.

'I heard the gunshots and turned back. I regret that I wasn't in time to help.' Luke swung out of the saddle and held out his arms. 'Come, it is an opportunity to stretch your legs. The immediate danger is past.'

Fiona allowed him to help her down, her mind now buzzing with thoughts of the people with whom she'd travelled. 'You saw the others? How were they all?' she demanded. 'Poor Bert had been shot and Mr Jackson hit over the head. But of course you must know that,' she rattled on. 'Oh, please don't say that either fellow has…' Her words tailed away and she blinked back a sparkle of tears. She had only known her travelling companions for a few days, yet so much had happened to unite them that they seemed like her old friends.

'Nobody perished from the attack,' Luke said gently. 'When I left them all at the Pig and Whistle they seemed as well as could be expected. The sisters—especially the younger—seemed to have controlled their hysterics. As for the two invalids, a doctor attended to Bert and Mrs Jackson adequately patched up her husband. The man seemed almost good as new. The couple were very concerned about you, though.'

'And I have been fretting over how they all do. Thank goodness they are safe. Had I known you'd seen them I would have made you tell me about them sooner.'

'*Made* me?' Luke challenged.

'Asked you, then…' Fiona amended, turning from him. 'I wouldn't like you to think *I'm* a bully, Mr Wolfson.' Her tone dripped irony.

'I wouldn't like you to think I am, either, my dear, but I fear you do, despite my selfless and costly efforts to rescue you,' he mocked.

'And why would it worry you what I think?' Fiona snapped, pivoting back, determined not to be bested in this verbal duel. 'You hold all the cards, as you made sure to impress on me, and are playing them close to your chest. I still know nothing about you or your association with Collins. But associated with him, indeed you are! And you're probably no better than he is!'

'Shall I take you back to him, Fiona, so you can know the difference between us?' Luke advanced a pace. 'No?' he taunted on seeing her blanch and retreat.

'I'm stuck with you, then… I doubt Jeremiah would refund my money, in any case.'

'But I will, sir, at the very earliest opportunity,' Fiona retorted, her pale complexion flushing with colour. She put her hands behind her to clutch at a thick tree trunk. His undue familiarity had unsettled her despite her liking the way his husky voice formed her name. 'Don't think for a second that you have bought me!' she whispered.

'But…I have…' Luke pointed out in an infuriatingly confident drawl. 'And it's unlike me to lose on a deal.'

'You will not lose! You will have my price and interest, too,' Fiona spat, tossing her face proudly aside. It was a moment before she realised she had no idea just how much it was that she owed him. And she was chary of asking. She had no money, not even the cash she'd saved for her travelling expenses. That thieving wretch Fred Ruff had pocketed her coins, despite sneering at the paltry amount. All she had left in the world was a gold locket, worn hidden beneath her bodice since her avaricious stepfather entered her life. The small oval had been her twenty-first birthday gift from her parents and was the only piece of jewellery she now owned. She'd be heartbroken to lose it. But she would hand it over to Luke Wolfson before they parted. From its worth she hoped he might recoup the many banknotes she'd seen him give to Collins and that there would be sufficient left to settle the cost of her coach fare from the King and Tinker to Dartmouth.

For weeks past her mind had been constantly occupied with her new job, but since this man had burst into her life she'd barely given a thought to being a governess. And she must, for what else was there for her? She just hoped that she still had a position to go to and her new master would be sympathetic to her tardy arrival, once he knew some of the facts behind it.

'There's no need for you to feel under any obligation to reimburse me.' Luke had spoken while kicking together some twigs. He squatted down with a tinderbox and put a light to the pile of kindling.

Fiona watched tendrils of smoke transform to baby flames as he teased the fire to take hold. She sensed he'd become bored with their cat-and-mouse game and was now being serious. 'I insist on settling my debts, sir,' she said distantly.

'From a governess's pay?' He slanted a look up at her.

Fiona bristled beneath his quizzical stare. Days ago he'd chided her for travelling alone as a vulnerable female, now she felt he was ridiculing her ability to earn enough to pay her dues. And, of course, on both counts he was right. He'd said her safety could turn out to be a burden on him…and so it had proved. As for her salary, she'd be lucky to save pennies from it after the cost of her board and lodging, and other necessities, had been deducted.

About to pull the locket into view with a flourish Fiona instead pressed her small hands to her stomach to smother its embarrassing gurgling.

'Are you hungry?'

She nodded, avoiding his eyes. She'd not eaten properly since having a beef sandwich at the Fallow Buck. When was that…yesterday, the day before? She realised she was losing track of time.

Having acknowledged she was famished, she suddenly felt quite giddy with fatigue, too, and sank on to her knees in case she swooned. 'Might I have a small drink from your brandy, Mr Wolfson?'

Luke took the bottle from the saddlebag and, pulling the cork with his teeth, upended it so the spirit poured in an amber stream to the ground. 'It's lethal,' he explained to Fiona, who was watching him with an indignant frown. 'A swig of that could kill you.'

'Why ask Collins for it, then?'

'I wanted him to think I trusted him enough to sell me a drinkable bottle. I tasted a drop earlier and knew it for poison.'

'So…if he thinks you've drunk some, and perhaps me, too, he might believe us to be dead in a ditch somewhere,' Fiona suggested.

'He might…' Luke gave a twitch of a smile, realising she had a quick intelligence. 'But I doubt it…' He stood up now the fire was blazing. 'Jeremiah Collins is not easily outwitted, and neither am I. I think we have each other's measure.' He hunkered down in front of her. 'If I go and find us something for breakfast, are you going to behave nicely and stay right where you are?'

Fiona's feline gaze flicked sideways at him; his lean stubbly jaw was mere inches from her and the warm male scent of leather and wood smoke about his person was pleasant and reassuring. 'If you're going to find a place to buy bread, I'll come, too.' She suddenly realised she didn't relish the idea of being left alone with the smugglers prowling in the vicinity.

'There's no bread to hand, but perhaps a rabbit or hare might let me snare them,' he explained, half-smiling. 'And I'll find us something to drink.' He glanced up. 'I spotted a heron earlier so there's water about.' He'd added that comment while getting into the saddle.

'Keep the fire alight, but don't use damp wood or it'll create smoke and attract unwanted attention,' was his parting advice.

Chapter Nine

A short time ago Fiona had been desperate to escape Luke Wolfson; now she wished she'd insisted on staying with him, she realised, as the sun climbed higher in the heavens and still he'd not returned.

Every unfamiliar rustle and creak made her start and peer apprehensively into undergrowth. She'd tolerate sharing her little woodland glade with wild creatures, but not with Jeremiah Collins's savages. She constantly fidgeted to and fro, on the lookout for approaching horsemen while her mind concocted dastardly betrayals as the reason why Wolfson had not reappeared. Pacing from oak to ash and back again, she'd soon convinced herself that he had tricked her into believing he'd gone hunting. In reality, he'd had enough of her and was bartering with the gang to get his money refunded. He'd told her to stay right where she was so Fred and Sam would quickly locate her and carry her, again bound and gagged, back to Jeremiah Collins's lair…

The sudden, unmistakable sound of a horse snorting made Fiona whip behind a tree trunk, heart pounding, in readiness to flee for her life. The sight of the chestnut being steered about a bush was so welcome that Fiona forgot herself and broke cover to run to him.

'You were a very long time.' She'd sounded like a carping wife, she realised, and lowered her eyes.

A quizzical sideways look from Luke let her know he also thought her a nag. But his smile was not *too* mocking as he dismounted. 'Sorry... I didn't think you'd miss me so much. I'm out of practice trapping.'

He dropped a brace of hare to the ground and immediately set about stoking up the fire that she'd forgotten to feed while in a stew over his absence.

'Do you know how to skin an animal?'

Fiona's retort, that she'd not missed him at all and was simply keen to get going, withered on her tongue. She gazed at him as though he were mad. The only hare she'd ever seen had been either running in a field or jugged in a pie. She found the idea abominable that she might strip a creature of its fur.

Having seen her pallor, Luke took out a penknife. 'Right... Gather up some more firewood while I prepare the carcase,' he ordered. 'Collect dry leaves, too, if there's not much seasoned timber to hand.'

Watching the first cut into the lifeless beast was enough to make Fiona spin away and start foraging on the ground. She didn't stray too far and soon was drawn back by the appetising aroma of roasting meat, carrying an armful of the driest twigs she could find.

As she dropped the kindling Luke immediately built up the blaze, then handed her his water bottle for a drink. She brushed together her gritty palms, then gratefully accepted, waiting for him to furnish a cup of some sort.

'Straight from the bottle,' he told her, turning the game slowly on the spit fashioned from a sapling branch braced between a pair of forked sticks.

Fiona watched him as he worked and juices dropped to sizzle and steam on the embers, curious as to how a refined gentleman came to acquire such marvellous skills.

And despite everything she sensed Luke Wolfson was from good stock and had the benefit of an excellent education. Her father had held a similar station in life, yet she was certain Anthony Chapman wouldn't have had the slightest inkling how to trap or camp or consort with villains.

When her father had been alive they'd been comfortably off and kept domestics to deal with menial tasks. Since her mother had remarried the cook had gone and a single maid had been burdened with everything, including cooking and serving at table. Fiona and her mother had feared poor Rose would hand in her notice before too long. Fiona realised the woman might by now have gone and Maude alone waited hand and foot on odious Cecil Ratcliff.

'Are you an officer serving in the army?'

'Not any more.' Luke hadn't raised his eyes from the browning meat while speaking.

Fiona pondered on how to make him divulge more about himself. She concluded that there was no subtle way of being inquisitive. Before she could stop herself she rattled off, 'Have you fallen on hard times? Have you joined those criminals to earn some money? Did you not really want to take part in kidnapping the duke's daughter?'

He slanted at her an impenetrable look and for a moment Fiona thought he might tell her to mind her own business. 'No, I've not fallen on hard times and, no, I wouldn't have been paid by Collins. As for the kidnap… you're right on that score; I didn't want to get involved because I thought it a stupid scheme from the start.'

'So why *did* you get involved?' Fiona was elated at getting him to spill a few beans.

'As a favour to a man I admire and to collect a fee.'

'So you *do* need the money.' Fiona pounced. Since her own downturn in fortune, she could understand how the prospect of destitution might ruin a previously upright character.

'No…I don't.'

'Why do it, then, with so much at stake?' Fiona was beginning to think he was deliberately talking in riddles to deter her from pursuing the subject.

'I'm starting to ask myself the same question.' Luke stood up, walking towards her.

He held out a joint of hare and Fiona took it, tossing it from hand to hand as it singed her fingertips. 'Hot…' she murmured with a bashful smile that incorporated her thanks. Her stomach was rolling in hunger and she took a cautious nibble, unable to wait for the food to cool. It was surprisingly tender and delicious and she told him so, then greedily tore again at the meat with her small teeth.

'Have you fallen on hard times, Fiona?' Luke had returned to the spit to break off a leg for himself while speaking.

Fiona wiped her mouth with the back of a hand, staring at him. She hadn't expected him to turn the tables on her. 'Why do you ask?' She took another bite of succulent meat and chewed slowly.

'Because…like me…you seem to be undertaking something at odds with your class.'

Fiona curled her legs under her on the ground and paid full attention to her food. 'My father died and my mother remarried,' she explained, sure he'd not remove his eyes from her profile until she did. 'Our circumstances changed. I felt it wasn't fair to burden my mother with the cost of keeping me any longer.'

'You don't like your stepfather,' Luke stated bluntly.

'No…' Fiona said, discarding the bone she'd stripped bare on the ground beside her. 'I should like to get going, Mr Wolfson. I was expected in Dartmouth this morning.'

'Why haven't you married?'

Fiona shot him a glance, shocked by his crude enquiry. 'I think that is none of your business, sir, and rude of you to ask.'

'I didn't complain when you pried into my life.' He sliced another joint from the cooked carcase and lobbed it towards her. It landed, perfectly positioned, on the grass next to her.

'I did not pry!' Fiona spluttered. 'I simply enquired…' She tailed off, knowing full well that she'd done her utmost to prise information from him.

He sent her a smile. 'If you want to know more about me, you'll have to furnish me with some answers in return. Quid pro quo, Fiona.'

'I'm a spinster because I've never received a proposal. And you? Are you married, and if not, why not?' she retorted in retaliation.

'I'm a bachelor…because I've never issued a proposal.'

'And had you done so, sir, you might still be a bachelor having been turned down,' Fiona pointed out sweetly. She ignored the silent laugh her barb elicited. He was obviously unrepentantly arrogant. 'Well...now we have that out of the way, I'd like to journey on, Mr Wolfson.' The savoury smell of the roast game, laying inches away, was tempting; she'd not eaten her fill, but she stubbornly resisted picking it up.

'I'm not ready to go. Eat your food and stop sulking.' Luke's white teeth ripped off what meat remained on the bone hovering by his mouth. The waste was thrown over a shoulder and he upended the water bottle against his mouth.

'Don't you dare order me about,' Fiona burst out, jumping to her feet. She felt irked at having been made to admit—to him of all people—that no man had ever wanted her as his wife.

'You say your stepfather won't pay out a ransom on you? I'm not surprised he won't have you back.' Luke pushed to his feet and kicked dirt on the dying fire. 'I doubt he's missing your acid tongue and lack of gratitude any more than I will when we go our separate ways.'

That comment made Fiona wince. 'Again you are being impertinent, Mr Wolfson,' she uttered coldly. 'You know nothing about my stepfather. If you did, you'd understand he'd lure me again under his roof as long as it cost him nothing.'

'I think you should explain what you mean by that.'

'And I think your explanations are due first, sir, so don't dare to interrogate me!'

Luke cursed beneath his breath for pushing her too far; he had been enjoying their lively talk despite the fact she could be the most insolent chit alive...and the most alluring. He wasn't sure why he found her fascinating, but the longer he was in her company the more he appreciated her mild loveliness. Here, amongst nature, she seemed to blend in. Her slender graceful body and fawn colouring reminded him of a woodland creature, as did her disposition. She'd attempt to bolt or snap at him the moment he made a move to touch her. And God only knew he was feeling tempted to do so.

Fiona sank her teeth into her lower lip to still its angry tremble. She'd thought they had established a tiny bit of harmony while preparing their meal, but it had soon evaporated. It was her own fault for having brought up the subject of her stepfather; she found it hard to suppress her despising when speaking of Cecil Ratcliff. Even the Collins gang were no worse, in her eyes, than the man her mother had vowed to love and obey. At least those wretches took their plunder openly rather than by stealth.

'I believe I've been more than fair with you, Fiona, but I realise that you have reason to think me a deceitful villain.' Luke broke the silence, hoping to soothe her.

'And are you a deceitful villain?'

'Not in the way you think, and only for the greater good,' Luke replied wryly.

'An answer that says little,' Fiona returned with a sparking glance. Her intuition told her that his casual manner concealed an unrelenting character. She was in the company of a soldier-turned-hireling who was used to giving nothing away. He was sparing with his information and his generosity, she guessed. Wolfson, if honestly acting as her saviour, would expect to be paid for his services.

'You need not fear that I cannot settle your fee.' Fiona fished the locket from inside her bodice and held it extended on its fine chain for him to see. 'I will hand this over when we reach the King and Tinker. It is solid gold and quite heavy,' she added, as she saw his eyes drop to it only fleetingly before returning to her face.

'I've told you I want nothing from you.'

'But I insist you take it.'

'Why?'

'Because I would not have you believe you have bought me, sir.'

'Forget I said that—it was a joke.'

'Not to me…'

'Then you must see yourself as a chattel more than I do.'

'I assure you I do not! I am my own mistress and nobody else's.'

'It never occurred to me you might be otherwise, my dear,' Luke drawled with lazy amusement, brushing a leaf off a sleeve.

She was a genteel spinster, not a prospective paramour, he reminded himself as he watched her blush beneath his insinuation. It was time to get going and find her a suitable chaperon to keep him at bay. Then, once she was on a coach heading west, he could have his belated meeting with Rockleigh before returning to London. The coming tête-à-tête deserved some preparatory thought, he impressed upon himself, as it was certain to turn unpleasant.

Luke knew he was attempting to force his mind to something…anything…that dampened the tormenting heat building in his loins. The longer he was with this provocative woman the more he felt sexual frustration gnawing at him. He avoided looking at her, concentrating on the imminent confrontation with his friend, wondering if it would be as well to ignore the appointment and head straight back to London. The idea of offering to marry Drew's niece because the silly chit wouldn't stop flirting and getting herself into scrapes was absurd and he was itching to tell Rockleigh so. But the matter would wait and perhaps in the interim his friend might accept he'd acted hot-headedly.

In his present irritable mood, Luke knew *he* might act hot-headedly and what had started as a minor problem could escalate to pistols at dawn. Better he got himself away from Fiona Chapman as soon as he could and follow Becky home. He'd pay his mistress one last visit before approaching the pretty redhead he'd seen at Vauxhall to replace her.

Then there was the question of Harriet Ponting. Once Luke had thought himself in love with the blonde. When she'd rejected his overtures on her parents' advice, he'd realised he wasn't, because he'd not felt heartbroken, just humiliated. After that he'd never again been tempted to find a wife, even though he'd since inherited land and wealth from his grandfather that made him a prime target for debutantes. Now he could afford to provide even a rich aristocrat's child with the sort of life she'd been reared to.

Harriet Ponting was still porcelain pretty and on the few occasions that their paths had crossed her big blue eyes had signalled that she still liked him. Luke knew she'd make a good wife; from a couple of brief amorous encounters they'd snatched when unobserved he'd guessed she'd also make a reasonable lover. Her social graces were more highly polished than his own, so he'd no qualms about her being a skilful hostess. It was time he started thinking about settling down for the benefit of future generations of Wolfsons.

He'd considered heading to Eaton Square to accept one or two of the invitations that always piled up on his desk during the height of the Season. Yet suddenly he felt no inclination to return to town to socialise and pick a wife. With startling clarity he knew that a mild physical attraction and good manners weren't enough to tempt him to remain faithful and give up carousing with courtesans like Becky. The idea of adultery was sordid to Luke. He knew a great many wealthy husbands did flit between two or more women, but for him the subterfuge made a mockery of taking vows.

Fiona was aware of his sudden preoccupation and of her inexplicable hurt at his implication that she was too plain for a gentleman to want her as a paramour.

But whatever careless remarks he lobbed her way Fiona had glimpsed the desire burning at the backs of Luke Wolfson's eyes. Simply because he could, he might take the opportunity to prove to her his powers of seduction while boosting his ego. And with a pang of raw emotion that stole away her breath, she realised that she wanted him to.

With clumsy fingers she undid the locket and stood up with it enclosed in her fist. She marched unsteadily over rough ground and very deliberately dropped the gold to the earth at his feet. 'I have worked out for myself that you are a mercenary of some sort. Your payment, sir, for rescuing me and escorting me to safety. You might as well take it now, as later.'

Luke gripped her wrist before she could withdraw

and slowly, with her struggling to free herself, brought her down to kneel in front of him so their faces were level.

'How do you know I'll keep my end of the bargain?'

'I don't,' Fiona breathed. 'But soldiers of fortune gain work through recommendation, I imagine, and if you cross me I will make it known you're corrupt.'

'You'd ruin my reputation, would you?' he murmured, amused.

Fiona gave a brief nod, wishing she'd not used the threat for it seemed to have had the opposite effect to its purpose. She was acutely aware of her imprisoned wrist and although his fingers had relaxed on her she knew they'd tighten in a second if she attempted to rise.

'Perhaps I might ruin yours first.'

Fiona's golden eyes clashed with his dark sultry stare. 'I think it rather late for that, sir. My reputation was in tatters the moment that highwayman tossed me over his shoulder.'

'Nothing to lose, then…' Luke's tone was silky, his eyes watching her tongue tip darting to moisten her top lip.

'Pick up your payment and take me to the King and Tinker!' Fiona ordered shrilly, aware that he was backing her into a corner with his clever words.

'I'm sorely tempted to do without any more of your snapping and snarling and leave you here.' Luke's voice was mellifluous, at odds with the threat in his words. 'Shall we call a truce for what remains of the ride to the inn?'

Fiona pursed her lips, but nodded while twisting her wrist in a renewed effort to liberate it. Unable to do so, she turned her head from him. 'I think it best we don't converse, sir,' she said icily. 'All we do is rub one another up the wrong way.'

'That's an interesting thought…' *And one I could have done without,* he inwardly mocked himself. He released her straining form so abruptly that she fell sideways on to the turf, her skirts askew, displaying her lissom shapely calves.

It was too much temptation for Luke to resist. As Fiona wriggled to straighten her petticoat he braced an arm over her, all thoughts of Harriet and Becky gone from his mind. Immediately Fiona became still, her eyes engulfed by a heavy-lidded blistering gaze.

Luke touched a long forefinger to her softly panting mouth. 'Let's not fight and argue, sweet,' he said huskily. 'We've some hours of travelling in front of us… Better we ride together as friends?'

Mesmerised by the soft finger outlining her lips, she could do no more than wait to see what he might do to her next. She had been kissed before by the more persistent of her suitors, but never, when with those gentlemen, had her heart battered at her ribs, as it did now, in a mix of excitement and trepidation.

Fiona watched his dark head dipping closer, his mouth nearing hers and although a sensible inner voice urged her to beat him off, she could not. He wasn't pinning her down as he had before when she'd fled from him; nevertheless, she felt trapped by her own need to have a small taste of being seduced by Luke Wolfson. Still he teased her as his face scuffed her cheek and his breath bathed an ear, then upwards skimmed his fingers to touch back from her forehead stray tendrils of silky hair.

He stroked his lips to a corner of hers and with a moan Fiona swung her head so their mouths collided.

Luke was lost in her sweet enthusiasm. A courtesan might put up a better fight before going down.

But he knew that Fiona Chapman had no sophisticated tactics to use to increase his desire; neither did she need them. She tasted smoky and sweet from the spit-roasted meat they'd eaten and he could sense a faint scent of lavender on her skin.

As his tongue skimmed her lower lip Fiona wound her arms about his neck, instinctively pressing up against him, to increase the chafing pressure of his chest on her bosom.

Luke drew her up further as he sensed her need, deepening the kiss, teasing her with the plunge of his tongue until she met him with shy touches of her own.

Somewhere deep in his consciousness he knew he should stop this madness before it went too far. But he was in an agony of arousal and his hands were already straying to open her cloak and slide within to caress her.

Fiona gasped as a large warm hand cupped her breast, teasing her nipple through her bodice. When his hand slipped free some buttons and thrust to touch her nude skin she moaned in delight at the sensation of hard fingers tantalising every inch of warm satiny flesh. His head lowered, his mouth circling the sensitive little nub before suckling hard and fast and making her cry out in wonder as fire streaked through her veins. Luke positioned her legs astride him, drawing back her skirts, but allowing her some modesty by not lifting them completely. He curved a hand about her nape, drawing her head down to his, tempting her back into their shared web of sensuality while loosening his trousers. The sweet feminine core of her felt slick as he teased her with a fingertip…then two…that began easing fractionally further into her. He knew that, virgin or no, she was ready for him and he'd only to free himself and ease her hips down to impale her, because he was more than ready for her.

Fiona's breath was rasping in her throat and the sound was so foreign that it startled her into parting her lashes. Her eyes merged with his, pleading for she knew not what. Despite drugging desire she understood she was risking everything for this man…a stranger who did deals with criminals. But it was the memory of something Collins had said that finally brought her to her senses. Luke Wolfson had a woman waiting for him at the inn they were about to head towards…

Luke sensed the change in her as she blinked, put up an inner struggle to defeat his boast of conquering a woman by seduction rather than force. Before she could push him away, he tumbled her so she lay sprawled beneath him, then very deliberately he touched together their lips before getting up with an oath exploding between his teeth.

He scooped up the gold locket from the peat and was gathering the mare's reins by the time Fiona had scrambled to her feet.

Slowly he approached her with such an impenetrable expression that Fiona stumbled back a pace, wondering how he could seem unmoved by what they'd just done. Without a word he lifted her on to the saddle, mounted, and within seconds the refreshed mare was hurtling out of the woods and towards the road.

His arm encircled her waist with such confidence

that Fiona knew he was challenging her to break her silence and object. But she'd no intention of speaking to him because she might betray feeling a dreadful jealousy for the mistress he had waiting for him at the King and Tinker.

Chapter Ten

'Yours, I believe, sir.' The fellow propelled the girl forward by her shoulder. 'You should take better care of her, or teach her how to behave.'

The Duke of Thornley gawped at the stranger who'd just addressed him as though he were an incompetent nanny who'd failed his charge. But what angered His Grace the most was having the upstart do so in front of his daughter while manhandling Joan to boot! And all at such an ungodly hour of the morning! He'd not been abed more than a few hours when a servant had woken him and told him he'd a visitor demanding an urgent audience.

Alfred Thornley had had a good dinner with his friend the squire and they'd swallowed much port and brandy to wash down the game that His Grace had magnanimously supplied from his own larder. He'd not reached home till three hours after midnight and had been helped up the stairs to his chamber by two trusty footmen. His head was thumping from over-imbibing and he was struggling to make sense of the scene in front of him.

'I beg your pardon!' he finally thundered. Alfred tightened the belt on his dressing gown with hands that shook with suppressed rage.

'And so you should.' Drew Rockleigh was in no mood for humouring the fellow, duke or no.

Yesterday evening he'd opened his door at gone ten o'clock at night not to the man with whom he had a grievance, but to a young woman searching for the same fellow. She'd told him she was a duke's daughter and he'd snorted disbelief at that. At first. Then he'd realised she was not some opportunistic doxy, but exactly who she said she was. Joan Morland would not tell him what she wanted with Wolfson or why she'd travelled late at night on perilous roads with just a frightened-looking youth driving her two-wheeled gig. Drew's increasingly wrathful demands for information had all been met with the same answer: it was a secret. Finally, in exasperation, he'd ordered the chit back aboard her transport and escorted her home.

'What the devil do you mean by that remark? Beg your pardon? Why should I, you young pup?' The duke planted his fists on his hips, his small black eyes sparking dangerously. 'What the deuce do you think you are doing here? What is it you want? Make it quick before I have you removed,' Thornley rattled off, his face glowing puce. 'Are you a madman?' he spat out in conclusion.

'Papa—' Joan started in a strangled voice, hoping to make her father cease insulting the fellow who'd brought her safely home. She was in terrible trouble, she knew, but her fears were for her father. She wanted His Grace to calm down in case he burst one of the blood vessels she could see throbbing at his temple.

She darted a quick look at the stranger. She guessed him to be about the same age as Luke Wolfson, but he was very fair rather than dark like the mercenary. He'd remained dour-faced and silent for the duration of a very strained homeward journey. She'd begged him to allow her to return in the way she'd arrived, with just Pip driving her. In that way she could have slipped in to Thornley Heights discreetly, in the same way she'd slipped out. But Rockleigh would not hear of it and had ridden at the side of the trap, right the way up to the vast front steps before hammering on the front door and bringing the footman running.

'Go to your room,' the duke snapped at Joan, wanting to deal with this matter in private. 'Why are you up so early, anyway? It can't be much past nine of the clock.'

Drew Rockleigh glanced at the girl, wondering if she was going to answer that one. She lowered her nervous eyes beneath the sardonic enquiry in his stare. 'Your daughter is not up early, Your Grace, she's not yet sought her bed. Last night she paid me a visit in the hope of finding Luke Wolfson, because she has an urgent message to give to my friend. More than that I cannot say…it is a secret, you see.'

Joan winced beneath the sarcasm she heard in Rockleigh's voice, but she kept quiet and tightened her fingers together behind her back until the knuckles showed ivory.

The duke remained facing his unwelcome visitor with a ferocious expression, as though he still believed him a raving lunatic. Then, after a full minute of unblinking deliberation, he very stiffly turned to his daughter, his eyebrows slowly elevating.

Joan hung her head, then with a shuddering sigh gave an imperceptible nod.

'Go to your room.'

Joan recognised that whispered tone of voice only too well; her father was enraged and she defied him again at her peril. 'Papa…please listen—' she began.

The duke had his open hand knocked aside in mid-air before it could make contact with his daughter's cheek.

'You may chastise her, if you will, later,' Rockleigh said, lowering his arm. 'First, I have more to say and would ask you to listen so I might get about my business without further delay.'

Joan, ashen-faced from her father's attempt to slap her, turned tail and, gripping her skirts, rushed to the stairs and disappeared up them.

The Duke of Thornley stalked to a nearby doorway, leaving his visitor standing alone on the marble flags. Before entering the room he turned, announced regally, 'I owe you my apologies and my thanks, it seems, sir. Do come in so we can become acquainted…there is much to discuss.' He flung open the door to the small library and stomped inside.

Maude knew she'd need to choose the time of her departure carefully. Her husband had been watching her again, and she hoped it was not because he'd guessed her intentions. Maude was under no illusion that Cecil Ratcliff would try to stop her leaving him because he loved or desired her. She aroused no sweet emotion in her husband, and never had, despite his ardent protestations when wooing her. She knew it all for lies now.

But, crafty as Ratcliff was, he couldn't disguise some aspects of his character. He was an arrogant fellow who put much store in his status and keeping up appearances. He would not want the neighbours, or the gentlemen he classed as his peers, to gossip behind his back that his wife had run out on him. Cecil would always want the upper hand and Maude suspected that he was ruminating on when to leave *her*. Of course, he would not do so while there were still things of value in the house that he might sell off to fund his roistering.

A small canvas was on the drawing-room wall that Maude had hoped had escaped his eye being muted in colour. But she'd noticed him in front of it the other day, fingering his chin, and her heart had sunk.

Having heard the crash of the front door, Maude trotted to the window that overlooked the street. Concealed by the curtain, she peeped from behind it as Cecil swaggered off along the pavement, hat at a jaunty angle, swinging her late husband's silver-topped cane as though for all the world it was his. And of course it was. Everything Anthony had owned was now Cecil Ratcliff's to do with as he would.

Seeing him flourishing her dear Anthony's favourite walking stick hurt Maude more than anything and she twitched the velvet back in place and made a snap decision.

At this time of the day Cecil would be going to his club and often didn't return till dinnertime. Maude knew she might have up to six hours' grace before he again was home to harry her with his snide remarks. Hurrying to the bed, she pulled out the packing case beneath it. She'd already told Rose they were taking a trip and to be prepared to leave at a moment's notice.

She'd also told the maid, unnecessarily, to keep her lips sealed on the plan. Maude hadn't elaborated because she hadn't needed to. Rose had eyes and ears and had given her mistress a knowing smile and a nod. The maid hated Cecil, too, no doubt because he'd treated her as a slave rather than a paid employee ever since he'd arrived.

Maude took some scissors from the dressing table then, perching on the mattress, drew a pillow towards her. Carefully she snipped the threads she'd put in a few days ago and withdrew her folded bank notes from where she'd secreted them inside the linen cover. She beamed, raising her winnings to her lips to kiss them in gratitude. After selling her few remaining items of jewellery she'd done a fine job of turning five pounds into fifty at Almack's faro table. It wasn't the small fortune she'd hoped for, but it would have to suffice because she could stand not another single day beneath the same roof as her husband.

She and Rose would travel to Devon to find her daughter. Once she'd begged for forgiveness from Fiona for subjecting her to Cecil's Ratcliff's odious presence, they would turn their thoughts to their uncertain futures. But Maude knew she must remain optimistic. Fate might yet smile on them. Something *would* turn up…and in case it did not, she was going to fetch the small oil painting from the drawing room and wedge it into her portmanteau. Even if it were not as valuable as she hoped, it might cover the cost of a week's board and lodging for them all.

Fiona realised that the brunette must have been watching for her lover's return. Barely had Luke dismounted in the stable yard of the King and Tinker when a voluptuous young woman hurtled out of the low sloping doorway and straight at him.

Without uttering a word Luke removed Becky's clinging hands and turned to Fiona to help her down from the chestnut mare. But his features were so tensely set that his mistress—and Fiona, too—could not but be aware of his latent anger, if unsure of its cause.

'Where have you been, Luke? Thank goodness you're back at last...' Becky rattled off with a winning smile, twirling a dark ringlet about a finger. When Luke continued to ignore her she flounced about to narrow her eyes on the woman with him.

Fiona had winced on hearing Wolfson's mistress quiz him over his absence using similar words to those she'd fired at him hours before when he'd returned from his hunting trip.

Planting her hands on her hips in a combatant manner, Becky demanded, 'And who is *she*?', while grabbing Luke's forearm in a way that seemed to Fiona both punishing and possessive.

The fact that his mistress had disobeyed him and returned to Devon to hound him rather than travel home with her dignity intact had stoked more than rage in Luke. He'd made it clear to Becky he didn't want or need her company, yet still she clung on determinedly. He realised that the fire had gone out of his anger and his lust for her, and disgust and pity had taken the place of those emotions.

Behind Becky was someone else Luke would rather not have encountered at this precise moment, leaning on the whitewashed wall of the inn. Rockleigh's face displayed mild amusement as he watched the scene, but Luke knew his friend well enough: Drew was here to exact a promise, not to be humoured. Disentangling himself from Becky's renewed clutch, he ignored both his friend and his mistress and turned to Fiona.

'I'll get you a room in the inn,' he stated quietly.

'There's no need, sir,' Fiona responded coolly. 'If there is a coach setting off west, at any time at all of the day or night, I wish to be on it.'

Luke watched her tigerish eyes flit past him to settle on Becky before skittering away. He knew there was no point in making introductions, or excuses; Collins had already done the damage on that score. At the time, Luke hadn't cared what was said. Now he did. He cared greatly that Fiona Chapman thought him a lecherous reprobate who dragged a woman with him on his travels to warm his bed.

'Surely you'll want some privacy to freshen up?' he suggested in a voice only she could hear, while fighting the urge to lift her again onto the horse and ride off with her into the unknown. And damn the lot of them. From Rockleigh's stance, he could see that the man had grown impatient waiting to resolve matters and was itching for a fight. And his mistress appeared to be similarly boiling with resentment.

The time spent with Miss Fiona Chapman might have been short and fraught with danger for them both, but it had been rather wonderful, Luke realised. And he didn't want it to end yet. Inwardly he mocked himself for confusing lust with something finer. The reason he wanted to keep Fiona's company was because the desire he felt for her remained unquenched. It was even now a weighty throb in his pelvis.

And it would stay that way, until Becky, or one of her ilk, soothed it for him. Fiona would avoid him like the plague now she'd met his mistress and he would do the decent thing and allow her to.

The idea of a wash and a rest on a proper bed was so tempting that Fiona was on the point of agreeing to take a room; then she remembered she had no money and she'd be damned before asking him to settle any bill other than that of her coach fare. 'I'm very well as I am, thank you,' she said, forcing a lightness into her tone that she was far from feeling. But she wouldn't have him think for a moment that the sight of his paramour bothered her.

Again Fiona's eyes were involuntarily drawn to the brunette. Despite a sullen droop to her full lips she was very attractive…and young. Fiona guessed that Luke Wolfson's mistress was at least five years her junior and for some reason that hurt more than feeling dishevelled and ugly in comparison. With small movements she brushed down her crumpled skirts, then attempted to twist her tangled fawn locks into a neat bun at her nape. She knew she must look a fright after her ordeal, but refused to feel apologetic or ashamed about it.

'I believe your friends are awaiting your attention, sir,' she remarked briskly. 'You need not think that I expect a long farewell between us. Thank you for the service you provided… I am glad it is over. If you will purchase my seat on a coach from your payment, I would be most grateful. Goodbye, Mr Wolfson.' She extended a hand and shook his fingers firmly before immediately turning away. She had seen the sardonic set to his mouth as she dismissed him from duty, and despite the hammering in her chest, and the weakness in her legs, she was pleased to be able to steadily walk away from him.

Thankfully she could approach the saloon bar of the King and Tinker without passing the young woman watching her with eyes brimming with suspicion and dislike. No doubt Luke would soon soothe the pretty brunette's sulks over a possible rival by saying Miss Chapman had been a client who'd unexpectedly landed in his path and that his fee for the mission had been a gold locket. He might give the necklace to her!

That awful thought shocked Fiona like a dousing with icy water, provoking a physical pain to twist in her gut. But aware of being still under observation she tilted up her chin and drew her cloak about her in instinctive protection. Her twenty-first birthday present from her parents had saved her from the Collins gang so it had been worth parting with such a precious gift, she impressed upon herself. Head high, she entered the low, thatched building determined to find the innkeeper and quiz him over the time of the next coach heading to Dartmouth.

While negotiating a warren of narrow corridors Fiona forced herself to forget the people outside and concentrate on mundane matters. She remembered that she must discover the whereabouts of her packing case. On the last occasion she'd seen the battered leather trunk it was being transferred with the other luggage from the damaged coach to the replacement Toby Williams had driven from the Fallow Buck.

In one of their less challenging conversations Wolfson had told her that the vehicle and remaining passengers had journeyed on, with his help, to the Pig and Whistle following the hold up and her abduction. Toby Williams had been distracted by his nephew's bullet wound that dreadful night, but Fiona hoped that the driver had had the good sense to leave her belongings at the Pig and Whistle for collection. She had nothing but the clothes she stood up in and on arriving at her destination must suffer the ignominy of requesting an advance on her wages. She could only hope that her employer would be sympathetic and hand over a few shilling for incidentals she might require.

A fellow of ample girth and bald of pate with a food-spotted apron hanging below his big belly suddenly rounded a corner, almost colliding with Fiona.

'Well, now, madam, what can I do for you?' He backed off a pace, looking surprised to see her wandering alone. 'Stanley Robley, patron of this establishment at your service, you see.' He followed up his introduction with a jaunty bow and a tobacco-stained beam.

'I am Miss Chapman, sir, and wonder if you can tell me when the next coach is leaving for Dartmouth? I shall need to stop at the Pig and Whistle en route.'

'One doo in tomorrow morning, but might be full, you see.' He sucked his teeth pessimistically. 'Most of 'em are—coachmen don't like empty seats, you see.'

'Yes…I see…Mr Robley,' Fiona concurred, feeling her spirits sink. In her agitated state it had escaped her mind that it could be a long wait for a vehicle to turn up with spare room on it. 'I am overdue in taking up my employment, so would be very grateful if you could secure me the very first available place, sir. Outside will do.'

Stanley Robley tapped the side of his nose while his other hand snaked out, palm up.

Fiona realised he was expecting her to either give

him an inducement for the favour she'd asked, or the cost of her fare, or perhaps both. Whichever it was she had nothing to hand over.

'Mr Wolfson is…umm…an acquaintance and he will settle with you.' Her voice had been level, but she couldn't prevent embarrassment colouring her cheeks. Her blush increased when she saw the landlord's goggling eyes slyly gleaming.

'Well… Of course I know *that* fine fellow and, being the soul of discretion, miss, never would repeat what you said.' He dipped his shiny head to whisper close to Fiona's ear. 'Specially not to his *other* girl. Hellcat she is!' he hissed. 'Nearly had my daughter's eye out with her claws and all my Sally was doing was serving Mr Wolfson his dinner, you see.'

'Mr Wolfson and I are just…' Fiona's indignant response faded away. The landlord's insinuation that she was another of Wolfson's paramours was not *so* far off the mark. How much of a hypocrite was she prepared to be? she taunted herself. She might try to block the memory of her shameful wantonness from her mind, but she couldn't lie to herself. Had Luke Wolfson not let her go when he did, she would have willingly let him take her virginity…just as he'd known she would. He'd made Jeremiah Collins cackle when bragging he could make any woman want him…and Collins had offered to buy her back when Wolfson had done with her. And to her utter humiliation it seemed he had done with her, without even bothering to complete the deed. He obviously preferred his jade to the buttoned-up spinster after all.

Mr Robley broke into Fiona's reflection. 'You and Mr Wolfson are…?' he probed, giving her a sala-

cious wink to reassure her any answer would be safe
with him.

'Mr Wolfson and I are simply business associates,'
Fiona burst out, then cleared her throat.

Again Mr Robley's fat forefinger patted his nose
and he endorsed his trustworthiness with a slow nod.
''Course…' he whispered. 'Doing business… I understand, you see…'

Exasperated by his attitude, Fiona turned away. 'Is
there a room where I might wait till the coach arrives?'

Again a pudgy palm wove towards her.

'Is there somewhere free to sit down?' Fiona sighed.

'Till morning?' Mr Robley queried with a squint
of astonishment.

'Yes…' Fiona said faintly. She'd not contemplated
the discomfort of having nowhere to rest her head overnight.

Mr Robley gave Fiona's arm a paternalistic pat.
'He's been a generous sort so I 'spect he'll stump up
for a room and dinner for you as well t'other one. Don't
you fret, I'll speak to him, about it, miss, you see—'

'You will not!' The idea that the landlord would demand Luke pay for her to be fed and watered as well
as his mistress was mortifying. Fiona was coming to
know Mr Robley and reckoned the landlord might want
a tidy profit from her board and lodging before eventually 'finding' her a seat on a coach, days hence.

As she could think of nothing further to say Fiona
gave the landlord a nod, then retraced her footsteps outside and was relieved to see that Luke and his companions had disappeared. Aimlessly she wandered about
the side of the building that led to a large kitchen gar-

den. Several paths criss-crossed beds filled with veg-
etables and herbs, and bathed in morning sun was a
wooden bench set against a mellow brick wall. She
walked towards it and sat down. The golden glow on
her face was pleasantly warm and Fiona was glad that
at least the weather was in her favour. To keep out of
the landlord's speculative sight she'd spend as much
time as possible waiting outside for the coach to take
her on to the Pig and Whistle. She gazed over the sun-
lit fields, thinking that she had missed much peace and
natural beauty by living in the metropolis for twenty-
five years. The signs of spring buds breaking open on
the trees and the fresh verdant landscape lifted her spirits, despite the problems besetting her. Her fingertips
skimmed the low bushes beside her and she breathed
in the scent of rosemary and sage, then picked some
purple-tinted leaves to chew on.

She didn't hear Mr Robley approach until he was
almost upon her. Fiona jumped up, wondering whether
he'd come to tell her that sitting on his bench and eating his herbs would cost her.

He was carrying a steaming plate of food and she
thought that odd as nobody else was outside to have
ordered it.

'Would you like to eat here? I can bring a table...'

Fiona glanced at beef stew and dumplings and felt
her mouth water. Stupidly stubborn earlier, she'd not
eaten her fill of hare and was still hungry. She glanced
away from the tempting meal, angry with the landlord
for going against her. 'Have you asked Mr Wolfson to
pay for my keep even though I said not to?'

'No...honest...' the landlord avowed, slowly shak-

ing his perspiring head to impress on Fiona his truth-
fulness. 'Never did say a word to him. Mr Wolfson
settled his shot and yours, before he went, you see, and
wouldn't hear no more said about it.'

Fiona had started off towards the inn as though to
find Luke and speak to him. Now she pivoted back.
'Went?' she echoed weakly. Despite what she'd said to
him about brief farewells, she'd imagined…hoped…he
might come and see her one last time before leaving.

'Gone off with his friends, you see.' Balancing the
plate in one hand, the landlord gave her arm a pat. 'The
other one's got her claws deep in him, that's what it
is, my dear. You're much nicer, I reckon.' Mr Robley
mimed the action of savage talons with his free fingers
and drew a tiny giggle from Fiona.

'That's better,' the landlord chirped. 'Plenty more
fish in the sea, eh, and where you're going, down Dartmouth way, there's sea aplenty.' He beamed at his little
quip and nudged Fiona with an elbow. 'Now sit you
down and eat this up.'

For some reason Fiona did as she was told and allowed him to place the plate and shiny cutlery on her
lap.

'You let me know what else you might like. There's
ale or tea or anything you fancy. All paid for…' He gave
her a sideways smile that transformed into a chuckle.
'Mr Wolfson might change his mind and come back
looking for you, I reckon, when he's got rid of t'other
one.'

Fiona picked up her knife and fork, wondering how
she would feel about that if he did.

The landlord watched contentedly as Fiona tucked
in enthusiastically to her dinner. He liked to know his

cooking was appreciated. He could be avaricious if the opportunity presented itself, but also a kindly, tolerant soul. He made a good living from gentlemen and young ladies, not always their wives, taking trips and stopping off at his hostelry, so had nothing against illicit shenanigans going on beneath his roof.

'When you've had your fill I'll have the gig brought round. Can't say it's a comfy ride, but as you're keen to get on—'

'What?' Fiona interrupted, using her handkerchief on her lips while frowning intently at him.

'Mr Wolfson's paid for the hire of my vehicle to take you on to the Pig and Whistle. He said you'd got to collect your case from there. You'll be able to get to Dartmouth from that tavern.'

Fiona surged to her feet, handing Mr Robley her half-empty plate. Seeing the disappointment on his face as he studied the half-eaten food, she blurted, 'Oh, thank you, it was delicious, Mr Robley, but I must get going, sir. If I don't turn up soon I won't have a job to go to.'

'Oh, well…if you must…' The landlord dug a hand in the pocket of his apron. 'Left you this, too, he did.' He handed over a small package, then nodded eagerly at it to hurry Fiona opening it. With a sigh Fiona did so, knowing he wouldn't go till his curiosity had been satisfied. She'd an inkling of what might be within, but it felt heavier than expected. On unfolding the parchment wrapper she glimpsed a glitter of gold. But it wasn't just her precious locket within: three sovereigns were stacked on top of the delicately etched oval. With the weight of her riches in one hand Fiona turned the paper, hoping to see a note from him, but the sheet was blank.

Mr Robley's jaw had slackened at the sight of the treasure but he suddenly clacked together his brown teeth and chortled. 'He *do* like you the best, you see...'

Chapter Eleven

She was finally drawing closer to her destination and the knowledge should have brought more contentment with it than it did, Fiona realised, as the gig set off west at quite a pace. She waved to Mr Robley who was flapping his dirty apron at her in farewell. As she settled back on the hard seat she put her pensiveness down to the likely reception she'd get from Mr Herbert when she eventually turned up days late.

The stable hand driving the one-horse contraption was called Bob and he was the landlord's son, he'd told her. Bob gave her a grin, but Fiona's eyes were drawn to a couple of older fellows who'd clattered off the cobbled courtyard to trot alongside the gig. When the road narrowed they dropped behind to follow it.

'Who are they?' Fiona asked.

'Them's me brothers.'

'Oh…' Fiona said. 'Do they also need to go to the Pig and Whistle?' She held on to her bonnet as a stray branch in the hedgerow scuffed it.

'They do today, miss, 'cos Major Wolfson's paid 'em to.'

'For what reason?'

'Escort duty, 'case we meet undesirables on the road. Michael and William have got guns on 'em, see.' He gave Fiona an admiring glance. 'Becky Peake don't get this special treatment. She just got put on the London mail last time he sent *her* home.'

So, it seemed that Mr Robley, despite his winks and nose-taps, wasn't the soul of discretion he'd said he was. The landlord had told his sons that she was one of Luke Wolfson's women. Only she wasn't...and neither did she wish to be! And it certainly wasn't the thought of never again seeing a mercenary that was making her feel oddly wistful, Fiona impressed upon herself, pursing her lips.

Becky Peake was welcome to him and the first opportunity she got to reimburse him, she would. She was glad to have her locket again securely beneath her bodice and, she had to admit, she was grateful for the sovereigns, too, although she wished he'd not been so ridiculously generous. One of the coins would suffice so she'd put the others away in their parchment wrapper, ready to be sent back.

Without money for her fare she would have been stranded at the Pig and Whistle. Although she'd already paid for a place on Toby Williams's coach she doubted he would be willing or able to take her on to finish her journey. If he were still at the hostelry he'd be watching over his nephew, and it would be a mean person indeed who'd expect him to abandon a gravely ill relative to drive her to Dartmouth.

Her thoughts veered back to the debt she now owed. She'd little chance of saving her locket's value and a sovereign. Even should she miraculously manage to gather the sum she'd no idea where to post his payment. Luke had told her nothing about himself, other than he was a bachelor who'd served in the army and was out of practice at trapping. Suddenly her mind pounced on the fact that he knew someone living locally. He'd been on his way to Lowerton to pay a visit on the first occasion they'd met. Nostalgically she recalled the stormy night he had built a fire to dry their clothes and they'd stood talking together in firelight while dripping trees made music in the background.

It all seemed now such a long time ago, yet only days had passed. Fiona wondered if the moody-looking fellow with Becky Peake was Luke's friend from Lowerton and whether they were all finished with Devon and returning to London. She'd never discovered the tale behind the aborted kidnapping of the duke's daughter and it irked her that she probably never would. She had suffered at the hands of the Collins gang because of it and felt she was at least entitled to know why.

Fiona sighed, wanting to stop dratted Luke Wolfson from dominating her every thought. Determinedly she turned her concentration to the people she'd travelled with on Toby Williams's coach. She wondered if the Jacksons and the Beresford sisters were now safely home. Fiona very much hoped they were. Yet she was worried that she'd not had an opportunity to beg them to guard their tongues over her abduction. No lasting harm had been done to her and she'd have liked to tell them so, if she could.

'I suppose you think you've been very clever, don't you?'

'What?' Luke was in no mood for jokes or for humouring his friend. He needed this argument with Rockleigh quickly sorted out so he could make sure Fiona had arrived safely at the Pig and Whistle.

Having taken Becky to the coach station, he'd left her there once he'd extracted her sulky promise to go straight home. Then Luke and Drew had travelled on to Lowerton. Luke no longer cared if Becky again defiantly loitered in Devon. He wouldn't be returning to the King and Tinker so if she went back there she'd be wasting her time.

A clinking together of crystal brought Luke's brooding thoughts back to the present. He was seated opposite Rockleigh at a table in the hunting lodge, a decanter and a glass midway between them on its surface. Another tumbler, half-filled with brandy, was shoved towards him over glossy mahogany.

'Turning the tables on me like that was a low trick. I'd not have thought you'd stoop to it.' Drew sat back in his chair, shrugging as though he blamed himself for being naive. He took a gulp of his drink.

'I've not the vaguest idea what the hell you are talking about.' Luke took a large swallow, too, returning the brandy to the table with a thump. He was still only half-listening to his friend's barbed remarks because images of Fiona's enraptured features were monopolising his mind. The silky feel of her skin and hair were ghostly phantoms beneath his fingertips, but it was her sweet instinctive response to his passion he couldn't forget. His hand clenched more tightly about the cooling glass as he became aware of the heat in his body. 'Can we get this business about Cecilia out of the way?' Luke began drumming some fingers on the tabletop. He'd turned sideways on his chair, a dark-sleeved arm resting on the back rail ready to push him to his feet. 'I'm sorry, Drew, but I've something vital to do.'

'Have you now? Well, sorry to hold you up.' Drew's drawling tone was scathing. 'But, by chance, I've also got something vital to do…and say. And you have more to apologise for than dismissing my niece as though she's one of your fly-by-night doxies.'

Luke discerned from his friend's tone of voice that he was about to hear something significant, and unpleasant, that was additional to the matter that had brought him here. His fingers ceased their tattoo. 'Enlighten me, then,' he invited with an impatient gesture.

'I've a meeting with the Duke of Thornley in the morning to impress on him that I will not be proposing to his daughter, despite his threats of dire consequences if I refuse to do so.'

Luke had taken an ill-timed mouthful of brandy; what he'd just heard made him choke, then splutter, 'If the Duke of Thornley, owner of five titles and six estates, would have you as a son-in-law, I'd sign up for it, Drew.' He dried his mouth with the back of a hand. 'No offence—I know you've got pots of money, but I fear you've not got the credentials where the fair Lady Joan is concerned.'

'Having compromised herself she's not quite so fair now…perhaps that's got a bearing on the matter of my eligibility,' Drew said silkily. 'But of course you know all of this. I made a few enquiries and was told she was planning to elope with a lover to get out of marrying some old roué her father found for her.' Drew cocked his head, resting his chin on forked fingers in a deceptively casual manner. 'I can't make up my mind if you're the old roué or the rake she's rumoured to want to run off with. Did you get cold feet and need a patsy? Or is it you're simply out to foist her on to me from spite because I've demanded you marry Cecilia?'

Luke's glass had hovered by his mouth and he'd stared at his friend over its rim while listening to Drew. The drink was placed back on the table and Luke stood up. 'I think you'd better explain that riddle.'

'I'd rather you did,' Drew returned, also getting to his feet.

The two men faced each other across polished timber, knowing that before too long a punch would be thrown. The silent atmosphere crackled as much from antagonism as burning logs.

'I've had recent business with His Grace, but what that is to do with you, I've no idea,' Luke said shortly.

'It's damn all to do with me!' Drew roared. 'And I don't appreciate being dragged into it so you can wriggle out of facing up to the consequences of kissing my niece at the Hancocks' ball.'

'I wasn't kissing the hoyden!' Luke bawled back. 'She was kissing me…after a fashion. She is only sixteen, after all.'

'Exactly!' Drew barked. 'And that's why you're damn well marrying her.'

'I'm not.' Luke spat through gritted teeth. 'And at the risk of repeating myself—if her mother had taught Cecilia the rudiments of good behaviour we wouldn't be having this conversation.'

Drew's lips tightened although the slur wasn't unjust. His sister had always been too wrapped up in herself to teach her only child her manners, especially around men. Cecilia had been his ward since his sister's widowhood and, like it or no, he'd been the closest

thing to a father the girl had had for three years past.
He'd already accepted that Luke was innocent in all
of this and had been prepared to apologise, days ago.
Drew knew it was his responsibility to do the best he
could for his spoilt niece, yet wished her sire had taken
a stick to her back years ago to discipline the wilful-
ness out of her.

Drew had said something very similar to the Duke
of Thornley about his shortcomings as a father and
about his daughter's wild character. Yet he'd instinctively prevented the old boy from chastising Joan with
a slap. And God only knew she was an infuriating individual; Drew had felt sorely tempted to shake the life
out of her when she refused to answer his questions
about why she'd risk everything to seek out Wolfson
at dead of night. Instead of an explanation the minx
had given him a challenging look.

Drew was determined to get the full story from
Luke because he couldn't believe the girl had called
on him by accident. If he discovered that Luke had
used Thornley's daughter as a pawn to get even with
him, he'd call him out. They had been at school and
at university together, but Drew had already accepted
that this evening their friendship might be irrevocably broken.

'Did you go to Thornley Heights looking for me
when I didn't show up? Is that where you met Joan?'
Luke demanded. He always kept details of his work
confidential so his friend knew no more than he had
business in the area.

'No, I didn't go looking for you,' Drew snapped.

'Well, how in damnation did you manage to put
yourself in Joan's path? Her father rarely lets her out

because of the Collins gang.' Luke had failed to make any sense out of his friend's tale.

'She rarely goes out…the shy little thing, yet here we are about to get engaged if the old boy has his way.' Drew gave a mirthless chuckle. 'Which he won't…'

Luke forked five fingers through his hair in exasperation. Memories of Fiona were again nagging at his mind, despite the gravity of his friend's predicament. He closed his eyes against the strength of the need to see her again. 'Look…whatever's gone on, Rockleigh, I can't help solve it. Whatever you've done—'

'It's not what *I've* done, is it?' Drew snarled. 'All *I* did was escort the chit home when she came here to find you.'

'Joan Morland came *here*?' Luke barked an astonished laugh.

'Indeed she did, alone…with just a lad driving her,' Drew stated.

Luke swore beneath his breath. His mind had pounced immediately on the only reason there was for Thornley's daughter to do that. He'd told Joan he wouldn't take on her father's contract, yet it seemed she'd not accepted his decision and had acted recklessly in her attempt to change his mind.

'Nothing to say?' Drew taunted, feeling his temper bubbling dangerously.

'How in God's name did she find out I was coming here?' Luke blasted.

'Well, someone told her and I imagine it was you. The way I see it, a woman would only take such a risk for a lover.' Drew's control exploded and he launched himself at Luke, swinging a right hook. Luke staggered, but hit his opponent back, harder. Drew fell, sprawling, across the table, sending the decanter skidding perilously close to the edge.

'We'll have to sort this out another time. I need to go,' Luke shouted. He knew he owed his friend an explanation if not an apology. But he'd not the time to spend talking now. He needed to catch up with Fiona to make sure she was safe.

Drew leapt between Luke and the doorway, barring his exit as he strode towards it.

'You're not going anywhere till I know the details. If you've seduced Thornley's daughter, then you can marry her.'

'What…and Cecilia, too?' Luke snarled sardonically. 'Bigamy's not my style.'

Infuriated, Drew bounded at Luke again.

'Don't be damned ridiculous, Drew!' Luke sidestepped and put out his hands in placation. 'I haven't seduced Lady Joan or even flirted with her—I barely know her.' He wiped a smear of blood from his mouth with a curled finger. 'I've only spoken to her a couple of times and your name and this lodge never cropped up between us. My business was with her father.'

'Did the duke know you were coming to see me?'

Luke searched his mind for such a conversation… and found one. A whistling sigh was expelled through his teeth. 'I told Thornley I was heading to a hunting lodge at Lowerton to see a friend before returning to London.' Luke leaned his back against the wall and tilted up his head, staring bleakly at the ceiling. If Joan had been eavesdropping on that occasion, or the duke had told her where his mercenary had gone, then she would have known where to head in an attempt to intercept him.

'So do you want to tell me all about it or are we going to fight some more?' Drew went to the table and poured himself a drink. He emptied the glass before adding, 'You blasted well owe me the truth, Luke.'

Luke couldn't deny it, so as briefly as possible he outlined his business in Devon with the Duke of Thornley. He also told Drew why he'd missed their first appointment, and how he'd helped stranded travellers whose coach had come a cropper. But he stopped short of mentioning Fiona and her ordeal at the hands of the Collins gang. That was too private, and, Luke realised, too precious, for even an old friend to know about.

Drew poured two drinks this time and moved one in Luke's direction.

'It sounds like some melodramatic romance novel my sister would read.' Drew shook his head in a mixture of mockery and despair.

'I know.' Luke crossed his arms over his chest. 'But unfortunately, it's no fiction.' He speared a glance at Drew. 'I'll speak to Thornley and explain.'

Drew snorted a mirthless laugh. 'His daughter's already tried that several times.'

'How do you know?'

'She sent me a note telling me so.'

'You've not blamed her in any of this, I notice.'

Drew shrugged. 'Young women can be impulsive and excitable—'

'Like Cecilia, you mean?' Luke interrupted drily.

'So, if you told the duke you were coming to see me, and he let on to his daughter about it, he's at fault.' Drew ignored the reference to his errant niece. 'I didn't have to escort Joan home, or put His Grace in the picture over what had happened. I could have packed her off in her trap and let her fall straight into Jeremiah Collins's clutches.'

'A point worth bringing to Thornley's attention to-morrow at your meeting,' Luke said. 'And while we're talking of gracious gallantry...no more did I have to bring Cecilia home from the Hancocks' ball that night before she disgraced herself any further.' He approached Drew, held out his hand in a peace offering. 'Send her off to her aunt's out in the sticks. Better still, send her off to finishing school somewhere.'

Drew took Luke's fingers, testing their strength with his own in a single shake. 'Do you think Thornley will send his daughter away? Not that he needs to—nobody knows but us and them.'

'What does she say about it all?' Luke asked. 'Apart from sorry.'

'I wouldn't marry him if he were the last man alive.' Drew had squeaked his answer in a childish treble.

Luke gave a gruff chuckle. 'Well, there you are, then. His Grace might huff and puff, but he'll give in to her in the end. Unless Joan Morland decides she wants you, you're quite safe.'

'Well...go on, then.'

Luke frowned.

'I know you're itching to get away so you can meet a woman. And it's not Becky, is it?'

'Becky's on her way back to London, as far as I know.'

'I'm heading back that way in the morning,' Drew said. 'Perhaps I'll catch up with the minx...'

'Be my guest,' Luke said.

'So...tell me about the woman who's got you dangling on a bit of string.'

Luke turned for the door, giving his friend no more response than a smile.

'The lady you were with at the King and Tinker?' Drew guessed. 'I reckon you've rescued that fair maiden…and put yourself in peril instead.'

Instead of telling his friend to mind his own business Luke made a rather rude gesture, but, worryingly, he immediately understood what Drew had hinted at.

It wasn't love…it was lust, he told himself, banging the door shut after him as he heard Rockleigh erupt in laughter.

Chapter Twelve

'Oh, how lovely to see you!'

Fiona had spotted the Jacksons as soon as the Pig and Whistle's creaking sign hove into view. She waved furiously in greeting, allowing Bob Robley to assist her down in the tavern's courtyard, then sped towards the couple. They appeared to have been awaiting her arrival, so she blurted, 'Did you know I'd be coming by today?'

Mrs Jackson took Fiona's hands in her own and gave them a fond squeeze. 'Indeed we did expect you, my dear! Mr Wolfson sent a note ahead of you to ask us to welcome you. Not that we needed him to tell us to do that! You cannot know how happy and relieved we felt to discover he had you under his care. It is wonderful to see you, you poor child.' Overcome with emotion Betty Jackson sniffed and enclosed Fiona in a motherly hug. 'Are you *well*, my dear?' She gave the younger woman a significant look, then glanced about to make sure that nobody was within earshot. 'You understand what I mean by *well*?' she hissed, raising her eyebrows, but her weathered features were shaped by concern rather than prurience.

'I'm very well,' Fiona answered quietly.

Mrs Jackson persisted. 'Mr Wolfson caught up with you in time, before those fiends…?'

'I was…am…perfectly fine,' Fiona interrupted with a faint blush. 'My dignity came off the worst,' she quipped. 'I was tossed about like a sack of potatoes.'

'Savages!' Mr Jackson interjected. 'I'd like to get my hands on those two.'

'Did they take you to that monster, Jeremiah Collins?' Betty Jackson whispered, aghast.

'I did meet him and he's a very insipid individual in the flesh.' Fiona gave her opinion of the notorious criminal.

'It's the quiet ones you have to watch,' Peter Jackson growled. 'The sooner the devil's at the end of a noose the better.'

Fiona nodded, feeling a little shiver race over her as she recalled Jeremiah's boast: *I've money to make and pleasure to take before I swing on Gallows Hill.* She sincerely hoped that the law caught up with him soon.

'Mr Wolfson is so brave!' Mrs Jackson's clasped hands were pressed to her bosom. 'How could he attain victory against such ruffians?' she asked rhetorically, eyes glowing with admiration.

'He is a military man, so used to employing tactics when skirmishing,' Mr Jackson opined. 'Nevertheless, praise where it is due for the feat of rescuing you so quickly, Miss Chapman.'

Fiona smiled faintly, wondering what the couple would think if they knew their hero was, or had been, a colleague of the wretch they'd see hung. And how would these fine people take knowing she'd come closer to being ravished by her saviour than by any gang member?

But Fiona knew she'd never discredit Luke Wolfson to anybody and not simply because of the service he'd done her. She sensed, deep within her heart, that he was a good man despite indications to the contrary and so little time spent with him to judge. But more than that, she felt oddly loyal to him, in the way she did to her mother. Maude had chosen to go ahead and marry Cecil Ratcliff despite her daughter's warnings about the man. Even before the banns had been read Cecil had tried to insinuate his fingers beneath Fiona's bodice on two occasions. Yet her mother had been angry to have her complain, insisting Cecil had simply been overzealous with his hugs. Now Maude knew the truth about the man she'd chosen to believe over her daughter, but it was too late. Maude had failed her child and no amount of bitter regrets would ever put things back as they'd been between mother and daughter.

'Mr Wolfson made us promise to keep quiet about your kidnapping,' Mrs Jackson whispered.

'Not that he needed to tell us to do that, either,' Mr Jackson emphasised. 'We would never have risked a slur on your reputation. We had faith in him when he promised to put things right.'

'Thank you for being so considerate...' Fiona said huskily with tears in her eyes. 'I *have* been worried about gossip.'

'We have spoken to nobody about what happened to you,' Mr Jackson quickly reassured. 'Obviously the Beresford sisters and Toby and Bert know, but I'm sure they'll heed Mr Wolfson's words on it and button their lips.'

'How is Bert? All of you have been constantly in my thoughts,' Fiona said earnestly.

'Bert is on the mend. Toby has travelled back to the Fallow Buck so he might be reunited with his own vehicle, if not his stolen nags. I doubt he'll see those again.' Mr Jackson sorrowfully shook his head.

Fiona realised that the loss of the coachman's animals would be a great blow to him.

'Toby planned to get Bert quickly home to his own bed from the Fallow Buck. On his last visit the doctor said the lad had made a remarkable improvement and should fully recover.'

'That's wonderful news,' Fiona breathed. 'And the Beresford sisters?'

'Oh, I imagine they're back at their own fireside now. They left with us their very good wishes for you.'

Fiona smiled on hearing that. All had turned out better than she had dared hope. If her employer were to be understanding about her delayed arrival, then her life would be no better, or worse, than before calamity struck.

'Well, let's find a quiet spot to sit down inside the inn. There's lots to talk about and I expect something to eat wouldn't go amiss.' Mr Jackson held out an elbow to both ladies and the trio proceeded into the Pig and Whistle.

'The duke would like an audience, sir.'

'I have an urgent appointment, but you may tell His Grace I will be back this way and will call in tomorrow to see him at Thornley Heights.'

'But it is of the utmost importance, Major Wolfson, he bade me impress that upon you.'

Luke walked out of the farrier's into warm sunlight so he might converse privately with Thornley's steward. He'd been forced to break his journey towards the Pig and Whistle because the mare needed shoeing. As well as heading there for Fiona's sake he had to return the horse to its owner and collect Star, full of beans no doubt after his enforced rest in a strange stable.

But Luke was being dogged on all sides by holdups. He cursed beneath his breath in frustration. He realised his obsession with Fiona Chapman was illogical, and out of character, yet still his mind persisted in returning to the spinster he barely knew, but desired so ardently that every fibre of his being seemed to have grown uncomfortably tense. He accepted, with wry self-mockery, that his desire for her company was probably not reciprocated. Indeed, he'd got the impression when they'd parted at the King and Tinker that she couldn't remove herself from his presence quickly enough. But he'd also noticed that she'd glanced at Becky with an amount of female pique and he'd enough experience with the fairer sex to recognise a jealous woman.

The smith walked out of his workshop, leading the mare. Having paid the fellow for his work, Luke turned again to the hovering steward. About to send him on his way by repeating the message he'd already delivered, he thought of Drew. His friendship with Drew had stood the test of time, but it might not outlast this crisis. He owed it to Rockleigh to speak up on his behalf and make the duke see sense about Joan's folly. Luke couldn't believe that Alfred Thornley would shackle his cherished daughter to a fellow she didn't want. His Grace, despite his undoubted fine intelligence, tended to act first and think second when in a passion over something. Luke had first-hand experience of the man's arrogance. He guessed that Joan's father had already calmed down enough to see the flaws in an enforced marriage. But he was too obstinate to admit he'd been wrong and was seeking a way out that would leave his pride intact.

If he rode hard for Thornley Heights then back again, he'd be delayed by no more than a few hours, Luke realised. He trusted the Jacksons to care for Fiona in his absence. And he did at least have the comfort of knowing that she'd arrived safely: he'd quizzed Robley's sons and been assured they'd seen her go inside the Pig and Whistle with a middle-aged couple.

Luke gave Thornley's man a brief nod. 'Very well— you may tell His Grace I will arrive by two of the clock this afternoon.'

Maude had never travelled on a mail coach before although she was no stranger to the hired cab. With a public hackney one had the chance to be private, rather than assailed by the touch and odour of strangers' bodies. She hoped the infernal bone-shaker would stop soon so she might get off to have some refreshment and cool down.

It was late April but the atmosphere seemed as hot as the month of June and the interior of the coach was smelly and steamy. Maude cast a jaundiced eye on her maid; Rose seemed unperturbed as she snored with her chin resting on her chest. Irritated, Maude realised that her servant had a better seat than she did being next to the window with air stirring her wispy brown hair. Maude wondered whether to wake Rose and tell her to change places, but of course that would entail bumping into the other occupants of the congested coach and Maude would sooner suffer cramps than risk physical contact with any of them. Stiffly, she straightened her legs beneath her skirts to ease their position.

She stopped fidgeting on hearing the blare of a horn. She avoided the eye of a labourer seated opposite who'd given her several lewd winks and beneath her breath muttered a little prayer which was answered: the vehicle slowed down and pulled into a wide tavern courtyard.

'Might we have a pot of tea, my girl, and some biscuits or cakes?' Maude asked the servant as she and her maid settled down in chairs by the hearth.

'I'll fetch scones and bread and butter with your tea, madam, if you like.'

Having received an agreement to her suggestion, Megan headed off with the order, her rosy lips forming a kiss for Sam as she spotted him through the window. She sashayed towards the kitchens, knowing her beau was watching her while using the currycomb on a horse.

If anybody suspected that her sweetheart was a member of the Collins gang, they knew better than to say so outright. Most local people took the view that the less said openly about the smuggling trade, the better. Turning a blind eye to nocturnal visits by fellows carrying kegs was accepted behaviour in this neck of the woods. Megan knew that her employer filled his cellar with contraband, but instead of personally taking deliveries, he'd leave the barn door ajar on an appointed night. So that he could honestly claim not to know the criminals he'd hide payment behind a brick in the wall for furtive collection. Since the landlord of the Cockerell had been found stabbed, no innkeeper had reneged on paying up for supplies brought on trust.

Megan had no family living close by; she'd left home in Exeter at sixteen to make her way in the world. The landlord and his wife provided her board and lodging and she had nothing but tips from the customers to put into her purse. So Megan appreciated that her Sam was often flush from running with a powerful man like Jeremiah Collins. In the past Sam had treated her to lengths of smuggled French lace and perfume.

Of course, Sam's parents suspected what he did to boost his meagre regular wages, and made no bones about it. With five younger brothers and sisters to feed they were grateful for whatever merchandise their eldest boy brought home. They asked no awkward questions as to how Sam came by sudden riches.

Maude gave the servant a gracious smile; the girl seemed keen to please, she thought, as Megan put down the tray filled with food and tea things and offered to pour.

Megan's pleasant expression turned sour when the maid started pouring tea and waved her away without offering her a tip.

'I do hope we find my daughter quickly.' Maude sighed as she watched Rose replace the teapot on the tray. 'How am I to know where to look for Fiona? It was bad of her to go off without leaving me her proper direction. Devon is a vast place.'

Rose gave her mistress a sympathetic look, but refrained from pointing out that Miss Fiona had probably been reticent so her stepfather didn't discover her whereabouts. Not that Mrs Chapman—Rose refused to think of her mistress as anything other than the late master's spouse—would have willingly betrayed her daughter. Rose knew Cecil Ratcliff for a bully. If he'd wanted to have Fiona brought home, he'd have eventually got out of his wife where to look for her. But Rose reckoned that Cecil had bigger fish to fry: she had opened the door to duns a few days ago. Now Cecil had almost emptied the house of furnishings, the property would be sold off next. In Rose's opinion, even if Mrs Chapman decided to return to the thieving wretch with her tail between her legs, she'd have nowhere to call home.

'I wonder if my daughter stopped here for refreshment?' Maude looked about the interior of the heavily beamed tavern. 'I'm sure she would have broken her journey as we have. Mayhap the serving girl might remember her,' Maude ventured brightly. 'It would not hurt to ask—she seems an obliging young woman.'

'More tea, madam?' Megan had quickly responded to the customer's beckoning finger. A few coppers as a tip could yet come her way.

'Do you know if Miss Fiona Chapman stopped at this hostelry? It would have been quite recently—she is my daughter, you see...' Maude tutted as the girl began loading crockery onto the tray as though deaf to her question. 'Did you not hear what I said, miss?'

'I... I don't recall that name,' Megan lied, flustered. 'Sorry... I've to wash up.' Picking up the tray, she hurried off.

'Well...really! It was a simple enough enquiry,' Maude huffed loudly. 'I'll ask the landlord instead.'

Megan heard that threat and immediately reduced

her pace to begin mulling things over. She stopped
and put down the tray on an empty table, then glanced
over a shoulder at the two women. Pursed-lipped, she
thought harder about things. She didn't like the fact
that her Sam was involved in holding up coaches, or
that he threatened people with guns to rob them. But
he'd sworn to her that it was Fred Ruff who'd fired the
shot at Bert Williams, winging him. Megan had been
mightily relieved when Toby Williams and Bert had
turned up yesterday to collect their repaired coach.
Bert had looked poorly, but at least he was again on his
feet; he'd even managed to give her a wink and she'd
teased him, what with him being a married man. But
neither of the Williamses had said a word about an abduction and naturally Megan couldn't say she knew one
had taken place when the coach had been held up. So
she'd realised that the two men were being respectful
of the victim's reputation.

Kidnapping was something new and *very* bad for
Sam to be involved in and Megan had told her sweetheart her thoughts on it. Not that he ever took any
notice of her; Sam was too eager to please his boss
because he liked his pockets jingling and he didn't intend mucking out stables all his life, so he'd told her.

But an idea was taking root in Megan's mind, making her slowly retrace her steps towards the seated
women. The Chapmans were not first-rate Quality; if
they had been, Mrs Chapman wouldn't be travelling
in a mail coach. But she was genteel and such people
hated scandals. The mother couldn't yet know what had
happened to her daughter, but when she found out she'd
want to protect Fiona's marriage prospects and whip
her back to London. In Megan's opinion, that couldn't

happen soon enough. The longer Mrs Chapman hung around asking questions, the more likely it would be that the whole story might emerge. The locals tolerated the Collins gang for the sake of cheap tea and brandy, but they'd be outraged to hear of an innocent woman's kidnap and furious if dragoons started turning houses upside down in their hunt for the perpetrators. Megan knew that if her sweetheart were arrested he stood little chance of acquittal.

Sam had told Megan of Fiona's eventual fate: Major Wolfson—who the gang suspected was a turncoat— had bought her from Collins to be his paramour. Jem had regretted bartering his prisoner and had sent Sam and Fred to snatch Fiona back, but they'd been given the slip. Miss Chapman was not the aristocrat's daughter they'd first thought her, but Wolfson's interest in her had piqued Collins. Jem had told his men he reckoned Wolfson saw Fiona Chapman as good for a profit as well as a roll in the hay.

'What is it you want?' Maude had turned and seen the serving girl hovering just behind.

'I think I do remember your daughter, madam…' Megan began in her slow country burr. 'I believe she was with a gentleman.' She lowered her voice and her eyes, as though embarrassed by the information she was imparting.

'A gentleman?' Maude echoed hoarsely. It had crossed her mind that Fiona might have a secret beau, but she'd dismissed it as too fantastic.

'His name is Major Wolfson as I recollect,' Megan added helpfully.

Maude had turned white and Rose sent her mistress a concerned look.

'And where might I find this fellow?' Maude croaked, glancing about as though anxious nobody should overhear the alarming news that her daughter might be a fallen woman.

'I've no idea, madam, but I do know he had business with the Duke of Thornley,' Megan said.

Chapter Thirteen

'Might that be him, do you think, ma'am?'

'I don't think so, Rose; he is not in military uniform,' Maude answered, squinting at the broad back of a tall fellow who was striding away from them towards his horse.

The gig Maude had hired at the Fallow Buck had turned through wide crenellated pillars and rattled along a mile of meandering tree-lined avenue before pulling up in front of a sweeping set of steps. She'd watched the darkly handsome young man athletically descending the shallow flight of stone two treads at a time, his long leather coat flying out behind him. He was certainly a dashing individual, but in her mind's eye Maude had an image of her daughter's swain—if indeed one *could* term Major Wolfson such. Maude had a depressing idea her daughter was possibly viewed as a mistress rather than a wife by the scoundrel. But she strove for optimism and to believe him honourable if predictably mundane. He would assuredly not be so distinguished looking as the gentleman in the distance, who was probably the duke's son. Fiona, Maude inwardly sighed, would be true to form and attract a suitor with little to recommend him. Possibly this *major* had just the prospect of his army pension to offer a wife.

It had been a great sadness to Maude that Fiona had not found an eligible chap like her younger sister. Verity was a vivacious charmer and had her glossy chestnut hair and petite figure to turn a man's head, whereas Fiona, being rather too tall and too bland in looks and personality in her mother's eyes, had been overlooked by the bachelors who'd come into her daughters' orbit.

But Fiona had not helped herself, Maude thought crossly; as a dutiful mother she had often bitten her tongue about her eldest girl's frustrating lack of ambition to catch a man. *'Why can you not be more like your pretty sister?'* would have been too cruel a comment to fire at Fiona. But to Maude's chagrin it had nearly rolled off her tongue on more occasions than she could count. Then, after Anthony died, assailed by loneliness and grief, she'd been glad to have Fiona's company…until Cecil wormed his way into her life and she'd again resented her daughter being under her feet. But only at first.

Maude knew she'd been wrong about Fiona in many ways. She should have heeded her eldest child's warning about Ratcliff's swinish character. But the most startling thing for Maude was learning that the girl she'd known for twenty-five years had an inner steel and a sense of adventure that she'd overlooked. It had come as a shock when Fiona had bluntly told her that Cecil Ratcliff was a lecher and not only that, but she was also off to Devon to start a new life so she'd never have to see him again. Might her homely daughter surprise her one more time by netting an eligible gentleman who'd propose to her and give her everything her heart desired? If such a miracle were to come to pass, Maude knew that all their troubles would be at an end. She'd live with her newly married daughter and son-in-law in their lavish home and Cecil Ratcliff could go hang!

These mixed musings and fantasies had passed through Maude's consciousness as she gazed up at the magnificent house. With a deep sigh she collected her thoughts and got down to the job in hand. 'Well, here we are, then,' she declared briskly.

The stable lad driving the gig was peeking nervously from under his brows at his grand surroundings. He'd never before been so close to the ducal residence and felt like a trespasser. His customer might be gentry from London, but he didn't believe she was of a class that hobnobbed with dukes any more than he was. 'Reckon I should've taken you straight round the back,' he muttered.

'Indeed, you should not!' Maude said indignantly, despite also feeling awestruck. She watched the handsome fellow galloping off into the distance, then turned her attention to the shrinking youth. 'Come help us down if you please. I have urgent business with this Duke of Thornley.'

The boy did as he was bid and watched, slack-jawed, as the lady marched to the steps and started up them. Arriving out of breath at the top, Maude took an inspiriting lungful of air, then hammered on the door.

His Grace had been on the point of returning to his study, having spent some minutes conversing with his butler after Wolfson had left. 'Who in damnation might that be?' He strode to the door in front of the ancient servant, muttering to himself, 'Has Wolfson remembered his manners and come to apologise?'

In fact, Thornley knew that the mercenary had nothing to be sorry about. The man had told him plain truths, as he always did. Grudgingly, Thornley was coming to like the fellow, even though he had learned some worrying and rather humbling things from Wolfson today.

Flinging the door wide, Alfred stared at the two middle-aged women on his step. He could tell the mistress from the maid, not just from their attire, but from the air of entitlement exuded by the person closest to him. 'And, pray, who might you be?'

'I am Mrs...Ratcliff...' Maude announced in her crispest accent. In common with Rose she hated giving her name as Mrs Ratcliff, but knew she must, as unfortunately, that's who she was now. 'I have come to speak to the Duke of Thornley on an urgent matter. Would you fetch him, please?'

'I have no need to...you are speaking to him, madam.' Thornley looked her buxom figure up and down then cocked his head at the maid hovering behind.

A silence ensued during which Maude felt her temper rising. How dare he make her stand outside while he boldly gave her the once-over as though she were some auditioning servant! She'd not expected the fellow to be so...imperious in tone and presence. And why he attended his own door was beyond her. Anybody might be excused for thinking *him* one of the hired help. 'I do not discuss my business on the front step,' Maude burst out, her bravado wavering.

'Well, I suppose you'd better come in, then,' Thornley said, and stalked off. Over a shoulder he instructed his butler to show his visitor to the blue saloon and enquire whether she would like refreshment.

After ten minutes the tea arrived. Maude and Rose sat perched on high-backed velvet chairs in a sumptuously furnished room. The blue saloon lived up to its name: a hue of a summer sky, adorned with puffy clouds and fat-cheeked cherubs, decorated the ceiling while the soaring walls were lined with watered silk in a toning pastel shade.

The clock chimed four o'clock, making Rose jump. The duke's servant poured tea for Mrs Ratcliff, then put down the pot.

'Please give a cup of tea to my maid,' Maude said firmly.

Thornley's lackey did as she was told, but with a pronounced arch to one of her eyebrows. Then she left, leaving the visitors alone. Before entering the blue saloon the butler had found Rose a chair in the hallway where she might wait while her mistress had an audience with the duke. But Maude would not hear of that and had insisted her servant accompany her, more from feeling nervous than egalitarian. Nevertheless, Rose had given her employer a grateful look and the butler a smug sniff on passing.

'Perhaps the duke has forgotten about your arrival, ma'am,' Rose ventured in a whisper on hearing her restless mistress's teacup clatter on its porcelain saucer.

'Perhaps the bumptious fellow has not forgotten but has no intention of giving me five minutes of his precious time,' Maude returned bitterly.

'The *bumptious fellow* shall give you ten minutes of his time, madam, but not a moment longer,' Thornley said drily, having just entered the room and overheard his visitor's sniping.

Maude blushed, put up her chin and pushed away her cup. 'Then I will state my business without delay, sir. I am looking for my daughter and have a report that she might be in the company of a Major Wolfson. I have also heard that you may know of that fellow's whereabouts. If you do, I would be grateful to have his direction.'

Beneath his breath Thornley made a sound, part-chuckle, part-groan. So Wolfson's doxy was refined enough to have a mother worrying about her. Yet Alfred was sure the boy he'd sent to the King and Tinker with a note for Wolfson had told him the courtesan's surname was Peake, not Ratcliff. Of course, he wouldn't be surprised to know the handsome major had more than one camp follower...

'I do know Wolfson but, alas, am not acquainted with your daughter. You have just missed the man, actually, but I expect you might find him at the King and Tinker, or perhaps the Pig and Whistle. I hope you are successful in your search.' Thornley turned for the door as though to leave. 'Do finish your tea... if you will.'

'That was *him*?' Maude exclaimed, jumping to her feet.

'Who was *him*?' Thornley asked a trifle impatiently.

'We saw a fellow leaving.'

'Yes...that was Major Wolfson, or Mr Wolfson as I believe he terms himself now.'

Maude almost stamped in frustration. 'Oh...but I

might have asked him about Fiona and have missed the chance.'

'Fiona?' Thornley had again been on the point of quitting the room, but pivoted back to stare at Maude.

'My daughter… Miss Fiona Chapman,' Maude snapped, sure the fellow hadn't paid heed to a word she'd said. Obviously he thought himself too important to bother with her. Rather haughtily she said, 'Thank you for your time and hospitality, sir. We must go now.' She wanted none of his tea, or his condescension, and for two pins would tell him so.

'No…please…sit down…stay a while so we might talk.' Thornley sighed, feeling a weight sink to his stomach.

That morning he had sent his steward looking for Luke Wolfson so he might quiz the mercenary over his friend Rockleigh. In no uncertain terms, Wolfson had told him that Drew Rockleigh was an exemplary individual with excellent connections, but he was his own man and would be coerced into nothing against his will. But Wolfson had had more to deliver than his friend's character reference: the major had gone on to relate a deeply disturbing story that had left Alfred feeling shocked and ashamed and deserving of his hireling's rebuke.

He knew himself to be arrogant and impetuous and had never before thought to curb those traits. He was the Duke of Thornley and had been bred to do as he pleased and damn the nay-sayers. But Heaven only knew he regretted the day he'd concocted the kidnap plot because never had he imagined how awful might be the consequences.

So, this was the mother of the brave woman Wolfson

had told him about. Less than an hour ago he had heard a tale about an abduction and a young woman's pluck and fortitude in coping with an ordeal that, Thornley was sure, might have deranged lesser females. He glanced at the lady who'd brought into the world such an intrepid soul. Yes…he could believe the connection true; Mrs Ratcliff was proudly challenging him with her stare—just like his late wife in that respect. Ethel would often tell him he might be a duke, but he was her husband first and he could get off his high horse.

Alfred felt duty-bound to inform the girl's mother about the dangers her daughter had faced and that the blame for Miss Chapman's ordeal could be laid at his door. But he didn't relish the doing of it. He hadn't wanted any lasting gossip surrounding his daughter's imaginary beau, so had known that at some time he'd have to expose all the details of his scheme to bring Collins to justice. He'd anticipated being hailed as a hero rather than an incompetent fool when his deception was made public.

The tale of Joan running off to elope had indeed pricked up the villain's ears and made him act, just as Alfred had intended it should. And Miss Fiona Chapman, an innocent in all of it, had suffered because of his half-baked plot. Luke Wolfson had impressed that fact upon him and Alfred knew that, had the two men been the same age, he'd not only have felt the full force of the mercenary's rage, but his fist, too.

Alfred would remain eternally grateful that the major had been in the vicinity to save the day; if Miss Chapman had been harmed Alfred's conscience would have tortured him till he died. A young lady's virtue, her dignity and self-respect—perhaps even her life—

had all been at stake because of him. Alfred thought of his own daughter. He had put Joan at risk, too: she'd never have gone out late at night looking for Wolfson but for the plot's existence. Oh, Joan had been all for the intrigue and excitement of it all, but she was still a green girl and should be allowed to indulge those sensations within a parent's protection. Now Alfred accepted that Drew Rockleigh deserved praise not punishment for the service he'd done Joan. Neither of them wanted the marriage he'd been determined to force on them and having Joan blaming him for her unhappiness would be a constant torment. So, etiquette be damned! If anybody dared start a whisper that the Duke of Thornley's daughter had been compromised, either by her imaginary beau, or by Drew Rockleigh, he'd sue them to kingdom come!

'I think you have something bad to tell me,' Maude said hoarsely. She had watched the duke's harsh features altering shape beneath some inner conflict that had left him looking worryingly grave. Instead of feeling relief at his softening expression, Maude had been alarmed by the change in him. 'Fiona has come to harm?' Maude whispered.

When His Grace said nothing, but paced to and fro pulling on his lower lip, reflecting on a way to couch bad news, Maude let out a small wail. 'It is all my fault! I've been stupid and selfish and a very bad parent. Why have I failed her when all I want is the best for my daughter? She would have been safe at home, had it not been for me.'

Thornley gazed at the woman who'd just voiced virtually word for word the self-abuse spinning in his own head. He knew that he had many apologies to make and

he might as well start straight away. Joan had chosen to
be reckless, but Miss Chapman's reputation had been
sullied through no fault of her own. Many folk were
privy to Fiona's ill treatment, some of them very nasty
characters. Alfred hated the thought of it, but feared the
scandal would eventually get out and ruin this woman's
daughter. 'Would you mind if your maid waited outside
while we converse privately?' he croaked.

'I would not mind, sir,' Maude whispered, giving
Rose a nod of dismissal. She would sooner be on her
own if she were about to hear of a disaster befalling
Fiona. Rose had served the Chapmans well over many
years, and was as loyal as the day was long, but Maude
knew that there were occasions when class differences
must be observed.

When Rose had been settled outside on a hall chair
Thornley closed the door and ambled towards Maude.
Stiffly he went down by her side and clumsily took one
of her hands, cradling it in his.

With increasing incredulity Maude had watched
him approach her and lower himself on creaky knees.
As soon as he touched her she instinctively withdrew
her fingers with a hiss of alarm.

Thornley patted her digits in reassurance, but left
them curled on her lap. Turning himself to a more comfortable position, he sagged on to his posterior, next to
her armchair. 'First let me start by saying I have heard
that your daughter has wit and courage and that it has
sustained her through a very unpleasant episode. I can
see from where your daughter might have got such qualities. Or perhaps you will tell me that Fiona favours
your husband.'

'My daughter detests my husband…as do I…but

we both loved her father very much,' Maude rattled off, still dazed to have made such an admission to a stranger.

'Indeed…that is a mixed blessing and I would hear more about it.' Thornley glanced at her, looking taken aback. 'But not now because I still have much to say. I must tell you something and beg your forgiveness when I have done for being the bearer of such bad tidings…' He frowned, wondering where to start to report to a mother that her unwed daughter had been vilely mistreated, and what's more, folk knew about it.

'My Fiona… She is not…' Maude licked her bloodless lips. Was he beating about the bush unable to say her daughter was gravely ill…and might *die*?

'Oh…no, no, she is in fine fettle!' Thornley burst out, having read Mrs Ratcliff's dreadful suspicions from her expression. He suddenly smiled, feeling rather better about everything. 'You are right, madam, there are much worse things might befall a parent than a scandal about a daughter. We are not at a wake, are we? Come, let us cheer ourselves up.' Thornley struggled to his feet while his visitor watched him with her eyes popping and her jaw sagging.

'I imagine—if you're anything like my dear departed wife—that you might prefer a drink of something stronger than tea.' He gave the bell pull a tug, then another. 'We must toast our children's good health, then worry about the rest later!'

Chapter Fourteen

Had Fiona but known it, she would have been astonished to learn that her attitude mirrored that of the illustrious Duke of Thornley, a man she'd never met.

Things were not so bad, she impressed on herself
in an attempt to combat pangs of melancholy. Gossip
could not kill her, but when thrown over Fred Ruff's
horse she might have slid off and cracked open her
skull during that mad gallop. Worse still, once she
was locked in that mildewed cell, bound and gagged,
her captors would doubtless have gone off about their
nefarious business. Had they met an abrupt end at the
hands of the militia, she, too, would have expired,
but not mercifully quickly, but in a drawn-out grisly
way! It was the terrifying thought that she might slowly
starve with nobody about to hear her muffled cries
that had spurred her to immediately attempt to escape.
She had much to be thankful for! She had her precious liberty, and her health, and good friends like the
Jacksons...

And the memory of Luke Wolfson's hands on her
body, trailing fire in their wake...

With a sigh Fiona cast him from her mind for the hundredth time that day. She had promised herself not to mope over him. She must accept that he was gone for good and probably hadn't given her, or their escapade, a moment's pause, since being reunited with his mistress.

Leaning her elbows on the wide gate at the side of the Pig and Whistle, she cupped her chin in her palms and gazed over meadow grass that swayed and gleamed beneath soft breezes and the setting sun. How would her mother take knowing about her eldest daughter's plight? Thank goodness Maude was in blissful ignorance of it all, she thought. But ever since Cecil Ratcliff set about defrauding the Chapman family Maude had toughened up, so she might cope better than expected when eventually Fiona recounted her tale. And she must; she'd hate it to come to her mother's notice on the grapevine.

Had her papa still been alive he would be distraught to know how badly things had turned out for his wife and spinster daughter. In his final months he'd mentioned leaving them financially secure, with no need to worry about paying the bills. But Anthony Chapman hadn't reckoned with his wife's silly vanity making her prey to a silver-tongued trickster. Her father's astute business deals, made to provide his widow with a comfortable pension, were now lining another man's pockets. Or they had been, Fiona reminded herself sourly, till her stepfather emptied his pockets at gaming tables and brothels.

It would have been easy for Fiona to rail at Maude, but she would not allow Cecil Ratcliff the added victory of turning mother and daughter against one another. He had often tried to drive a wedge between them, no doubt so he could mistreat both women under his roof without them seeking mutual support. He hadn't succeeded; though the parting between Fiona and Maude had been strained, there had been tears and affection on both sides.

Familiar laughter reached Fiona's ears, breaking into her introspection. Through one of the Pig and Whistle's mullioned windows she could see Peter and Betty Jackson. They were seated comfortably, partaking of an after-dinner tot, happy in each other's company. Her parents had liked to settle down together in such a way. But Fiona had not seen her mother laugh in a long while now.

Earlier Fiona had eaten supper with Mr and Mrs Jackson, and a very good dinner of mutton hotpot it had been, too. Naturally the couple had been curious to know where she was heading, and why. After all they'd been through together, Fiona believed that they had proved their friendship and trustworthiness. She told them honestly that she'd travelled from London to take up employment in Dartmouth. Betty had said she'd heard of the Herberts and that nothing bad had reached her ears about the family. That had lifted Fiona's spirits a little. If Mr Herbert was good and kind he was sure to be sympathetic to her tale of the coach being delayed by highwaymen. And that was the extent of the story she would relate!

Fiona had wanted to stretch her legs before retiring to her chamber for the night. Tomorrow morning she must say farewell to the Jacksons, who were heading inland to Woodstone while she carried on journeying west.

Being considerate sorts, the Jacksons were trying

to put a brave face on things for her. But Fiona feared human nature was much the same whether people were peasant or peer: salacious rumours would always be of great interest when a young lady's reputation was at stake. And heaven only knew there were stories about her now to give a gossip a field day.

The first twinges of self-pity assailed Fiona. Had fate been kinder to her, and that accursed vehicle of Toby Williams not broken down, none of it would have happened. The ruffians had been waiting for night to fall to rob innocent travellers braving the dark lanes. It had been very bad luck that Megan had misconstrued her identity from an overheard conversation at the Fallow Buck, then shared the misconception with her beau. Sam and Fred were not the sharpest tools in the box and had pounced too readily on the idea of her being the duke's daughter, hoping for high praise from their boss and a fat slice of profit from her ransom.

She owed her freedom, her comfort, perhaps even her life to Luke Wolfson. She should have thanked him properly rather than going off in a huff because his mistress had been waiting to welcome him at the King and Tinker. Now it was too late; he was no doubt halfway to London with his friends and had already forgotten her…

Her head dropped forward as she swayed on her feet, yearning to have his sweetly teasing fingers roving her skin once more. Fiona spun about to thump her back against the gate and stare up at the first stars studding a pale night sky. 'I'm glad he's gone…' she groaned in a whisper, desperate to convince herself of it.

'You're glad who's gone…dare I ask?'

Fiona snapped down her face, gazing unblinking at his beautiful gypsy features as though seeing a ghost. 'Jeremiah Collins…' She finally forced the fib through her quivering lips. 'What are you doing here, sir? I thought you'd travelled to London.' She made a small gesture, then turned away from him quickly lest she betrayed how happy and confused she was to see him.

'Who told you I'd gone to London?'

Fiona scoured her mind for an answer. In fact, Mr Robley at the King and Tinker had said Mr Wolfson had left with his friends but not where he'd headed to. She'd placed Luke in the metropolis because she brooded about him, and what he might be doing, far too much.

'I… Nobody told me… I just assumed you'd go there with your friends.' Fiona swiftly changed the subject. 'Mr Robley gave me your packet. I must thank you for your generosity. But it was uncalled for, Mr Wolfson. I am glad to have back my locket, but will replace its value with cash as soon as I'm able. As for the three sovereigns you gave me…' She dug in the pocket where she had stored his precious parcel of gold. 'I must return two to you straight away.'

Luke moved closer to her, enclosing her wrist as she would have thrust the parchment-wrapped money in his direction.

'You were glad I'd gone. Have you changed your mind now I'm back, Fiona?'

She looked away from those penetrative dark eyes. Of course, he'd known all along she was thinking… talking of him, whereas he probably had Becky Peake at the back of his mind. 'I'm certainly happy to have the opportunity to thank you properly for rescuing me,' she answered brittlely.

'My pleasure…' Luke raised her imprisoned fingers, chivalrously touching his lips to them.

Fiona avoided his gaze. She didn't need to look at him to know that his suggestive comment would have strengthened the amusement glimmering at the backs of his eyes. 'Why have you come here, sir?' she demanded, snatching back her hand. 'Is your purpose simply to mock me some more before you carry on with your life as normal? My life will never be normal again! I might be a disgraced woman but I'm certainly not a toy to be trifled with.' Again she thrust the coins at him and this time he took them with a sigh, slipping them into his pocket.

'I've never thought of you as such. Neither have I underestimated what you have endured. You're the bravest woman I know.'

His unexpected praise humbled Fiona; she even felt rather embarrassed by it. She'd heard simple sincerity in his voice and that was very pleasing. But she must not let his opinion matter too much; soon they would part ways for good.

'What *normal life* are you rueing the loss of, Fiona?' Luke asked, plunging his hands in his coat pockets. 'You've left home to get away from your stepfather and intend to take up paid employment in a profession that is likely to make you miserable. Do you still hanker for such an existence as that?'

'You don't know anything about me!' Fiona burst out. 'Who told you I dislike my stepfather?' she continued, ruining her determination not to speak about anything personal.

'You did… Have you forgotten already?' Luke replied. He approached her, moving a hand as though to draw her close, but Fiona whipped aside, greatly alarmed that he might have guessed Cecil Ratcliff had treated her in a very inappropriate manner. Nobody knew about that apart from Maude, and perhaps Rose. Not that Fiona or her mother had mentioned it to their maid, but Rose had a keen eye and a sharp mind. Nothing much happened in the household that passed the woman by.

'So I have an idea of why you quit London to journey west. Do you know what brought me this way?' Luke asked quietly.

'How could I, sir, when you've made it your business to keep it all a secret,' Fiona retorted.

'I've not intentionally concealed anything from you. When we were outrunning the gang I said I'd no time to explain, but now things are different. So, in answer to your previous question—what am I doing here at the Pig and Whistle?—I've come specifically to see you, my dear. You wanted me to tell you about my involvement with Jeremiah Collins, didn't you? Are you still interested in hearing about it?'

Fiona raised her eyes to his and through the dusk could see his fixed gaze was no longer lit by mockery, but by another, truer emotion.

'Yes…if you will, sir.' Fiona dipped her head. 'An explanation is in order, I think, so must thank you for taking the trouble to come out of your way to give it to me.'

'Have you told anybody you suspect me to be in cahoots with the gang?' Luke turned his head to glance at the Jacksons, still ensconced by the tavern's fireside.

Disquiet needled Fiona as she slowly gave a shake of her head. Perhaps his purpose in coming was to discover if she'd exposed him as a criminal, rather than to honourably explain himself.

Luke braced his hands against the gate, close to Fiona's side, and stared out over the darkling meadow. Somewhere out in the wilderness that held a tang of brine blown off the sea, a curlew called and was answered by its mate. After a moment in which they faced in opposite directions, enclosed in pastoral peacefulness, Fiona turned about and she, too, propped herself on the timber rail to gaze at the horizon.

'I quit the army last year, but still accept commissions suited to my profession,' Luke began in his rich baritone. 'I took on a contract for the Duke of Thornley. A day or so later I went back to see him to cancel it as the two of us didn't see eye to eye on vital aspects of the plan's structure and execution. My aim was then to return to London and forget all about the deal.'

Fiona digested that, then darted a bemused glance at his profile. Surely he was not about to tell her that the duke had somehow plotted to have his own daughter kidnapped by some villains! For what purpose? To prevent the young woman marrying the man she wanted? And why would Luke Wolfson's help be sought? Fiona found the answer to that last conundrum almost immediately: a duke would not deal directly with the scoundrels. He would need a go-between…somebody who might be able to infiltrate the gang and pretend to be in league with them. But the duke would not want his daughter harmed, just taught a lesson. And His Grace's mercenary would protect the girl while pretending to be her abductor.

Fiona had forgotten to seem aloof and rattled off the sum of her conjecture, moving closer to Luke in her eagerness to have his response to it.

'You've almost worked it out, sweet, so you'll understand my misgivings about strategic flaws.' Luke smiled sardonically. 'It was hardly going to fool a crook like Collins for very long.'

'Does the duke not *like* his daughter to risk her life in such a way?' Fiona gasped.

'He loves Joan very much and would have risked his own life before hers. The tale of Thornley's daughter running off to wed a lover was concocted. The duke's idea was for a woman to impersonate Joan, then when Collins was lured into the open in the hope of netting a huge ransom for the discreet return of the runaway bride, the villain and his accomplices would be captured and finally get their day in court.'

'Well, none of it came to pass!' Fiona snorted derisively. 'And it would have been exceedingly good luck if it had succeeded.'

'Indeed…' he concurred.

Fiona stole a glance at Luke's rugged profile; he had sounded very scathing, as well he might! He'd cancelled the contract with the duke and had been on the point of returning to the metropolis when he found himself again embroiled in rescuing a damsel in distress, albeit the wrong one, and for no reward!

'So…if a false rumour had not been put about concerning Joan's secret elopement, those dullards Sam and Fred would have stolen my money, but left me be.'

'I'm sorry you suffered, but I'm not sorry that I met you.' Luke pivoted on the elbow he'd planted on the top of the gate, facing her. The hand idle at his side was raised so a leisurely finger could trace the delicate contours from her temple to jaw. 'I'm not sorry, either, that I had the chance to rescue you, or to get to know you better during that short time we shared. It wasn't enough. I still want more of you...' he said huskily.

Slowly he straightened, removing his lounging arm from the timber and very deliberately sliding it around her narrow waist to draw her closer. 'Just a day or so apart, yet I've missed you, and I don't believe you've not felt the same way about me. We've unfinished business, Fiona...that's the main reason I've come to find you.'

He lowered his face and intuitively Fiona angled her head sideways and back, sighing as they fitted together like pieces of a puzzle. He swept his warm lips across her throat to take her mouth in a leisurely, drugging kiss.

From behind a daze of sensation Fiona reminded herself that he'd still answers to give her. But the tantalising touch of his tongue tip against hers was enough to make her gasp and open up to his artful probing. When his hand caressed from her spine to the buttons on her bodice she instinctively put an arch in her back to entice the skilful fingers infiltrating her clothes to fondle her nude skin.

'You've no need to fret over gossip, sweet,' Luke murmured as he stroked the warm plump flesh he'd exposed beneath her chemise. 'And no need to fret over your employment, either. The fellow will understand you quitting your job, given the nature of what you've been through...'

'But he must not know!' Fiona's whispered cry was smothered beneath the sweet assault of his lips. She clasped his abrasive chin to force back his head an inch. 'Nobody must know what happened to me...' she breathed into his preying mouth. 'Or I will be unable to earn a decent living anywhere.'

'You've no need to earn your keep, Fiona,' Luke growled, tantalising a small ear with nips and kisses. 'I'll protect you...care for you...give you everything you'll ever want. Just tell me what it is you desire...'

A burst of intense joy swamped Fiona and she nestled her cheek against his shoulder. With a tiny sob of astonishment she realised that pure love was at the centre of the conflicting emotions this man aroused in her. In just a few days she'd finally fallen deeply, instinctively in love. And he must love her, too, or why would he want to marry her when he didn't have to...

Her lashes parted and the throb of joy faltered, then faded as her reason revived. He hadn't mentioned marriage...or love. And thank goodness that she hadn't, either!

What a fool she was! Fiona inwardly railed at herself. She'd simply read into his declaration what she wanted to hear. Yes, it was a proposal of sorts, but now, recalling it word for word, she saw it was similar to that delivered by her stepfather. He had also promised to give her gowns and trinkets, while attempting to thrust a hand beneath her skirts. And all the while he'd been raiding her inheritance—money put by for her dowry—so he could carry on carousing with his dubious friends.

She'd believed Luke Wolfson had a wedding on his mind because, unconsciously, that's what she wanted... what she'd always wanted. From the first moment their eyes had met through driving rain she'd felt attracted to him in a way that defied logic. Oh, he was wonderfully handsome, but it was more than mere good looks drawing her to him. She'd sensed between them existed an affinity that she'd never experienced with anyone other than her birth family.

When she'd been Jeremiah Collins's terrified prisoner she'd trusted Luke Wolfson would rescue her from the gang. And he had not let her down. But now he would; saving her from a life of servitude, or from her ruined reputation, was a chivalry too far. And why should he marry her? Did she think she now had a hold on this mercenary's affections because they'd shared intimacies a wife would allow a husband? How naive and unsophisticated he would think her, compared to Becky Peake!

If he guessed her awful mistake he might laugh... or feel embarrassed. He could be no more uncomfortable than she was! She must never disclose how close she'd come to throwing her arms up about his neck and blurting that she'd be delighted to be his wife.

Fiona had grown stiff in his arms, but didn't yet push away. Even relinquishing the bittersweet comfort of his warmth and strength was hard to do. She remained quiet, conscious of his silence, and of puzzles still unsolved.

Why would a man who already had a beautiful young mistress want an older, plainer woman in his bed? The solution she found made her burn with humiliation. She'd never save enough money to settle his fee, so he was offering to take payment in kind, allowing her to keep her precious locket, and to save her blushes was wrapping his lust in generosity. Then, when he'd had his money's worth, no doubt he'd turn her out. Perhaps he might even give her a reference to ease her path towards employment as a governess!

Disentangling herself from his embrace, Fiona raised her hands, intending to fumble beneath her collar for the clasp of the locket, but her fingers were arrested in mid-air and held steady at her shoulders.

'What are you doing?' Luke asked quietly.

Fiona shook him off, attempting to step back, but he gripped her elbows, jerking her against him.

'You mistake my character, sir. Thank you for your kind offer, but I still intend to keep a roof over my head by teaching children, rather than sleeping with gentlemen,' she said with a faux sweetness.

'Gentlemen? How many lovers did you anticipate having, Fiona?' he rasped.

'None…' She flung back her head, her tawny gaze clashing on eyes that gleamed between lengthy jet-black lashes.

'None? You intend to remain celibate? Do you not want children?'

'Only within wedlock,' Fiona answered coolly. She would not allow him to upset her fragile equilibrium with his taunts.

The throaty chuckle he gave lacked humour. 'You're after a husband, but not a lover, is that it?'

'I'm not looking for either, but if I were I'd want a gentleman I can respect and trust!' Fiona snapped.

'And desire?' Luke purred. 'I fit the bill on that score, even if you don't respect or trust me.'

Fiona had backed away against the gate, but he pursued with slow deliberate steps, bracing an arm either side of her, trapping her as he lowered his head towards hers…

'Mr Wolfson…is it you? Are you there, sir? Is Miss Chapman with you? Oh, for a pair of young eyes! It is grown quite dark and I left my spectacles inside…'

Chapter Fifteen

An expletive, forcefully ejected through Luke's teeth, preceded him straightening up. As he turned about he subtly brushed his mouth across Fiona's lips, still invitingly parted in a soundless wail of horror from recognising Mrs Jackson's cheery tones.

'Ah…it *is* you, sir!' Mrs Jackson was peering myopically into the twilight. 'And there *you* are, Miss Chapman. What a wonderful surprise to see your saviour again!' Betty beamed at the couple as she hurried closer. 'You two young people must have lots to talk about before we all leave this…' She cast a dramatic glance over a shoulder before whispering, '*This dreadful episode* behind us and finish our journeys.' She patted Luke's sleeve. 'But do both come in and join us. My husband will be pleased to see you, sir. You mustn't just go off as you tend to do without saying a proper goodbye,' she playfully scolded Luke. 'I've come to see if Miss Chapman would like some warm milk or chocolate ordered before bedtime. With so much to do tomorrow I expect an early night is in order for us all.'

'I… Yes…that sounds nice,' Fiona burst out, aware

of a very ironic look singeing the top of her head at the mention of bedtime. 'Chocolate…' She quickly gave her choice of beverage, relieved that Betty didn't appear to have noticed anything untoward.

Perhaps the Jacksons were beyond being shocked by her behaviour, Fiona wryly reflected. When she'd first met the couple they'd seemed alarmed that she was travelling without a companion. Heaven only knew what they'd think of her now if they discovered what she'd been up to moments ago with the gentleman at her side!

'You mustn't take a chill, Miss Chapman.' Luke's mild tone was at odds with him briskly pulling her cloak edges together.

'How considerate,' Mrs Jackson praised, blinking adoringly at her hero.

It took Fiona a moment to recover from his abrupt ministration and to realise the reason for it: she glimpsed an edge of her lacy chemise and, horrified, realised that her unhooked buttons had been exposed to view. Blood surged into her complexion and she silently gave thanks for the dusk and for Betty's forgetfulness. Had the woman been wearing her spectacles…

Discreetly tugging at her clothes, Fiona accepted the arm that Luke extended to her. She knew she owed him at least a glance of gratitude for preserving her modesty, but she could not do it. Betty clutched Luke's other elbow and began chattering about the richness of the lamb hotpot they'd enjoyed for supper.

'Ah…capital to see you, sir!' Mr Jackson had made quite a sprightly leap to his feet on seeing Luke accompanying Betty and Miss Chapman into the tavern. Solicitously he began rearranging chairs so that ev-

erybody might sit close by the fire. 'I must shake you
by the hand, Mr Wolfson, and do allow me to procure
you some brandy. It is the least I can do after such a
noble effort on Miss Chapman's behalf.' Peter Jackson
glanced furtively about before hissing, 'Awful business!' He shook his head, continuing to pump Luke's
fingers.

As Fiona sank back into her chair she wished the
couple would quit referring, even obliquely, to her dratted abduction. She wished, too, that the hero of the hour
would go away and leave her be! Yet seconds after the
landlord had brought a bottle and glasses she learned
that Luke was, indeed, staying for just a short while
and her heart vaulted to her mouth in consternation.

'But surely, sir, it is best not to travel so late?' Peter
had previously asked whether Luke intended taking
a room at the tavern and had received a reply in the
negative.

'I'm used to riding at night,' Luke said, taking a
sip of the brandy Mr Jackson had insisted on pouring for him.

'You must make sure your guns are loaded and
ready for use,' Mrs Jackson instructed in a motherly
way.

'I always do, ma'am.'

A silence developed during which the married couple exchanged several significant glances. Suddenly
Mr Jackson burst out, 'I have to say, Miss Chapman,
that I'm sorry I was stubborn that night.' His veined
cheeks flamed. 'It was my fault we got caught by those
rogues. Had I listened to Toby Williams and turned
back towards the Fallow Buck all might have ended
differently—'

'And I must also say sorry.' Betty interrupted her husband's apology to insert her own. 'I wanted to journey onwards when we should have heeded the driver's advice.'

'There's no need for any mention of it.' Fiona sounded forgiving although the thought had crossed her mind that they'd been foolish and selfish to overrule Toby Williams. 'You've been good friends to me and I'm pleased to see that you are recovering well from that crack on the head, sir.'

'It would take more than that tap to do me down,' Mr Jackson boasted, conveniently forgetting how he'd suffered and complained at the time. 'Besides, it was my own fault.' His expression again turned sheepish.

'All is now forgotten.' Fiona glanced about at her cosy surroundings to indicate she hoped the matter closed.

'So graciously done...' Mrs Jackson leaned towards Fiona, clasping her hand in gratitude. 'Are you sure you do not want to set the authorities on those rogues? They should not get away with treating you so abominably.'

'No! I'm very well, as you can see...as I have already said...' Fiona rattled off. Carefully she disentangled her fingers, then rose to her feet. 'I think I shall ask the landlord for that chocolate. I'll order a cup for you, Mrs Jackson.' She knew that the moment she was out of earshot the Jacksons would again discuss her. But Fiona needed to escape Betty's probing questions and Luke's dark, preying gaze. Close to him she felt stifled by the heat of his desire and the ambivalent thoughts storming her mind were making her light-headed.

'I wish she would turn around and go home to her family,' Mrs Jackson whispered before Fiona had moved more than a yard.

A small, unseen grimace was Fiona's only reaction to the overheard remark as she carried on, with an admirably steady step, in search of the landlord.

'Hush…' Peter said. 'Now, we don't gossip, do we, my dear. Miss Chapman wants no more talk of it.'

'Hmmph… I'm sure that Miss Chapman considers Mr Wolfson as trustworthy as we, after all he has saved her virtue and her life.'

Peter shrugged in defeat.

'She is going to Dartmouth to be a governess, you see,' Betty hissed, gazing earnestly at Luke.

'Miss Chapman has told me all about it,' Luke said, finishing his brandy.

'Ah…she has, has she?' Peter mumbled, ignoring his wife's smug nod.

'Mr Herbert is known as good stock. We aren't personally acquainted with him, but we know people who are,' Betty carried on as though deaf to Mr Wolfson's heavy hint to change the subject.

'Yes…yes…' Peter cut across his wife. 'We cannot vouch for people, though, can we, if we don't know them well?'

'That's why I'd sooner see the poor lamb go back home to her mother.' Betty pulled her shawl this way and that. 'She seems such a sweet, genteel young woman— things cannot be so bad that she must leave all she knows and loves in London to school a stranger's children.'

'Miss Chapman is independent and quick-witted— assuredly she knows what she is doing.' Luke knew that Fiona wouldn't appreciate being talked about behind her back…especially by him. He got to his feet, executing a farewell bow. 'Thank you for the brandy, sir.'

Peter lunged to his feet to again shake Luke by the hand and mutter good wishes and hopes for a renewal of their acquaintance. Betty extended her fingers, too, acting coy when Luke briefly raised them to his lips. Then with a smile and farewell that couldn't be mistaken for anything but final, he said, 'My best wishes go with you for a safe journey home. I'm off to the stables to see if my horse is sufficiently rested to set upon the road.'

Having found the landlord and asked for two cups of chocolate, Fiona dithered outside the kitchen door into which the fellow had disappeared. She was reluctant to return to the saloon and face more questions or well-meant advice. Part of her wanted to spend every available second that remained with Luke; she knew he was simply being polite in tarrying a while with the Jacksons. That other, logical, corner of her mind was urging her to avoid him completely because the pain of parting would worsen the more she saw him. She knew she must forget about him and his tacit offer of protection at a price.

But she couldn't; at present overriding all sense and reason was an unbearable thrill trembling her from head to toes, the like of which she'd never before experienced.

She was twenty-five years old yet had never before aroused such ardency in a gentleman. Now she had, and the man who wanted to make love to her was the man to whom she'd given her heart. Would it be so bad to lie naked with Luke Wolfson and bask in his passion if she couldn't have his love? The maelstrom of emotion battering her person caused her to sway on her feet and she sought support from the wall, her warm palms flat against cooling plaster.

She couldn't deny that his taunts had hit home: she *did* desire him…and she trusted Luke would treat her well as his paramour. If she could conquer her indignation and dreadful disappointment that another woman was sure, one day, to be his wife…what matter if she accepted the crumbs offered to her for as long as he tossed them her way?

'You seem to be lost in thought again,' Luke said huskily.

Startled, Fiona swung about, wishing she'd heard him approach. 'I've a lot to think about,' she blurted, managing a wavering smile.

'Me included?'

An immediate denial was teetering on the tip of her tongue. But the mockery in his eyes was directed more at himself, making him appear oddly vulnerable.

'Yes…' she murmured. 'You were on my mind, sir… amongst other things.'

'Were you thinking you might come to trust and respect me, Fiona, if I strive to improve my behaviour?'

'And how might you do that?' she asked, suppressing a smile. As well as being the most handsome man alive he had a self-deprecating humour she found appealing. Luke Wolfson, she realised, had qualities that any woman would find attractive in a husband. And no doubt he possessed other, sensual skills, temptingly tasted by her, but to which his mistress could fully testify.

Luke leaned his broad shoulders against the wall op-

posite and crossed his arms so they diagonally faced
one another in the narrow corridor. 'I might quit seeking dangerous escapades as though a boy tasting excitement for the first time.'

'Is that why you're a mercenary? For the thrill of
it?'

'Most probably...'

Fiona had to admit that did make him sound immature. Most soldiers would surely only risk their lives
for their king or their pay. 'You really don't need the
money from such work?'

His sensual mouth twisted aslant in a way that
looked oddly bitter to Fiona. Most people would be
happy to announce they were well off.

'My grandfather left me a bequest,' Luke stated distantly.

'My grandmother left me a bequest,' Fiona answered
simply. She told him things she never mentioned to
others. It was as though he held the key to her tongue
as well as her heart.

'And what happened to it?' Luke asked gently.

Fiona's eyes slid sideways to merge with his dark
stare. She could tell he knew...as he knew everything
about her without her needing to utter a word. But he
must never know she'd fallen in love with him; that
was a secret she must bury deep.

'My stepfather spent it,' she informed him briskly.
'Which was typical of his selfishness. So now I am not
a minor heiress, but a governess.'

'And what else has he taken?'

Fiona stiffened against the wall, her nails digging
into flaking distemper. So...he had guessed that, too,
had he? She lifted her eyes to his face but could read

nothing there. His gaze was relentless, as always, demanding she bare her soul as well as her body to him. 'He...' Fiona moistened her lips. 'He took liberties and believed he had a right to my bed as well as my mother's, promising me nice things in return for my compliance.'

'He forced himself on you?'

'Not...to the full extent. He tried to kiss and touch me and he became unpleasant enough to make me want to leave.' Fiona lifted her chin, challenging him with a stare. If he felt disgusted to know she'd been mauled by a man charged with caring for her, he gave no sign. But there was a livid white line circling his mouth, stark against the depth of his tan.

'Did you tell your mother about it?'

Fiona nodded. 'She didn't believe me at first. Now she detests him as greatly as do I.' Fiona clasped her hands before her. 'I worry about her being left there alone with him.'

'And is she worried about you, do you think?'

'I believe she is...yes.'

'Will you go home, then?'

Fiona frowned at him. 'What is there for me to go back to? Nothing will have changed, and if it has, it will be for the worst. My stepfather has almost stripped the house of everything of value to fund his carousing.'

'You believe him a fortune hunter,' Luke stated.

'I believe he is a corrupt individual and I wouldn't be surprised to learn that what he told my mother about his background is a pack of lies.'

Luke's thick eyebrows were drawn up in enquiry.

'He said he hailed from Surrey and had been decorated during his army career, even serving under Wellington. He was a very smooth talker, at first…until he had my mother pinned beneath his thumb.'

Luke frowned. 'His name?'

'Cecil Ratcliff.'

'I also came under the Iron Duke's command, yet I don't believe I'm acquainted with Ratcliff.'

'Then you may think yourself fortunate!' Fiona said pithily.

Their eyes merged through the murky flickering shadows thrown by the corridor's wall candles. For a moment Fiona felt tempted to cross the tiny space that separated them and launch herself into his arms. She knew he would comfort her and how she longed for such. But then he spoke quickly and harshly, breaking the spell.

'There's a better life waiting for you than teaching other people's brats for a living.'

'There's a better life waiting for you than pursuing criminals for pay you don't need,' Fiona shot back. 'You, sir, are in the privileged position of being able to play at having a career and may stop at any time you choose. I am not so lucky.'

'I take what I do seriously,' Luke said quietly. 'And if you think that money brings with it happiness and contentment, I can assure you it does not.'

Fiona sensed he was about to add something, but he turned from her, shielding his expression while pacing along the corridor. Puzzled by the change in him she thought he might leave without another word, but he retraced his steps. Cocking his head to one side, he stared pitilessly at her until, flustered, she blurted out, 'I have applied for a teaching position and I intend to

take it up. I would be a poor wretch indeed if I backed
away from a new challenge before giving it a try.'

'You deserve better,' Luke returned.

'It is what I want to do.' It was far from the truth,
but she'd bristled at his domineering tone. 'It is what I
shall do,' she added determinedly, hoping to convince
herself as well as him.

Luke extended dark fingers towards her, trailing a
fingertip down the side of her forearm. 'I want you…
you know that,' he said throatily. 'Why do you persist
in making things hard for yourself?'

Fiona threw up her face to the ceiling and gave a
sob of laughter. So he thought it would be hard for her
to bow and scrape for her pittance of a salary, did he?
No…being relegated to the outer circle of his existence
while he lived his charmed life with his wife and their
children…now *that* would be hard for her.

Then she thought of Becky Peake and wondered if
the brunette might get Luke down the aisle. Their attachment obviously ran deep and Luke must trust his
mistress, too, or he wouldn't have brought her with
him on such a dangerous mission.

That led Fiona to reflect on another puzzle to which
she'd not yet had an answer. Who had been in line to
play the part of the duke's daughter had Luke decided
to carry on with Thornley's kidnap plot?

'You said you initially agreed to get involved in the
duke's scheme, so you must have had an accomplice
who was prepared to impersonate Joan Thornley.'

'I did…somebody I know…' A corner of Luke's
mouth quirked in half a smile as he anticipated what
sharp question might come next.

'You chose to draw your mistress into danger, despite knowing the plot had so many holes in it?'

Turning his head, Luke squarely met Fiona's accusation. 'I chose to leave Becky in London, but she took it upon herself to follow me here. As a rule I work alone and the inclusion of a female accomplice was another reason I decided to quit the contract almost before the ink had dried on it.'

'It was selfish of you to use your lover's devotion to your advantage.'

'Becky needed no persuasion to get involved. And it's less a case of devotion than possessiveness.'

'I see…' Fiona murmured, understanding why his mistress would risk a lot to stay close and keeps tabs on him. The brunette was no doubt aware her lover had a roving eye. Fiona wondered if Becky had guessed Luke had attempted to seduce her. Or perhaps the woman was confident of her hold over him and believed he'd never fully stray. And so far he hadn't fully strayed… at least not with her. 'And where is Becky now?' Fiona blurted.

'Probably with my friend, Drew Rockleigh, travelling back to London.'

'Did she go willingly?'

'She'd sooner have returned with me, but she'll find Rockleigh an adequate companion.' Luke smiled slightly.

'And if she doesn't perhaps she'll again come after you.'

'If she does she'll not find me so tolerant of her unwanted presence,' he returned coolly.

'You sound heartless…' Fiona murmured.

'You'd sooner I dragged her around with me?'

'You may treat your camp followers as you will, sir. They are none of my concern and neither will I ever join their number.' She'd snapped like a jealous shrew and Fiona forced herself in the next quiet moments to appear relaxed because his mouth had slanted in amusement.

'My relationship with Becky is finished now. You've no reason to fret over her, Fiona.'

'I can assure you I do not!' The lie was rattled off as Fiona flushed to the roots of her silky fawn hair. She had dearly hoped to keep from him that she viewed Becky Peake as a rival.

'Oh… I thought you'd be sitting with your friends, Miss Chapman.' The landlord had barged backwards out of the kitchen door and swung about to face her. He was holding a tray laden with two cups of chocolate. Seeing Fiona's companion, he gave a low bow, dropping the tray obsequiously close to his knees.

'Major Wolfson…what would you like, sir?'

Luke glanced at Fiona, a wicked glint just visible beneath lazy lids.

'Nothing from the kitchens, thank you… I'm just off to the stables.'

'Ah, settling your shot, then, and on your way, are you, Major?' the landlord said, disappointed to know such a flush fellow was leaving so soon. Every local innkeeper knew how free Major Wolfson was with his tips. Having batted a look between the couple he mumbled about taking the drinks through to the saloon.

'Are you returning to London now?' The question burst out of Fiona.

'Eventually… I've a score to settle first.'

'With the Duke of Thornley?' Fiona asked with a frown.

'No… I've said all I needed to, to His Grace.'

'You're not going after Jeremiah Collins?' Fiona gasped in shock. 'Why?' Their differences now seemed unimportant; she was anxious that Luke might again risk his life rather than give up being a hireling. 'I wish you would not go after him, sir. You are badly outnumbered by his gang and might be ambushed and captured.' Seeing that her comment had not made him stop and reflect, she blurted, 'Besides, if you provoke Collins he might spread dirt about me from malice.'

'I've said I'll take care of you in every way necessary,' Luke returned quietly.

'There are some things that cannot be put right with a pair of duck-foot pistols…or a gift of sovereigns.' Fiona sounded exasperated. 'I'll not allow my future to become a game of chance, dependent upon men's whims and favours.'

'I'll not abandon you, Fiona.' Luke took a step towards her, a crooked smile softening his hitherto stern expression.

'And what of Becky Peake? Did you abandon her? Will you renew your acquaintance with her when back in town and spread your time and generosity between us?' Before he could answer she carried on, her tone now level and composed. 'Thanks to you I'm on my way to take up my position in Dartmouth tomorrow.' She evaded him by pacing slowly to and fro until he again propped himself against the wall, hands plunged into his pockets. She knew he was watching her from beneath heavy lids and kept beyond his reach. 'You have helped me in putting my life back on track, and in return I'd like you to also have a future in front of you. If you pursue that fiend Collins…' Her voice tailed away and she kept her back to him to protect the glitter of tears in her eyes at the dreadful idea of him being killed or maimed.

'I came to Devon to rid the area of the gang and I'll leave when the job's done.'

Fiona pivoted on a heel. 'But…you've cancelled the contract with the Duke of Thornley!' she argued, coming closer to him in her agitation. 'Why make it your business?'

'Because it is my business and I don't need a contract. Now it's personal between him and me. And Collins knows it.'

'Miss Chapman…come along, my dear, your chocolate will get cold.' Betty Jackson had hove into view and seen the couple, face to face, in the corridor. 'Do have another brandy with us before leaving, Mr Wolfson,' she cajoled. 'It will save my husband sinking the lot and falling asleep.'

'Thank you, ma'am, but I'm setting off now.' Luke turned a relentless gaze on Fiona. 'Come with me!' His demand was honeyed with persuasiveness.

Fiona drew a ragged breath, hovering for a second on the cusp between agreement and refusal before giving an almost imperceptible shake of the head.

Luke continued to drill his eyes into a crown of fawn hair as though waiting for her to change her mind. 'Miss Chapman…' he finally murmured, before stepping away from her and giving a nod that encompassed both ladies. 'I wish you all safe onward journeys.'

'And we return you the same sentiment, Mr Wolfson. Oh, indeed we do!' Betty exclaimed.

'Don't worry, my dear, I'm sure you'll see him again.' Betty gave Fiona's quivering arm a squeeze as the door closed on Luke's departing figure.

Fiona mumbled something indistinct in response to the woman's comfort. She was just overwrought with all that had gone on! she told herself impatiently as a tear trickled from the corner of an eye.

'I know he likes you.' Betty winked and tapped the side of her nose. 'Just between us… I remember my courting days.'

Fiona bit her lip, realising that the woman was hinting she'd seen more than she'd let on when they'd all been outside earlier.

Chapter Sixteen

Cecil Ratcliff shoved away his half-empty coffee cup. With a look of utter distaste he picked up the piece of soggy toast on his plate, then in a fit of temper flung it to the floor. At breakfast time he desired eating broiled kidneys and poached eggs, juicy ham and freshly baked bread, not a slice of thinly buttered toast without so much as a dollop of jam to tempt the palate.

The woman he'd employed as a servant, since his wife absconded taking her maid with her, barely raised her head at the sound of his snarling. Dolly carried on sweeping out the fire, although there was no fuel in the outside bunker to bring in and burn in the grate. The scuttles were empty, too, and only a few small logs remained piled by the fireside. In an attempt to hide the gaping hole beneath the mantelpiece the maid continued scrunching up old copies of *The Times* and lobbing the paper balls over the fender.

'Get me something palatable for breakfast,' Cecil snapped, irritated that his servant had ignored his tantrum.

Dolly pushed herself to her feet. 'Nothing in the larders, Mr Ratcliff. I had to cut the mould off that bread before I could toast it.'

That blunt remark brought a furious glow to Cecil's unshaven cheeks. 'Go to the grocer's, then, you insolent chit. Tell them to send the boy round with every supply we lack.'

Dolly had only been with him for three days. Already she'd had enough. He was a mean swine who expected all the luxuries of home provided by a single servant for a pittance of pay.

'Did you hear what I said?' Cecil roared as the maid continued swiping together her sooty palms. 'You insubordinate hussy, get to the shop and put in my order,' he bellowed.

'You want goods from a grocer, you find yourself one who'll take your order,' Dolly returned shortly. 'Every shopkeeper around says the same—they'll not be coming back here till you've paid what you owe.' Dolly pulled off her apron and flung it on the floor. 'You can have back your job. I'm not surprised the other one went. You're a slave driver, that's what you are.'

Dolly was glad she'd not unpacked her things. She'd had an inkling she might not be staying long. Having stormed up to the attic room that had been her chamber for the two nights since she'd arrived, she jammed her few belongings into her carpetbag's open mouth and was lugging it downstairs in a trice.

Cecil was waiting for her by the banisters, a faint smile turning down the corners of his mouth. 'Don't you want to have your pay, Dolly?'

Dolly hesitated. Even if it were only pennies, it would come in handy. 'If you want to give it to me, sir, I'd be much obliged to have it.'

Cecil nodded slowly. 'I think you deserve something...'

As she reached the bottom tread he held out his closed fist, but instead of opening his fingers to reveal a few coins he backhanded Dolly, knocking her to the ground.

The maid was allowed to crouch, whimpering, at his feet for no more than a few seconds. Ratcliff hoisted Dolly up by her collar and dragged her to the door. Flinging it open, he tossed her on to the top step, then with a boot against her backside sent her crashing to the pavement.

On hearing Dolly's howl Cecil slammed the door, then set off towards the drawing room with a satisfied smirk. Within moments he'd forgotten about the servant and was putting his mind to more important matters. There was not much left in the house to sell, but the small portrait on the wall would fetch something at the pawnbroker's and Solomon had expressed an interest in seeing it.

Cecil gawped, open-mouthed, at the space where the picture had hung. He was sure that Dolly hadn't taken it. For the short while she'd been in his employment the lazy slut had rarely moved from her warm spot in the kitchen. He glanced about at dusty surfaces on a few unattractive items of furniture that remained. Cecil tried to bring to mind when last he'd clapped eyes on the canvas, but since Maude had bolted, he'd been out more than usual and came home every night deep in his cups. He always went straight to bed and hadn't set foot in the drawing room in days.

Maude... His thoughts pounced on his wife and his eyes narrowed. The woman he'd married hadn't been the biddable mouse he'd taken her for. She'd certainly surprised him by running off. Perhaps she'd not fled empty-handed, but had stolen a valuable painting to speed her path away from him.

Spitting an oath, Cecil pulled out drawers in the sideboard and emptied the few remaining bits of silver cutlery on to the top.

'Ah…Mr Ratcliff…back so soon,' the pawnbroker purred, beetling from the back of his shop to welcome his prolific client. 'Now, what have we this time?' The elderly fellow slid his spectacles up the bridge of his nose and passed a jaundiced eye over the mismatched collection of knives, forks and spoons that Cecil had emptied on to the counter.

'I thought you said you might bring a painting in for me next time, sir,' Solomon mentioned.

'Yes, I might…if I can find it,' Cecil snapped. He didn't like the fellow's familiar tone. But Solomon paid good prices so Cecil bit his tongue. 'It's probably of little value in any case: very small and dull, and the frame is damaged.'

'Ah… I know it, sir,' Solomon said, lowering his eyes. 'Your wife's late husband bought that one from me some years ago.' Indeed Solomon did know it and would have been very pleased to see it again. After he'd sold it to Anthony Chapman for a few pounds he'd re-alised it had been a Dutch master and worth a lot more than he'd got for it.

Cecil had picked up on the pawnbroker's sly inter-est and he ruminated on the reason for it while finger-ing the silverware on the counter. 'Mr Chapman knew about art, did he?'

'No…no…' the pawnbroker lied. 'As you say, the painting is small and dull…unattractive.' He shrugged. 'But business is business and I take a look at everything. Bring it in when you find it.'

'I will,' Cecil said through his gritted teeth, pocketing the cash Solomon handed over for the cutlery.

For some minutes Cecil stood outside the shop with his head sunk towards his chest while he cogitated. Although it was easy for a person who didn't want to be found to lay low in the heaving metropolis, he had a hunch that his wife was no longer close by. He imagined mother would have followed daughter; he'd not been able to break the bond between them despite his best efforts to divide and conquer. Previously Cecil had had little interest in Fiona's whereabouts…but he did now.

Maude had only recently run off so Cecil was confident that somebody in the coaching company would know in which direction she'd travelled. With a brisk step he set off to find the proprietor. On rising that morning Cecil had not been bothered about bringing Maude home, but suddenly he was determined to catch up with his errant spouse.

'There is a gentleman below asking to see you, Miss Chapman.'

Fiona's heart vaulted to her mouth. She'd been sorting through the few things in her travelling trunk, but now dropped the lid on it and gazed, wide-eyed, at the landlord's wife. 'Is it Mr Wolfson?' she eventually forced out as her heart continued to batter at her breastbone.

Mrs Brewer shook her head. 'He looks to be a well-to-do fellow and needs to speak to you urgently and privately, so he said. He wouldn't give his name.'

Her disappointment at knowing Luke had not come back was subdued by a prickle of uneasiness. Fiona quashed her fears with logic; it was highly unlikely her stepfather would have discovered where she was, let alone put himself to the bother of pursuing her.

'I'll be down directly. Perhaps you would have one of the lads bring down my trunk. Is the Dartmouth coach soon due in?'

'Should arrive before noon—the weather is as fine as can be, so I'm sure we'll be hearing a blast of the horn soon.' The landlady followed up the information with a reassuring beam.

Fiona followed the woman down some narrow creaking stairs to the saloon bar where a stout gentleman was standing with his back to her, his hat caught beneath an arm. He twisted about on hearing Fiona pass over the threshold.

'You are Miss Chapman?' he clipped out, giving her a sharp top-to-toe summary.

'I am, sir, and perhaps you would acquaint me with your name?' Fiona had bristled and taken an instant dislike to the fleshy-faced fellow staring at her through a pair of round spectacles balanced on his bulbous nose.

'I, Miss Chapman, am your employer. Or I was.' Mr Herbert strode to the door and closed it. 'For your own good,' he explained his move to closet them privately. 'I doubt your reputation could be more damaged, but in the spirit of attempting to do what I can to help, I'll keep what I have to say very quiet and concise.'

Fiona felt her stomach lurch; the horrible man need

not add anything at all for her to know that gossip had started about her and the highwaymen. But she put up her chin and politely waited for Mr Herbert to do his worst.

'I expect you now realise that I am Mr Stanley Herbert. Word has reached my ears that a misfortune overcame you and your fellow travellers en route to Dartmouth.'

'It did, sir,' Fiona confirmed levelly, realising he had pursed his lips in readiness to have her admit to her disgrace.

'And is it true that you, Miss Chapman, suffered abduction at the hands of these miscreants?'

'I… Yes, that's correct…but I am in good health, as you can see, sir.' Fiona suddenly felt heartsick. She had no wish to be constantly reminded of the vile incident, but her greatest fear was that her livelihood was about to be whipped away.

'Physically well, you may be, Miss Chapman, but I think you know that your life, and your prospects, have been irreparably damaged.' Mr Herbert's voice was low and slow, as one might enunciate an opinion on an immeasurable tragedy. He blinked rapidly behind his glasses. 'I was annoyed to find you did not arrive at the appointed time. Now I know the circumstances behind the delay, I can sympathise with your dreadful plight, but of course my duty to my daughters' moral welfare is paramount.' He shook his head, approaching her. 'Here…take this…' Mr Herbert handed over five shillings. 'It is an amount of compensation and I hope it will help you. I also hope you find work in another area where people remain in ignorance of your stigma.'

Fiona marched to the table and tipped from her palm

on to its surface the coins he'd given her. 'I have no need of your sympathy or your charity, sir.' Her pride had revived and her tigerish eyes clashed on his affronted stare. 'I can see now that we would not have suited one another in any case, so am glad to have met you sooner rather than later.'

Mr Herbert's chest expanded and he grew florid. 'Indeed, Miss Chapman, we would not have suited!' he wheezed out. 'My daughters have had a lucky escape. I will bid you farewell.' With small fast steps he strutted to the exit, then returned to retrieve his five shillings. With his puffed-out chest straining his waistcoat buttons, he again approached the door and shut it noisily behind him.

It was the sound of the fanfare from the approaching mail coach that startled Fiona from her daze. She had been standing stock still, her head thumping from the effort of trying to decide what to do next. After she settled her bill at the Pig and Whistle she would have some change from the sovereign Luke had given her, but there was nowhere near enough in her purse to get her back to London. Even should she decide to return to the metropolis she would never again set foot in her stepfather's house.

Her friends, the Jacksons, could not help her, either. They had all parted company earlier that morning, with hugs and tears in abundance. The couple had given her their direction and insisted on having Fiona's promise to write to them as soon as she had settled in at the Herberts. Then they had climbed aboard the trap that was taking them home. Even Mr Jackson had looked suspiciously dewy-eyed as he took the reins and called out to Fiona every good wish for her future health and happiness.

So she was quite alone and regretted having pressed Luke to take back his coins. How she needed them now! But she did not rue for one minute having refused to take Mr Herbert's conscience money. She was glad she had found out what a horrible man he was.

But beggars couldn't be choosers, she impressed on herself when her indignation had been tempered by realism. Unpleasant as her work and her life might have been at Dartmouth she would have had shelter till she could find the means to move elsewhere.

Fiona's troubled thoughts were dragged to the present by the clamour in the bar next door. New arrivals had disembarked from the coach and trooped into the inn for refreshment before journeying on.

Fiona propped her warm forehead against the cool glass of the mullioned windowpane and watched the hubbub outside. The team of horses was being unharnessed from the dusty contraption and the busy ostlers brought to Fiona's mind memories of Toby and Bert Williams.

'There's a lady turned up on the coach asking for Mr Wolfson.'

Fiona spun about to see the landlady closing the door behind her. Mrs Brewer looked slightly awkward. 'I know the major has gone on his way, but my husband said that the two of you were friendly…so do you know where he has headed? The lady seems anxious to catch up with him.'

'Did she give her name?' Fiona asked, although sure she already knew the answer to that. So Becky Peake had not given up her chase! Fiona was assailed with a mixture of anger and admiration that her rival would continue to humble herself for Luke Wolfson's sake.

Suddenly the door was flung open and Maude hurtled in. 'I thought I recognised your voice. Oh, Fiona, my dear child! How glad I am to have found you!'

The landlady diplomatically withdrew on realising that a family reunion was about to take place. Of course she'd heard the rumours about what had happened to Miss Chapman, so could imagine that the poor mother—if that was who the woman was—had much to say to the ruined daughter.

Shocked to the core at the sight of her mother surging towards her with Rose trotting at her side, Fiona gripped the nearest chair for support. 'Mama! What... what on earth—?' The rest of Fiona's stuttered question was cut off as Maude enclosed her daughter in a breathtaking hug.

'Oh, my dear, I'm so, so sorry that you have suffered abominably...'

Fiona gently disentangled herself as her sense returned. She held her mother's hands and gazed into Maude's wet eyes, feeling very close to blubbing herself. 'How did you know where to find me?'

'The duke said that Mr Wolfson would be at either the King and Tinker or the Pig and Whistle, and would know your whereabouts.' Maude gulped. 'He wasn't at the first inn so I came here in the hope of questioning him. But now I don't need to, for I have found you!'

'You've spoken to the Duke of Thornley about me?' Fiona pounced on one of many astonishing facts circling crazily in her mind.

'Yes…yes…or I wouldn't have known to come here,' Maude garbled.

'And His Grace told you that Luke Wolfson knew me?'

'Well, he did, but he wasn't the first to mention that fellow and you in the same breath. A young hussy at the Fallow Buck said that you were with the major and she pointed me in His Grace's direction to find out more. So off we set to Thornley Heights and I met the duke and what a tale I heard!' Maude wailed.

'Young hussy?' Again overwhelmed by her mother's report, Fiona found one thing to immediately ask about. Overriding all else was the thought of Becky Peake being still in the vicinity to hound Luke.

'Her name was Megan,' Rose interjected helpfully, having hitherto listened to and watched the fraught exchange from a distance.

Fiona drew her mother, tottering, towards a chair and made her sit down. Then she sank down beside her on the rug. For a moment she remained quiet and still, assembling her thoughts. Then she raised her head and gave her mother a wobbly smile. 'It is good to see you, Mama, and I wish that we had better news for one another. But we must not despair. We will get by…we always do.' She enclosed her mother's shoulders in a hug as Maude stifled a sob. 'First you must tell everything that has happened to you and then I'll tell you my news…good and bad.'

'Oh… I know, you are ruined,' Maude wailed beneath her breath. 'The duke told me so and very sorry he is, too, because it is all his silly fault that you got dragged into this. But what good is sorry?' Maude wrung her hands. 'He seems a decent man and has said

he will make amends…but how is that to be achieved?'
Maude flung up her hands in exasperation. 'When I
demanded he tell me, he had no answer to give. What
will he do? Will he buy you a husband?' She snorted
her dubious opinion on the likelihood of that.

'I don't want a husband bought for me, Mama,'
Fiona returned forcefully. She threw back her head,
moist eyes blinking at the ceiling. Oh, she knew that
in the circumstances paying a nice chap to marry her
and salvage her reputation would be a sensible, if humiliating, option. Indeed, Fiona had heard of instances
when a genteel woman had been discreetly married to
a fortune hunter following an unfortunate slip on the
lady's part. But Fiona knew she had not made a slip
and she knew there was only one man she wanted.

Luke Wolfson had desired taking her with him, as
his mistress, and suddenly she was regretting turning
her back on that offer more than she was sorry for having given him back his shiny gold coins.

'Tell me what else the duke said, Mama.' Fiona sat
back on her heels and waited for her mother to resume her account. Her hopes of keeping bad news from
reaching her mother's ears—or at least breaking it to
Maude herself—had been dashed. Fiona realised that
Mr Herbert would not be alone in having heard the
gossip. The countryside was probably buzzing with
tales of the lady and the highwaymen, each version
more lurid than the previous one, thrilling everybody
with its awfulness.

Some twenty minutes later mother and daughter
had finished talking and were gazing quietly at one
another.

'So…this Wolfson is just your saviour rather than
your beau?' Maude said, a touch disappointedly. 'When
I spoke to His Grace, he was cautious in what he said
about you and the major. Perhaps he thought I might
have a fit of the vapours knowing you had an admirer.'
Maude glanced at Rose who had taken a chair by the
window and appeared to be absorbed in some cro-
chet work, pulled from her reticule. 'I wondered if you
might have succumbed to Wolfson's charms, you know,
Fiona.' Maude managed a weak chuckle. 'I saw him
leaving the duke's house, you see, but had no opportunity to talk to him. He is very handsome.' Maude
angled her face to watch for Fiona's reaction.

'Yes, he is…' Fiona agreed in a murmur, a tiny smile
tilting her full lips.

'You like him, but fear that he is put off by those
rogues having manhandled you.' Maude slapped her
lap in exasperation. 'And how I wish I might have given
that Mr Herbert a piece of my mind. How dare he speak
to you so! But none of this would have come about
but for my stupidity…' Maude ended on a sorrowful
sigh. 'If only I had not married Cecil.' She clutched
her daughter's hands, bringing them to her bosom. 'If
I could turn back the clock I would. Please forgive me
for being a silly vain woman.'

Fiona nodded vigorously, unable to speak. She hated
seeing her mother upset, but her burgeoning sorrow
at having let Luke go off and leave her was closing
her throat with anguish. Piously she'd told him she'd
sooner be a governess than a mistress, but even before
Mr Herbert had dismissed her, she'd known she'd told
a lie and would fly to him in an instant if she could.

The night through she'd tossed and turned upstairs

in her comfortable bed. At one point she'd got up and padded to the window to stare at the heavy moon, knowing he was somewhere close, beneath the same silver orb. And with a fervour she'd not employed since her dear papa was on his deathbed she'd prayed for the well-being of a man she loved. Then she had felt annoyed with him for troubling her so. He had rejected what most people wanted despite having the wherewithal to provide himself with a permanent home in polite society. It was a great puzzle to Fiona why Luke chose not to enjoy the safety and comfort his wealth and status could provide.

'What will you do?'

Maude broke into Fiona's introspection with a quavering demand for information. She'd been watching her daughter's delicately sharp features being shaped by fierce concentration.

'The first thing I will do is get us some refreshment.' Fiona stood up, determined to buck up on seeing such concern in her mother's eyes. 'It will all seem a little better after a nice cup of tea and some of Mrs Brewer's ginger cake.' At the door Fiona hesitated and turned to look back at her mother. 'Have you left Mr Ratcliff for good?' She refused to give her stepfather anything other than a formal title.

'I shall never go back to him! I'd sooner enter the workhouse!' Maude declared dramatically. 'And I'd not be surprised to see him there, too…or the Fleet! He has sold everything we once had.'

'Apart from your late husband's small painting, ma'am,' Rose reminded without looking up from her needlework.

'Oh…we have something to sell!' Maude gleefully

clapped her hands. 'I had quite forgotten about that picture packed in the trunk.'

Fiona was pleased to see her mother's smile and went off to find Mrs Brewer and order their tea. But she knew there were still many problems ahead of them all. If the Duke of Thornley were prepared to make amends to them in some way then she'd as soon he compensated her mother so Maude might have a modest home and shelter.

She needed nothing for herself; she knew with a kind of serene acceptance that fate had already decreed her future. Luke Wolfson was a dangerously enigmatic man but wherever he was…that was where she would go…in the hope he still wanted her.

Chapter Seventeen

Megan moved closer by sidling from table to table, furiously polishing the wooden tops, hoping to eavesdrop on the conversation between the two men. The landlord of the Fallow Buck was a gregarious fellow, willing to pass the time of day with any patron and he seemed to have a lot to say to the haughty-faced individual.

It was a name overheard that had drawn Megan closer…and there it was again… *Mrs Ratcliff*. Megan knew *that* woman…and her daughter, Fiona Chapman, and she reckoned that this traveller must be a relative, come looking for the two of them.

She resumed swiping her cloth over ale-spotted oak as she noticed the gentleman was watching her from beneath his brows. Perhaps he thought she had crept closer because she fancied him.

The landlord wandered off and Megan was about to follow him to probe for information about the stranger when he spoke to her.

'And what might your name be, my dear?'

Innocently, Megan glanced up at him. 'I'm Megan.

Would you like me to get you some refreshment, sir?'
she asked politely.

Cecil Ratcliff slumped down into a chair at the table
Megan had been cleaning. 'Indeed you may…a bottle
of port and a plate of beef with bread and cheese and
pickles,' he listed out. 'And if a decent cigar is to be
had in this place, bring that, too.'

Megan dipped her head. One of those, was he?
Plenty of wants but most likely a tight-fist…like his
wife, if indeed he was Mrs Ratcliff's husband. Megan
went off to the kitchens and while preparing the food
alongside the landlord, got answers to the questions
she casually asked. She learned that the fellow was indeed Mr Ratcliff and he *was* enquiring after his wife
and stepdaughter.

'He seemed a churlish sort,' the landlord summed up
Cecil Ratcliff, while slicing juicy beef from the bone.
'I don't reckon his wife will get to keep that picture. I
wish I'd not mentioned seeing it now.'

'Picture?' Megan echoed with a frown.

'Mrs Ratcliff couldn't get the lid of her packing case
shut. I gave her a hand and noticed she'd got a small
painting wedged inside. I only mentioned it in passing, but Ratcliff seemed glad to know about it.' The
landlord raised his bushy eyebrows at Megan. 'Perhaps
it's an heirloom…and, no, he is not having one of my
cigars so say we've no stock.'

Megan turned away with the loaded plate of food,
heading for the door. She reckoned that Sam might
want to hear about Mr Ratcliff arriving in Devon and
about an heirloom.

Jeremiah Collins had been snapping and snarling at
his men since the fiasco with Miss Chapman. In turn

Sam had been snapping and snarling at Megan. Collins didn't like deals to turn sour on him and the kidnapping escapade had netted him just a few pounds from Wolfson when he'd been expecting ten times as much in ransom. Megan wanted her and Sam to be married because she loved him despite his faults and bad connections. Once they were wed she was sure she could lure Sam away from Collins's gang. But in the meantime she was certain if she gave Sam some useful information to pass to Jeremiah then all might be well again between them and they'd start walking out together once more. Perhaps, before Ratcliff was reunited with his family, he might be tricked into believing that his stepdaughter was still in danger and stump up a ransom. That would be sure to put a smile on Collins's face. As far as Megan could see there was no risk in such a plot...but much to gain...

The Duke of Thornley was also beset by thoughts of Cecil Ratcliff and had been since the day Maude had come to visit him, looking for her daughter.

Following his talk with Maude that day he'd brooded on what she had disclosed about her wretched marriage. Alfred had liked Maude and wanted to do everything he could to make her life comfortable and that of her blameless daughter. He felt he owed them both that much. He'd guessed what Maude wanted above all else was for her and Fiona to be rid of the man making their lives a misery. So he'd acted on that hunch. Alfred wasn't sure that the document in his hand would do the trick, but it was certainly intriguing enough for him to harbour a glimmer of hope.

The duke's man of business had returned from London just that afternoon, bringing with him a report of his investigations into Maude Ratcliff's reprobate of a husband. With a sigh Alfred tossed the parchment on to the shiny yew table and sat down, chin cupped in his hands. It all seemed outlandish, but then, of late, much of his life was like that, so he imagined other people's lives were, too. He made a snap decision to send servants to scour the coaching inns and find Maude… perhaps now reunited with Fiona…and invite her to Thornley Heights so he might share with her some astonishing news. Of course, were it authentic, it would present the woman with a fresh set of problems. But Thornley felt it only right to give Maude the chance to have her say on it.

'I hoped I'd be seeing you again quite soon.'

'Always happy to oblige,' Luke drawled as he circled Jeremiah Collins, levelling a pistol at the man's chest. 'But I think you're lying.'

'How astute you are, Wolfson,' Jeremiah scoffed through his gritted teeth. In fact, he was cursing his unexpected visitor to damnation and also the fellows who were supposed to be guarding the churchyard. He imagined that Wolfson had overpowered the dolts. 'And what have you done with Ruff and Dickens?' he smoothly enquired.

'Nothing that a good physician won't be able to cure.'

'I'll knock them out again when they come round.' Jeremiah chortled. 'I must get myself some better help.'

'You won't need it. You're packing up business. We're off to see the magistrate.'

'I don't think I'll come…but thank you anyway for

the offer,' Collins spat caustically. 'I guessed from the start you were up to no good.' In fact, he'd known nothing of the sort. When the major turned up in Devon, offering his good connections and expertise in exchange for a slice of the profits in kidnapping the Duke of Thornley's daughter, Jeremiah had been keen on the idea. He hated those above him in the pecking order, and though Wolfson fell into the category, the major had sounded like a man carrying a chip on his shoulder. He'd seemed a kindred spirit to Jeremiah…but of course it had been a clever ruse on Wolfson's part.

Influential as he was in his own way, Jeremiah would never have had the audacity or the opportunity to attempt the kidnap of a powerful aristocrat's child. When the major had outlined his scheme and told him he had Thornley's ear, and that of their mutual friend, the Duke of Wellington, Jeremiah had listened intently.

Naturally, Jeremiah had had the major's credentials checked by a militiaman who was not averse to taking a bribe. Everything had checked out as it should. Still, Collins had been wary. Why would a fellow who moved in such exalted circles want to bite the hand that fed him? He'd demanded an answer direct from Wolfson and had been told that there were private reasons—not for discussion—for him wanting to even scores and make some money in the process. Jeremiah had accepted that as it fitted in with the major's brooding moodiness. But he bitterly regretted now letting avarice blind him to the fellow's true character. He'd fallen for it hook, line and sinker rather than making Wolfson prove himself further.

By the time Jeremiah's suspicions started outweighing his greed it was too late. Those numbskulls that worked for him had taken it upon themselves to abduct the wrong woman.

'And how is Miss Chapman?' Collins jibed although inwardly seething, and investigating every angle to outwit and kill his daunting adversary.

'She is very well,' Luke said, pocketing the pistol. At present he had no need of it. Ruff and Dickens were out cold and tied up out of harm's way. Luke knew he could take Collins easily in a straight fight and the man didn't appear to have a weapon on his coatless person. Nevertheless, Luke was on his guard. The smuggler could have a knife concealed, probably in a boot, just as Luke did himself.

Luke glanced to right and left in the church. All was quiet and still and the candles burning at the end of the pew where Jeremiah had been seated, drinking brandy, shed a blurry light on his foe's sinister features.

Then he heard it: a scratching noise and a faint shout.

Luke's dark eyes whipped back to Jeremiah. 'You've somebody imprisoned down there?'

'Nobody important.' Jeremiah flicked some indolent fingers. 'Not to me at least; perhaps you'll think differently as you're smitten with the man's stepdaughter...or has that fire already extinguished?' Jeremiah smirked. 'I told you I'd buy back the buttoned-up spinster when you'd done with her.'

Luke had withdrawn the pistol again and was walking backwards towards the stairs that led below, keeping Jeremiah in his sights. He could scarce credit what the man had said, yet didn't think that Collins was lying, either.

'You've got Ratcliff?'

At Jeremiah's bored nod Luke snorted a harsh laugh. 'Why? You fool! The man's being dunned, he's hardly going to find a ransom for himself or a stepdaughter who loathes him.'

'Being dunned, is he?' Jeremiah tutted sarcastically. 'I doubt those creditors know he has a valuable painting. Or rather his wife has it in her possession.'

'Bring him up!' Luke snarled. Of all the things that could have gone wrong during his mission to bring Collins to justice he hadn't thought it would be something as unpredictable as Cecil Ratcliff's untimely appearance!

He'd had from Fiona's own lips that she and her mother detested Ratcliff, but Luke couldn't allow Jeremiah to murder the fellow, which he would once he discovered no cash was to be had for Ratcliff's release.

Fiona was a sweet fair-minded person; she had every reason to loathe the man her mother had married, but she wouldn't want his death on her conscience. She'd blame herself for running away and drawing her stepfather into danger. And the thought of Fiona's future happiness being threatened stabbed at Luke's guts like a hot knife. He'd known for a long while that he was falling in love with her, but had suppressed the emotion by trying to convince himself that he was confusing lust with finer feelings. He regretted propositioning her when he could just as easily have asked her to marry him. It seemed incredible that in such a short time he should be so enslaved and ready to settle down. But with calm acceptance he knew it to be true. There'd been nobody in his past, and he sensed that neither would any woman in the future match up to Fiona as his future wife and the mother of his children.

'Get him up here!' Luke's bellow brought Jeremiah to his feet.

'I'll bring the fellow up when Mrs Ratcliff arrives and hands over the painting.' Jeremiah threw back his head and hooted a guffaw. 'You really don't know, do you, that the whole family is now congregated in the neighbourhood?'

Luke lunged at Jeremiah, curling a large, savage hand about his throat, prepared to throttle the devil to get every scrap of information out of him.

'Mrs Ratcliff was first to come searching for her daughter, then the stepfather turned up. I have spies out—these things soon reach my ears…sooner than they do yours, by the look of things,' Jeremiah wheezed out merrily. 'I imagine you might have some explaining to do when the chit's belly starts to swell.'

Shoving Collins away before he succumbed to the temptation to strangle him, Luke gritted with specious softness, 'Bring the fellow up here.' He raised the pistol. 'Or I will kill you and God knows you'll not be meeting your maker before time.'

A few moments later Cecil Ratcliff was pushed, stumbling, up the same stone stairs from which, not long ago, Fiona had emerged into dim candle flame. Luke, staring, thought his eyes were deceiving him. Then, on striding closer for a better inspection, he noticed the cunning light in the fellow's pale eyes and knew he wasn't mistaken.

Luke glanced at Jem Collins. 'This is Cecil Ratcliff?'

'The very same,' the smuggler croaked through his crushed windpipe, his mean eyes darting between the two men.

'Tell him who you are.' The pistol moved slightly to encompass the prisoner.

'Cecil Ratcliff. And who pray are you?'

'Your erstwhile commanding officer, Rowland…not forgotten me already, surely?' Luke said softly. Lieutenant Charlie Rowland might have cut his sparse hair short and shaved off his beard, but he was still recognisable as the army deserter and all-round blackguard Luke knew of old.

Cecil licked his lips. 'I've no idea what you're talking about.'

'Of course you have—you're still up to your old tricks, then. But your time's up now, just as it is for him.' Luke jerked his head in Collins's direction.

'What in damnation?' Jeremiah snarled, glowering at his prize. 'If your wife's not on her way with that canvas, you've not long to live.' In a deft swooping movement that attested to much practice, Jeremiah had whipped a blade from his boot, then leapt to hold it to Cecil's throat.

'His wife's not on her way.' Luke advanced on the two men. 'His wife's in Bedlam, and since committing her he's had at least another two bigamous marriages that I know about, not including the one to Miss Chapman's mother. He's also had more sojourns in the Fleet than you've had kegs of brandy off Dawlish Beach.'

'Don't listen to him…he's lying. I don't know him,' Cecil spluttered before realising that both men were enemies and his greatest peril was from the fellow pressing the knife to his jugular.

'You've got yourself a pig in a poke, Jeremiah,' Luke stated coolly. 'The authorities will be almost as keen to apprehend this felon as they will you. You might

as well let him go. He's bankrupt…he always is…'
Luke cocked the loaded pistol in a very deliberate way.
'Who's carrying the message to Mrs Ratcliff?'

Jeremiah licked his dry lips. His informant in the
dragoons had told him to take care if crossing Wolfson
as the man had a fearsome reputation with a range of
weapons, both on and off the battlefield.

Jeremiah knew he risked a bullet in the brain before
he'd finished slicing his captive from ear to ear. But
he managed a careless shrug, his free hand gesturing
obscenely his refusal to answer any questions.

Luke suddenly barked a laugh. 'Ah… I see… Dickens was on his way, was he, when I caught him saddling up outside.' Luke got great satisfaction from
knowing that Fiona's mother wasn't about to burst in
and swoon at the sight before her.

Jeremiah knew he must upset Wolfson's equilibrium
to have a chance of escaping. At present his lethally
composed opponent would be difficult to conquer. If
Wolfson overpowered him, his next stop, after gaol,
would be Gallows Hill.

'Whoever you are, I doubt you knew that this fine
major has been tumbling your wife's daughter. What
do you think about that, eh?' Collins muttered close to
Cecil's ear, but loud enough for Luke to hear.

Cecil darted a resentful glance at Luke. So he'd
had more luck bedding the wench, had he? But Cecil
wasn't about to let on that Fiona had rejected him. He
gave as listless a shrug as was possible with Jeremiah's
heavy arm about his neck. 'She's a harlot ready to lift
her skirts for any fellow. She's soothed many an itch
for me.' He growled a ribald laugh.

Luke knew it for a provocative ploy, yet even so

he was consumed by an irresistible urge to leap at the sneering pair and batter them.

Collins glimpsed a flicker of raw emotion stretching Wolfson's lips flat on his teeth and seized his moment. He gave his captive an almighty shove, reinforced by a boot against Cecil's backside that sent him crashing into Luke. Luke stumbled under Ratcliff's unexpected weight, giving Jeremiah the second he needed to lunge forward. Momentum had taken Cecil to his knees and, caitiff that he was, he cowered there, arms up over his head, as Collins charged forward with the knife, steel glinting in the candlelight.

A vicious knife-swipe sliced Luke's shoulder, but he managed to protect himself from further injury by swaying backwards on his heels. Swinging his head round in a brutal movement, he caught Collins's profile. When the smaller man staggered from the blow Luke followed up by delivering a single hefty jab to the smuggler's chin, snapping together his sagging jaw. Once Collins was sprawled senseless on the flags Luke removed the blade from his opponent's limp fingers.

He swung a look over a shoulder as he heard a scurrying sound and was just in time to see Cecil Ratcliff frantically crawling on hands and knees, then jumping to his feet to flee from the church. Following a frustrated curse, Luke turned back to Collins and hoisted his comatose form on to his shoulder, then went outside in pursuit of the other man.

'Be still or I'll use this pistol,' Luke shouted at the fugitive dodging between headstones. 'You know I can hit you from this distance.' In a sliver of moonlight Luke saw his quarry duck down behind a rock angel. Quickly, keeping Cecil in his sights, he flung Jeremiah over his stallion, lashing together the unconscious man's hands and feet with the reins as a precaution.

Free of that burden, Luke began to stalk Ratcliff through the graveyard, shoving the pistol back into his coat pocket. He knew he had no need of it. The bigamist looked to have grown fat on his three years of parasitic living since deserting from the army. Had he not absconded he would have been court martialled, possibly executed for thieving supplies from the army store he'd been charged with overseeing.

Cecil stood up slowly as though about to turn himself in, but instead he threw the fistfuls of stones he'd gathered from the ground. Luke crouched down as a pebble scored his scalp, but Ratcliff's desperate tactic had gained him little other than a few more yards of turf covered. Luke sprinted forward, tackling his wheezing torso to the freshly dug soil beside an open grave.

'I can make it worth your while to let me go,' Ratcliff gasped, struggling to get free of the forearm on his throat, pinning him down. 'I've that painting to recover, Wolfson. You can have it, I swear,' he cravenly wheedled. 'Once I catch up with my wife she'll hand it over in a trice. It's yours…and on good authority it's valuable…'

'You've got two choices in the matter,' Luke said with deceptive softness. 'You can beg forgiveness for ever having laid your filthy hands on Fiona Chapman, or you can spend the night in there.' Luke jerked a nod at the open grave. 'I'll blanket you with earth to make sure you keep warm.'

'You're no better than me where that chit is concerned. Will you apologise to her for bedding her?'

Cecil spat. 'What does it matter? She's ruined now. Collins told me what's gone on. No gentleman would touch her with a bargepole once he knows smugglers have taken their sport with her. She'll end as a penny whore in Whitechapel if I don't put a roof over her head. You might as well keep your mouth shut on it all, Wolfson, for the sake of those two women. They've no choice but me.'

'You're wrong about that,' Luke said as he hit Ratcliff in the mouth with all the force he could muster from close range. He dragged the snivelling wretch up by the collar, in much the same way that his prisoner had hauled Dolly to her feet days before.

'I'm tempted to kill you, but I won't.' Luke thrust Cecil from him as though he felt contaminated by his proximity. 'You're not worth a murder charge. The law can decide your fate.' He grinned suddenly, and drew the pistol from his pocket. 'Two for the price of one… not a bad night's work.' Shoving Cecil in front of him, he headed back to Star.

Chapter Eighteen

'Please calm yourself, Mama,' Fiona whispered.

She sent a glance over a shoulder to where the Duke of Thornley had diplomatically withdrawn to allow mother and daughter to digest his solemnly imparted news that Cecil Ratcliff was a bigamist, amongst other things.

Maude scrunched her wet handkerchief in her fist. 'The cheating swine! To do something so vile and immoral to an innocent woman is beyond bearing!' She scrubbed again at her bloodshot eyes.

'Yes, I know, Mama,' Fiona soothed. 'But you are not his legal wife after all—you said you regretted marrying him so perhaps it is not all bad.'

'I have allowed a man—an odious individual at that—to take intimate privileges only given under vows to a husband,' Maude spluttered in a voice of suffocated outrage.

Fiona drew her mother towards a chair and made her sit down, then shot a look at the fellow hovering by the window with his hands clasped behind his back.

Earlier that afternoon, mother and daughter had

been drinking their tea and discussing where to head on departing the Pig and Whistle, when the duke's servant had turned up with a message for Maude. Thankfully it contained just an urgent summons to Thornley Heights. Had it been any more explicit Fiona knew her mother might have swooned dead away in the tavern's saloon bar, then even more people would know that, unbelievably, the scandal surrounding the Chapman women had just deepened.

The letter had intrigued both mother and daughter and they'd agreed that they should accept the invitation and go straight away to see His Grace. So they'd packed up their things with Rose's help, then all ridden in the coach provided by the duke to solve the mystery.

Obliquely, Fiona had been glad to have a distraction to prevent her constantly thinking about Luke. Had he been injured in the confrontation with Collins? Had he sensibly decided to avoid danger and return to London after all? But the most pressing uncertainty was where to go to find him.

At the Pig and Whistle she'd been mulling over ways to tell her mother that she'd fallen in love and was prepared to follow Luke Wolfson to the ends of the earth if need be. She'd now need to bite her tongue on that secret a while longer; it would be too cruel to add to her mother's anguish when Maude was already on the point of hysterics.

Fiona glanced up as the drawing-room door opened and a young woman entered. Having approached the duke for a brief conversation, the petite brunette then hurried over to Fiona and Maude.

'Papa has allowed me to come and speak to you,

Miss Chapman. I'm so very sad to hear of your troubles.' Joan cast a sympathetic look on Maude's bowed head.

'You must be Joan Thornley.' Fiona straightened from her crouching position close to her mother's chair.

'I am… Oh, sorry to be rude—I should have introduced myself straight away.' Joan held out her hands and warmly clasped Fiona's fingers. Following a quick glance at Fiona's mother, still propping her contorted features in her hands, Joan drew Fiona aside. 'I know you have also suffered through no fault of your own,' she whispered, looking chagrined. 'I very much regret that as well.'

'Hush… I am fine…' Fiona said kindly, as the young lady began blinking back guilty tears. 'But I'm not sure my mama will quickly recover from this dreadful blow.' Fiona knew Maude must feel the greatest fool alive. Although her mother now hated Cecil, at one time the woman had thought herself in love with her second husband. She had put her faith and trust in a man who'd given nothing but lies and deceit in return for sincere affection and loyalty.

'I expect Major Wolfson acquainted you with our half-baked scheme to catch the smuggling gang.' Joan had kept her voice low while looking very sheepish.

'Yes…he did…'

'You were very brave, Miss Chapman; I couldn't have asked for a better impostor—' Joan broke off, blushing and biting her lip. 'Sorry, that was a daft thing to say.' Soon she'd bounced back to resume excitedly, 'It must have felt as though you'd been swept up in a Gothic novel. Luke Wolfson is such a handsome and brave hero and the whole thing is exceedingly romantic.' Again Joan frowned at what she'd said. 'I know why Papa got cross with me. I do sound like a very silly and flighty girl sometimes. Yet I'm almost twenty.'

'It *was* quite thrilling—in hindsight, of course,' Fiona ruefully admitted. 'I was terrified at the time, but tried not to let on to those villains. Besides, I trusted in Mr Wolfson to rescue me,' Fiona concluded softly.

'If I tell you something, will you promise not to breathe a word to a soul?' Joan asked.

Fiona had been on the point of returning to her mother's side, but noticed the duke had pulled up a chair close to Maude and was talking to her in an undertone.

'I am disgraced, too!' Joan hissed, rather tactlessly. 'But thankfully only my papa and the major's friend know about it. Oh, and Pip, too. He drove the gig that took me to see Mr Rockleigh, you see, but Papa has threatened the boy to keep quiet on pain of losing his livelihood. My father is still very angry at me for taking such a risk, but eventually he'll calm down—'

'You went to see Mr Rockleigh?' Fiona interrupted Joan's rattling report. She recalled Luke had told her that his friend Drew Rockleigh had set off back to London.

Joan nodded. 'I was trying to help with the plot to capture Jeremiah Collins, you see. I knew only the major could outwit the devil. So believing Wolfson at his friend's hunting lodge I went off to find him, late at night, behind Papa's back.'

'I'm guessing your plan went awry.' Fiona sounded calm despite her shock at hearing what the young woman had done.

'Mr Rockleigh was on his own at his hunting lodge.'

Joan grimaced. 'Thankfully Papa has now seen sense over trying to make the poor man marry me. *I* compromised *him* if anything…' Joan sighed. 'I refused to have him, but I expect Mr Rockleigh must hate me for causing him such trouble, especially as he brought me home safely.'

A small muffled noise from Maude drew Fiona hurriedly back to her mother's side, fearing yet more bad news was to be had.

'You are very good to us, sir,' Maude gulped. She put away her handkerchief and turned to Fiona, making an effort to compose herself. 'His Grace has kindly invited us to stay the night at Thornley Heights as his guests, Fiona. Then in the morning he will escort us to London to sort out this terrible mess.'

'Oh, capital!' Joan burst out. 'I love to have company and I adore London.' She gave her papa a twinkling smile, just in case he had intended leaving her behind. 'I shall pack a few things after dinner. I'm so looking forward to it.' She linked arms with Fiona as though they were old friends. 'We have so much to talk about.'

'I must let Rose know what has been decided.' Maude made to rise, but the duke stopped her with a hand on her arm.

'My daughter will send a message down to the servants. I expect your maid is taking refreshment.'

Fiona smiled although privately feeling rather melancholy. She yearned to see Luke again, but accepted any meeting would be delayed by this latest calamity. There was no urgency to be with the man she loved, other than to revel in his closeness. She knew to abandon her mother would be selfish; besides, she trusted that Luke would still want her, whether it was in a day, or a month's time, that they were finally reunited.

He might be a gentleman who in his time had dallied with a variety of women, but she believed him fair and honest. She was sure that he'd fulfil the promise he'd made to care for her and protect her.

Given time, and a successful result against the smugglers, she guessed that Luke would journey to Dartmouth, believing her to have taken up employment with the Herberts. He wasn't fickle; he'd not give up his pursuit of her too easily. And if he did…then he was not the man she believed him to be.

'I have spent far too much time lately riding in carriages…' Fiona mused, partly to herself, gazing out of the window at drifting fluffy clouds.

'I'll warrant none of those contraptions were anywhere near as luxurious as this one,' Maude returned, nestling further into supple hide squabs. Although they had been journeying for almost two hours the woman was still in awe of the splendid crested coach that was taking them to the metropolis. She ran her appreciative fingers over the upholstery for the hundredth time.

'Papa does own some very nice vehicles,' Joan piped up. She had insisted on riding with the ladies rather than with her father. So Maude and Rose shared one spacious seat and the two younger women sat opposite. The Duke of Thornley was travelling ahead with his valet in another impressive conveyance, flanked by liveried outriders. 'When I turned seventeen he bought me a landau so I might parade around Hyde Park with my friends.'

'Do you visit London often?' Fiona had wondered

why the younger woman wasn't enjoying the London Season. Most spinsters of Lady Joan's age and elevated status wanted to be part of the vivacious social whirl in town in springtime.

Joan pulled a face. 'Since Mama passed away my father has withdrawn into his shell. And taken me with him,' she added rather wistfully. 'But I don't begrudge comforting him as best I can. My parents liked to spend time in Devon and were so very happily married...' Joan frowned and shot a look under her brows at Maude.

'Lucky people indeed...' the woman muttered sourly.

'So you will relish this unexpected outing,' Fiona burst out, keen to keep a light atmosphere. She'd been surprised that Joan was not even engaged. She was a very pretty young woman and with such wealth and connections would attract a horde of eligible suitors. But Joan obviously knew her own mind and had rejected her father's choice when hapless Drew Rockleigh compromised her. He was a very handsome fellow, Fiona recalled, but other than that he might have nothing to recommend him.

'Indeed, I am delighted to be going to town!' Joan had been peering out of the window at passing scenery, but now settled back and clapped her gloved hands in excitement. 'When we arrive in Mayfair the first thing we must do is arrange a big party...' She hesitated and glanced at the unhappy woman in the corner. 'If you would like to, of course.'

'That sounds a splendid idea.' Maude bucked herself up. She might be dejected on her own account, but she knew she must not look a gift horse in the mouth. There was never likely to be a better opportunity to re-launch her daughter into society and find her a husband. Maude knew it was Fiona's last chance. A twenty-five-year-old spinster was more of an age to be a debutante's chaperon at the marriage mart, than her friend or rival. Maude discreetly assessed Fiona's profile; her daughter had turned up her face to allow the sun streaming in the carriage window to gild it. She seemed prettier, Maude decided, her hair blonder and her complexion peachier. Her daughter's usual air of serenity seemed subdued by a vibrant, if rather secretive, happiness. Maude had guessed that Fiona had a hankering for her handsome rescuer and was harbouring fantasies of a happy ending with him. What girl would not fall in love with such a dashing hero? Before Maude had even learned of the service Wolfson had done her daughter she had thought he appeared to be a charismatic man.

Of course the major knew all the details of Fiona's disgrace so could not be counted on for anything other than his discretion—which the duke, during their private talk yesterday, had assured her Wolfson had gladly given. If Fiona's dreadful ordeal leaked out she would be shunned, but Maude's flagging spirits where her daughter was concerned were boosted as she reminded herself that they now had the patronage of the Duke of Thornley. Few would dare question the calibre of the friends of such a rich and influential man.

Maude settled back with an air of resignation. As far as her own situation was concerned she knew she must make the best of a bad hand. She *had* wished her marriage to Cecil had never taken place…and it seemed she'd got her wish, albeit courtesy of a very shocking and humiliating set of circumstances. She lifted her chin an inch, knowing she must find some of the grit her daughter had in abundance and stare down any malicious gossips.

Fiona heard her mother's tiny satisfied sigh and, feeling pleased by it, she relaxed. She could scarce credit that so much had happened in so short a space of time.

Having spent a comfortable night in a sumptuous chamber, mother and daughter had risen early, as had the rest of the household. The duke had said at dinner the previous evening that he wanted to set off for London immediately after breakfast and indeed that had happened. At the crack of dawn the house had been a hive of industry as the servants finished the preparations for their master's trip to town and served up a huge repast that seemed to Fiona barely necessary as she was still feeling full from the twenty courses or so of dinner from the previous evening.

Despite the thick mattresses and silky smooth sheets Fiona had slept little with her mind crammed with worries. At one point she had given up trying to count sheep and had got up and stared out of the window into blackness where Luke's face seemed to haunt every cloud and shadow. Now, the rocking of the coach and her exhaustion combined to lull her and her lashes dropped over her weary eyes.

She wasn't sure for how long she slept but she awoke with a start and quickly looked at her companions to note they, too, had nodded off. She realised then what had brought her awake: the coach was slowing down and bumping over ruts formed by a multitude of other carriage wheels that had turned into this tavern courtyard. Inwardly Fiona groaned; she had been inside many such establishments lately and would have preferred to journey on.

'Why are we stopping?' Maude came awake with a start and craned her head out of the window.

'It is the Halfway House,' Joan said, rubbing her sleepy eyes. 'We always break our journey here. Papa will bespeak us a private room so we might have some refreshment.'

'Oh, no!'

Fiona had been gazing at some drizzle trailing down the leaded windows when she heard Joan's muted gasp of dismay. Moments ago they had been shown to the back parlour of the Halfway House. Joan had been about to take a fireside chair while Fiona continued to stretch her stiff legs, promenading to and fro in the cosy room. Now she returned to Joan's side, but the young woman, with a wary glance at her father who was ensconced with Maude on a sofa, skipped to the door. It had been left slightly ajar by the landlord who'd gone to fetch their food. Quickly Joan pushed it shut.

'What is it?' Fiona asked in concern.

'*Who* is it? That's what you should have asked.' Joan swivelled her eyes in a show of exasperation. 'I just spied Mr Rockleigh in the corridor! I hope Papa does not see him. I think they are under a very fragile truce following my visit to the man's lodge.' She sighed. 'Oh, what a bother and such bad luck to run into him here!'

'Are you sure it was him? Was he alone?' Fiona frowned.

The two young ladies stepped to the window so they

might talk more privately under the guise of observing the worsening weather.

Joan shook her head. 'Oh, he was not accompanied by his friend, the major,' she explained quietly. 'He had a dark-haired young woman with him.'

'I see…' Fiona tried to curb her dreadful disappointment. Just for a moment she had imagined that Luke might be under the same roof as her, but she realised it was more likely his mistress was instead. It was a puzzle why Luke's friends had not already reached London and the only solution Fiona could come up with caused her heart to thump in anxiety. Had Becky Peake and Drew Rockleigh been waiting for Luke to join them before journeying on? Fiona felt the pain around her heart increase as her mind pounced on a dreadful reason for his delay in turning up. Luke might even now be lying murdered in that desolate graveyard that the Collins gang used as a hideaway.

'I hope he is planning on leaving soon,' Joan fretted in a whisper. 'Papa is unpredictable. He might blow his top, or sink into one of his moods if they unexpectedly come face to face.' She shot a look at the door. 'Perhaps I should go and see if I can find the dratted fellow and warn him to conceal himself.' She nibbled at her lower lip. 'I must find an excuse to slip away…'

'I'll go,' Fiona said hoarsely. 'We've not been introduced, but I know what Mr Rockleigh looks like. I'll explain the situation to him.'

'Oh, would you? That is very kind.'

Joan's grateful smile helped Fiona swallow her misgivings over her impetuous offer. She felt desperate to have any news of Luke that she could, although she was naturally reluctant to accost people she didn't know.

A meeting with Becky Peake was especially daunting to her. Yet she also had a morbid wish to come face to face with her rival and perhaps with womanly intuition gauge just how entwined in Luke's life the woman was.

Fiona hurried out into the corridor with her mother's bewildered expression imprinted on her mind. Of course the woman would be sceptical about her excuse that she was in need of a little fresh air. They had all only recently come indoors after all…and it had turned to rain.

Chapter Nineteen

The Halfway House was a far larger inn than any that Fiona had previously frequented.

The maze of intersecting corridors that ran into back and side annexes was busy and she was relieved that most of the travellers appeared too harassed to bother about her slender presence weaving through the throng.

A very rotund fellow barged impatiently past, causing Fiona to ram a flat palm on the top of her bonnet to prevent it being knocked askew. She then resumed scouring the crowd for a pretty brunette or a strikingly fair-haired gentleman. Instead of clapping eyes on either of those individuals she rounded a corner and spied a handsome tanned face.

She might only have got a glimpse of his profile before other people surged forward to block her view, but it was enough for Fiona to recognise Luke. She'd know him anywhere, she realised, even in a darkened room. Her senses were attuned to him, like an animal scenting its mate. And then her fanciful yearning was quashed and she was jolted to harsh reality.

Becky Peake was with him. The crowd surrounding the couple dispersed and, snatching her chance, the brunette pressed her mouth to her lover's. Luke removed his mistress's arms from about his neck and turned…

Astonishment transformed his features, then he took a pace forward, shaking off Becky's fingers as she again reached for him.

'I thought you and your mother were staying at Thornley Heights.' Luke had reached Fiona in a few long strides, taking her hands in his.

Fiona moistened her lips, wondering how he knew she'd been the Duke of Thornley's guest, or that Maude had joined her in Devon. But seeing him being kissed by the mistress he'd said he'd finished with had ignited a fiery reaction within that overpowered her reason. She snatched back her hands. 'We were at His Grace's house, but left this morning to travel to London,' she answered frostily.

'I need to speak to you on a very important matter, Fiona,' Luke said huskily. He thrust his fingers through his glossy raven hair. 'Actually, there are numerous things I must say to you privately.'

'I see…and these matters are so vital that you travelled in the opposite direction to that in which you expected me to be.' She glanced past at the woman watching them through narrowed eyes. 'Your mistress is waiting for you, sir. I doubt we have anything left to say to one another.' Fiona knew she was acting like a jealous shrew, but she couldn't control herself. She was desperately keen to know what had occurred between Luke and Jeremiah Collins, but then realised he might have forgone a confrontation with the smuggler in favour of chasing after his paramour.

Luke's mouth slanted in sardonic contemplation of Fiona's indignant, blushing face. 'If you allow me to explain, my dear, seeing me with Becky will seem quite insignificant to you, as indeed the meeting is.'

Fiona raised furious eyes to his. 'Your arrogance and conceit is breathtaking, Mr Wolfson. Why would that woman matter to me?'

'I wasn't convinced last time you said you were indifferent to what I get up to,' he drawled, taking her arm and steering her towards the door that led outside into the courtyard. 'I'm no more persuaded now. But you will listen to everything I have to say whether you like it or not.'

'Unhand me!' Fiona hissed, trying to wrench her elbow from his grip.

But he forced her with him into the cool damp afternoon and before she knew it they were protected from the drizzle and from view by a large privet bush. When Luke removed his hand from her arm Fiona flung herself around to glare at him with sparking tawny eyes. 'To my previous complaints about your character I now add that you are the most ill-mannered man alive. Don't you dare rough handle me! And you have abandoned your mistress without giving her the courtesy of a word of explanation.'

'She needs none. Becky knows about us and that she is no longer my mistress. And I didn't want her farewell kiss just now.'

That steely announcement stunned Fiona into silence for a few moments. 'What does she know about us?' she eventually asked hoarsely.

Luke rubbed a hand about his bristly jaw; Fiona recognised then the weariness about him and his dusty dishevelment. He looked like a man who had ridden hard and had little rest. Suddenly she felt ashamed of her behaviour.

'We'll talk about that later. I've some news about your stepfather that I think you should know immediately although I'm loath to upset you.'

Fiona put an unsteady hand to her forehead. So, gossip about Cecil Ratcliff's bigamy had already spread. 'I know what you are going to say,' she murmured. 'So it will not come as a shock…although it is a surprise that the scandal is already out.' She sighed in defeat. 'The Duke of Thornley reported to my mother yesterday that Ratcliff is a bigamist who uses aliases.'

'Is that why you didn't travel on to Dartmouth? Did you forgo your employment to comfort and support her?'

Fiona guessed that he'd been to the Pig and Whistle looking for her. He would have learned from the landlord that a crested carriage had taken mother and daughter to His Grace's home. Luke obviously didn't know, though, that her employer had also turned up at the inn with no good deed in mind.

'Mr Herbert learned of my kidnapping and came to the Pig and Whistle to say he thought me unfit to be near his daughters following the incident.' Fiona's voice betrayed just a hint of the hurt she'd felt at being so rudely rejected.

'He insulted you? The bumptious dolt! I've a mind to go to Dartmouth and—'

'You will not!' Fiona interrupted quickly, gripping Luke's arm in emphasis. 'Please do not… It will just make matters worse.' She allowed him to draw her closer in comfort, leaning into his warmth and strength as though it were the most natural thing to do. 'I would have had no option but to quit the position in any case when Mama showed up.'

'Bad luck and heartache seem to dog you, don't they?' Luke said softly, gently soothing her with caressing fingers that moved from her cheek to cradle her scalp. 'Did you mother travel west looking for Ratcliff, or for you?'

'Ratcliff?' Fiona raised her eyes to Luke's face. Then her puzzlement transformed to horror. 'Oh, no! Never say the swine is close by.' She gazed back at the inn, inside which her mother was comfortably ensconced with the Duke of Thornley.

'He is…but there's no need to fret, Fiona. He is under guard and can't bother you.' In as few words as possible Luke explained how he had come across Ratcliff as Jeremiah Collins's prisoner and recognised him as a thief and deserter who'd served, under a different name, in his regiment.

Their eyes remained locked together for several moments after Luke stopped talking. Finally Fiona dragged her wide amber gaze up to the heavens. 'It is too much!' She took a pace away, then quickly returned. 'So not only is he *not* my mother's husband, but he is *not* Cecil Ratcliff, either? *That* name is one of his aliases, I take it.'

Luke gave a grave nod. 'He has changed his name several times to escape justice. His crimes are many after all and he knows a long prison sentence is the best he can expect once apprehended.'

'Why did Collins kidnap him?' she asked in despair. 'The spendthrift has nothing but IOUs to hand over.'

'I gather he pursued your mother towards Devon

because she stole a painting from him. He believes it valuable…and Collins somehow came to hear about it. He wanted to attempt to trade Ratcliff for the canvas.'

'*Stole it?*' Fiona burst out in an outraged hiss. 'That small painting belonged to my father, and whatever that odious man might think about his rights to it, *we* believe it to be ours.'

'If Ratcliff were your mother's legitimate husband, the law would see it differently, but never mind that now,' Luke added gently on noticing moisture beading Fiona's lashes.

Fiona smeared away the angry tears and composed herself with a little sniff. 'The fiend should rot in gaol for what he has done.'

'And will your mother feel the same way about his fate?'

'I think Mama would like the chance to throw the key to his cell into the depths of the sea!' Fiona replied flatly.

Luke released her and prowled to and fro, looking reflective. 'Do you want me to turn him over to the authorities?'

'Why…where is he?' Fiona marched after Luke, cocking her head to read his expression. 'What have you done with him?'

'Nothing…yet. He's locked away in a barn and can't escape. Drew's gone off to guard him. But I wanted to speak to you first before delivering him to the magistrate.' He gazed solemnly at her. 'I couldn't add to your woes and I couldn't be sure your mother wouldn't choose to stay loyal to Ratcliff, no matter what. If you want him set free…just say.'

'You would do that for me even though he has a catalogue of crimes to answer to?'

'I'd do anything for you, Fiona…you should know that by now…' Luke said huskily. Suddenly he was again before her and his mouth swooped, covering hers in a hard swift kiss. 'If I let him go he'll simply disappear from your lives. It's how he operates. Once his fraud is uncovered he runs for cover, then emerges elsewhere to prey on another unsuspecting female.'

Fiona bit her lip, thinking. She glanced up at Luke and gave him a faint smile; he had been very kind, considering their feelings before making any decision on Ratcliff's fate. 'He should be punished…' she uttered slowly.

'I agree…'

'But it is up to Mama, she must decide.'

'Shall we approach her now and bring an end to the matter?'

Fiona nodded. 'Mama is sitting with the Duke of Thornley…'

'*Thornley's* inside?' Luke snapped his gaze to the inn.

Fiona smiled ruefully. 'He's been very good to us. We overnighted at Thornley Heights and he is accompanying us to London in order to help sort out the mess we're in.' Fiona shook her head ruefully. 'We none of us had any idea that *the mess* has met us halfway.' Fiona sighed. 'Perhaps His Grace might turn back when he finds out and that will disappoint Joan. She is very much looking forward to her sojourn in town.'

'Joan is inside, too?' Luke's dark eyebrows shot up. Fiona suddenly clapped her hand to her mouth in consternation. She had forgotten her promise to Joan to run an errand.

'I was out in the corridor looking for your friend, as a favour to Joan. She caught sight of Mr Rockleigh and wanted to warn him to keep his distance from her father.'

'You know about that fiasco, do you?' Luke's tone held a mixture of amusement and exasperation.

'The kidnapping plot had some bad consequences,' Fiona said with some understatement.

'And His Grace is obviously feeling very guilty over the way it affected you,' Luke observed. He dipped his head, teased a delicate earlobe with his lips and warm breath. 'I rode this way looking for my friend simply to enlist his help. I'd rather have followed you to Thornley Heights, but I needed Drew to guard Ratcliff while I attended to other things. Drew and I served under Wellington together so he knows of Charlie Rowland, as we knew Cecil Ratcliff to be.'

'You have put yourself to some trouble over the vile wretch.'

'I had to—I knew you would never be content until the matter was settled. So you may tell Joan that my friend Drew is out of harm's way and no need to fret on that score.'

'And Becky Peake?' Fiona breathed.

'No need to fret on that score, either.' Luke dropped his hands away from her, but his loving expression intensified. 'Becky might claim that she wants only me… and she does…but we both know it's not true. She appreciates the things I give her and I've appreciated her company. But for me it's over. And for her…another generous man will do.' He smiled ruefully. 'I caught up with her and Drew quite quickly because they'd been enjoying staying at a variety of inns on their leisurely return to town.'

Fiona's lips softly parted in astonishment. 'You mean, your friend has stolen Becky from you?' she burst out.

'Not exactly—he's providing a service,' Luke answered diplomatically. 'And I've no objection to that whatsoever. Neither has Becky, although she was delighted to see me, as you witnessed. She likes to keep her options open—it's what women in her position do.'

'I see...' Fiona could feel the heat travelling from her throat to her cheeks. Was he obliquely giving her a first lesson in the ways and expected behaviour of his paramours? Had he just hinted that his mistress was expected to go quietly when her time was up? 'I should return to the others,' Fiona said. 'They will all be wondering where on earth I have got to.'

On cue, Joan appeared in the doorway that led back inside the tavern. 'Oh, there you are, Fiona,' she called. 'I thought I spied your bonnet behind that bush.' Joan rushed outside, then came to an abrupt halt on seeing somebody else, better concealed behind the privet.

'Major Wolfson!' Joan beamed and gave Fiona a rather arch glance. 'Well, this is a nice surprise. You are travelling with your friend, I expect.' She turned to Fiona. 'Have you warned Rockleigh off?' She grimaced. 'Papa is sinking some brandy and one never knows how that might affect him. He'll either be very mellow, or a bear with a sore head.'

'Mr Wolfson has just told me that his friend has already left,' Fiona quickly informed her. 'There was no need or opportunity for me to speak to him.'

'Oh...' Joan sounded a trifle disappointed and slipped her hand through the crook of Fiona's arm. 'Perhaps he will turn up in London.'

'We might not need to travel on...' Fiona shot a glance at Luke, hoping he might take over explanations. Her head had started to pound with the amount of information crammed within it. And then there was the question of her future with Luke, if indeed she had a future with him. She believed that his relationship with Becky was finished and that he still wanted her to replace the brunette. But for how long? Would he allow her to be taken on by one of his friends when he grew bored with his *buttoned-up spinster*?

'Let's go inside and find the others, then everybody will hear what I have to say,' Luke said, leading the way back to the tavern.

'So...the blackguard is safely apprehended?'

The moment Luke had finished his concise account of capturing Jeremiah Collins the Duke of Thornley demanded absolute confirmation of his arch-enemy's fate.

'Delivered to the magistrate and under lock and key,' Luke replied before taking a sip of brandy.

'Capital! I owe you a sum of money, sir,' Thornley boomed out. Then he glanced at the ladies. 'We'll speak of it later.'

'There's no need. I went after Collins on my own account rather than yours.'

His Grace looked rather taken aback at that blunt comment, but appeared not to take offence. He employed the decanter instead, then offered Luke a refill.

'What of Dickens and Ruff?' Fiona asked. She knew

that the young smuggler deserved his comeuppance, yet still felt sad that, with his life before him, Sam might have forfeited his future with Megan for the noose…or if he were lucky, years of hard labour.

Luke shrugged. 'I told the dragoons where to find them tied up. I imagine Collins's two cohorts have now joined him in gaol.'

'Quite rightly!' His Grace announced. 'Those types deserve no quarter. With Collins gone I expect another gang will form in time. It is the unfortunate way of things along this coast.'

Fiona knew it to be true; she recalled how savage young Sam had been when she made her escape from her dank prison. If pushed to choose between obeying his master, or sparing her life, he would have followed Jeremiah Collins's orders.

After a moment Fiona realised that her mother had remained very quiet, seated alone on the sofa. She sat down beside Maude and took her chilly hands between her palms. The woman had listened quietly to Luke's account of finding Cecil incarcerated by Collins. She had looked too shocked and despondent to speak a word on hearing that he had followed her simply to lay his hands on the painting she had in her possession. Fiona guessed that her mother harboured a grain of duty, if not affection, for the man she'd believed to be her husband.

'What should Mr Wolfson do with Ratcliff, Mama?' Fiona asked quietly enough for their conversation to be private. 'He will free him on your say so—'

'No!' Maude hissed in an undertone. 'I would not have some other poor wretch go through what I have had to endure at that man's hands. I have some concern for Cecil. I'm not sure why after the way he has treated me. But both men *must* be punished. It is the only civilised way.'

Fiona's fingers tightened on the thin digits in her clasp. 'You are right…and I'm proud of you for being so strong.' She gave her mother an encouraging smile.

'I'm so proud of you!' Maude croaked, raising her glistening eyes to her daughter's face. 'I cannot describe how sorry I am that any of this came about, my dear.'

'Hush…' Fiona rubbed vigorously at her mother's quivering fists, clasped together in her lap. 'All will get better now.'

'Are we still to go to London, Papa?' There was a great deal of persuasiveness in Joan's voice, indicating the answer she hoped to receive.

'I suppose so, my dear, if it is what you all want.' He glanced at Maude.

Maude turned her enquiring eyes on her daughter.

'Miss Chapman?' The duke turned to Fiona for her decision.

'Yes…let's carry on to town, if we may.' Fiona gave Luke the most fleeting of glances and thought she saw him respond with an almost imperceptible nod. From that she drew comfort that he wanted her to know that once his business in Devon was finished he would come after her.

Chapter Twenty

'Wake up, Fiona… Wake up!'

Fiona blinked her heavy eyes. Then, as the sound of a voice calling her name penetrated the fog in her mind, she pushed herself on to an elbow amidst plush coverings on her comfy feather bed. Her mother's wide-eyed visage wavered into view behind the burning candle the woman was holding aloft.

Fearing yet another disaster was about to be revealed, Fiona swung her legs over the edge of the bed, ready to get up.

'What has happened, Mama?' There was a tinge of weary resignation in Fiona's tone as she searched for her slippers in the wavering light brightened by a glow of logs smouldering in the grate.

'The duke has asked me to marry him.' Maude sank down on the edge of the mattress.

So vacant-eyed did her mother seem that Fiona sensibly removed the flame from her weak fingers lest she dropped it and set fire to the blankets. Having deposited the sconce on a side table, she sat beside her mother, studying her expression.

'Do you think he is a madman?' Maude slurred in a whisper.

Fiona blinked, moistening her dry lips. 'Perhaps you misheard him, Mama.' She was aware that her mother smelled of sherry.

'*Will you marry me, Madam*, were his exact words.' Maude livened herself up. 'He has taken quite a lot of port. Perhaps he is drunk, not mad.'

'And what response did you give?' Fiona breathed.

'Well, I said I would marry him, of course, before quickly retiring for the night. I thought it best to humour him in case he acted yet more bizarre.' Maude giggled. 'Me…a duchess…just think, Fiona—'

'You *would* marry him?' Fiona interrupted. 'But you don't love him and are barely acquainted…' She bit her lip, aware of being a hypocrite. She barely knew Luke Wolfson but she believed she loved him and wanted to be his wife.

'I didn't know that vile creature I walked down the aisle with a year ago; yet I thought I did.' Maude gave a fierce wag of the head. 'Love! Pah! I need no more of that. I loved your papa and now I know that was enough! At least the Duke of Thornley has his credentials all about him.' The grand furniture and velvet bed hangings in the chamber drew Maude's appreciative eyes. 'No person would dare gossip about you if you are the Duke of Thornley's ward.' Maude sighed. 'I doubt the fellow will recall it in the morning when he is nursing a sore head.' She stood up unsteadily and started to disrobe. 'That will be a shame, for he is a nice gentleman… He reminds me of your papa.' Maude unlocked her packing case and haphazardly pulled out some things in search of her nightgown.

'Had Joan retired for the night at that point?' Fiona found it hard to believe that His Grace would have proposed while his daughter was listening.

'She went up to bed just after you, so we were alone. There were no witnesses.' Maude sighed, pulling ineffectually at her gown in an attempt to get her arms out of the sleeves.

Fiona helped her mother with her buttons, then to don her nightgown. She watched the woman climb unsteadily into the other huge four-poster and draw up the covers to her chin. Although shocked by what she'd heard Fiona could find no questions to ask.

Her mother might fear His Grace was under the influence, but Fiona doubted the Duke of Thornley, drunk or not, would blurt out something so consequential without realising the enormity of what he'd done. The man had said he wished to make amends to them, but to offer her mother marriage? Fiona couldn't deny it was a solution that would rectify everything in one fell stroke. Her mother's shame and embarrassment over Cecil Ratcliff's bigamy would disintegrate and her own situation would be vastly improved. There would certainly be no need for the stepdaughter of a duke to become a gentleman's mistress...unless she really wanted to...

On hearing the first soft snore coming from her mother Fiona massaged her tired face with her fingers. She wished she, too, could climb back into bed and fall fast asleep, but she knew such comfort would be denied to her. She had slumbered for more than an hour already and now felt depressingly alert following her rude awakening.

They had arrived in Mayfair late that afternoon and

had been shown to a magnificent chamber on the first floor of the west wing of their host's mansion. Joan had wanted the guests to have maids, but Maude had politely refused. Fiona knew that her mother was concerned that the duke's servants would see the state of their oft-darned nightgowns and petticoats.

Earlier, on rising from the dinner table following a lengthy and delicious meal, Fiona and Joan had played a few hands of rummy while their parents continued depleting the decanters. Fiona had then retired for the night, wanting some private time to mull things over in her mind and think of Luke. Surprisingly, he'd barely entered her mind when she fell asleep shortly after her head snuggled into the downy pillows.

But she concentrated on Luke now while perching on the edge of the bed. She knew he would not yet have returned to London. They had all parted company at the Halfway House; the duke's party had set on the road towards London and Luke had set off in the opposite direction to relieve Drew Rockleigh of his duty guarding Ratcliff. The man she'd believed to be her stepfather would by now be in prison.

Fiona wondered if Becky Peake and Drew Rockleigh might also have arrived in town. But those two were swiftly pushed to the back of her mind. It was Luke who dominated her thoughts. Would he soon come to visit? If he did, and again propositioned her to be his mistress, what then?

With a sigh, Fiona sank down on to the bed and curled up, resting her cheek on her clasped hands. She had promised to go shopping with Joan tomorrow, and she was determined to enjoy the outing, so she must empty her mind again and fall asleep or she would make a very dreary companion.

'Are you getting up, Mama? Fiona pulled back the curtains, allowing sunlight to stream into the bedchamber.

Maude burrowed further into the covers, avoiding the golden beams. 'My head is aching,' she whimpered.

Fiona redrew the heavy curtains till just a chink of light remained. 'It is almost two o'clock. I am going out with Joan soon. Will you come?'

'I want to…but I cannot…' Maude mumbled. 'I shall not take another glass of sherry in my life, I swear.'

Fiona went to sit by her mother, shaking her shoulder to gain her attention. 'Do you recall what you told me last night?'

Maude peeped over the edge of the blankets. 'Yes, I do.' She struggled to a seated position. 'Was His Grace at breakfast earlier?'

'He was. He looked bright as a lark and as though he can hold his drink far better than you.'

Maude sank into the pillows. 'Well…I expect that he is a more regular tippler and I suppose a serious talk with him must be in the offing.'

'Indeed…' Fiona said on standing up. She knew it was best to leave her mother to ponder alone on something as personal as another marriage proposal. She didn't want to influence Maude on her future because she realised her time at home had come to an end. Her life had changed the moment she set off for Devon and would never be as it once had, whatever transpired between her and Luke. Fiona had tasted freedom and found it suited her despite the pitfalls that were the price to pay for independence.

'I know you very much like that fellow Wolfson and so I suppose the other news I told you came as a blow.'

Fiona turned back to frown at her mother. 'What news are you talking about, Mama?'

Maude again struggled up, looking concerned. 'I should not have said anything… I would not have, had I been thinking straight when I came up to bed.'

'I fear you were thinking straight, Mama, because you told me nothing about Mr Wolfson. You only repeated the duke's proposal.'

'Oh…' Maude bit her lip. 'I didn't tell you what His Grace overheard while at his club yesterday afternoon?'

Fiona shook her head and perched again on the edge of the mattress, feeling curious. The Duke of Thornley had taken himself off to St James's within an hour of the travelling coaches rolling to a stop in front of his magnificent Mayfair town house. Joan and a host of servants had been left to attend to his guests while he sought the company of his gentlemen friends. But His Grace had returned in good time, and good spirits, to dine with them all.

'You said it concerned Mr Wolfson,' Fiona prompted. Her mother's reticence in finishing what she'd started was making her uneasy. Had Maude been told something very detrimental to Luke's character?

'Are you in love with him?' Maude asked bluntly. On seeing her daughter's immediate blush she gave a sigh. 'I'm sorry, my love, but His Grace heard some gentlemen talking about Luke Wolfson's betrothal.'

'Betrothal?' Fiona breathed.

Maude nodded. 'It might just be baseless gossip, but I'd sooner you heard it from me, my dear, than from others.' Maude patted at Fiona's fingers, tilting her head to read her daughter's expression.

'Well…if it is true that he is taking a wife, I suppose it is his own affair,' Fiona said with a levity she was far from feeling. She stood up with a ready smile and bid her mother farewell, aware of Maude watching her quick retreat from the room.

A few minutes later Fiona was descending the stairs, with her temples thudding, lost in troubled thought. Luke had informed her that he had never asked anybody to marry him and she'd believed him speaking the truth. Since that conversation had taken place he had been in Devon. If he were to be married, he must have recently proposed to somebody in the West Country… so had Becky persuaded him to make an honest woman of her?

The pounding in Fiona's head increased. She also believed Luke had told the truth about finishing with Becky. But the scorned mistress might be back in town by now and playing games. Perhaps Becky had been starting rumours in the hope they might become true for her. Fiona sighed, pulling on her gloves, in readiness to depart for the shops. She would not cast Luke into the role of liar and cheat. She would put her trust in him and not torment herself with overheard gossip. Impatient as she was to know more about it she must wait till he came to see her then ask him calmly about the rumours.

Fiona spied Joan waiting by the great door and speeded up towards her. She had said nothing to the duke's daughter at breakfast about their parents' blossoming friendship. Fiona guessed that if His Grace had meant his proposal to be taken seriously he'd want a sober talk with his intended bride before he mentioned a word about it to his daughter.

A gentle nudge in the ribs from Joan made Fiona drop the mother-of-pearl buttons she was examining.

'Look! Mr Rockleigh is just over there and he has seen us. I'm sure his companion is the brunette he was with at the Halfway House. Now I've had a better look at her I can tell what sorts *he* consorts with!'

The rattling information certainly gained Fiona's attention. Startled, she followed the direction Joan was indicating with a pair of lively eyes.

'I believe you're right…it is Mr Wolfson's friend,' Fiona murmured with surprising calm considering that Becky Peake was glowering at her from beneath a feather-embellished bonnet.

'He's coming over!' Joan squeaked while apparently absorbed in selecting a reel of French lace.

Indeed, Drew Rockleigh was approaching them and Fiona's heart began hammering beneath her ribs. She took a calming breath and drew herself up in her shoes. Her immediate instinct had been to march over to Becky and demand to know if Luke had asked her to marry him. But she knew she must not. With perfect attention to etiquette Drew Rockleigh had abandoned his *demi-rep* companion to examine fripperies at the counter while he joined them.

'How nice to see you, Lady Joan,' Drew said suavely.

'Is it?' Joan returned tartly. 'I am surprised, sir, that you feel that way, all things considered.'

Drew gave a gruff chuckle and turned his attention to Fiona, growing serious. 'And you must be Miss Chapman. Luke has spoken about you. I'm pleased to be able to introduce myself to you at last.'

'I'm glad to meet you, too, sir.' Fiona returned a pleasant greeting although anxious to know *what* had been said about her. She didn't wait long to find out.

'Luke has often praised your courage,' Drew informed her. 'And from what he has told me, I must add my admiration to his. But enough has been said on the unfortunate matter and I'm sure you'd sooner leave it be.'

'And I, too, would sooner no more was said on *the unfortunate matter,*' Joan chipped in sourly, drawing another wry glance from Drew.

As Rockleigh turned his attention to Joan and they continued to have a prickly exchange Fiona felt her eyes drifting in Becky Peake's direction. The woman appeared to have been waiting to gain her attention. Fiona was beckoned, then, when she hesitated in obeying the audacious summons Becky again crooked her finger.

As though to reassure Fiona that their meeting would be discreet Becky screened herself behind rolls of fabrics standing on end. Women like Becky knew their station in life; a genteel female would be sullied by talking to a notorious courtesan.

The temptation to find out more about Luke's betrothal was irresistible; Fiona's womanly intuition was telling her that Becky wanted to speak to her about that very subject. Stepping away from her companions, still engaged in a bout of lively bickering, Fiona joined Luke's mistress in a colourful forest of silks and satins.

'You're Miss Chapman,' Becky stated bluntly.

'I am, and I believe you're Miss Peake,' Fiona returned, meeting the woman's challenge in similar vein.

'Luke has told you about me, then.' Becky sounded triumphant.

Fiona wasn't prepared to reveal anything about her private conversations with Luke, so merely replied coolly, 'Did you want to discuss something in particular?'

'Of course...' Becky smirked. 'And you know very well what it is, don't you? Now don't go all coy or pretend that it's a surprise to you that Luke and I are lovers.'

'I never act coy, nor do I employ pretence,' Fiona retorted clearly.

'I'm glad to hear it.' Becky felt grudging admiration for her rival's forthright manner. She might be genteel and past her prime, but it was plain Fiona Chapman was no shrinking violet. 'I shan't pretend, either, then,' Becky said. 'I know Luke wants a dalliance with you. But we've no need to be jealous of one another. You're not his first fancy and you won't be the last, but he always comes back to me.' Becky was a robust liar; most of what she'd said she knew to be false. Luke had made it clear their relationship was over. Then when she'd quizzed him over Miss Chapman, the strange look in his eyes had told her everything she needed to know but he wouldn't say. He was in love—not with the simpering miss who'd come to town to try and hook him for the second time, but with the quiet mouse he'd rescued from Jeremiah Collins. At close quarters Becky could grudgingly see that the refined lady who'd stolen Luke's heart had qualities a man might find attractive. Her eyes were a fascinating shade of hazel and her fawn hair was thick and glossy. She was not as buxom as Becky, but her figure was nicely curvaceous.

Becky might profess not to be jealous, but Fiona guessed the opposite were true. She wasn't going to get dragged into a catfight over Luke Wolfson in the middle of a drapery. She'd been wrong in thinking that Becky was about to crow about being Luke's future wife. And it would be the height of bad taste for her to bring up the subject of his rumoured betrothal, much as she craved finding out more about it.

'Don't sulk.' Becky gripped Fiona's arm, tugging her back as she would have moved away. 'Luke will give you a pension when he grows bored with you. He's very generous, if you please him.' Becky deliberately fingered the pretty gem pinned to her collar. 'You're not his usual type, but he'll take fair-haired women, for a change.' She twirled a long brunette ringlet about a finger. 'Even if he does wed Miss Ponting, he'll keep me close by.'

Becky smiled on seeing a flicker of raw emotion clouding Miss Chapman's cat-like eyes. 'Ah…he has not let on about her, has he? He chased after a debutante a few years ago.' Becky sighed theatrically. 'But back then, you see, he was a lowly lieutenant with nothing but his looks to recommend him.' Becky gained a mean comfort from the hurt intensifying in Fiona's eyes. 'The foolish chit took her mother's advice and rebuffed him. But now he is one of the most eligible bachelors around she is trailing after him like a puppy dog.'

An insolent look raked Fiona from head to toe. 'She is rather like you in a way—older now than she wants to be and hoping she'll not get left on the shelf.' Becky crossed her arms over her middle in a contented way.

'If you have nothing of importance to say, then please do not waste any more of my time.' Fiona managed to dismiss the woman's spite although she was feeling light-headed with tension and close to tears.

'His marriage does not bother you?'

'Not in the slightest,' Fiona returned with barely a betraying tremor in her voice.

'I think you *do* employ pretence...' Becky chortled. 'You're a poor liar, Miss Chapman. Quality such as you want husbands, not lovers. You thought he'd do the decent thing because of your connections.' Becky glanced past Fiona at the Duke of Thornley's daughter. 'Luke's still a bachelor because he favours keeping company with me rather than getting leg-shackled to any snooty madam.'

'And you're welcome to him,' Fiona uttered in a suffocated tone. With that parting shot, she slipped out from behind the rainbow screen of fabrics, passing Drew Rockleigh, with a strained smile, as he made his way to rejoin his companion.

Fiona's heart was beating a slow tattoo beneath her bodice as she pored over her hostile exchange with Becky. The woman had seen through her defensive pride to the core of her being. Of course she wanted to be married to the man she loved, but Becky's few coarsely spoken remarks had finally helped her bury her hopes and dreams beneath reality.

Luke *had* finished with his mistress and he *did* want her as Becky's replacement—Fiona trusted that to be true. Becky had lied on that score, but there was a ring of truth to the younger woman's talk of Luke's past. Some years ago he'd chased after a debutante and been turned down. Since then his prospects had improved and the lady who'd spurned him was in town to let him know she'd changed her mind. Now Fiona knew exactly what the Duke of Thornley had overheard and recounted to her mother when they were both tipsy.

Fiona had wondered whether she'd cope with being Luke's mistress, shut away in a corner of his life when he married and raised a family. She'd wondered if she might endure that twilight existence that would grow darker as they aged until his time and affection for her finally extinguished. A brusque exchange with a woman who knew Luke better than she did had lifted the blinkers from her eyes. It would be intolerable and she ridiculed herself for having thought she might equal Becky's role and attitude where Luke Wolfson was concerned. Over the past frantic weeks many people had praised her courage. But once intimately bound to him, would she ever be brave enough to quietly withdraw from his life when he wanted her to rather than have him despise her?

Fiona focused on Joan, noticing the young woman was waiting impatiently for her.

'What did *she* want?' Joan nodded at the door through which Becky Peake and Drew Rockleigh had departed. 'I saw you having a quiet word with her. I won't tell, I promise.'

'It was nothing important,' Fiona answered, bringing her quavering tone under control with a cough. 'Did you win?' She swiftly changed the subject to avoid any further mention of Becky.

'Win?'

'You sounded as though you were sparring with Mr Rockleigh.'

'Oh, that… I always win. I imagine he lets me,' Joan

admitted ruefully. She looked thoughtfully at Fiona. 'Were you sparring with *her* a moment ago?'

Fiona's answer was a neutral smile. 'I was on the point of buying some nice buttons a moment ago.' She opened her reticule to find some coins. 'My blue pelisse could do with brightening up.'

'As you won't admit to fighting over Mr Wolfson I imagine you lost the battle—'

'I did not!' Fiona blurted before realising she'd been tricked into saying too much.

With an arch look Joan led the way back to the button display.

Chapter Twenty-One

Two more days had passed before the moment arrived that Fiona was both longing for and dreading. As she placed down her novel on the dressing table and peered wide-eyed at her reflection in the mirror, she again pondered on what might have delayed him.

Over the past long days and nights she had tormented herself with the idea that he had by now proposed to Miss Ponting. Becky's boast that Luke would sooner keep his freedom and her company than get leg-shackled seemed less likely the more Fiona had thought about it. Besides, her mother had now confirmed what Becky had told her about Luke's connection to the Pontings. He *had* courted Harriet a few years ago and been rebuffed.

The duke had taken Maude to the theatre one evening and the Pontings had been there, too, her mother had reported. High-instep people, Maude had described them, although nowhere close to being in His Grace's league, the woman had added with a smirk. The daughter was rather an obvious beauty, she had carried on with a sniff, being too blonde and too pale of complexion. Maude's attempt to encourage Fiona had had the reverse effect, especially when she'd let slip that gossip was now rife about Luke Wolfson renewing his pursuit of Harriet.

Fiona knew she should not feel so hurt or surprised by the news. A well-bred, eligible bachelor would naturally want to pass his name and wealth on to future generations of Wolfsons. In the past he'd seemed quite bitter when mentioning family life, but surely if he intended to quit working as a mercenary, a wife and children would figure in his plans…

As Miss Chapman was still seated and appeared to be entranced by her own reflection, the maid added, 'Mr Wolfson is waiting for you in the morning room. Shall I arrange for tea?'

'Umm…no… I believe his visit will be brief. Is my mother back?' Fiona asked normally despite blood streaking so rapidly through her veins that she felt faint. Slowly she gained her feet, gripping the edge of the mahogany table and swaying into it for support until her knuckles turned white.

'Not to my knowledge, Miss Chapman.'

Fiona was glad that Maude and the duke were still out on a shopping excursion. She knew that Joan was with her friends, visiting an exhibition of Greek artefacts at a museum. In fact, Luke's timing for a very private conversation between them could not have been better. Perhaps his mercenary's propensity for meticulous preparation had made him plan it that way. But she was glad that there would be no witnesses and that she might have an hour or so in which to recover from this final parting.

* * *

When Fiona entered the morning room Luke stayed quite still for a moment, simply regarding her with hungry dark eyes. Then he relinquished his lounging position by the mantelpiece and strode to meet her, immediately taking her cool hands in his warm grip.

'I've missed you,' he said huskily, his fingers tightening on hers.

'I've missed you, too,' Fiona replied, believing him sincere. He seemed about to embrace her and, much as she yearned to have him do so, she slowly withdrew her hands and put distance between them. He looked wonderfully distinguished and handsome, as usual, but she knew the closer they were, the more he touched her, the harder it would be for her to say what she must. Several times she'd rehearsed this little farewell speech and her good wishes for his future, yet phrases slipped away to hide in the corners of her mind.

'What's the matter?' Luke asked bluntly, moving to a position where he could read her expression. 'Are you cross that I've not turned up sooner?' He gave her a boyish smile. 'I've a good excuse for the delay.'

'I'm sure you have…' Fiona wouldn't let rancour into her voice. He owed her nothing, not even an explanation for his tardiness. They both knew that his business was his own. The only offer he'd made was to care for her as his mistress.

'Are you interested in hearing where I've been?' Luke asked, plunging his hands into his pockets.

'I have some news for you, actually,' Fiona blurted, achieving a level, conversational tone. She could tell he was alert to her reserve despite her best efforts to conceal it. In turn, he'd become guarded. 'It is a rather exciting and very unexpected turn of events.' Fiona injected some lightness into her voice.

Luke raised his thick eyebrows in polite enquiry, but Fiona sensed that he was brooding on the reason for the change in her. He had, unseen by family and friends, snatched a farewell kiss from her in a fleeting private moment before she'd boarded the coach at the Halfway House. Then he had mounted Star and, from a vantage point on the brow of a hill, had watched the cavalcade of Thornley vehicles till it disappeared from view. The blossoming intimacy and affection between them Fiona had hugged to herself like a warm shawl as the conveyance dipped and swayed over ruts on the final leg of the journey to town. But that serenity was gone now, crushed by reality. If she succumbed to the longing to be with him at any cost, she risked an intolerable future veering between joy and despair.

'My mother has received a marriage proposal from the Duke of Thornley. She has accepted. The betrothal is not yet common knowledge so you are one of the first to be told. His Grace is to put an announcement in *The Times* at the end of the week.'

'That is a surprise.' Luke's response held mild interest.

Fiona was somewhat taken aback by his attitude. She knew him for a cool, undemonstrative man, nevertheless she'd expected more of a reaction than that. 'So…it will affect me,' she added briskly.

'In what way?' Luke asked, strolling to again prop a hand against the mantelshelf.

'In…in the matter of…our attachment,' Fiona stammered out, cringing inwardly at her jumbled explanation. She so wanted to match his composure. She elevated her chin, squarely met his attentive eyes. 'You asked me to be your mistress on two occasions. I expect you have taken from my…affectionate responses…that I have tacitly agreed to your proposition and my words to the contrary were sham modesty.' She plunged on quickly, as warmth fizzled in her cheeks. 'I admit I was tempted to accept when everything in my life seemed turbulent, but now my circumstances have changed.'

'And have your feelings for me changed?' Luke's tone was flinty. 'Or are you simply trying to tell me that the stepdaughter of a duke deserves better than a retired army major?'

'I am trying to tell you that being shunned by my family, and in time by you, sir, is what I find unacceptable,' Fiona flared at him. Every good intention to remain logical and unruffled fled from her mind to be replaced by indignation.

'You are able to easily turn your emotions on and off, are you?' he asked quietly.

'No…I am not!' Fiona enunciated. 'Brave you might think me, but I am human and have weaknesses. I cannot bear the hurt awaiting me if I turn my back on every code I've known. If I go with you I risk heartbreak and ostracism.' Her tawny eyes raked his impassive features. 'Do not cast *me* in the role of mercenary,' she added in a suffocated whisper. 'Or imply that I have misled you. That would be too rich, coming from you.'

Luke glanced at his dark hand stark against the pale marble supporting it. 'What has Becky Peake told you?' His tone was pitilessly demanding.

Fiona's lips parted in surprise, then were pressed together in a mutinous line. Of course, he might have visited Becky and his friend Drew before coming to see her. Becky had been shamefully spiteful to her in the drapery so Fiona imagined that, of the two, Rockleigh might have mentioned witnessing the clandestine conversation between the two women.

'What did the infernal woman say?'

Luke strode towards her so fast that Fiona skittered backwards. Again he stopped himself touching her although she saw that he wanted to. His outstretched fingers were jerked back and rammed into his pockets.

'I've had a report of your meeting from Drew so you might as well tell me.'

'It matters little what we spoke about as I'd already heard the news she wanted to flaunt in my face. My mother told me about some gossip that is flying around town about your betrothal. Becky Peake merely confirmed she'd heard it, too, although apparently it doesn't bother her one bit as she is confident of remaining your mistress when you take a wife.'

But for a muscle tightening close to his mouth Luke would have appeared unmoved by what he'd heard. 'I told you I had finished with Becky. Do you think me a liar?'

'No…' Fiona admitted faintly. 'I think you were telling the truth and poor Becky isn't happy about being put off.'

Luke barked a laugh. '*Poor Becky* is already ensconced in an apartment owned by a young viscount. So her talk of undying devotion to me is far-fetched.'

Fiona blushed. 'I see… I'm sorry,' she said automatically.

'There's no need to be. I'm happy she is settled so quickly. I believe Drew made the introduction—the viscount is a friend of his.'

'Would that I had some of her spirit,' Fiona muttered ironically.

'Explain that…'

She averted her face, but gave him his answer. 'Becky saw a future with you as nothing to be afraid of, no matter what you chose to do, or who else you chose to spend it with.'

'I imagine you are again hinting at me having once courted Miss Ponting. I recall telling you that I had never proposed. Do you think I have lied about that?'

Fiona bit her lip, unable to remember Becky's exact phrasing about Luke's pursuit of a debutante. 'Whether you fell to bended knee or not is unimportant—you wanted Harriet Ponting as your wife!' she argued with renewed vigour. 'Had she been receptive to your suit you would now be her husband.'

'But she wasn't and I'm not,' Luke pointed out mildly. 'There is nothing for you to take exception to…not even the fact that I briefly paid attention to a woman in my youth.'

'*Your youth?*' Fiona echoed sharply. 'You are now thirty and chased after Miss Ponting not that long ago. I hardly think you were a green boy at the time.'

'Very recently you accused me of being woefully immature… How much worse do you think I was when aged twenty-five?' he asked with mordant self-mockery.

The moral high ground seemed to be slipping away beneath her and Fiona keenly felt her lack of sophistication. 'You think it all amusing, don't you?' she stormed, a teary sheen burnishing the gold in her eyes. 'Well, I do not.' She marched away from him, then swung about, quivering fingers clasped in front of her. 'You're right—you are still woefully immature. I am not a toy to be trifled with. I am a human being and deserve some consideration and respect. You might pick your mistresses on a whim and perhaps you also chose Miss Ponting with the same lack of care.' Fiona edged up her chin, despite feeling utterly forlorn. 'Thankfully her parents were vigilant on her behalf and I can look after myself. I will never accept such cavalier treatment from you or any other man.'

'So…of what are you accusing me, Fiona?' Luke asked. 'You seem to think me fickle, incapable of true feelings…yet at the same time the idea of a serious past attachment to Harriet Ponting upsets you. Which is it you want me to be? A rogue or a gallant?'

I want you to be only mine… Fiona bit her lower lip to prevent the plea exploding from her. She gasped in a calming breath. 'I did not know that you might soon be wed.' While gazing soulfully into his earthy brown eyes she blurted, 'Did Miss Ponting break your heart when she rejected you? I have sensed on occasions that you feel hurt…bitter even…about something in your past.'

In exasperation Luke turned his face up to the ceiling with a gesture of disbelief.

'I'm sorry if you think it's an impertinence to ask… but can you not see that it makes a difference? You should have told me if you are still brooding on another woman.'

'I'm not bitter or brooding because of another woman…not in the way you mean, in any case,' Luke said quietly, dark fingers pinching the bridge of his nose as though to ease his strain.

'In what way then are you feeling bitter?' Fiona persisted. For a moment she thought he would either ignore her question or take himself off. But again he raised his eyes, this time to moderate his expression rather than his temper. Suddenly he seemed steelier, master of his emotions.

'You asked me once why I worked as a mercenary when I'd no need of the money.' He glanced at her. 'The truth is I did need the money from those endeavours… not to pay bills but for my own self-respect.' He paced to and fro as though undecided whether to say more. 'My grandfather bequeathed to me everything he owned and it was a considerable amount of cash and property. I was nine years old when he disinherited his son in favour of his grandchild. When I was twenty-seven I took what should have been my father's birth-right. By then it no longer mattered that my father had hated me from the moment I'd usurped him. All the family I'd known were dead…my benefactor the last to go.'

Fiona became very still, shocked at what she'd heard. She was tempted to move to comfort him. But she feared if she did he'd bottle up the rest and she wished to ease the burden of his unhappy memories.

'My father and grandfather had fallen out over a joint business venture that failed—cargo from the In-dies that was lost in a storm. My father never recov-ered financially, but my grandfather made back his money and more besides. The rift between the men never healed and worsened when I was dragged into their fight.' He studied the floor this time, stubbing the toe of a boot against the oak boards. 'My mother blamed me and also my father and his kin for destroying our happy family and her comforts. She separated from my father although a divorce was out of the question. She took me to live in the Berkshire countryside with an elderly aunt of hers while my father stayed in the city.' He paused. 'I attended Harrow school, but was never invited to my father's home. By the time I went up to Oxford he had been dead two years. He'd drunk himself close to death many times, but he couldn't recover from tumbling down the stairs in a bawdy house.' Luke gave a sour, reflective laugh. 'I spent most school holidays with Drew and his family in Kent. The Rockleighs are fine people.'

Fiona could not bear listening to the strengthening huskiness in his voice. She rushed to him, tentatively touched his arm, her heart squeezing when she felt the tension in him.

'You feel guilty, but you should not,' she whispered. 'It is not your fault that your elders…people who should have cared for your well-being…made you a pawn in a spiteful game. You were just a boy.'

'I know…' Luke nodded. 'But still I do, even after all this time. Had my grandfather gone first I would have gladly given everything to them the moment the bequest was executed.' Luke curled his fingers over the small white digits soothing him. 'My father expired over a decade ago and my mother followed him to the grave a few years later. She'd requested to be buried in the Wolfson plot, by my father's side. My grandfather was eighty years old and still holding grudges. But I fought him and eventually he relented and allowed his daughter-in-law to be laid to rest on his land.' He paused. 'My mother always wished to stay with her husband, but she did her duty and removed me from living beneath his roof and his wrath. But she never let me forget she'd suffered for it.'

'Oh, I'm so sorry…' Fiona hung her head, feeling ashamed. 'I shouldn't have pressed you to say anything about it. I know you have aired some very private thoughts. I swear I'll never betray your trust.'

Luke turned to fully face her, gazing down at her with immense gravity. 'My inheritance was a curse, not a boon, and that's why I wished to carry on earning my living. If I brood on anything in my past it's that, not a failed love affair. When a moody young man I vowed I'd give away the lot the day the will was read. My mother despaired on hearing that plan. In her eyes such an action was a greater insult than that perpetrated by her father-in-law.' He frowned. 'If she'd outlived the old boy I would have given her whatever she desired.'

'I do understand why you would want to do that.' Fiona's voice trembled with sincerity. 'But…I'm glad you didn't have a chance to test the scope of your generosity, or her avarice.' She sighed. 'Money and corruption are often bedfellows. And if it helps you at all…what you have told me has made me reconsider my own situation.' Quickly she explained, 'Ratcliff let slip that he knew about my small bequest. Perhaps he wormed his way into our lives to lay hands to it.' In her sweet attempt to boost Luke's mood Fiona enthused, 'In any case, I no longer care about Ratcliff. We…my mama and I…have you to thank for our salvation where he is concerned. The Duke of Thornley and Joan also owe you a debt of gratitude for apprehending vile Jeremiah Collins.' She smiled shyly into his velvet-brown eyes. 'So, you see, being in possession of your hateful inheritance has done good, in its way. Without his grandfather's wealth spurring him to soldier on, Major Luke Wolfson might have retired to the life of a town fop.'

'*Town fop*…is that how you see me?' But he chuckled gruffly, hugging her to him. 'I think you, Miss Chapman, are all I need to stay hale and hearty and happy.'

Fiona's smile faded. Now he seemed to have returned to his normal self, anxieties were again pricking at her mind. She felt more closely bound to Luke following their intimate talk. But she was still haunted by uncertainty over his feelings for Miss Ponting. Carefully she withdrew from his possessive embrace and gazed up into his preying eyes.

'I'm sorry to ask, but I must know—are you still in love… Is Miss Ponting right to hope…to expect…?'

The unfinished question throbbed between them, timed in seconds by the pendulum of the large wall clock.

'I know I should have told you I'd fallen in love,' Luke eventually said very softly.

'Will you marry her?' Fiona's voice was a hoarse whisper,

'If she'll have me…' Luke's smile was barely there. 'First I have to impress on her my sincere apologies if she believes I have ever treated her with a lack of consideration or respect. Of all the people I have ever known she is the most deserving of such homage.' He paused for a moment following that vehement declaration. 'I must also convince her of my intention to improve my behaviour. And I will change, for her…just for her…because no other woman will do…so if she turns me down…'

Luke left the rest unsaid. He approached Fiona and stood very close. Very slowly he smoothed the satiny line of her jaw with gentle knuckles before tilting up her chin so she couldn't avoid his eyes. 'Please look at me, Fiona,' he begged.

After a fractional hesitation Fiona raised her lashes, her heart wedged dizzyingly in her throat. She yearned to hear him say that he loved her, but he simply rewarded her shy smile with another tender caress.

'I love you, Fiona… Oh, I want you, too… You're a fire in my blood and have been since the first night that I met you. Even drenched through you looked ravishing to me. I recall almost telling you so at the time and earning your mistrust because of it.'

Fiona remembered very well the incident on that first night they'd met. He'd given her his coat to wear and she'd felt spellbound while they'd talked by the firelight.

He skimmed his lips over a satiny crown of fawn hair. 'I've tried to fool myself that seducing you will suffice and ease my desire to be with you. But it won't do. I want to be by your side in and out of bed. Most of all I want to protect you and our children from every disappointment and harm. I know I can't do that, however hard I try.' He tilted up her chin with five curled fingers. 'There'll be times when bad luck and worries will afflict us as a family…but we'll fight it all together…if you'll be very kind and have me as your husband.'

As the little muffled sob of joy broke in her throat he enfolded her to his chest, rocking her within his embrace.

'I can't lie and say my intentions towards you were

honourable from the start. After such a short acquaintance you can't blame me for thinking that the need for you was simply a base one.' His tone was growing increasingly wolfish, but he slid a reverential kiss on her brow. 'I soon realised that what I felt for you ran far...far deeper than lust.' He chuckled on seeing the blush spreading on her cheeks, then took her mouth in a profoundly drugging kiss.

Just a touch of his tongue teasing her lips made Fiona melt into him. She opened up immediately to the skilful caress, her hands climbing his muscled chest to rest on his shoulders before her slender fingers linked behind his head, urging him closer.

He loved her...wanted to be her husband... The wonderful words circled soft as butterfly wings in her consciousness. And her own declaration was filling her mind ready to burst forth. But she couldn't relinquish the exquisite sensation of their fused mouths to utter anything at all. His hands were undoing buttons on her bodice, then unlacing her chemise. Fiona shivered in glorious anticipation as finally...finally warm firm fingers slid, then moulded over her silky, sensitive skin. Arching her back, she gave herself up to the stroking hands drawing her closer to a blissful frenzy.

Luke growled deep in his throat, lifting her and settling her calves about his hips before striding to the sofa. He went down with her, his mouth pressing hot and hard against her lips, the delicate dips at her collarbone, before moving lower to tantalise thrusting rose-tipped breasts peeking at him from between the loose edges of her gown.

Fiona cried out in delight as he suckled the sensitive little nubs, drawing first one then the other into his mouth to be tasted and tantalised with tongue and teeth.

'I love you, Luke,' Fiona gasped, bucking and writhing beneath his erotic fondling.

'I should ask you properly to be my wife.' Luke cupped her enraptured face between his palms. 'You deserve better than this,' he groaned. 'Yet if you don't quit wriggling, sweetheart, I might not be able to stop.'

'No...don't stop...' Fiona burst out, drawing a rough laugh from him as she tugged his face again down to hers.

Gently he kissed her. 'You are a very wanton young lady...much to my surprise and delight,' he murmured. In a swift abrupt movement he sat Fiona up, tugging together her clothes. Then he gazed into her smoky amber eyes just visible beneath a dusky fringe of bashfully lowered lashes.

'Let me put your mind at ease over that youthful courtship.' Luke brushed a thumb over Fiona's lips, pulsing from his passionate assault. 'I did kiss Harriet Ponting a couple of times during our courtship. When her father told me not to call on her again my pride was badly dented, but I wasn't heartbroken. Two years later I inherited my grandfather's wealth and the Pontings made it clear they'd welcome my visits.' He paused. 'I felt no inclination to get to know Harriet again. In fact, when our paths have crossed I've simply been polite to the family.' He frowned as though aware he seemed callous. 'I realise now it was infatuation...not love. I had decided to get married before my grandfather died and my army pay was all I had to offer. I wanted a wife to accept me for who I was rather than for what another man's money made me.'

Fiona leaned forward and pressed her soft lips to his cheek. 'You have my love and my respect and if you wish to give away your inheritance, I will not object.'

'I know, Fiona…and that's why I'm determined to keep it so that every luxury and comfort will be yours.' He sank from the sofa to humbly plant a knee on the floor, taking both her hands in his. 'Will you marry me, Miss Chapman? I swear I'll improve and be worthy of you and our children.'

'I wouldn't have you change a single thing, sir, for I very much like you the way you are.' Fiona shaved his jaw with her palms, savouring the abrasion against her stroking fingers. 'I would still adore and want you even if you carry on with your dangerous missions.'

'Would you indeed?' Luke gently teased.

'Well…as long as you were at home with me for a good deal of the time,' Fiona amended stoutly.

'Or perhaps you could be my accomplice and join me on my travels. We make a good team, you and I,' Luke said. 'We could set up in business ridding the country of outlaws…'

'Now you're mocking me…'

'No… I'm not… I'm trying to tell you…in my woefully immature way…that I've no further need of such thrills. Those ghosts that refused to let me enjoy my inheritance have gone now.' Luke rose to sit beside her, drawing her back against the sofa with an arm about her waist. 'You, Miss Chapman, have brought about a rather wondrous change in me. For many years I've craved finding that contentment I knew as a youngster, before my grandfather blighted my life with his riches.' The crooked smile he gave her was appealingly bashful. 'I suppose what I'm trying to say is that you have soothed my troubled soul…and helped me find peace…and I can't do without you.'

'I'm so glad about that,' Fiona whispered, nuzzling his cheek.

'As a lad I loved the fields and open spaces about my grandfather's estate in Essex, even during a cruel winter. I'd like to settle down in the country and raise our family. But if you prefer a lively social life we can live at our Eaton Square town house during the Season. Wherever we are…London or Essex…I'll be happy so long as you're with me.'

'I feel the same way about you.' Fiona laid her head against his muscled shoulder, feeling quite serene. 'And I think I might like country living. I'd barely set foot in rural parts before seeking employment in Devon. Yet as soon as I returned to London I knew I missed that vivid scenery. In town all seems grey by comparison.' Fiona gazed up into Luke's face, harking back to the first time their eyes had merged through the dusk. His complexion had been glistening with rain, his snowy linen shirt a stark contrast against his bronzed skin and she'd thought him as dangerous and foreign as the alien landscape. 'I thought we were very different people. Yet it seems we are quite alike.' After a harmonious silence she tilted up her face to his. 'Is there no villainy in Essex to occupy you while I fill a nursery with our sons and daughters?' Just an hour ago Fiona would have been astonished, and not a little embarrassed, at the thought of talking so openly about having babies. But it seemed the most natural thing in the world to chat with Luke about bearing his children.

'Surely it's a bit early to talk about that, when you've

not yet accepted my marriage proposal, Miss Chapman,' Luke reminded her, not wholly in jest.

'Oh, of course I'll marry you,' Fiona answered on a yearning sigh. 'I would marry you tomorrow, Luke Wolfson, if I could.'

'Tomorrow?' Luke asked, an amused glitter in his eyes.

Fiona nodded vigorously. 'Today…' Her tone held utter conviction. 'I would marry you this minute, Luke.'

'Good… Do you want to know why it's taken me a while to join you in town?'

'Was it to do with my stepfather?' Fiona asked doubtfully.

'No… Ratcliff was quickly taken into custody in Devon. He will be dealt with in due course.' Luke drew a jewellery box from his inside pocket. 'I went shopping to get you this.' He turned the casket, lifting the lid to display a domed emerald encircled by glittering diamonds. 'I have lots of inherited gemstones, but I wanted you to have something of your own that was free of the taint of the Wolfson family's sadness.'

'Oh, Luke…it's beautiful…' Fiona cried, touching a single digit to the rich green stone.

Easing the ring from its velvet nest, he slid it on to her betrothal finger.

'I would have become your mistress knowing you loved me, you know.' Fiona moved her fingers allowing the light to spark on the gems.

'But you might have left me at some time,' Luke replied wryly. 'I couldn't risk that.' He drew her into his embrace. 'I wanted to tell you sooner that I loved you. I almost did on occasions. But there never seemed to be a right time. The smugglers…Becky…your mother and stepfather…they all got in the way.' His mouth covered hers in a kiss of wooing sweetness that nevertheless was powerful enough to leave her lolling against the velvet cushions, craving more.

A sudden crash of a doorway and voices outside made Fiona grip tight to Luke's shoulders and stifle a giggle. 'Mama is back with the duke.'

'I can't wait long for us to be man and wife.' Luke stroked her cheek. 'I expect your mother and stepfather will have a glittering affair despite both having been widowed.'

'Mama does class it as her second marriage. She says what occurred with Ratcliff was a pantomime. They do talk about having a large party, too.' Fiona's eyes darted to the door as though she expected the newly betrothed couple might burst in on them at any moment. She struggled up to a decorous sitting position beside Luke.

'Do you want such a celebration for yourself?' Luke asked, his sultry gaze roving her beautifully flushed face.

'No…not at all.' Fiona twisted the weighty stone on her finger, polishing it with a thumb. 'I've never been one for lavish entertainment.' She gave him a twinkling smile. 'I might make a disappointing hostess, you know.'

'Nothing about you disappoints me…' Luke paused. 'And I'm hoping you won't disappoint me now and look shocked when I ask if you will…'

'Whatever it is, I will…' Fiona suggestively coiled her arms about his neck, resting her head on his shoulder. 'I trust you, you see, Luke, and love you so very much.'

Luke rewarded her devotion with a sweetly seductive kiss. 'When I went shopping for your betrothal and wedding rings I stopped off to get a special licence,' He breathed against her bruised lips. 'I want you as my wife before the sun sets on today.'

Fiona held his face back from hers, searching his eyes for humour. But there was none, other than that wry self-mockery that seemed to be his constant companion.

'Are you brave enough to risk coming with me and throwing in your luck with mine? Shall we share one last adventure before we settle down to sensible domesticity and a barrage of questions in the morning?'

Fiona nodded, eyes brimming with joy and excitement. 'Of course, but I insist on having some terms, sir.'

'Name them,' Luke said gruffly.

'I must leave my mama a note or she will fret dreadfully.'

'Agreed.'

'And…' Fiona hesitated, afraid that he might think her next request unattractively outlandish and very forward.

'Tell me…for I've a mind to carry you off and have my wicked way with you without delay,' Luke groaned.

'I should like to spend our wedding night in the open beneath the stars, with a fire to warm us and the scent of roasting game in the air,' Fiona breathed, her eyes vivid with excitement. Familiar, delightful sensations were tormenting the depths of her abdomen, and her breasts tingled and grew weighty as erotic thoughts flooded her mind.

Luke dropped his head to hers and just touched together their smiling lips. 'We certainly are made for one another, Fiona… That memory haunts my mind, too. I feared it might remain an unfulfilled fantasy to make love to you on the ground beneath the stars.' His tongue tip circled her lips, plunging to taste hers. 'Are you sure you wouldn't rather a feather mattress and silk sheets for your first time?'

Fiona blushed, nipped a corner of her lower lip with small pearly teeth in an unconsciously alluring way that drove Luke wild with desire.

'An earthy bed it is, then,' he growled, thrusting ten fingers into her dishevelled locks and tilting her face to his so he might feast again on her lips.

'I hope the night is mild.' Fiona's murmured comment was gruff with laughter.

Luke's kiss deepened, shooting spears of heat through her.

'I won't let you get cold, sweetheart. You'll be burning till dawn, I promise…'

* * * * *

THE RAKE'S RUINED
LADY

Chapter One

'Of course I do not understand!' Beatrice Dewey's blue gaze was fixed on her fiancé's face in shocked disbelief. 'How is any woman supposed to comprehend that the man she believes will shortly be *her* husband must marry another?' She pressed pale, quivering fingers to her brow. 'Repeat to me your news, please, and furthermore tell me why I should accept it.'

Colin Burnett's deep sigh displayed his regret. He stretched a hand towards Beatrice but she evaded his comfort in a swish of pastel muslin.

'Tell me, Colin! An explanation—a dozen explanations if I wish to have them—is the least you owe me.' Beatrice turned back to him, eyes sparking icy fire.

Ten minutes ago Mrs Francis, the Deweys' housekeeper, had interrupted Beatrice's letter-writing to announce that Dr Burnett had called on her. Beatrice had joined her fiancé in the front sitting room with a sunny smile, proving her gladness at this unexpected visit. Her happiness had started to wither before he'd uttered a single word: she'd read from Colin's demeanour that something was dreadfully wrong.

Not for a moment had she believed him jesting when he had quietly informed her that their wedding must be called off. Colin was not one for levity; neither was he a man who liked a drama. Beatrice could tell this predicament was causing him equal embarrassment and sorrow, but was conscious that he seemed nowhere near as wounded as was she at the idea of them parting.

'You know if there were any other way around this I would take it. I want you as my wife, Beatrice. I love you—'

'I don't see how you can love me…not really,' Beatrice interrupted harshly, 'if you are prepared to jilt me because you'd sooner have money.'

'It is not just about the money, my dear.' Colin sounded pained, and a trifle exasperated by her accusation. 'My family's reputation and estates are founded on the baronetcy. The Burnetts were granted the title as long ago as the Norman Conquest and it has passed through our male line ever since.' He cast his eyes heavenwards, seeking inspiration. 'If I reject the title and estates everything will be returned to the crown. How am I to explain that to my relations?'

Beatrice gave an impatient shrug. Her fiancé's logical reference to history and his kin, when her heart was breaking, was simply increasing her indignation.

'My uncle was not an easy man to fathom,' Colin continued doggedly, thrusting his fingers through a shock of auburn hair. 'He was known as an eccentric, but had I for one moment realised what madness he planned I would have privately set lawyers the task of finding a loophole to wriggle out of his stipulations. As it is, I must bow to his whim or lose everything.'

'So instead of forfeiting your birthright and choosing to remain much as you are: a country doctor of modest means—which is the person I fell in love with—you would dance to a dead man's tune to have his fortune and his title?'

Now her shock was receding anger was bringing Beatrice close to tears. She wouldn't beg the man with whom she'd planned to spend her life to honour his proposal, neither would she attempt to shame him into doing so. If he went ahead and married his cousin Stella instead of her then Beatrice knew she would have learned something vitally important and deeply upsetting about Colin's character. And also about her own: she had previously believed she'd become a reasonable judge of people.

'If you have chosen to comply with the terms of your uncle's will, then there is nothing more to be said,' Beatrice whispered. 'All I would ask before you leave is that you find the courtesy to explain to my father why he has wasted his money on my wedding day.' Hot brine squeezed between her lashes and she averted her face.

'I will of course make any financial reparation necessary,' Colin vowed stiltedly.

As he took her elbow to turn her towards him Beatrice flinched from his touch as though scalded. 'I think you should go now, sir.'

'Please don't hate me, Beatrice…I couldn't stand it…'

'I have a lot more to stand than you, I think.' Beatrice gazed stormily into eyes that were pleading for compassion. 'Please do not beg me for anything. Especially that I should not hate you for squandering three years of my life and destroying my future happiness.' She distanced herself from him, an odd lethargy enveloping her. 'In truth I do not hate you, Colin…I am coming to realise that I pity you for allowing a person you barely knew to dupe you and dictate to you.' She smiled sourly. 'I've let you kiss and caress me, yet despite our intimacy I never really knew you. I'd not imagined you capable of acting in such a callous and selfish way.'

Beatrice noticed the faint colour rising in his cheeks at her wounding criticism.

'It is because I refuse to act selfishly that I must give you up.' Colin cleared his throat. 'I have a family duty to uphold…'

'What about your duty to me?' Beatrice cried. But she knew it was too late. If he were to change his mind and refuse his birthright to marry her instead things would never be right between them. She could never recapture the person she'd been just twenty minutes ago, when excitedly smoothing her hair and gown before speeding down the stairs to joyfully welcome her fiancé and ask him to stay to dine with them.

He too would be different: outwardly Colin might claim to have forgiven her for making him forfeit his inheritance. Inwardly his bitter disappointment might fester and grow until it destroyed the love he professed to still have for her.

'I made a mistake in giving you my heart, but in time

I will appreciate you handing it back to me. The pain will pass now I have come to understand your character better.' Beatrice paused, a part of her relishing the hurt she had brought to his eyes with that brutal comment. But she was not by nature spiteful and the feeling soon faded. 'My father is in his study. Please call on him before leaving and do the honourable thing. He is not a wealthy man, as you know, and has scrimped to buy my trousseau.'

'My uncle was fifty-five and if he knew he was not long for this world he kept it to himself. Had he been old and infirm I would have had more cause to check on the terms of my inheritance.' Colin strode to block Beatrice's path as she made to exit the room.

'I've had explanations enough,' Beatrice rebuffed coolly. 'There is no need for you to tarry longer. I hope you find your new wealth and status make up for what you and I have lost.' She withdrew a small garnet ring from her finger and held it out. 'Yours, I believe. Now, please let me pass.'

Colin's lips tightened at Beatrice's frosty tone but he took the gem and pocketed it, standing aside. 'I've suffered too…I'll never forget you…'

Beatrice heard his plaintive farewell as she closed the parlour door. With her eyes filled with burning water she approached the stairs. She would wait in her bedchamber till Colin left, then go and see her father.

Beatrice knew her papa would need comforting over this calamity as much as she did. Walter Dewey had liked Dr Burnett as his physician and as his future son-in-law. Colin had promised financial reparation and she hoped her father would not be too proud or too angry to accept the cash.

Her sister, Elise, would be shocked to discover she was not shortly to be a matron of honour. Elise lived in Mayfair and had done her best to persuade her kin to join her as permanent house guests following her marriage to Viscount Blackthorne. Alex had a fabulous mansion on Upper Brook Street. But Walter Dewey had insisted a quiet pastoral life suited him. Beatrice had also been happy to remain in bucolic bliss in Hertfordshire as her physician fiancé was living and working in the vicinity of St Albans.

Now Beatrice wondered if Colin had always wished to improve his prospects from that of country doctor, and if so whether he might immediately move to town with his intended wife to enjoy what remained of the season.

At twenty-five, Beatrice accepted that in the eyes of the world she was past her marriageable prime. Most of the friends she'd made during her debut were now married with children. Colin's future bride was not known to Beatrice—unsurprisingly, as she'd just learned her rival was some seven years her junior and had just made her come-out. Bea had digested that much about Stella Rawlings before shock had snatched away her senses, leaving her momentarily deaf to the horrible details of Colin's visit.

The light tap on the door brought Bea's head up off the pillow. She had been dozing on her bed's coverlet while waiting for the sound of the doctor's departure from her house, and her life. Beatrice knuckled her tired eyes as she went to the door, realising she'd cried herself into a deeper sleep than she'd wished to have.

'Papa!' Beatrice frowned in consternation. 'You should not have come upstairs!' She sent a searching glance over her father's stooped shoulder. 'Did Mr Francis help you with the climb?'

Walter Dewey waved away his daughter's concern as he made slow progress into her bedchamber assisted by a wooden walking stick. 'Norman is out hunting rabbits for our dinner.' He explained the manservant's absence. 'My small struggle is nothing to the pain I know you must be suffering my dear.'

Walter eased himself down into the armchair by the window. Raising his tired eyes to his daughter's wan face he shook his head to indicate he felt lost for words.

'Dr Burnett has gone?' Beatrice croaked.

'He has, and with my opinion of him ringing in his ears.'

Beatrice dropped to her knees by her father's chair and took a dry, withered hand between her soft palms. 'Please don't be upset over it, Papa,' she whispered, fearful for his health. She could hear his laboured breathing and see a greyish circle outlining his lips. 'My heart will mend...'

'You have a resilient ticker, then, my love,' Walter remarked wryly. How many times now has it been broken in two by some fellow?'

Beatrice knew her father was referring to her past romances that had foundered—usually because the gentleman involved had no money and could not afford to get married. How ironic that this time she must remain a spinster because the reverse were true. Her fiancé had recently received his inheritance and with it a demand to jilt her.

'Had this confounded Sir Donald not died when he did, leaving his odious terms and conditions, you would shortly have been Mrs Burnett.'

Walter gazed levelly at his daughter's upturned face. Beatrice had always been a beauty; some said she was fairer than her younger sister, who had bagged herself a nobleman three years ago. Walter thought them equally wonderful, in their own ways, although he wished Beatrice resembled her younger sister in one aspect: Elise had chosen to give her heart just the once, and very wisely.

Two previous rogues—besotted by Beatrice's golden-haired loveliness, Walter was sure—had encouraged his elder girl to think they would propose, then bitten their tongues at the last minute. In both cases it had transpired that they must fortune-hunt for a bride, being penniless.

Out in the sticks and cut off from the cream of polite society he might be, but Walter was cognizant with marriage mart standards: Beatrice's chances of finding a spouse diminished with every failed romance and every year that passed.

In Walter's opinion Beatrice was as lovely at twenty-five as she'd been when half a decade younger. Her creamy complexion was smooth and unblemished and her blonde hair appeared as shiny and abundant as it had been when she was a teenager. Her figure was enviably slender, yet curvaceous enough to catch a man's eye, and her vivacity made people take to her instantly. Yet still his elder girl remained at home with him because he'd never had the means to provide either of his daughters with a dowry.

Elise had married a millionaire who'd stated bluntly that the privilege of marrying Walter's daughter was payment enough. Unfortunately a similar good and generous fellow had never crossed Beatrice's path, catching her eye.

Colin Burnett had come closest to walking her down the aisle, and thus Walter despised him the most.

'Do you think Burnett truthfully had no idea of the clause in his uncle's will?'

Beatrice gave a little nod. 'I believe him sincere on that; as for greatly adoring me and never forgetting me, that I now find harder to swallow.' Her father's thin fingers closed comfortingly on hers. 'Did Colin offer to pay back the cash you spent on wedding preparations?' Bea asked huskily.

'He did,' Walter confirmed, bringing his daughter's hand to his cool lips.

'It is only fair you are not left out of pocket because of him. You will take what is due to you, won't you, Papa?' Beatrice used the heel of her hand on her cheek to remove a trickle of tears.

'Indeed I shall!' Walter forcefully concurred. 'I admit there was a moment when I felt like telling him to take himself and his money off to rot in hell…but I didn't.' He rumbled a chuckle. 'He might be getting off scot-free from a breach of promise suit but he won't wrig-

gle out of my expenses so easily. Mark my words, my
dear, Burnett will get his comeuppance for treating you
so shabbily.'

'Letters for me?' Elise Blackthorne jumped up from
her dressing table stool as her maid approached, prof-
fering a silver salver.

Excitedly the viscountess rifled through the post,
ignoring elegant cards inviting her to society parties,
to find what she was looking for. She frowned; it was
from Hertfordshire but bore her father's spidery script
rather than her sister's neat slanting hand.

'I shall not need you for an hour or so, Maria.' Before the maid left her bedchamber Elise asked, 'Is the
viscount eating breakfast?'

'He has gone to the stables, my lady. Shall I send one
of the boys to give him a message?'

Elise shook her head, satisfied she would see Alex
before he went about his business for the day. She still
felt sated from his lovemaking that morning and knew
she should get dressed. If he came back to find her in
a lacy negligee they might once more tumble onto the
silk sheets, limbs entwined. Elise wanted to get to Pall
Mall early today because the dressmaker there had recently given her a fitting and she was impatient to see
the beautiful blue satin gown she would wear when matron of honour at Bea's wedding.

Elise corresponded regularly with her sister and relished reading about all the wedding preparations. A
local seamstress was making Bea's gown, although the
bride to be was keeping the style of it a secret. Mrs Gar-

ner had a workshop based in St Albans and had served the Dewey family for over a decade. Walter had never had the means to provide his daughters with many new clothes when growing up and their debuts had thus been modest affairs.

'What have you got there?'

Else twisted about at the sound of her husband's husky baritone.

Alex came closer and dropped a kiss on her bare shoulder. His fingers continued to caress his wife's satiny skin as he glanced at the parchment in her hand, recognising the writing.

'Your father has sent you a letter.'

Elise twisted about in the circle of her husband's arms. 'I'm just about to read it, Alex, so don't...' Her breathy plea was cut off as his mouth slanted over hers and he drew her closer.

'Oh...Alex...' Elise giggled, but her protest was half-hearted as she melted against him.

'It's your own fault,' he growled. 'What's a man to do when his gorgeous wife parades about half naked?'

'Whatever he likes, I suppose,' Elise breathed against his preying mouth.

'Right answer, sweetheart...' Alex purred and, swinging her up in his arms, headed for the bed.

Chapter Two

'There was a time when it was hard to shake you off my shoulder; now I need to make an appointment to see you?' Alex Blackthorne's ironic comment drew an apologetic grin from his best friend. However, the fellow's narrowed gaze remained fixed on the razor sweeping a path through stubble towards a lean cheekbone.

Hugh Kendrick swirled the implement in a china bowl filled with soap-floating water before turning to face the viscount. 'You know I'd sooner come to watch the fight with you, but I've promised Gwen a trip to Epsom races this afternoon.'

Alex sank into a hide chair in his friend's bedchamber. Obligingly he shifted to one side, allowing Hugh's startled valet to rescue an elegant jacket that his master had discarded over the back of the upholstery.

'Besides, if your wife wasn't out of town you wouldn't want my company, would you?' Over the top of the towel mopping his face Hugh hiked a dark eyebrow at Alex.

'True…' Alex sighed, flicking a speck from a thigh breeched in fawn cloth.

He was feeling at a loose end since Elise had gone to Hertfordshire to visit her family. It was puzzling that Walter Dewey had written a letter containing a coded message that he would like Elise to visit as soon as she was able.

Alex felt rather guilty now for distracting his wife from immediately reading her note on the morning it had arrived. It had been some hours after the post was delivered that Elise had finally retrieved the paper from amongst their warm, crumpled bed sheets. Mere moments after breaking the seal she'd thrust the letter beneath Alex's nose, announcing that she'd deciphered her father's few odd sentences and was certain that a crisis had occurred. Elise could never bear to be parted from her infant son, so Adam had gone to Hertfordshire too, and at Alex's insistence Maria had accompanied mother and child in one of the luxurious Blackthorne travelling coaches.

'You look browned off,' Hugh remarked, shrugging into his shirt. For several minutes he had been contemplating Alex's frowning expression as he stared into space with his chin resting atop fingers forming a steeple. Hugh guessed his friend was already missing his beloved wife and son.

The two men had been friends for decades, despite the fact that for most of that time their statuses had been poles apart. Hugh had been the underdog, with nothing much to claim to his credit other than his popularity and his family connections. His late father had been an upstanding fellow, a minor peer of the realm who had seen the best in everybody. Unfortunately that blind faith had been particularly strong where his heir was concerned. Others, however, could see what a corrupt, calculating character was Toby Kendrick. On taking his birthright following his father's demise, Hugh's brother had become even more of an unbearable wretch.

But Hugh no longer had reason to feel resentful over the bad hand life had dealt him as the second son of a gentleman who believed in primogeniture. Neither had he reason to feel lucky that Viscount Blackthorne had chosen him as a life-long comrade. Hugh might not have a title to polish, but he now had every other advantage that his illustrious friend enjoyed, including a fortune that his acquaintances coveted and that dukes would like their debutante daughters to share in through marriage.

'It's odd for my father-in-law to call Elise home.' Alex finally stirred himself to answer while standing up. The last time his wife had been summoned in such a way Beatrice had sent word because their father had fractured his collarbone in a fall. Naturally Walter had wanted to have both his beloved daughters by his side... just in case the injury had proved fatal.

'Do you think some harm might have again befallen him?'

'Walter wrote the letter himself, so I doubt he's bedridden.' Alex shrugged. 'It's probably all about Beatrice's wedding day. Elise is matron of honour...' He grimaced bewilderment at the workings of the female mind.

Hugh glanced up to find his friend's eyes on him. 'Yes...perhaps it's just about the wedding,' he muttered, resuming buttoning his cuffs.

'You don't ask about Beatrice any more.' Alex began adjusting his cravat in the mantel glass now Hugh had left the space free.

'Does she ask about me?' Hugh countered, picking up his jacket and pegging it on a finger over a muscular shoulder. He preceded his friend towards the door.

They were heading towards the top of the stairs before Alex answered. 'You can't blame Beatrice for wanting to forget all about you after the way you behaved.'

Hugh's mouth tilted sardonically. 'Indeed...so it seems a bit pointless asking about her, doesn't it?' He plunged his hands into his pockets. 'A lot of water has passed under the bridge since then...'

'And for you...most of it flowed in India...' Alex remarked dryly.

'So it did...' Hugh said in a similar vein. 'I hope everything goes well on the big day.'

He moved ahead of Alex, descending the stairs at quite a speed.

On reaching the cool marble vestibule of Hugh's grand town house the friends waited for the butler to announce that the curricle had been brought round. A moment later they clattered down the stone steps, then stopped to exchange a few words before going their separate ways.

'Come along to Epsom with us if you're kicking your heels. You might back a few winners and cheer yourself up by raising your bank balance.' Hugh was speaking ironically; he knew very well that his friend's accounts were in no need of a boost. It was his spirits that were flagging.

The startling change in his own fortunes still gave Hugh cause to smile inwardly. Just two years ago he'd had reason to watch carefully every penny he spent. Now he could purchase a stable of prized Arabs and watch them race at Epsom—or anywhere else—if that was his whim. Yet Hugh realised that his enthusiasm for a day out with his favourite mistress was waning and he felt oddly deflated.

'You expect me to play gooseberry to you and the lovely Gwen?' Alex scowled. 'I don't think I will, but thanks for asking.' He clapped a hand on Hugh's shoulder. 'See you in White's later in the week, I expect.'

'It's a bit late to let Gwen down with an excuse.' Hugh sounded irritated by his conscience.

'Quite right…keep the lady happy,' Alex mocked.

Gwen Sharpe was a celebrated Cyprian known to select as lovers affluent gentlemen who could provide her with the finer things in life. Hugh certainly fitted the bill, following a bizarre stroke of luck that had made him one of the wealthiest men in the country.

'I'll be back before ten tonight. Do you fancy a visit to the Palm House to cure your boredom?' Hugh called over a shoulder as he approached the kerb to take the curricle's reins from his tiger.

Alex snorted a laugh. 'I'm a married man…are you trying to get me hung?'

Hugh shook his head in mock disgust. 'You're under the thumb…that's what you are.'

'And I'll willingly remain there…' Alex returned, grinning.

The Palm House was a notorious den of iniquity

where gambling and whoring went hand in hand. Men of all classes—from criminals to aristocracy—could be found mingling in its smoky environment from midnight till gone daybreak. At early light the club would spew forth its clientele, the majority of whom would stagger off with sore heads and empty purses.

Hugh set the greys to a trot, wishing he could shake off the feeling that he'd sooner return home than go to Epsom with Gwen. His mistress was beautiful and beguiling, if gratingly possessive at times. Any man would want to spend time with her... And yet Hugh, for a reason that escaped him, wanted solitude to reflect on a romance that had long been dead and buried. The woman he'd loved three years ago was now about to become another man's bride, so what purpose would be served by brooding on what might have been?

With a curse exploding through his gritted teeth Hugh set the horses to a faster pace, exasperated by his maudlin thoughts and the fact that his friend had chosen this morning to remind him that his sister-in-law's marriage was imminent. Beatrice Dewey was firmly in his past, and Gwen and Sophia, the courtesans he kept in high style, would serve very well for the present. If in need of deeper emotion he could head out to India and spend some time with somebody he'd grown to love...

'What do *you* want?'

'That's a nice greeting, I must say.'

'Are we to pretend I'm pleased to see you?' Hugh folded the newspaper he'd been reading whilst breakfasting and skimmed it over the crisp damask tablecloth.

He lounged into a mahogany chair-back, crossing his arms over the ruffles on his shirt. Sardonically, he surveyed his older brother.

Uninvited, Sir Toby Kendrick pulled out the chair opposite Hugh, seating himself with a flourish of coat-tails. He then stared obstinately at a footman until the fellow darted forward.

'Coffee—and fill a plate with whatever is over there.' Toby flicked a finger at the domed silver platters lining the sideboard whilst giving his order. He turned sly eyes on his brother, daring Hugh to object.

The servant withdrew with a jerky bow, a fleeting glance flying at his master from beneath his powdered wig. Hugh gave an imperceptible nod, sanctioning his brother's boorish demand to be fed.

All of the servants knew—in common with the *ton*— that Hugh Kendrick and his older brother did not get on.

Sir Toby's dislike of his younger brother had increased since Hugh's wealth and standing had eclipsed his own. Toby had relished what he deemed to be his rightful place as loftiest Kendrick. Now he'd been toppled, and in such a teeth-grindingly, shocking stroke of luck for his brother that Toby had been apoplectic when first hearing about it. Knowing that he wasn't alone in being bitter was no consolation to Toby. His brother was popular, and more people had been pleased than jealous of Hugh's success.

Their mother and their sister had been overjoyed— no doubt because they'd both benefited from Hugh's generosity. Toby had received nothing from Hugh other than a bottle of champagne with which to toast his luck.

In the event Toby had refrained from smashing the magnum to smithereens on the step and downed the prime vintage at record speed, drowning his sorrows.

'No broiled kidneys?' Toby used a silver fork to push the food about on the plate that had just been set before him.

'I don't like kidneys,' Hugh replied. He sat forward in his chair. 'Neither do I like being disturbed by visitors at his ungodly hour of the day.' He got to his feet. 'Are you going to tell me what you want? Or have you just turned up for a free breakfast and the opportunity to try my patience?'

Toby shoved away the plate of untasted splendid food, a curl to his lip. 'All that cash and you can't find yourself a decent cook?' he chortled.

'As you've no appetite, and nothing of moment to say, it's time you went on your way.' He addressed the footman. 'My brother is leaving. Show him out.' Turning his back on Toby he strolled to the huge windows that overlooked Grosvenor Square, idly surveying the busy street scene.

The servant attempted to conceal his satisfied smirk on springing forward to do his master's bidding.

'You're getting a bit too high and mighty, aren't you?' Toby barked, his cheeks florid.

'Perhaps I spent too long studying you when growing up,' Hugh drawled over a shoulder.

Toby whacked away the footman's ushering arm, stomping closer to Hugh. 'Very well…I have something to discuss,' he snarled in an undertone.

'Go ahead; but be brief. I have an appointment with my tailor.'

'Might we repair to your library and be private?' Toby suggested sarcastically.

Hugh glanced back at the servants clearing the breakfast things. He sighed. 'If we must…' He strode for the door without another word and once in the corridor approached the library at the same exasperated speed.

Toby trudged behind, his footsteps muffled by the luxurious carpet. Inwardly he squirmed at having to come here, cap in hand, and beg his brother for a loan. Not so long ago he had been the one the others in the family came to when in need of cash. It had given Toby immense pleasure to make them dance to his tune for their coins; even his mother had had to humble herself to extract her allowance from him. But now she had no need to because Hugh had provided her with a generous pension—something her dear late husband had omitted to do.

Sir Kenneth Kendrick had relied on his son and heir to provide fairly for his successors, proving that he might have doted on Toby but he had never come to know his eldest son's true nature.

'I need two hundred pounds urgently,' Toby blurted as soon as the door was closed behind him.

'Is that a request for a loan?'

'You know damn well it is,' Toby spat. He swiped a hand about his mouth, aware he'd need to control his temper if he was to get the cash and keep the duns at bay. Hugh might be open-handed where his mother and sister were concerned, but his generosity to Toby was a different matter.

Hugh leaned on the library table that almost spanned from one end of the oak-panelled room to the other. He drummed his long fingers in slow rhythm on the leather-topped furniture. 'I've already handed over a thousand pounds in less than six months.' Hugh watched his brother's lips whiten in anger at that reminder.

'I didn't realise you were keeping a tally of the paltry sums.' Toby flung himself down in a chair, affecting ennui.

'As I recall, one thousand pounds wasn't a paltry amount when I came to you many years ago and begged for your help in securing Sarah's future.'

Then Toby's meanness had run so deep that he'd denied his only sister the cash she desperately needed after she'd been compromised during her debut. With their father gone it had fallen to Hugh, impecunious at that time, to rescue Sarah's reputation. He'd managed to scrape together a dowry—the majority of the cash borrowed from Alex Blackthorne—thus tempting a decent chap, lacking prospects, to put a ring on his disgraced sister's finger.

Inwardly Toby railed at himself; he'd laid himself wide open to that barb. 'The little madam deserved to be taught a lesson for acting like a strumpet.'

'Our sister did nothing wrong other than to trust one of your friends to act as a gentleman. She was seventeen and not worldly-wise,' Hugh coldly reminded him.

Toby snorted derision. 'Well, she was worldly-wise after her folly…so a lesson well learned about promenading after dark with randy men. You—and she—should thank me rather than criticising.'

Hugh moved his head in disgust. 'I wonder sometimes if we are related. You really are the most obnoxious character.'

'Are you questioning our dear mama's virtue?' Toby guffawed. 'She'll not thank you for hearing that repeated. Perhaps I might tell her.'

He eyed his sibling calculatingly, feeling confident that Hugh would relent rather than risk upsetting their widowed mother. The dowager was approaching sixty-five and would be distraught to know her elder son risked a spell in the Fleet because his debts were out of control.

'I've had enough of you...take yourself off...' Hugh snapped in exasperation, turning for the door.

'What's wrong? No money left? Sent too much out to India, have you? Toby's voice was low and sly and he concealed a smirk at the look of intense hatred he'd brought to his brother's face.

'I'll arrange for a bank draft later in the day,' Hugh said, just before quitting the room. 'Now, if you don't mind, I need to be elsewhere...'

Toby strutted after him, looking exceedingly pleased with himself.

'If you come again demanding me to bail you out of gambling debts you'll be wasting your time. I won't care what you say...'

'Won't you, now...?' Toby drawled provocatively. 'Gambling debts?' He smoothly changed the subject. 'It's nothing so vulgar, my dear fellow. Serena has expensive tastes in jewellery, if you *must* have the details...'

Toby wasn't referring to his prospective fiancée's taste but to that of his mistress. Hugh knew his brother had set up Serena Worthing in a smart apartment, and even with a marriage contract under discussion it seemed Toby had no intention of putting her off to concentrate on his future wife.

'Well, whatever it is…whoring, drinking, gambling… you'll pay for it yourself in future.'

'If ever our positions return to what they were…what they *should* be…I'll remember this conversation and all those others where you've had the damnable cheek to moralise.' Toby pointed a stout finger at his brother. 'Before you got rich and Blackthorne got married the two of you were constant petticoat-chasers. Blackthorne might have eased off now, but you're worse than ever since you got back from India.' Toby thrust his face close to Hugh's jaw. 'Tell me…what it is about an exotic beauty that fires a man's blood so…?'

'You sound jealous of my popularity with the ladies.' Hugh shoved his brother away and strode on along the corridor. 'Show yourself out.'

Chapter Three

'I'm sorry Papa worried you enough to bring you racing to Hertfordshire yesterday. I had no idea he'd summoned you home just because the wedding is off.' Beatrice bounced her baby nephew on her knee. 'Of course it is wonderful to have you visit, Elise, and this little chap has grown so big since I last saw him.'

Elise had been pouring tea into bone china, but on hearing the quaver in her sister's voice she put down the pot and crouched down by the side of Bea's armchair. 'You don't need to be brave with me, my dear. I know how dreadfully hurt you are.' She pressed Bea's fingers in comfort.

Beatrice avoided Elise's astute gaze, blinking rapidly at the window to one side of her. 'It is all right...really it is...it has been nearly a week now since...' She tried to name the person who'd caused her heartbreak but found his name stuck to her tongue.

As her nephew gurgled, giving her a gummy smile, Bea fondled his soft pink cheek with a forefinger.

'Another few days and I will be right as rain—won't I, Master Adam?'

'Well, I know I would not be, if it were me who'd been so cruelly jilted,' Elise announced pithily. She shook her head in disbelief. 'I'd never have imagined Dr Burnett to be a callous or a fickle fellow.'

'I'm glad I wasn't the only one who mistook his character.' Beatrice sighed. 'I can't forgive him for abandoning me in favour of family duty, yet since I've had time to calm down I understand why he did so.'

'Then I think you exceedingly over-obliging!' Elise exclaimed. 'Love should override all else in my book.'

'In a perfect world…perhaps…' Beatrice returned philosophically. 'I think matrimony and Beatrice Dewey are destined to remain strangers.'

'Never say so! There is a husband for you…he just has not shown himself yet.' Elise attempted to draw her sister from her glums with a provocative comment. 'As I recall, there was nobody more determined to be a wife and mother than you.'

Beatrice chuckled wryly at that reminder. Indeed, there had been a time when she'd driven her poor sister to distraction, so keen had she been to settle down with a nice fellow and raise a little family of her own. After several false starts she'd met Colin and finally thought her ambition was within her grasp. Now, for some reason, she felt tired of struggling towards that particular dream…

'You girls are up early.' Walter Dewey entered the sunny front parlour, supported by his stick. He gave his daughters an affectionate smile, thinking it nice to have them both together again at home, and with the added bonus of his handsome little grandson.

In Walter's opinion the child was a perfect blend of his parents: he had the viscount's brown eyes and sturdy build and his mother's sharp chin and fair hair.

'Did you sleep well?' he asked Elise. 'I heard young Adam having a grizzle just before dawn broke.'

'He was wet so I changed his nappy,' Viscountess Blackthorne said, as though it were the most natural thing in the world to tend to her baby herself rather than give Adam to his nurse.

Following their parents' acrimonious divorce, Elise and Bea had been reared by their papa in straitened circumstances, so were accustomed to being useful and practical in mundane matters. Both young women were quite happy to dress themselves and knew how to cook and clean. When younger, the sisters had taken to painting their bedrooms and made a capable job of it, much to their papa's surprise and delight.

'Don't look at me like that, miss,' Walter mildly reproved, having caught Beatrice frowning at him. 'I know you believe I'm at fault because your sister has better things to do than commiserate with us that you've been put back on the shelf—'

'I certainly do not!' Elise cut across her father. 'There's nothing more important to me than being here with you, although the reason for it is upsetting.' She gave her sister's cheek an affectionate stroke. 'Bea is certainly not on the shelf, Papa! How can she be when she is so pretty and looks not a day over eighteen…?'

'Oh…Elise!' Beatrice choked. 'A very nice compliment but it really is too much.'

'Perhaps I exaggerated just a little. You could pass easily for twenty-one and that is certainly not over-egging it.' Elise cocked her head to assess her sister's countenance. Beatrice was still one of the loveliest young women of her acquaintance, and in the *haut monde* Viscountess Blackthorne certainly came into contact with some vaunted beauties.

For the first time in days Beatrice chuckled with genuine amusement. 'Papa's right: I might be on the shelf…' she pulled a little face '…but I'm not sure it worries me; at present I'm fed up with gentlemen and romance.'

'That will pass.' Walter flapped a hand. 'Every young lady craves her own home and family.'

'Are you trying to get rid of me, Papa?' Beatrice teased her father.

'You know I am not! You may stay with your old papa for as long as you wish…but to tell the truth I was looking forward to walking you down the aisle before these old legs finally give out on me.'

'And so you shall, Papa,' Elise reassured him, getting up from her place by her sister's chair. Having tested the tea that she'd abandoned in the pot, Elise found it now unpalatably lukewarm.

'Your Aunt Dolly will be very sad to have this news,' Walter muttered, sinking into a seat.

'She loves a wedding,' Elise reflected, settling by her papa on the sofa.

'She travelled here to attend your nuptials uninvited,

as I recall.' Walter dredged up a chuckle at the memory of his widowed sister turning up out of the blue on the eve of the wedding, expecting to be housed and fed.

'And Mrs Vickers accompanied her,' Elise chipped in, fondly dwelling on her countryside wedding at the local church. It had been a quiet, yet wonderful occasion, with just her family about her. She glanced at her sister, wondering if Bea was musing sadly on the fact that Colin Burnett had acted as Alex's groomsman that fine afternoon.

'I rather liked Edith Vickers,' Beatrice remarked brightly. She had indeed been thinking of Colin's role in her sister's happy day and pounced on the first thing that came into her head to chase memories of him from her mind. 'How is Mrs Vickers? Do you ever see her?'

'Oh…of course…you would not know for I've not had a reason to mention it.' Elise frowned. 'Sadly, Mrs Vickers passed away.' She leaned forward to impart an exciting titbit. 'There was quite a brouhaha when it came to light that she had not been as hard up as she'd believed herself to be. When Edith's husband died his creditors pounced and left her in very reduced circumstances. But they left alone the deeds to a strip of land in India because it was deemed to be barren. Mrs Vickers bequeathed it to her nephew, Hugh.'

'Hugh Kendrick?' Walter snarled.

He recalled that name. When Beatrice had gone with her sister to London several years ago Mrs Vickers's nephew had shown undue interest in Beatrice, raising her hopes that he might propose. Walter had been enraged to know the fellow hadn't the wherewithal to take on a wife so must fortune-hunt for a bride. He'd been angry at himself, too, knowing that if only he had put by a dowry for his daughters his elder child might have been settled before the younger, as was the proper way of things.

'Oh, I'm sorry to hear of her passing.' Beatrice wiped dribble from her nephew's mouth with her hanky. 'I expect Aunt Dolly misses Edith. They were good friends, weren't they?'

'So…the land was not worthless?' Walter guessed, returning to the crux of the matter.

'It was not,' Elise confirmed, clapping her hands in glee. 'Alex was delighted for his friend when he found out about his good fortune. Of course there were many green-eyed people not so pleased at the turn of events, and Sir Toby Kendrick led the pack—'

'What happened?' Walter butted in impatiently, his gnarled hand clutching tightly at his stick, turning the knuckles white. Walter loved a good tale of Lady Luck turning up unexpectedly. Many a time over the years he had wished that elusive minx would smile on him when his marriage and his business had crumbled, leaving him desolate with two teenage girls to bring up alone.

'The strip of land contained some mines, long ago abandoned as dry. Hugh went to India and had them re-investigated from curiosity and they turned up a seam of fine diamonds. So now Hugh Kendrick is very rich, and I for one am overjoyed for him.'

Beatrice blinked in astonishment at her past love's extraordinary stroke of luck. 'Yes…good for him…' she said quietly.

'Good for him?' Walter barked. 'Another fellow who broke your heart, as I recall.'

'I do seem to attract rogues.' Beatrice's tone was rueful rather than bitter. 'I'm sure it's my own fault,' she added with a twinkling smile. 'You have warned me not to be so impetuous, haven't you, Papa?' Bea knew that in the past, especially in her pursuit of Hugh Kendrick, she'd been not only impetuous but foolhardy.

Walter glanced at his jilted daughter. He'd been right to call Elise home, he realised; just a few days ago Beatrice's low spirits had worried him. Now, with her sister close by, she was recovering far better than Walter had dared hope. It had always been a great comfort to him that his girls were good friends as well as close kin. He knew of families where siblings resented one another— especially when one child did better than the other. But Beatrice had only been happy for her younger sister when she had caught herself a handsome aristocrat to wed, and Elise with her open, sweet nature never attempted to lord it over her less fortunate sibling.

'It's a shame Edith didn't pop off a few years ago,' Walter said. 'Her rogue of a nephew would have received his bequest earlier and been in a position to call on me for your hand.'

'Papa!' Beatrice cried, half-amused, half-outraged. 'Poor Edith! I am sad to hear of her demise no matter what benefits it turned up.' She gestured airily. 'Besides, it all turned out for the best; after that little sojourn in London ended, and with it my friendship with Mr Kendrick, I had only been home a few days before I was feeling relieved that he'd thrown me over.' She tickled

Adam, making him giggle, while adding self-mockingly, 'I quickly met Colin and fell in love all over again.'

'On the rebound,' Walter muttered darkly. 'And look where that got you.'

'Hugh *is* still a bachelor,' Elise piped up, subtly siding with her father.

She had also thought at the time that her sister had transferred her affection to Dr Burnett far too quickly after Hugh's rejection. Not that Hugh had carelessly withdrawn his suit; at the time he had confided in Alex to feeling mortified at not being in a position to propose to Bea. Elise had thought him brutal in making a clean break with her sister, yet had come to realise it had been the decent thing to do. The couple's mutual affection had started stirring gossip, and the town tabbies loved nothing better than to amuse themselves shredding an innocent's reputation.

A girl who too obviously set her cap at a gentleman, then failed to get him to put a ring on her finger, invited opprobrium. Worse still, if it had been discovered that Beatrice had advertised for a husband in a gazette, like a vulgar hussy, the Dewey sisters would have been hounded out of town during the season they'd been house guests of the Chapmans. In the event a scandal *had* broken, but Elise and Alex had been the butt of it and it had quickly died away when Elise received Alex's marriage proposal.

'I understood Hugh Kendrick had set his sights on Fiona Chapman's inheritance.' Walter had been reflecting, as had his daughters, on the drama of three years ago.

'Fiona deterred him from proposing, I believe, know-

ing as she did that his heart wasn't in it.' Elise glanced
at Beatrice, who seemed oblivious to the hint and continued playing pat-a-cake with Adam.

'That young woman must have been kicking herself
ever since.' Walter growled a laugh. 'I expect she has
had the scolding of her life from Maude.' He mentioned
Fiona's mother with obvious fondness. The Chapmans
were good people and had remained loyal to the Deweys
through good and bad times over the decades.

'Verity is increasing with her first child.' Verity
Clemence, née Chapman, was a very dear friend of
Elise's. 'I have only just found out!' She answered Bea's
unspoken question, flashed by a pair of expressive blue
eyes. 'I believe the babe is not due till late autumn.'

'She must be thrilled, and so must be Mr and Mrs
Chapman.' Beatrice sounded wistful. 'It will be their
first grandchild...'

A bang on the door caused the room's occupants
to abruptly cease their lively conversation and look at
one another in surprise. Elise jumped up to peer discreetly out of the square-paned window. 'We are on the
point of having a visit from Mrs Callan and Victoria,'
she groaned.

'The grapevine has done its work, then,' Beatrice
acknowledged wryly.

'Would you sooner I sent them away?' Elise feared
that her sister was right: the vicar's wife and daughter
had come to pry about the broken engagement rather
than politely socialise.

'Everybody will know sooner or later, so I must get
used to the idea of facing down the stares and whispers.'

Bea stood up, handing Adam to his mother. 'Let's get it over with now, while I'm feeling ready to deflect any amount of sly comments.'

Elise's smile combined admiration and encouragement for Bea. 'I'll tell Betty to show them in.'

A few minutes later Elise was back with her family in the front parlour, exchanging a resigned smile with Bea as they heard voices in the hallway heralding their visitors' imminent appearance.

'We came as soon as we heard,' Mrs Callan announced with theatrical sympathy, surging into the room. She halted abruptly, causing her plump daughter trailing in her wake to collide with her. Nudging Victoria, to alert her to the presence of aristocracy, Mrs Callan bobbed low to the viscountess, who was rocking her son in her arms.

'We are indeed honoured to see you today, Lady Blackthorne. Ah...you have brought your little son to see his grandpapa.' Ethel Callan fluttered a hand to her throat to indicate her regret in what she was about to say. 'Of course it is a shame that such calamitous news brings you back to Hertfordshire.'

'I come to Hertfordshire gladly, for good or bad news.'

'Oh...of course...' Mrs Callan approached Beatrice, taking her hands in a thin, dry grip. 'Shocked! It is not too strong a word!' She gave Bea's fingers a vigorous shake. 'Deeply disappointed also, to discover that nice Dr Burnett would heartlessly abandon you like that.'

'We have discovered he is not so nice, have we not, Mama?' Victoria piped up.

'Dr Burnett had his reasons for doing what he did

and I have accepted them, so that is that.' Beatrice's voice was cool and held an air of finality as she firmly withdrew her hands from the older woman's clutch. She was not about to be drawn into complaining about her loss. Whatever she said would be repeated ad infinitum in the village.

'Do take a seat, madam, and you also, Miss Callan.' Walter's fist was quivering on his stick as his annoyance increased. Just as he'd been daring to hope Beatrice seemed more cheerful these two were likely to overset her again with their false pity. He knew for a fact that Victoria had done her utmost to snare the doctor herself. It had gone round the locality that the minx had concocted ailments simply to get the fellow to make a house call. Her father had moaned to Walter that he owed Burnett a tidy sum on account of his spinster daughter's antics, and no gain made from it.

Ethel Callan settled down, with much smoothing of skirts, in a vacant chair by the fireside, and her daughter perched on the sofa next to Walter.

'We were just about to have some fresh tea,' Beatrice announced. 'I'll ask Mrs Francis to bring two more cups and a fresh pot…' Her voice tailed off as another rata-tat on the door was heard. Inwardly she groaned, fearing yet more ladies had come to gleefully commiserate with her. 'I'll go this time.' She sent Elise a subtle wink that conveyed she'd sooner her sister fielded questions for a short while.

Chapter Four

In the hallway Beatrice spied the comforting figure of Mrs Francis ambling towards her from the direction of the kitchen.

'I'll attend to the door.' Bea gave the housekeeper a smile. 'Would you make some tea for us, please, and bring it along directly? The sooner we have been hospitable the sooner our guests might decide to be on their way.'

Betty Francis twitched a smile, understanding the quip. 'Don't you worry. I'll be quick as I can with the refreshments, but maybe I'll just dawdle a moment and see how many cups we might need.' The woman's grey head pointed grimly at the door. Betty knew very well why people were calling on them, and wouldn't be surprised to see Squire Thaddon's wife outside with some of her friends, keen to join the inquisition that was taking place in the front parlour.

'I suppose that might be wise,' Bea said wryly.

'The rumour mill's been grinding overtime, no doubt

about that,' Betty muttered darkly. 'Might be you'll open up and I'll need to break out another tea service.'

Betty Francis and her husband Norman had been with the Deweys for approaching twenty-five years and felt very protective of the family. Betty had been like a mother to the girls when the hussy Mr Dewey had married ran off to her lover. If she bumped into the doctor Betty would cheerfully wring his neck for breaking Miss Beatrice's heart. But she'd heard from the butcher's boy, who'd pedalled over earlier in the week, that Colin Burnett had wasted no time in upping sticks and moving away.

With one hand Beatrice smoothed her sprigged muslin dress, while the other tucked blonde tendrils behind her small ears. Forcing an insouciant expression, she opened the door. Extreme astonishment caused her smile to freeze on her full pink lips.

'Hello, Beatrice; you look well...'

'Why...Mr Kendrick...I...that is...we were expecting somebody else,' Beatrice finished faintly, having finally snapped herself to attention.

'You remember me...I'm flattered.'

Beatrice attempted to rouse herself from her stupor. Her heart had begun to thud erratically and the pearl buttons on her bodice were quivering with every breath she took. But if her visitor noticed her bosom's alluring movement he gave no sign; Hugh Kendrick's eyes were politely fixed on her blanching face.

'I'm sorry to startle you, and hope I've not arrived at a bad time...'

'No...not at all...' Bea fibbed. 'Please...do come in,

sir.' She belatedly remembered her manners and drew to one side, aware that Betty was hovering behind, watching and listening to their strained conversation.

'Just one more cup, then, please, Mrs Francis.' Beatrice was thankful to have a reason to turn to the housekeeper and compose herself, simply to avoid a pair or relentless hawk-like eyes.

She *had* recognised Hugh straight away, yet marvelled at having done so. The person before her little resembled the gentleman she had fallen in love with three years ago. His thick hair was still conker-brown, worn rather long, and his eyes were deepest hazel, fringed with ebony lashes; but there all similarity ended. Once he'd had an appealing fresh-faced demeanour and had worn modestly styled attire. Now his lean, angular face was sun-beaten and bore lines of dissipation. His elegantly tailored suit of clothing, dusty and creased from the journey, proclaimed him a man who could afford to be carelessly indulgent.

So far they'd exchanged few words, all of them polite, yet Bea felt unsettled by his lazy confidence. Once Hugh Kendrick would blush endearingly the moment she entered a room; at present she found his hooded amber gaze intimidating rather than flattering. As Beatrice pivoted about to again invite him into her home she sensed a pang of regret that he was no longer a charming young fellow but an aloof stranger who possessed an alarming virility.

'I expect you're busy with wedding preparations.'

His quiet comment caused Beatrice to snap her darkening eyes to him, wondering if he was being deliberately sarcastic. His tone had been as unemotional as were his features, but she quickly realised it was unlikely he'd yet heard her bad news. Her sister had only found out a few days ago on reaching Hertfordshire, and Elise's husband remained in ignorance of what had gone on.

'It's none of my business, I know. My apologies for mentioning it.' Hugh had sensed her frostiness increase at the mention of her marriage. She had good cause to dislike him, and he'd often cursed the reason for it.

But not any more. He'd been too broke to have her— the only woman he'd really wanted—and following several humiliating and vain attempts at fortune-hunting a bride he'd done with love and marriage. Now he could buy himself all the female company he needed, and renew it when he grew bored with the women in his life.

Hugh's mouth slanted in self-mockery as he recalled that a joyful wedding reception had been taking place the last time they'd been in one another's company.

Alex Blackthorne had been married in Hertfordshire at a country church with few people in attendance, but he had bestowed on his bride an extravagant party when they arrived back in Mayfair. No expense had been spared and the lavish affair had seen ambitious society brides emulating it ever since.

During the celebration Hugh remembered Beatrice and her father keeping their distance from him. He had taken against the fellow escorting Beatrice even before Alex told him that Beatrice Dewey had become engaged to Colin Burnett.

'What do you want, sir?' Bea asked coolly, although

her complexion had grown warm beneath his relentless scrutiny. She felt wound as tightly as a spring, but the thrill of being so close to him, enveloped in his musky sandalwood scent, was not easily conquered. If he'd just stop staring at her, she thought crossly, she might manage to calm down and stop turning over in her mind what had happened between them years ago.

At Vauxhall Pleasure Gardens, Hugh had singled her out, paying her such attention that a crowd of envious women had closed in on them to eavesdrop. The giddy elation of that warm midsummer evening and the following days, anticipating her next meeting with Hugh, were not easy to forget. Neither was the memory of her happiness disintegrating when he bluntly told her he couldn't see her again.

'We have some neighbours visiting. I do not want to seem inhospitable, sir, but it might be better if you do not join us.' Mrs Callan's hoarse laugh had jolted Beatrice to the present. 'My father has not forgotten or forgiven that once we knew each other...that is, he recalls that our brief friendship turned sour,' Beatrice hastily amended, blushing. They had most definitely not *known* each other—in the biblical sense or any other. She had mistaken this man's nature and sincerity just as she had with Colin.

'I regret that we parted before I knew you as well as I would have liked.'

'I cannot echo that sentiment, sir.' Hugh's amused tone had deepened the colour staining Beatrice's porcelain complexion. '*My* only regret is that I ever became acquainted with you at all.' Stolen kisses and caresses, snatched during their brief moments alone, were at the forefront of her mind, putting a disquieting throb low in her belly. Bea feared he might also be recalling their passionate moonlit trysts, and his next soft comment proved her intuitive.

'I don't believe you wish we'd never met when we had such a delightful time.'

'Then you should curb your conceit, because it is the truth,' Beatrice snapped, avoiding the sultry glint in his eyes. 'Once again I must ask you what you want. I cannot believe you have simply come to see me and reminisce—'

'I won't keep you long from your friends,' Hugh interrupted smoothly. 'Nice as it is to see you, my dear, it's a far more vital matter that brings me here uninvited.'

Bea was aware of the arrogance in his tone and felt her hackles rise. No doubt now he had increased his prospects he felt she should feel flattered by his attention. Before she could step away from him he'd strolled back towards the door as though he might leave.

'I have some urgent news for Alex. Would you fetch him, please, so I might speak to him?' Hugh's exasperating thoughts made him sound harsh and domineering. Beneath his breath he was cursing himself for finding her country freshness sweetly appealing after Gwen's cloying presence. Once he'd touched and caressed Beatrice often, and with her full consent. Any sudden move from him now was sure to result in a swift slap, so he'd distanced himself to avoid temptation.

'Alex?' A small frown crinkled Bea's brow. 'Why, I cannot get him, sir…he is not here. Elise arrived a few days ago with baby Adam but we have not seen Alex. Is he on his way, then?'

'I imagined he would have arrived by now. He left before me. His butler said he'd travelled into Hertfordshire so I came directly here, assuming he'd be with Elise.'

On the long hard ride towards St Albans he'd been wondering how he'd feel again when he saw Beatrice. In his youth he'd been infatuated plenty of times, impoverished just as frequently, by pert beauties with expensive tastes. But he'd put all of them from his mind. Beatrice Dewey he'd not been able to forget. He'd explained it away by blaming mutual friends for keeping the winsome blonde haunting his thoughts. But Hugh suspected that what presently occupied Beatrice's mind was her brother-in-law's safety. She was no doubt imagining that Alex had come a cropper on the road, and Hugh naturally wanted to soothe her fears on that score.

'If he'd broken an axle, or one of his horses had gone lame, I would have passed him en route,' Hugh softly reassured her. 'Alex might have taken a break at a tavern.'

A furrow appeared in Beatrice's smooth brow, testament to the fact she was not entirely convinced by that argument. 'I shall let Elise know you are here; she'll want to speak to you if you've come on her husband's account.'

Swiftly Hugh moved to apprehend her, catching her wrist in a firm grip. 'It might be best not to tell her anything till I locate Alex. I don't want to unduly upset Elise if there is an easy explanation for the viscount's absence.'

'Yes…I understand…' Beatrice croaked, her skin heating beneath his clasp. She'd proof now that Hugh Kendrick had kindly sought to allay her fears over her brother-in-law's tardiness, despite suspecting all might not be well. But it was the sensation of Hugh's touch— far more assertive than she remembered it to be—rather than anxiety for Alex that was making her captured flesh quiver.

Slowly Hugh withdrew his hand, and this time Bea heard a syllable of the oath he emitted as he jammed his hands in his pockets and walked off.

'Oh, there you are, Bea…I wondered where you had got to…'

It was too late to prevent Elise knowing the truth: Bea's prolonged absence had prompted her sister to nip out of the front parlour in search of her. With Adam cradled against a shoulder, obscuring her view, Elise hadn't at first noticed the gentleman by the door.

'Hugh!' Elise hurried towards him. 'What a lovely surprise to see you! Why have you not joined us in the parlour?' she burst out. Elise's sparkling gaze veered between the couple, lingered on Bea, wordlessly enquiring what had brought about this unexpected and exciting turn of events.

'Mr Kendrick has come here with important news for Alex.' Beatrice didn't want to worry Elise, but knew her sister would eventually discover the reason behind Hugh's visit. 'We expect he'll turn up soon, having stopped for a drink.'

'Alex didn't say he would come after me but I won't be surprised if he does.' Elise smiled contentedly. 'He's probably at the Red Lion. He doesn't like Papa to fiddle and fuss and spend his money on unnecessary comforts just so he might bed down here for a night or two.'

'Of course…that's where he is.' Beatrice sighed in relief. When Viscount Blackthorne had been courting her sister he would often lodge at the inn at St Albans.

Elise was swaying her drowsing son while frowning at Hugh. 'If you've come all this way it must be bad news. Please tell me what it is for I shall only fret if you do not. Has something awful happened in the few days I've been away?'

'I'm afraid that your mother-in-law has scarlatina.' Hugh comforted Elise with a sympathetic smile as one of her hands flew to cover her shocked gasp. 'The physician thinks she will recover well but at her age there is an obvious risk…' His voice tailed off. 'She has been asking to see Alex.'

'Of course…he must go immediately to her side. I should return too.' Elise was very fond of her mother-in-law and knew the woman doted on Alex, her only child.

'It has been wonderful to see you, but Papa will understand why you must cut short your visit.' Beatrice strove to remove Elise's worry over leaving so soon after arriving in Hertfordshire.

The doorknocker was again loudly employed at the same moment that Betty reappeared, shuffling towards them, bearing a tray laden with a silver tea set surrounded by some delicate bone china.

'If it's more nosey Parkers here to tattle they can come back another time,' the housekeeper stated with salty directness. 'We're right out of tea anyhow, till Norman gets back from town with the provisions.'

Being closest to the door, Hugh did the honours, opening it to find Alex on the step.

The viscount gave his chum a quizzical look while proceeding inside, but was prevented from asking the most obvious question. His wife hastily handed her precious burden to her sister, then launched herself at him to hug him about the waist in a show of welcome and comfort at the news she must soon break. Gently Elise urged her husband towards a small alcove by the stairs so they might quietly converse.

'What's it all about?' Walter demanded waspishly, emerging from the parlour and pulling the door shut behind him. 'You're not going to abandon me with those two, are you?'

Leaning heavily on his stick, he fished out his spectacles and put them on so he might get a closer look at what was occurring. He peered from one to the other of the people crowding his narrow hallway. 'Ah…capital! I see my son-in-law has dropped by to join us…why are they whispering?'

Walter didn't wait for a reply to his question about Elise and Alex huddling together a yard or so away. His attention had already moved on to a person he felt sure he recognised. When the fellow's identity popped into his mind his gaze narrowed angrily on Hugh Kendrick's tall, distinguished figure.

'Ha! I *do* know you! So you've heard, have you, and come to speak to my daughter and me? Well, Bea won't have you now, no matter how much money you've got from your diamonds. And neither will I. You had your chance years ago, so be off with you.'

In the ensuing silence Betty shuffled forward with the heavy tea tray, and never before had Bea felt quite so grateful for their housekeeper's peevishness.

'Is some kind person going to open the door?' The woman huffed out. 'My arms are giving out with the weight of this lot.' Betty rested a hip against the wall for support.

Courteously, Hugh unburdened the elderly servant, allowing her to enter the parlour. She gave him a wide smile when he carried the tray inside and put it down on the table, causing the two seated ladies to gawp admiringly at him. Hugh nodded politely before retracing his steps, leaving Betty behind the closed door setting the cups and Mrs Callan and Victoria frantically burbling in low voices.

'You may quit my house, sirrah.' Walter pointed his stick at Hugh. 'Beatrice, come into the parlour, do. I've exhausted every topic of conversation I can think of that avoids mentioning a fickle scoundrel upsetting my daughter.' Again his rheumy eyes settled accusingly on Hugh.

Walter beckoned to Elise and Alex, then disappeared inside the parlour, oblivious to his elder daughter's mortification or Hugh Kendrick's cynically amused expression.

'I'm sorry my father was so rude just then.' Beatrice's voice was hoarse with chagrin and she found she could not meet his eyes. She feared he'd understood her father's oblique reference to her having been jilted. Eventually it would all come out and Hugh Kendrick, along with other acquaintances who resided further afield, would discover Beatrice Dewey's wedding had been cancelled, but she didn't want his pity, or his questions, today.

'I've poured the tea if you want to go in and drink it before it goes cold,' Betty announced, still sounding tetchy as she closed the parlour door and stomped off down the corridor.

'Just take tea with us, Alex, before setting off to see your mother; Papa will like it if you do.' Elise tenderly removed her drowsing baby from Bea's embrace. She'd seen the wisdom in her husband's argument that he could travel faster alone to London. 'I can explain all about the dowager's illness to Papa when the ladies leave.'

Elise gave Hugh a look of heartfelt gratitude, then the preoccupied couple joined Walter in the parlour, leaving Beatrice behind and in two minds as to whether to follow them. But running off and letting Hugh Kendrick see himself out would be rude and cowardly. Beatrice hoped she was neither of those things. Today Hugh had acted as a true friend to her brother-in-law; the least he deserved in recompense was a little hospitality before setting again on the road.

'I'll go to the kitchen and get you some refreshment. You should have some tea at least…'

Hugh caught at her shoulder as she turned to go. 'Your father's churlishness doesn't bother me, but I'd like you to explain to me what caused it.'

Beatrice tipped up her chin, met his eyes squarely. 'I

have already told you that he has not forgotten or forgiven you for pursuing me when I was younger.' The
sensation of his long fingers again restraining her was
making her skin tingle and burn. She glanced signifi-
cantly at the tanned digits curved on rose-sprigged cotton. 'If you don't mind waiting in there I will fetch your
tea.' Beatrice indicated a door further along the hallway.

'Am I to be held in solitary confinement?'

Hugh sounded less amused now—haughty, even, Bea
realised as his fingers fractionally tightened on her before dropping away. But though her defences were rising
she knew he had a point. 'I admit it is unfair treatment,
sir, when you have performed a mission of mercy for
your friend. I beg you will tolerate my elderly father's
foibles. It is not just you he is set against; he is protective of his daughters and hostile to any person who
might have harmed us.'

'Is Dr Burnett such a person?' Hugh asked bluntly.

'I will explain to Papa how generously you have behaved when our visitors have gone.' Fearing he might
repeat his question about Colin's role in all this, Beatrice quickly took two backward steps before carrying
on towards the kitchen.

Chapter Five

'Who's the handsome stranger?' Betty asked in her forthright way, having assessed Beatrice's tortured expression. 'I've not seen him here before but I reckon he knows you…and rather well in my opinion.' She wiped her damp hands on her pinafore then plonked them on her ample hips.

Beatrice had closed the kitchen door and then her eyes while leaning against the panels, her head tilted up in an attempt to control her whirling thoughts. She pushed away from her support and with a sigh took a seat at the floury-topped table. 'He's a good friend of the viscount's,' she finally answered, picking up a warm biscuit from the dozen or so cooling on a rack. Beatrice loved a freshly baked treacle biscuit and usually would have taken a greedy bite and got a ticking off from Betty for not letting it set properly. But she put it back, unable to quell the queasiness in her stomach spoiling her appetite.

'So…this fellow is also a friend of yours, is he, Miss

Beatrice?' Betty crossed her arms over her chest, awaiting a reply.

'Once he was…or I thought as much. But I was
wrong about him as well.' Beatrice frowned at her fingers, clasped in front of her on the table. She'd banished
Colin from her mind and refused to mention his name.
'Would you put the kettle on, Betty? Mr Kendrick has
done the viscount a good turn by conveying news from
London. He deserves some tea before setting off home.'

The housekeeper gave Beatrice an old-fashioned
look. 'I'll do that for him, and I'll even bring him along
a few of those.' She tipped her head at the biscuits. 'No
matter what your father thinks of the fellow, I took to
him— 'cos he's a gentleman not too high and mighty
to give a hand to the likes of me.'

'He hasn't always been a wealthy man, so I expect
he is used to fetching and carrying for himself,' Beatrice murmured, almost to herself.

'Sometimes them that comes late to luxury are the
worst sort, with their penny-pinching and lording it.
They don't want to go back to scrimping and scraping,
and doffing caps, you see. He's not like that. I'd stake
my life on it.' Betty imparted her wisdom on the subject of upstarts.

Bea planted an elbow on the tabletop and sank her
sharp little chin into a palm. She couldn't agree with
Betty's estimation of Mr Kendrick's modesty. She'd
seen a very imperious glint in his eyes earlier that had
impressed upon her, almost as much as had his cool
tone of voice, that he was no longer the ordinary man
she'd once known…and loved.

'Off you go, then, and keep him company and I'll be along directly.' The housekeeper nodded at the door.

'I think I'd sooner stay here with you and wait till the tea's brewed.'

'I know you would,' Betty said. 'That's why I reckon you should go and sit with him and show him what you're made of.' She wagged a finger. 'You, Miss Beatrice, are not a coward. If I can tell he frightens you I reckon he already knows.'

'He does *not* frighten me!' Beatrice asserted, sitting straight in the chair and blinking at Betty.

'In that case you'll remember your manners and have a nice chat about the weather with him while the kettle boils,' Betty returned bossily. 'I'll be by in about ten minutes with a hot pot of tea and a plate of biscuits.' She turned away. 'But those two in the front parlour aren't getting any; Vicar's wife maybe, but not a charitable bone in her body by my reckoning. And the daughter's not much better.'

Betty glanced over her shoulder as she heard the chair scrape back. Her puckered features softened in a smile as she watched Beatrice marching towards the door, a determined set to her full mouth.

'Tea won't be long…do sit down, sir.'

Beatrice had entered the morning room to find Hugh standing by the unlit fire, contemplating the view through the window. His long fingers were drumming on the oak mantelpiece, making him seem impatient, and Bea wondered if he'd decide to leave without waiting for refreshment. The idea that he might depart before she'd proved to him her indifference to his arrival prompted her to burst out with some conversation.

'I hope that the dowager will soon recover. I have only met her once or twice but found her to be very nice,' Beatrice rattled off. She had decided to steer their chat in the direction of mutual concerns. In that way she might avoid his hard stares and lazy mockery. 'My father will be sad to hear that she's ailing. He also likes Alex's mother…'

'I'll attempt to find out how she managed to charm him,' Hugh remarked dryly. He strolled to an armchair and sat down.

Beatrice perched on a seat opposite, inwardly sighing that she'd suffered an early defeat. 'How are your family keeping, sir?' she asked brightly, recollecting that he had a younger married sister. 'Have you nephews or nieces?'

'One of each,' Hugh replied, sitting back and planting a dusty boot atop one knee. His fingers curled close to his mouth and he regarded her through dropped lashes. He knew she was anxious to avoid answering personal questions but, vulgar as his curiosity might be, he wanted to hear from her own lips that her wedding was off.

Elise's urgent summons to the countryside, taken together with Walter Dewey's recent bitter comments about scoundrels upsetting his daughters, pointed to the fact that Beatrice was not after all getting married. Hugh wanted her to tell him herself, because in that way he could judge her reaction and whether she had instigated the break-up with Dr Burnett.

'How old are your sister's children?' Beatrice doggedly continued, keeping an eye on the clock. Betty had said she would bring the tea in ten minutes; Bea was sure that five must already have passed. Yet the hands seemed to have crawled only fractionally about the face of the timepiece ticking on the wall.

'Luke is seven and Lucinda five.'

'Such nice names,' Beatrice remarked, on realising he wasn't about to add anything to the drawled information. Abruptly she got to her feet. 'I should open the door wider for Mrs Francis or she will struggle entering with the tray. Indeed...I should carry it for her...'

Bea had a plausible excuse to escape the strained atmosphere, but Betty's warning about acting cowardly rang in her ears, holding her on the spot. Today there'd been nothing in Hugh Kendrick's behaviour to which she might take serious offence. So far he'd been unfailingly civil... And yet she knew Betty had spoken the truth: she *was* fearful of him, and not simply because he might at any moment launch an unwanted question at her.

The fever on her flesh where his hands had been, the butterflies circling in her stomach, all were indications that she was not immune to this man, and she dearly wanted to be. It might be three years since they'd kissed and caressed one another but the memory of it was strengthening with every minute that passed. There was an unbearable tension between them and she knew he too was dwelling on that shared intimacy.

Never had Colin Burnett kissed her so hard and long that a vivid colour had stained her lips for hours. Never had he, during their long engagement, pulled open her bodice and drawn whimpers of delight from her when his mouth teased her breasts.

In a brief courtship Hugh Kendrick had done those things and more before it had all turned to ashes.

But he was different now, and she must be too. Behind the screen of his long lashes amusement was competing with lust in his hazel eyes. He might still desire her but he no doubt found his younger self—and hers—risible in hindsight. He now possessed riches… and power and influence. She could tell that from his every mannerism and utterance. He was no longer a man used to being denied what he wanted, whereas once everything…even she as his wife…had been out of his reach. Now, of course, he could pick and choose from society debutantes for a bride.

Well, she wouldn't want him as a husband now! Beatrice inwardly exhorted herself. Her papa was right: even had he raced here on hearing she was free, to beg her to accept his proposal, she'd not have him! He'd had his chance and could go away, back to his fine life, and leave her in peace. She had earlier said to her father and sister that she'd done with men and marriage and she'd meant it. The idea of living out her days as a spinster, doting on her nephew rather than her own offspring, was not a *vastly* depressing future.

She moistened her lips, feeling calmer and ready to force out a little more conversation. 'I shall no doubt hear Betty approaching.' Beatrice returned to her chair and sat down. 'There is no need to leave you alone again.'

'Thank you…'

Beatrice shot him a look, noting his ironic tone, but if he wanted to interrogate her, let him. She now felt prepared for any challenge he might throw down.

'The weather is cool for the time of the year.' Bea again broke the silence, irked that she was the one making all the effort to be sociable. 'Have you a little conversation about your journey?' she suggested with faux sweetness. 'For instance…did you drive here or come on horseback?' She again glanced at the snugly fitting dusty jacket encasing his broad shoulders. She imagined his valet would be horrified to see the state of it.

'Horseback; it seemed the quickest way to travel with urgent news.'

'And did it rain during the journey?' Beatrice asked, causing him to smile.

'Just a few spots…'

'Oh…well, I'm glad you kept dry at least.'

'I appreciate your concern.'

Again Beatrice flicked an acid look at him from beneath her lashes, then glanced at the clock. Fifteen minutes had passed. She hoped Betty was not deliberately hanging things out because she had taken to Hugh Kendrick and wanted him to stay a while…

'Do I make you nervous, Beatrice?'

Bea snapped her sapphire eyes to his watching gaze. 'Of course not! What makes you think that, sir?'

'I fear you are about to wrench apart that handkerchief.' He jerked a nod at the scrap of linen, taut between her rigid fingers.

She'd unconsciously been twisting it for minutes. Quickly she tossed aside the thing that had betrayed her.

'I should leave and let you get back to your guests.' Hugh stood up.

'No!' Beatrice jumped to her feet, instinctively stepping towards him. 'Please—' She broke off, unsure of what she had been about to say but realising that she honestly did not want him to go yet. 'I could not in all conscience allow you to journey home without something to drink. Would you prefer a glass of port? You have come a very long way with unpleasant tidings.'

'I believe you were already dealing with an unpleasant matter and I've made things worse.' He drove his hands into his pockets, tilting his head to watch her averted expression. 'Were you, Beatrice, dealing with a family crisis when I turned up?'

'No…' She swung a beautifully poised mien towards him. 'I am no longer marrying Dr Burnett, so there has been something for us, as a family, to discuss, but it's done now.' She fluttered a gesture. 'No crisis at all… far too strong a word for the situation…'

Hugh stared out of the large casement at the garden. 'The man's a damnable fool.'

Beatrice moistened her lips, mortified that from her casual explanation he'd easily deduced that she'd been jilted rather than the other way around.

He pivoted on a heel, gave a self-deprecating laugh. 'You seem unlucky enough to attract such types and I'm sure you don't deserve to, my dear.'

'You know nothing about me now. Please do not feel obliged to embroider your condolences.'

Beatrice realised it was high time to show him out before the annoying lump in her throat choked her. Why was she feeling close to tears because he'd said something nice about her and offered his sympathy?

Without asking if he would oblige, the housekeeper came in, holding out the tray for Hugh to carry to the table. She also gave him a smile and, Beatrice was sure, a wink. A moment later Betty had withdrawn, leaving a silence that was shattered within seconds by the clock chiming.

Beatrice busied herself pouring tea. 'Please be seated again, if you wish.' Suddenly voices in the hallway drew her attention. 'The vicar's wife and daughter are leaving...'

'I'm sorry I kept you from them,' Hugh murmured, choosing to prop himself against the mantelpiece rather than take a chair.

For the first time since he'd arrived they exchanged a proper smile.

'Please don't apologise, sir, for their company was no loss on my part, I assure you.' Bea put a cup of tea near the five bronzed fingers splayed on the mantelshelf.

'I'm certain your father and sister did sterling work on your behalf.'

'They are both protective of me and will see off the tattlers.' Beatrice sipped tea, placing down her cup with an unsteady hand that rattled together china. 'Mrs Callan and her daughter wished to let me know how shocked and sorry they are to hear I'm to remain a spinster, so are bound to be disappointed to have lost my company after just a few minutes. But I would not have our neighbours…or anybody for that matter…think that I am hiding away, embarrassed and heartbroken, so must go over to the vicarage later in the week to allow their sympathy full rein.'

Hugh smiled. 'And are you? Heartbroken, I mean? You're too fine to allow that dolt Burnett to embarrass you…'

'Why bother asking how I feel now? You didn't care before!' Bea cried, before sinking her small teeth in her lower lip to stem the list of accusations ready to be launched at him. Abruptly she turned and snatched up the plate of treacle biscuits, bitterly regretting that she'd let her suppressed anger at *his* defection, rather than Colin's, simmer and boil over. 'Please, have a biscuit. Betty would like you to…' She slid the plate next to his untasted tea on the oak mantel.

'Of course I damn well cared!' Hugh gritted out, curving his fingers over her forearm to keep her close when she would have swished away. 'Did you believe me that callous?'

Bea prised away his fingers from her body, flinging him off when he would have kept her hand imprisoned in his. But there was a smile pinned to her lips when she said, 'I'm sorry, sir…please think nothing more of it. I'm just a little on edge after recent events or would not have spoken so.'

She made a concerted effort to still her madly drumming heart. She would not allow him, or any man, to make her act like a hysterical harpy. She had, just an hour or two ago, felt relatively at peace with the prospect of returning to her life as a spinster and living at home with her father. Now, since Hugh Kendrick's arrival, old yearnings and emotions that she'd thought she'd successfully conquered were again pricking at her mind, making her feel restless.

'I must not keep you any longer,' she blurted. 'I expect you will want to speak to Alex before he heads off to see his mother...'

A skewed smile was Hugh's reaction to being summarily dismissed. 'Perhaps I should not have made my presence known to your guests earlier,' he said quietly. 'Will our absence from the parlour have given rise to more speculation and added to your troubles?'

Bea had been occupying her nervous fingers by shifting crockery to and fro on the tray. Now she turned about with a frown. 'I admit I had not thought of that...' *And I should have.* The phrase rotated slowly in her mind. She'd concentrated on the Callans being absorbed by her jilting, but of course they'd also be intrigued to have the details of what had kept Miss Dewey and Mr Kendrick elsewhere in the house during their visit. Mrs Callan was renowned for an ability to craft a salacious rumour from little other than her own imagination...

'Your family are sure to have explained the situation,' Hugh reassured her. 'It would indeed be a travesty if you were to be the subject of conjecture because of me when nothing at all exists between us...does it?'

'Nothing at all,' Bea fervently endorsed. 'And, as you say, my sister and father would have made that quite clear when explaining that I was attending to your needs...your hospitality,' she quickly amended, managing a fleeting smile despite his amused expression acknowledging her infelicity. 'Besides, in a short while people will no longer be interested in me but chasing new and more interesting tales.'

Unfortunately Beatrice knew that was not strictly true in this neck of the woods: London might boast fresh scandals every week, but in the sticks it might be six months or more before the old biddies found something as entertaining as Beatrice Dewey's being jilted to chew over at their afternoon get-togethers. They'd also be intrigued to know that soon after the cancellation of her wedding to Dr Burnett she'd been having a private talk with a handsome stranger.

Bea raised a hand to her throbbing brow, realising she was not quite as indifferent to cruel gossip as she'd believed herself to be. If a rumour started, and travelled to London, that shortly after being jilted she'd tried to charm Hugh Kendrick, she'd be mortified…especially if he got to hear of it…

'I'm setting off in a moment. Do you fancy a lift back to town? You can tether your mount to the curricle.' Alex had given a cough to herald his arrival before fully entering the morning room and addressing his friend. Behind him came his wife, using a knuckle between Adam's soft lips to pacify him.

'He is hungry, and wet too. I shall take him upstairs.' Elise gazed into her husband's face. 'Promise you will come and say goodbye before leaving.'

Alex cupped his wife's cheek with a loving hand. It was answer enough for Elise and she went off, content.

'So…you are still here, Mr Kendrick.' Walter limped into the room. 'I believe I mistook the reason for your arrival, sir. I've learned you have done my son-in-law a good deed and for that I'm grateful.'

Hugh bowed, accepting the oblique apology for his host's earlier brusqueness.

'Drink your tea, then, and stay to dine if you wish. I can see that Beatrice has been keeping you company and holds no argument with you. So I cannot either, I suppose,' Walter grumpily concluded.

'Thank you, but I am setting on the road again.' Hugh graciously declined Walter's off-hand invitation.

Walter shrugged and ambled off towards his study.

'I shall also take my leave,' Beatrice said. 'I wish you both a safe journey, and please give the dowager my best wishes for a speedy recovery.'

Her brother-in-law received a spontaneous hug, Hugh a formal bob. A moment later she was slipping from the room, only fleetingly hesitating at the door to discover if Hugh was watching her.

He was. And it hadn't gone unnoticed by Alex either.

'Don't even *think* of a dalliance there, or you'll have me to answer to this time, not her father.'

Hugh dispassionately met his friend's steady gaze. 'I get the distinct impression that Miss Dewey finds it difficult to tolerate my company. There'll be no repeat of what went on, trust me.' He hesitated, then strolled to the window. 'Does she know about my life in India?'

'I've not had reason to tell my wife all of it, so I doubt Bea knows much at all other than that you're now rich from your Indian mines. Neither, I hope, is she interested in any of it.'

Hugh nodded slowly, lips thinning in a grim smile.

'Are you thinking of cutting off your ties abroad?'

Hugh's sharp glance answered Alex before he heard his friend's reply. 'My ties in India are permanent and non-negotiable.'

'That's what I thought...' Alex said deceptively mildly. 'So I repeat...stay away from my sister-in-law or suffer the consequences...'

A moment later it was as though no tense exchange had taken place between them.

Alex said, 'I want to get going. Norman Francis will bring your horse round from the stable and we can be on the road in ten minutes...'

Chapter Six

'Why don't you come with me to London?'

While speaking Elise continued folding a lawn petticoat, then packed it away in readiness for departure later that morning. Her maid was attending to the baby's things, neatly piling them alongside her mistress's garments in the travelling trunk.

When Beatrice continued cooing at Adam, Elise renewed her effort to persuade her sister to have a sojourn in town. 'You'll enjoy the shops in Oxford Street and I'll introduce you to some nice people.' She waved aside Bea's dubious frown. 'There are some nice ladies, I swear. In fact I'd say some of the matrons in this neighbourhood are worse tattlers…'

'I can't think who you might mean,' Beatrice replied drolly.

'In any case it is high time you said hello to the Chapmans. Verity would love to see you. She'll tell you all about the babe she is expecting…' Elise bit her lip, realising it was insensitive to enthuse over another woman's marital bliss to a dear sister who had recently been jilted. 'Fiona is naturally still at home with Mr and Mrs Chapman, and I'm sure she'd adore having your company.'

'There's no need to fuss over me, Elise.' Beatrice raised her eyes from the baby's rosy face to give her sister a serene smile. 'I'm better now, honestly, and will bear up here with Papa.' She held the baby aloft, rolling him to and fro and making him giggle. 'The shock of it all has been short lived, I assure you. Isn't that so, Master Adam?'

'The shock of what, exactly?' Elise quipped. 'Seeing Hugh Kendrick or losing your fiancé?'

'I no longer think of Colin as a loss but as a hazard I avoided.' Bea got up from the clothes-strewn bed where she'd played with her nephew and handed him to his nurse. Helpfully, she started to assist her sister with packing. She felt her profile growing warm beneath Elise's determined stare. 'Oh, all right, I admit Mr Kendrick's appearance did shake me up a bit. But I'm over that too.'

'I wasn't hinting that you should come with me so you might see Hugh again,' Elise fibbed. She had seen the way the couple had reacted to one another yesterday and it had stirred in her an idea that they might still harbour feelings for one another. Hugh had not taken his eyes off her sister and Bea had certainly not seemed indifferent to him in the way a woman should if an old flame—now completely forgotten—turned up out of the blue.

Following his upturn in fortune Hugh was highly sought after by top hostesses and fond mamas with

debutantes to settle, but Elise knew he wasn't courting
any well-bred young lady. Of course she heard the gossip, like everybody else, and knew he associated with
female company of a very different class. Although
Elise liked Hugh, he was an unashamed philanderer,
and that fact dampened her enthusiasm for Beatrice
again falling for him. The last thing Elise wanted was
for her beloved sister to again have her dreams shattered by a man.

'I suppose I ought to tell you that Hugh is known as
an incorrigible rake who keeps company with demi-
reps. I have to admit, though, that Alex's reputation
was vastly embellished upon by excitable ladies before
we were wed.' Elise smiled wryly; she'd not forgotten
how jealous she'd felt, hearing about Alex's paramours.

'Thank you for the warning,' Bea said mildly. 'I'm
not surprised to know it; he seems very different now
from the man I once knew. Anyhow, his sordid habits
and so on are of no interest to me. I don't care how he
spends his time.'

Elise gave her sister an old-fashioned look. 'You
might have sounded a little more convincing, my dear.'

Beatrice raised her eyes heavenward, miming exasperation, making her sister chuckle.

'Papa won't mind at all if you stay in town with me
for a week or two. Mr and Mrs Francis attend to all his
needs—'

'No…' Beatrice interrupted, giving her sister a winning smile. 'But thank you for the invitation.' She knew
what Elise was up to: finding her a replacement for
Colin. Although Bea was swayed by an offer to visit

dear friends in the metropolis, the idea that Hugh Kendrick might believe she'd followed him home to put herself in his way was terrifying enough to quash the temptation to accept.

Elise huffed in defeat. 'I don't know what you are afraid of. I have told you that Papa and I fielded every question that Mrs Callan batted over about your association with Hugh. I made a point of letting them know he had courted our friend Fiona Chapman to put them off the scent.'

'And I do thank you for it. But I am not afraid, Elise, of gossip or of Hugh Kendrick.' Bea knew that was not quite truthful and hastened on. 'So, I will remain here, quite content, though I pray your mother-in-law will recover.' Bea looked reflective. 'She was very kind to us at your wedding reception and made sure Papa and I had servants dancing attendance on us. She introduced us to so many people, and Papa was glad to renew his acquaintance with her that day. He told me he had liked her late husband too.'

'Susannah is a dear soul…' Elise frowned, folding linen with renewed vigour. 'I must quickly get back and visit her. I'm sure the doctor is right, though, and she's already on the mend.'

Beatrice comforted her sister with a hug. 'She will be fine, Elise. The dowager will be up and about again in no time…'

'I should like to attend.'

'Are you feeling up to the journey, Papa?' Beatrice asked in concern.

The post had arrived just ten minutes ago. Alex's bold black script had been on one of many letters Bea, with heavy heart, had brought to her father's study. Walter had opened it at once. There had been a note for her too, from Elise, but Beatrice had slipped that into the pocket of her skirt and would read it later.

The other letters, she surmised, were replies from the guests who'd been informed by her father last week that the wedding would not be taking place. She recognised Mr Chapman's hand, and also that of her Aunt Dolly on two of the five sealed parchments. Bea felt sure all would contain messages of sympathy and encouragement for her, but she didn't yet want to know about any of it.

Neither did Walter, it seemed. Bea's father left untouched the pile of post and continued sighing and polishing his glasses with his handkerchief.

'Are you sure the journey will not excessively tire you?' Beatrice rephrased her question in an attempt to draw her father's attention.

'I will bear a few discomforts to pay my respects to Susannah Blackthorne.' Walter dabbed a handkerchief at his watering eyes. He put his glasses on, then held up Alex's letter so he might again scan the sad news that his son-in-law's mother had passed away. The funeral was to be held in a few days' time and Alex had offered to send his coach for Walter and Beatrice so they might join the mourners at Blackthorne Hall. He had added that he hoped very much they would attend as his mother had enquired after the two of them only recently.

'You will come as well, my dear, won't you? I should not like to travel alone.' Walter raised hopeful eyes to his daughter.

'Of course I shall come with you, Papa!' Beatrice replied. 'I would not want to miss it.'

Walter nodded, content. 'I shall write a reply and get Norman to quickly despatch it to Berkshire. I don't like imposing on the viscount's generosity but we must accept the use of his transport.'

'Alex will be cross if you do not! I expect he and Elise are feeling very low and will be glad to see us as soon as maybe.'

'As a family we lately seem to be in the doldrums more often than not.' Walter dropped the letter to the desk, drawing forward his quill and a plain parchment. 'Susannah was a very vivacious woman...and more than ten years my junior.' He dipped the pen into ink. 'I'm getting quite ancient now...'

'Don't be so maudlin, Papa!' Beatrice dropped a light kiss on the top of her father's sparsely covered crown. 'You are a mere spring chicken.'

She could tell he was feeling quite depressed at the news of the dowager's death. Bea had noticed that as he aged her father acted increasingly sentimental when hearing about sad or happy events.

As Walter's quill began scratching on paper she turned for the door, informing him, 'I'll start to pack a few things.'

Beatrice took down her carpetbag from the top of the clothes press. She blew dust off it and set it on her bed's coverlet. It seemed she would be taking a trip to stay with her sister after all, but glumly wished something nicer had prompted it.

As the viscount's well-sprung travelling coach bounced over a rut the letter in Bea's hand fluttered from her fingers to the hide seat. She retrieved it and recommenced reading. It had arrived that morning, before she and her papa had set on the road for Berkshire, and had been sent by Fiona Chapman. Bea had known the identity of the sender as soon as she spied her name written in elegant sloping script. But it had only been moments ago when her papa, seated opposite, ceased chattering and started dozing that she'd drawn her friend's note from her reticule and unsealed it.

As expected, the message bore very kind and sincere wishes to boost her morale following her jilting. Bea had already received fulsome sympathy from Aunt Dolly and Fiona's father. Walter had shown to her the letter from Mr Chapman and Bea had had to smile at Anthony's robust defence of her reputation. In his honest opinion Walter's daughter was too good for the physician in any case, and the whole matter was a blessing in disguise for Beatrice. Anthony had emphasised that observation with a very large and forceful exclamation mark that had punctured the paper.

'My sentiments exactly,' Walter had barked, perking up on reading it. Then he'd promptly helped himself to port from the decanter on the edge of his desk.

But now, as Beatrice's blue gaze landed on the final paragraph of Fiona's letter, she gasped at the startling news it contained. Mr Kendrick, Fiona wrote, had put a flea in Colin Burnett's ear over vulgarly flaunting his new fiancée before anybody in town had been given the news that he'd jilted his former bride-to-be. Bea's eyes sped on over the paper. The clash had taken place at her sister Verity's home, Fiona informed her, and Mr Kendrick had threatened, *very discreetly*—Fiona had underlined those two words—to throw the doctor out if he didn't go before people started asking awkward questions. Colin had bowed to Mr Kendrick's dictate and slunk off with his tail between his legs, Fiona penned in conclusion, before signing off with affection and good wishes.

Beatrice felt her heart thudding in consternation and her cheeks glowing despite the breeze from the window. The last thing she'd wanted was any fuss about the affair, because it would be sure to give an impression that she was bitter and jealous over it all. And whereas for a short while those emotions *had* overtaken her, they had now faded away. Or so she'd thought…

Beatrice slowly reread that ultimate paragraph. She *was* irked that Colin could treat her so shabbily when less than a month ago he'd said it was her he loved and would marry if only he could. She pondered then on Stella, and whether the girl was pretty, and if Colin had quickly fallen in love with her.

In which case, Beatrice impatiently scolded herself, *he is the most dishonest and fickle man alive and you should pray you never again are foolish enough to be taken in by his like.*

Having mentally shaken herself, she turned her thoughts to Hugh Kendrick. So he had championed her, had he? She wondered why that was. Their recent meeting had been frosty, if civil. She stared through the coach window and twisted a smile at the passing scenery. Perhaps the aim of his gallant intervention had been to impress Fiona. Beatrice recalled that he had courted her friend a few years ago; perhaps Mr Kendrick was of a mind to do so once more as they were both still single and Fiona was a minor heiress. At her sister's wedding reception Hugh had partnered Fiona in the ballroom and Bea recalled thinking they had looked happy together...

Bea folded the note without again looking at it, putting it back into her reticule, then rested her head against the squabs. Behind her drooping lids two couples were dancing and laughing. The gentlemen had both once professed to want her as a wife. Beatrice huffed a sigh, wishing for a nap to overcome her so she might have a respite from her irritating fantasies.

Wearily she again watched the verdant landscape flashing past, but the same thoughts were haunting her mind. Colin and Stella would be the first to get married: no long engagement for him this time, as he now had enough money to set up home immediately. If Hugh Kendrick were intending to propose to Fiona, and her friend were to accept him, Bea would make sure she was one of the first to send congratulations...

'You are sighing louder than the wind outside.' Walter had one eye open and was watching his daughter's restless movements from beneath a thick wiry brow.

'It is rather gusty...' Bea pulled the blind across the window to protect the coach interior from draughts.

'Have you read your letter?'

'Mmm…' Bea guessed her father was keen to hear what was in it.

'I have lately shared my missives from London with you,' Walter wheedled, giving her a twinkling smile.

Beatrice smiled, swayed by his mischievous manner. 'Oh, very well… Fiona Chapman has written to me more or less echoing her father's thoughts on Dr Burnett.'

'Oh…is that it? No other news?' Walter queried. He'd watched his daughter from between his sparse lashes while she'd been reading and had been sure he'd heard a muted cry of dismay. Not wanting to immediately pry, he'd waited till she seemed more herself before letting her know he was awake.

Walter had felt very protective of Beatrice since the doctor had broken her heart. The more she put a brave face on it, the more he desperately wanted to make it all come right for her. He'd guessed the cause of her distress was reading about some antic of Burnett's reported in her letter.

'I've just had news that Colin turned up at Verity's house, but it was made clear he was unwelcome, so he left.'

Walter struggled to sit upright. 'Did he, by Jove?' Gleefully he banged his cane on the floor of the coach, grunting a laugh.

Bea nodded, suppressing a smile at her father's delight on hearing about her erstwhile fiancé's humiliation. 'Miss Rawlings was there too.'

Walter thumped the cane again, in anger this time. 'How dare he treat you like that? Damned impertinence he's got, squiring another woman so soon. I've a mind to bring it to his notice.'

'I believe Mr Kendrick has beaten you to it, Papa…'

'So it was that fellow, was it?' Walter nodded. 'That's twice he's done us a favour in a short space of time. Hugh Kendrick has just gone up considerably in my estimation. I suppose I must find an opportunity to tell him so.' He grimaced, remembering how rude he'd recently been to Hugh.

Beatrice settled back into the seat, niggling anxieties again assailing her. Just how much of a good deed had Mr Kendrick done her? She feared that embarrassing rumours about the jilting might even now be circulating, and would only be worsened by talk of two gentlemen— both past loves of hers—arguing in public over her.

Chapter Seven

'Alex seems to be bearing up well.'

'Oh, he is a stoic soul and keeps busy all the time to take his mind off things.' Elise met her sister's eyes in the mirror. 'But I believe at a time like this he misses having brothers or sisters to talk to.'

Beatrice was seated on her sister's high four-poster bed, watching the maid put the finishing touches to Elise's coiffure. At breakfast that morning Alex had seemed very composed, despite it being the day of his beloved mother's funeral. It was the late dowager's daughter-in-law who was having difficulty turning off the waterworks.

As Elise stood up from the dressing stool, pulling on her black gloves, Beatrice relinquished her soft perch and embraced her sniffling sister. 'Alex has you to comfort him, my dear…and I'll wager he's told you already that's enough family for him.'

Elise nodded, wiping her eyes. 'Susannah wouldn't want any wailing; she said so before falling into a deep sleep. Of course she knew the end was near, but she slipped away peacefully.' Elise suddenly crushed Bea in a hug. 'Thank you for coming.'

'Did you honestly think I would not?' Beatrice asked gently.

Elise shook her head. 'I knew you would not let me down.'

'You have never let *me* down, have you?' Bea stated truthfully, remembering a time when Elise had been unstintingly loyal. Elise, though exasperated with her, had continued risking censure despite Bea's shockingly selfish and daft actions. To her shame, Bea knew her behaviour had been at its worst during her infatuation with Hugh Kendrick. She'd made quite a fool of herself over him, much to Elise's dismay. But today Bea was determined to banish thoughts of her own upset from her head. And that was not an easy task as Elise had let on that Hugh Kendrick was due to attend the funeral if he could escape his commitments in London.

'Come…dry your eyes again,' Bea prompted gently. 'If we are to visit the nursery before we go downstairs Adam will not want to see his mama blubbing.'

Having left the darling baby in the care of his nurse, the ladies joined the other mourners. A hum of conversation, interspersed by muted laughter, met the sisters on entering the Blackthornes' vast drawing room. It was crowded with people and Beatrice was glad that the atmosphere seemed relaxed despite the sombre occasion. They headed towards their papa, who was standing by the wide, open fire. Walter was alternately warming his palms on his hot toddy and on the leaping flames in the grate. It was mid-May, but the weather was cool for the time of the year.

'I hope the showers hold off,' Alex said, turning from his father-in-law to greet his wife and sister-in-law.

Elise slipped a hand to her husband's arm, giving it an encouraging squeeze.

'Are you warm enough, Papa?' Bea asked. 'Would you like a chair brought closer to the fire so you may be seated?'

'I'm doing very well just where I am, thank you, my dear. My old pins and my stick will keep me upright for a while longer.'

'You must sit by me in the coach when we follow the hearse to the chapel—' Elise broke off to exclaim, 'Ah, good! Hugh has arrived; he's left it to the last minute, though.'

Beatrice felt her stomach lurch despite the fact she had discreetly been scouring the room for a sight of him from the moment she'd entered it. Casually she glanced at the doorway and felt the tension within increase. He looked very distinguished in his impeccably tailored black clothes, and she noticed that several people had turned to acknowledge his arrival.

'Has it started to rain?'

Alex had noticed the glistening mist on his friend's sleeve as Hugh approached.

'It's only light drizzle, and the sun's trying to break through the clouds.'

Hugh's bow encompassed them all, but Bea felt his eyes lingering on her so gave him a short sharp smile.

'Come, my dear...' Alex turned to Elise, having noticed a servant discreetly signalling to him. 'The carriages are ready and it's time we were off.'

The couple moved ahead and Beatrice took her father's arm to assist him. Hugh fell into a slow step beside them, remaining quiet as they filed out into the hallway.

'You must get in the coach with Elise, Papa.'

'And you will come too?' Walter fretted.

'If there is sufficient room I will; but you must ride with Elise in any case.'

Beatrice was used to walking. Living in the country, she often rambled many miles in one day, especially in the summer. She walked to the vicarage to take tea with Mrs Callan and her daughter when no immediate excuse to refuse their invitation sprang to mind. She'd also hiked the four miles into St Albans when the little trap they owned for such outings had had a broken axle and no soul passed by in a cart and offered her a lift. A march to the chapel at Blackthorne Hall was an easy distance to cover for someone of her age and stamina. But her father would struggle to keep his footing on the uneven, uphill ground.

Bea glanced at the people in the hallway; many looked to be decades her senior. From glistening eyes and use of hankies she guessed that Susannah had been truly liked by her friends, neighbours and servants.

'I've no need of a ride, Alex,' Bea whispered, nodding at some elderly ladies close by, dabbing at their eyes. 'There are others more deserving.' She stepped outside onto the mellow flags of a flight of steps that cascaded between stone pillars down to an expanse of gravel. At least half a dozen assorted crested vehicles were lined up in a semi-circle, ready for use. The glossy-flanked grey and ebony horses appeared impeccably behaved as they tossed regal black-plumed heads.

Beatrice noticed that a column of mourners was snaking towards the chapel. Pulling her silk cloak about her, she started off too, at the tail-end of it.

'The sun seems reluctant to escape the clouds.'

Beatrice's spine tingled at the sound of that familiar baritone. Hugh Kendrick was several yards behind but had obviously addressed her as no other person was within earshot. He seemed to be casually strolling in her wake, yet with no obvious effort he had quickly caught her up and fallen into step at her side.

'It is an unwritten law that funerals and weddings must have more than a fair share of bad weather.' Bea's light comment was given while gazing at a mountain of threatening grey nimbus on the horizon. To avoid his steady gaze she then turned her attention to the rolling parkland of Blackthorne Hall that stretched as far as the eye could see. The green of the grass had adopted a dull metallic hue beneath the lowering atmosphere.

'Were you preparing for showers on your own wedding day?'

Beatrice was surprised that he'd mentioned that. A quick glance at his eyes reassured her that he hadn't spoken from malice. She guessed he wanted to air the matter because, if ignored, it might wedge itself awkwardly between them. She was hopeful he shared her view that any hostilities between them should be under truce today.

'I was banking on a fine day in June, but one never knows…and now it is all academic in any case.'

A breeze whipped golden tendrils of hair across her forehead and she drew her cloak closely about herself. She scoured her mind for a different topic of conversation but didn't feel determined to rid herself of his company.

'It seems the dowager was liked and respected by a great many people. My father has sung her sincere praises and those of her late husband.'

'They were nice people. The late Lady Blackthorne was always kind and friendly to me. I was made to feel at home when I spent school holidays with Alex here at the Hall.'

Bea smiled. 'You have known each other a long time?'

'More than twenty years.'

'I expect you were a couple of young scamps.'

'Indeed we were…' Hugh chuckled in private reminiscence, then sensed Bea's questioning eyes on him. 'Please don't ask me to elaborate.'

'Well, sir, now you've hinted at your wickedness I feel I must press for more details.' A teasing blue glance peeked at his lean, tanned profile.

'Just the usual boyish antics…climbing trees, catching frogs and tadpoles, building camp fires that rage out of control,' Hugh admitted with a hint of drollery.

'A fire…out of control?' Beatrice echoed with scandalised interest.

'It was a dry summer…' Hugh's inflection implied that the drought mitigated the disaster. 'Luckily for us the old viscount remained reasonably restrained when learning that his son and heir together with his best friend had burned down a newly planted copse of oak saplings while frying eggs for their supper.'

Beatrice choked a horrified laugh. 'Thank goodness neither of you were injured.'

'I burned myself trying to put the fire out…' Hugh flexed long-fingered hands.

Bea had never before noticed, or felt when he'd caressed her, that area of puckered skin on one of his palms. She recalled his touch had always been blissfully tender. Quickly she shoved the disturbing memory far back in her mind before he became puzzled as to what he might have said or done to make her blush.

'It was quite an inferno,' Hugh admitted. 'It frightened the life out of the viscountess; she made Alex and me amuse ourselves indoors for the rest of the holiday. We rolled marbles with bandaged hands till we were sick of the sight of them. Even when the physician told us we were fit to be let out we were kept confined to barracks. But I wasn't sent home in well-deserved disgrace.' His boyish expression became grave. 'I could give you many other instances of Susannah's kindness and tolerance.'

Beatrice realised that Hugh was as moved by Susannah's passing as had been the weeping ladies in the Blackthornes' hallway. But of course he would not show the extent of his feelings: once, when a personable chap rather than a diamond magnate, he might have been less inclined to conceal his sadness behind a suave mask. Quietly she mulled over the theory of whether gentlemen felt it was incumbent on them to foster an air of detachment as they became richer.

'And what mischief did you get up to in your youth, Miss Dewey?'

Bea glanced up with an impish smile. 'Young ladies are never naughty,' she lectured, before tearing her eyes free of his wolfish mockery.

'I seem to recall a time, Beatrice, when you were very naughty indeed…'

'Then I advise you to forget it, sir, as it is now of no consequence,' she snapped. She tilted her chin and strode on, but no matter how energetic her attempt to outpace him he loped casually right at her side.

'But you don't deny it happened?' he provoked her.

'I have nothing to say on the subject other than you are very ill-mannered to bring it up.'

'My apologies for upsetting you…'

He'd spoken in a drawling voice that made Bea's back teeth grind together. 'You have not done so,' she replied, in so brittle a tone that it immediately proved her answer a lie.

'Of course we were talking about childhood. I alluded to a time when you were most certainly a woman, and I admit it was not fair to do so.'

Bea said nothing, despite his throaty answer having twisted a knot in her stomach. She again contemplated the countryside, presenting him with her haughtily tilted profile.

'So, did you enjoy your schooldays? How did you spend them, Beatrice?' His tone had become less challenging, as though he regretted having embarrassed her by hinting at her wanton behaviour with him.

'When we lived in London Elise and I were schooled at home by Miss Dawkins,' Bea responded coolly. A moment later she realised it was childish to remain huffy. He'd spoken the truth, after all, even if it was unpalatable. 'I was almost fifteen when we moved to Hertfordshire, so there was little time left to polish me up. Papa did engage a governess for Elise, and the poor woman did her best to prepare me for my looming debut.' An amusing recollection made her lips quirk. 'She despaired of my singing and piano-playing and told Papa he had wasted his money buying an instrument that neither of his daughters would ever master.'

'What did Walter say to that?' Hugh asked, laughter in his voice.

'I cannot recall, but I expect he was disappointed to have squandered the cash; we were quite hard up by then—' Beatrice broke off, regretting mentioning her father's financial struggle. Hugh, in common with many others, would know that her parents had divorced amidst a scandal that had impoverished Walter Dewey. It had been a terrible time for them all and she didn't intend to now pick at the painful memory.

'I expect you missed your mother's guidance during your come-out.'

Hugh abhorred hypocrisy so avoided judging others' morality. He was no paragon and had had illicit liaisons with other men's wives, although neither of his current mistresses was married. He therefore found it hard to understand why Arabella Dewey had left her husband

and children. In polite society the customary way of things was to seek discreet diversion when bored with one's spouse. But it seemed Arabella hadn't been able to abide Walter's company. Hugh found that rather sad, as he sensed the fellow was basically a good sort and the couple had produced two beautiful girls.

Arabella had passed on years ago, when still in her prime, but not before she'd scandalised the *ton* by abandoning her husband and teenage daughters to run off and live with her lover.

'Aunt Dolly did her level best to take me under her wing and turn me into a sweet debutante,' Bea finally answered, having reminisced on that dear lady's efforts to obtain invitations to top social functions so she might attract a suitor.

'Thank goodness she failed,' Hugh muttered. He put up his hands in mock defence as Bea glowered at him. 'It's a compliment, I swear. In my experience debutantes tend to be vapid creatures.'

'I'm surprised you know any well enough to be able to judge.' Unfortunately Bea's sarcasm had not been spoken quietly enough.

'What do you mean by that, Beatrice?'

What *did* she mean by that? Beatrice thought frantically. She'd rather not let him know that Elise had told her he was a notorious rake.

Ignoring his question, and his scorching stare, she chattered on. 'My father paid handsomely to get us vouchers for Almack's that year, but it wasn't a successful season for me.' She stopped short of elaborating on her failure: some hostesses had spitefully shunned them because the gossip over her parents' divorce was still doing the rounds.

'What did you mean by your comment?' Hugh demanded, undeterred. His firm fingers circled her wrist, turning her towards him. 'Why would I not know such young ladies?'

Beatrice shook him off, then set on her way again. 'I know you liked Fiona Chapman, but she is rather too old to be called a deb.' She was thankful that excuse had popped into her head. Moments later she regretted having drawn her friend into it; in mentioning Fiona's age she'd sounded bitchy and jealous. Besides, Fiona was only a year her senior...

'I still like Miss Chapman very much,' Hugh said levelly.

'And so do I like her very much. Actually, I had a letter from her just days ago,' Beatrice blurted in emphasis.

She sensed the same quickening of her heart as she had on first absorbing the disturbing fact that Hugh and Colin had argued about her in public.

'Did the letter have good news for you?' Hugh asked. He'd immediately guessed what information Fiona might have passed on.

'I think you probably know the answer to that.' Beatrice twisted towards him, eyes blazing accusingly. She was tempted to give him a piece of her mind about risking her reputation in such a way, but the lych gate was now in view and beyond it, standing by some ancient leaning headstones, was her father, supported by his stick. He raised a bony hand, signalling to her to come to him, just as Elise also gave her a wave. With a curt dip for Hugh she sped ahead to join her family, filing into the chapel.

Chapter Eight

'I suppose I must speak to the fellow,' Walter grumpily announced.

Beatrice removed her father's port from his fingers, setting it on the table before he spilled it down his front.

They were sitting side by side on a small fireside sofa and had been observing the company attending the wake. Alex and Elise were the perfect hosts, moving through the room talking to the mourners. From elderly estate servants, now retired, to the Duke of Rodley, who'd arrived on horseback from the next town with two bottles of best cognac strapped to his saddle, all were being graciously thanked for their kind messages and tributes.

'Would you like me to fetch you some pastries from the buffet, Papa?' Beatrice had noticed her father again reaching for his depleted glass of port. He was drinking too much, as was his wont. Over the years Walter's daughters had had to ask their manservant to take their father to bed when he'd been unable to rouse himself due to over-imbibing.

'Another fruit tart might be sufficient, my dear. I have room for just one.' As his daughter rose from the sofa, he added, 'And will you bring the fellow over to me so I might talk to him before he leaves?'

'Do you know that he's soon leaving?' Bea asked, glancing at Hugh's dark figure surrounded by some jolly people.

'The viscount told me his friend Kendrick intends returning to town today. I imagine he will not set on the road after dark…not in this weather.'

Walter turned to the dismal grey afternoon beyond the enormous casements. The fire to one side of them had been hissing and spluttering as the driving rain dampened the apple-scented logs. After the funeral service they had been lucky to return to the Hall before the worst of the rain set in.

'Will you fetch him over?' Walter nagged. 'I'd sooner not struggle up out of this chair to go to him and eat humble pie with strangers present.' Walter sighed. 'Yet it must be done. My conscience will not allow it to be otherwise.'

Hugh's group were loudly toasting Susannah's life. Alex's mother had left strict instructions that she wanted no maudlin speeches at her wake but a thanksgiving for the blessing of a wonderful life shared with an adored husband and beloved son.

Moving gracefully through the throng towards the dining room, Bea angled her head in an attempt to drag Hugh's attention from his lively companions. He now seemed oblivious to her presence, and yet before, when walking to the chapel with him, it had been impossible to escape his taunting amber gaze. She'd no intention of approaching him to loiter meekly at his shoulder, waiting for an opportunity to interrupt.

On passing over the threshold into the dining room she glanced over her shoulder, and her heartbeat quickened as his eyes clashed on hers. She felt a burst of elation that had nothing to do with being a step closer to carrying out her father's task. She'd experienced similar excitement years ago, when she'd easily lured his attention every time she quit or entered a room.

Turning her head, Bea carried on towards the buffet table—but not before she'd noticed him concealing his private smile with a sliding forefinger.

He'd made no move to leave the group and Bea fumed. If her wordless plea for an audience wasn't plain enough for him to act on he could forgo having her father's apology and her farewell before he left for London!

'Are you still hungry, Beatrice?' Hugh's eyes skimmed over her slender figure swathed in black silk. 'You certainly look as though a little more sustenance might benefit you.'

'You...you think I am too thin?' Beatrice stammered. His comment had irked, and his swift approach had startled her. Her gaze dropped to the intricate folds of his cravat, pinned with a sizeable diamond. Sourly she wondered whether he'd dug it up himself.

'You seem less...buxom than I remember.'

Bea's soft lips parted in a mixture of astonishment and indignation. She'd never realised he'd thought her fat.

'Well, I'm happy with my appetite!' she breathed. 'I

never eat too much, and I think it impertinent of you to make such a comment.'

'Am I to pretend I know nothing of your body when I can recall it quite clearly within my embrace and pressed to mine?'

'Please say no more!' Bea hissed. 'I find that remark even more unmannerly,' she spluttered, blushing scarlet.

'I apologise, then; I merely intended a passing observation that your figure appeared more curvaceous when you were younger.'

He was quelling his humour with a frown, and she guessed he was deliberately riling her because of their prickly parting at the chapel earlier. 'Please do not explain and add insult to injury. Your opinion of my looks is of no consequence to me in any case.'

Beatrice turned to the pastries and began loading a plate with them while her cheeks continued to burn.

'If you are about to accuse me of being a glutton, this food is for my papa.' In her agitation, it had slipped her mind that Walter desired just one fruit tart. Swishing about with a laden plate she moved on.

'Did you want to speak to me on a matter?'

Beatrice halted, moistening her lips. She'd also forgotten she'd drawn him to her side with a come-hither glance.

'I…I did want to have a word with you. My father would like you to join him for a chat before you go.'

'Of course I'll speak to him.' Hugh glanced back towards the drawing room, locating the sofa on which Walter was ensconced. 'It would be my pleasure.'

'Thank you,' Bea replied stiltedly.

'Shall I accompany you now?' Hugh suggested mildly.

'If you wish to, sir.'

Hugh's heavy sigh brought Bea's eyes darting to his bronzed face.

'I beg you will not put yourself out for us, though,' she said acidly. 'My father would not want that.

'It is *you* putting me out, my dear. Have you forgotten my name that you continue calling me sir?'

'Indeed I have not, *Mr Kendrick*,' Bea returned sweetly on passing him.

'Will you let me know what Mr Dewey wants to talk about so I might prepare my defence?' Hugh asked wryly, falling into step with Bea as they wound a path around knots of people.

'You are not about to be ticked off, I assure you.' Bea was unable to repress a smile at his ironic tone. 'I believe Papa wishes to apologise to you.'

'And how have I redeemed myself in his eyes?' Hugh politely led the way past a long sofa encircled by chattering ladies. A few yards on, at a quieter spot, he turned back to Bea. His hand was idly planted against the wall, completing her casual entrapment by his powerful body.

'Papa was most grateful to you for coming to Hertfordshire to convey the news about the dowager's ill health. I expect he wants to impress that on you.'

'I recall he said something similar to me at the time,' Hugh murmured, his eyes lingering on Bea's mouth as her pearly teeth attacked her lower lip. 'I doubt he'd make an issue of repeating it. So what else is on his mind?'

'If we carry on to him I'm sure he will tell you,' Bea returned.

Barely were the words out when a sudden clap of thunder made her gasp and stumble. She would have dropped her pastries but for Hugh's steadying hand on her shoulder. Beatrice felt her heart thudding unevenly and the silk of her sleeve seemed to grow unbearably hot beneath his palm. She gave an embarrassed laugh.

'Heavens! That frightened the life out of me.' She glanced about to see that she hadn't been the only lady startled by the storm. Fans were whizzing and a few smelling salts bottles were being wafted amidst nervous giggling. A small crowd had gathered at the windows to watch lightning zigzagging across the heavens.

Bea's gaze was captured by eyes that had lost their golden tint and now burned like coal embers. His fingers began moving in a slow caress, increasing pressure, as though he would feel her skin beneath the barrier of fabric. Her eyelids became weighty, slowly falling beneath the narcotic effect of his secret seduction.

'Please don't... I...' She finally listened to the inner voice protesting wildly at her behaviour. She sensed he might dip his head and kiss her while she acted like a mindless idiot enthralled by his touch. And at such a time and place as a wake! Despite her chagrin she felt unable to physically move away from him and raised her eyes to beseech him for leniency.

As Hugh withdrew his fingers in a slow stroking movement Bea expelled a breath, darting glances hither

and thither, relieved that people were still too preoccupied with the storm to have noticed their indecent
intimacy.

Hugh took the plate from Bea's shaking hand. 'I'm
glad I wasn't responsible this time for giving you the
jitters…or was I?' he challenged.

In a moment he was resuming their conversation
as though nothing had happened, although Bea felt
strangely light-headed.

'As you seem reluctant to help me prepare for a chastisement, let me stab a guess at the bee in your father's
bonnet.' He paused before asking abruptly, 'Did you
tell him what was in Fiona's letter?'

'Of course…' Bea replied after a second spent wondering how he could change so quickly from charmer
to interrogator.

'Ah…so I imagine I'm about to be told to mind
my own business where Colin Burnett is concerned.'
Hugh's moulded mouth slanted sardonically.

'Actually, you are wrong,' Bea answered, flustered,
because just as she'd been recovering her equilibrium
he had again upset it. He had a knack of being too forthright for comfort. It was something else he'd acquired
along with his money, she was sure, but she wouldn't
be intimidated by it any more than she'd allow his prac-
tised philandering to steal her composure. 'It is I who
would ask…insist…you do that. My father, on the other
hand, seemed pleased to hear about your uninvited in-
terference in my affairs.'

Bea stared pointedly at his imprisoning arm until
lazily he removed it from where it had been propped

against the wall. She took immediate advantage of her liberation and carried on towards her father, forcing herself to a leisurely pace so it would not seem she was cravenly taking flight.

'Papa seems in good spirits.' Elise sipped tea following this observation.

'I think he has sunk rather too far into good spirits.' Bea put down her bone china cup.

The sisters were side by side on a window seat and had been watching fat clouds travelling over the insipid sky through the square-paned glass. They had turned their attention to their father, still huddled on the sofa by the fire, now with a group of male companions. By his side on the velvet upholstery was the Duke of Rodley. His grace had been topping up Walter's glass with his fine cognac for at least fifteen minutes while gregariously holding court. Opposite, in a wing chair, sat Hugh Kendrick, also with a replenished brandy balloon and an air of indolent interest in the duke's conversation. Just moments ago Alex had also joined the gentlemen. He was leaning on the back of the sofa while, at the duke's insistence, partaking of his late mother's favourite tipple.

A cosy atmosphere had descended on the drawing room. Most of the guests who lived locally had departed, keen to get home since the storm had blown south. Others, with long journeys in front of them, had taken up the Blackthornes' offer of accommodation at the Hall while the roads remained bad.

Hugh Kendrick had not bowed to Alex's insistence

that he stay because it would be madness to risk life and limb in such abominable weather. He planned to get going before dusk, much to his host's disgust.

'I think I shall go and see Adam before dinnertime.' Elise found it difficult to spend long periods apart from her little boy.

'Dinner?' Bea choked a laugh. 'I have eaten very well already, Elise.'

'Oh, the gentlemen will expect their dinner; and their port and cigars,' Elise declared ruefully, thinking of her husband's predilection for a smoke and a drink when they had male company. 'Will you come with me and say goodnight to Adam?'

'I shall peek at him in the nursery later,' Bea promised. 'For now I shall keep the ladies company.' With a nod she indicated the elderly women she'd seen drying their eyes in the hall earlier. Bea had been introduced to them and recalled that the silver-haired individual with a remarkably hooked nose was called Lady Groves. On her black satin bosom was pinned a huge mourning brooch. The name of the other lady had momentarily escaped Beatrice's mind.

'Lady Groves came in her brother's stead as he is poorly,' Elise informed her helpfully. 'My mother-in-law was Lord Mornington's *chère amie* for a very long time. He is heartbroken to lose Susannah and it has made him quite ill.'

'Poor man...' Bea murmured.

'Lady Groves and Susannah were friends; they were about the same age, I believe, and were widowed at about the same time. Mary Woodley, Lady Groves's companion, lost her husband in the Peninsular wars.'

After Elise had gone off to the nursery Bea settled in a wingchair adjacent to the ladies with a cheerful, 'The clouds are fast moving away, thank goodness.'

'I shall be glad to set off home tomorrow if the water on the roads has drained away.'

Mary Woodley was a lesser mortal than her noble benefactress in the eyes of polite society. But Lady Groves saw her companion as her equal and treated her as such, despite her friend's impoverishment. She also treated Mary to those things she could not afford to purchase for herself, due to her subsisting on her late husband's meagre army pension.

'I'd rather stay here a while longer, Mary, so flooding doesn't bother me.' Lady Groves's greedy black gaze roved her sumptuous surroundings. 'It is the first time I have visited Blackthorne Hall but my brother told me it was a wonderful sight.'

'But what about the Whitleys' *musicale,* Gloria?' Mary mildly complained. 'I do not want to miss that in case that flibbertigibbet turns up with her aunt, causing us all to gawp at her. Very strange behaviour...very strange indeed.'

'I heard that Miss Rawlings wasn't even officially invited to the Clemences' that evening.' Lady Groves tutted at such vulgar conduct as gatecrashing. 'Country bumpkins!'

'Miss Rawlings?' Beatrice echoed faintly, too shocked at hearing her rival's name to take umbrage at Lady

Groves's all-encompassing insult to people like herself who hailed from the shires.

'I doubt you would know her my dear.' Lady Groves patted at Bea's fingers, tightly curled on her lap. 'She is a gel about eighteen and new to town—from the Yorkshire area, we believe, don't we, Mary? She is out this year and is being chaperoned by her aunt. Nobody knows much about them, you see…but the bold chit seems determined to change that.'

But I think I might know about her… The words rotated in Bea's head but she managed to keep them from tripping off her tongue. It seemed these two ladies were ignorant of her being jilted, and therefore didn't know that the '*bold chit*' they spoke about had stolen her fiancé.

'Dolly Pearson told me that the aunt says her charge is secretly engaged.' Mary was pop-eyed while giving this news.

Lady Groves snorted her wordless opinion on that. 'If Miss Rawlings *does* have a fiancé I'll wager the fellow is unaware of her flirting.' She inclined forward to whisper, 'I saw her fluttering her eyelashes at…' She left the sentence unfinished but her eyes darted sideways to where the gentlemen were grouped. 'If she thinks she has a chance of snaring *him* she'll be sorely disappointed.'

'No respectable young lady has a hope of catching Hugh Kendrick's eye,' Mary scoffed behind the fingers fluttering in front of her lips. 'He has no interest in debutantes, no matter how irresistible they find him.'

'No wonder he's oblivious to decent gels with those

two doxies fighting over him. Then there's the shocking *other business* to keep him occupied...' Lady Groves rumbled.

'*Other business...?*' Bea echoed the phrase back at the woman.

Lady Groves looked extremely discomfited by her slip, but nevertheless patted again at Bea's fingers before attempting to change the subject.

'Is Mr Kendrick a villain?' Bea insisted on knowing, and received a shocked look from Mary Woodley at such impertinence as cross-examining Lady Groves.

'You are a sweet innocent and need not know the details of a gentleman's behaviour when he is freed from the restraints of a civilised society...' Lady Groves said, fingering her throat in embarrassment.

'I assure you I am not about to swoon on hearing that Mr Kendrick has female friends.' Bea realised she sounded vulgarly inquisitive, and very unladylike, but she couldn't help herself. She craved to know more.

'Miss Rawlings and her aunt *did* leave the Clemences' early with a gentleman but I've no idea who he was,' Mary burst out, returning to gossip she deemed more seemly. 'I was coming out of the retiring room and saw the trio suddenly disappearing down the stairs.'

'I didn't see the fellow, but possibly he was her father, come to take her home before she disgraced herself,' Lady Groves sniffed.

'He seemed far too young for that, Gloria!' Mrs Woodley disagreed. 'Perhaps Dolly might know who he was. She seems to find out everything first, though I doubt she spotted the fellow either, for his arrival and departure seemed as one.'

'Dolly Pearson is my aunt.'

Beatrice could think of nothing more to say at that point. She knew she should feel grateful that the argument between Hugh and Colin had been very discreet, and few people yet knew the details of it. But preying on her mind was the scandal concerning Hugh to which Lady Groves had referred but had refused to explain.

'I do recall, now you mention it, that you are related to Dolly.' Lady Groves beamed, having fully recovered from her shock at Miss Dewey's audacity a moment ago. 'My brother, Lord Mornington, told me that your sister was Dolly's niece. I've always found Mrs Pearson a charming woman,' she added graciously. Glancing at Mary for a comment, Gloria found the woman peering beneath her pale lashes at the group of gentlemen. 'What's the matter with you, Mary?' she asked.

'Do you think Mr Kendrick overheard us talking about him?' Mary whispered, aghast. 'He seems to be staring at us rather too frequently, Gloria.'

Lady Groves frowned thoughtfully, then looked at Beatrice. 'You were talking to him earlier, weren't you, my dear?'

'Yes…I was…' Bea avoided looking his way, although she felt the side of her face burning and wondered if he'd guessed that she'd just heard an intriguing hint about his sordid way of life.

'He is your brother-in-law's good friend, is he not?' Mary Woodley picked up on her ladyship's unspoken thought that Miss Dewey might have caught Hugh Kendrick's interest.

'I believe they've known each other since their schooldays,' Bea answered with a neutral smile.

'Do *you* have a beau, my dear?' Lady Groves had already taken a surreptitious look at the young woman's pretty white fingers and noted they lacked any rings. 'A sweet gel like you must have admirers buzzing around like bees about a honeypot.'

Mary discreetly nudged her companion in the ribs, having just brought to mind a stunning titbit. Dolly Pearson had told her recently that a swine of a country doctor had jilted her niece. No names had been mentioned, and Mary had taken little interest in the tale as she'd doubted she'd know such provincial folk. But it seemed she did! Obviously the niece in question could not be the viscount's wife, and that only left...

'I am not being courted,' Bea answered as cheerfully as she could. 'Well, I did promise Elise I would visit the nursery and see baby Adam before he goes to bed.' She rose gracefully. 'Apparently we are all to be given dinner soon.'

'Such charming hosts,' Lady Groves murmured. 'I hope Mr Kendrick changes his mind and stays. I should like to have a chat with him.'

'I'm afraid *I'm* hoping he will disappoint you,' Beatrice murmured beneath her breath, walking away. She had seen the sudden intelligence on Mary Woodley's face and knew that Dolly hadn't after all kept the news of her jilting to herself. Philosophically, Bea realised people would soon know—and besides, what occupied her now was imagining how debauched Hugh might have become in the years since she'd last known him.

The two ladies exchanged a look as soon as they judged Miss Dewey was at a safe distance.

Lady Groves shook her head. 'I doubt it, Mary. She might be his friend's sister-in-law, and a beauty too, I must add, but rather mature to seriously catch the eye of such an eligible gentleman. She is the senior of the two gels and it must be galling for her to have nothing when her sister has done so well. Miss Dewey could pass for twenty with that perfect complexion…but she must learn to control that forward nature.'

Mary nodded vigorously. 'She is twenty-five; Dolly told me her niece's age and said she'd be lucky to come so close again to her wedding day. I expect the doctor has found someone younger and more demure and that's why he jilted her!'

'Jilted?' Lady Groves sounded horrified. 'Poor child! That *is* a setback. Gentlemen like to think they've won a prize with a wife, not a cast-off—'

'Hugh Kendrick has just watched Miss Dewey leaving the room, Gloria,' Mrs Woodley interrupted excitedly. 'I think he likes her…'

Chapter Nine

A ghostly shroud appeared to be hovering over the sodden ground as Bea stepped out of a side door onto shingle. Following yesterday's downpour a thick early-morning mist had formed and cool droplets tickled her complexion as she crunched over gravel towards the stable block. While surveying the pearly landscape she drew in a deep breath, savouring its earthy effervescence. It was barely seven o'clock and, apart from the servants, nobody else was yet up at Blackthorne Hall.

Bea was kitted out in sturdy boots and one of her sister's riding habits, with a hat sitting jauntily on her fair tresses. As she jumped a puddle, one hand on the brim to prevent her hat flying off, she felt inexplicably joyful, considering the ordeals of the last few weeks. Others might pity her, and think there was little in her life to celebrate, yet Beatrice was determined that failed love affairs would never crush her while she had Elise and her papa close by. And her little family was expanding all the time: yesterday, after dinner, when the gentlemen had taken port and cigars, and Lady Groves and Mary Woodley had settled down in the drawing room to play cards, Elise had quietly confided to Bea that she suspected Adam might soon have a little brother or sister.

While pondering on the lovely idea of a little niece to cherish alongside Adam, Bea realised being a spinster aunt held a certain warm appeal. Vigorously she brushed a splash of mud from the fine cloth of her sister's bottle-green skirt. The viscountess had a collection of the most exquisite silks and satins stitched by feted *modistes* and would press on Bea any garment she might praise—not simply to borrow, but to keep. Bea understood the sweetness behind Elise's generosity but rarely accepted such lavish gifts, quipping that there was little need for pearl-encrusted ball gowns in her neck of the woods.

Having traversed a courtyard, Bea glimpsed the stables situated beyond a walled physic garden. As she approached the neat shrubs and plants some of her child-like delight at being up early on this fresh new morning dwindled. The sight of the herbs had reminded her of Colin. His work as a doctor had necessitated him knowing about natural remedies for ailments and Bea had taken an interest in the healing powers of plants too.

Her fingers brushed against rosemary spikes, filling her nostrils with a pungent perfume. Suddenly she crouched down, unable to pass by without touching the velvety leaves of lady's mantle, cradling their watery jewels. The image of tiny diamonds jolted her upright, thinking of another gentleman who had the power to disturb her peace of mind.

She marched briskly on, trying to shake off the unwanted memory of Hugh's degeneracy. Mulling the secret scandal over in private, she'd guessed, from Lady Groves's hint, that it had occurred abroad, and that Hugh's investment in India held the clue to the outrage he'd committed. When she'd joined Elise in the nursery yesterday she'd asked her sister—quite casually—if she could shed any light on the matter alluded to by Lady Groves. The viscountess had given a little shrug, reminding Bea that Hugh was a notorious rake and saying that she doubted he'd remain celibate just because he was on foreign soil.

Bea had already arrived at the same conclusion: the idea of Mr Kendrick having foreign affairs, as well as a few closer to home, had probably sent the elderly ladies into a tizz…but it certainly didn't surprise *her*.

Of course Bea knew the only way to find out for sure what it was all about was to ask him…and she'd no intention of doing that! Why would she bother when she didn't care a jot what he got up to…?

'You're up early, Beatrice.'

'So…so are you, sir.' Bea had swivelled about and automatically stuttered a reply, despite her amazement at seeing the very person who'd been intruding on her thoughts.

Hugh was emerging from the first stall she'd passed, leading a large chestnut horse. 'Are you riding alone?'

'I am… Elise told me last night she would not stir herself before ten o'clock. She and Alex often like to lie in…' Bea cleared her throat, wishing she'd kept her answer brief.

'I'm sure they do…' Hugh muttered, glancing at the house.

'I thought you would by now be in London,' Bea blurted, unable to curb her curiosity at his reappearance.

'I'm sorry to disappoint you,' Hugh drawled. 'But it was foolish of me to suppose I'd get even as far as Enfield last night. Half the road had been washed away by the flooding so I turned back after a couple of miles.'

Bea found the idea of him, unbeknown to her, sleeping beneath the same roof rather disquieting. And if he had returned to the house he hadn't joined them at dinner yesterday. 'You stayed at the Hall last night after all?'

'I was tempted to,' he said huskily. 'Too tempted…' he muttered at the leather he was tightening on the chestnut's flanks. 'I put up at the Red Lion instead.'

His tawny eyes ran over her smart figure and returned quizzically to her lovely face. He was too polite to voice the obvious: that she was dressed in her sister's expensive finery. Bea's gloved fingers adjusted the tailored jacket; she wasn't too proud to hide the fact that she wore borrowed clothes. Besides, he already knew her father's income wouldn't stretch to such luxuries.

'Elise kindly loaned me one of her habits,' she said carelessly.

'And very becoming it is too.' Hugh fondled the chestnut's ears soothingly as the stallion continued nudging him to gain attention. 'Will you accompany Elise to London when she returns there?'

'No, we are going back to Hertfordshire this afternoon.'

'The roads will still be hazardous to travel on.'

'My brother-in-law has given us a good sturdy coach and the driver is skilled. The journey to Berkshire was very comfy despite the potholes.'

Bea was aware that they were politely skirting about the obvious. Much as she wanted to forget him holding her close yesterday, the incident constantly played over in her mind. And she believed he was also brooding on it. A solid heat seemed to be building between them, despite the yard or two of cool atmosphere separating their bodies.

'Molly, is it, for you, ma'am?'

A young stable lad had poked his head above the door, startling Bea with his question about her choice of ride.

'Yes…thank you…' Bea managed a smile for the youth. 'She suits me very well,' Bea explained as the ensuing quiet stretched. 'I always take her out when I visit. I hope she remembers me…'

'You're not easy to forget,' Hugh muttered. 'You were right in thinking your father wished to thank me yesterday for reminding Burnett of his manners.'

'Are you hinting I should follow his suit?' Bea crisply enquired. 'Because if you are I must disappoint.' She avoided a pair of preying eyes, glad of the distraction of clopping hooves ringing on cobbles as the ostler led a small dappled horse towards her.

Once the lad had assisted her in mounting the mare Bea felt energised and calmer. She smoothed Molly's nose, murmuring affectionately as she heard her snicker softly. The opportunity to ride was a great treat for Beatrice; Walter Dewey hadn't owned any quality horse-flesh for many years. In her early teens Bea had shared the use of a pony with Elise and they had both delighted in galloping about under their father's strict supervision. Then the sisters' world had crumbled when their mother had abandoned them and their father had bankrupted himself trying to win her back.

Bea had retained a modest skill, despite the inter-mittence of being in the saddle, and she wanted to sa-vour her morning constitutional. She dipped her head at Hugh in farewell, trotting on towards the beckoning open space off to the south.

'Do you mind if I join you?' Hugh had swung eas-ily onto the stallion's back, bringing his prancing under control within a matter of seconds.

'Not at all…' Beatrice called over a shoulder. 'Don't feel obliged to try to keep up, though…'

With that bold challenge she prodded her mount into action and Molly sprang forward immediately, cover-ing ground.

As soon as Bea had leapt the small brook that edged the meadow she gave Molly her head. The mare might be small and pretty but she was a wiry little animal, and Bea's exhilaration soared as stinging air battered her soft cheeks. She laughed softly, racing on, but it was just seconds later that she registered the thud of hooves clos-ing on her. She knew when he reined in to allow her to retain the lead as the drumming rhythm subtly changed tempo. Bea allowed Molly to slow down too, reluctant to appear determined to outpace him in some silly con-

test. She'd known from the start that docile little Molly
was no match for the sleek thoroughbred on her tail.

Having reached the valley where the brook fed a
fast-flowing stream, Beatrice slackened the reins so
the mare could take a drink and crop grass.

Hugh came to a halt some yards away, then dismounted. He strolled over, wordlessly extending his
arms, inviting her to get down.

Bea hesitated, then went to him because she could
see he imagined her wary of his touch. And she wasn't
afraid of him. Neither had she any need to be. In an instant he'd lifted her easily, swung her about with giddy-
ing speed, then put her down on the turf and walked off.

Feeling flustered by his efficient handling, she wandered towards the water's edge, glad to stretch her legs,
while he tethered the stallion to a branch.

'He's a fine beast.' Beatrice was keen to make conversation. The tense silences between them seemed
more awkward than an exchange of barbed remarks.
'He must be new; I don't recall seeing Alex ride him.'

'He's mine.'

'You brought your own horse with you?' Bea turned
about.

'I rode him here; I left London quite late and I didn't
want to miss Susannah's funeral.' He came slowly
closer. 'Travelling across country is quicker than using
a carriage on the roads.'

He assessed Bea's thoughtful expression.

'You're wondering why I didn't make it home yesterday, in that case.'

Bea nodded, aware of his eyes roving her flushed

complexion, making her wonder if mud had flown up from Molly's hooves to dirty her face as well as her hands.

'I found I didn't want to go home, Beatrice. I wanted to stay here for a while longer...'

Beatrice turned away, then bent down to dip her fingers into the cold water, sluicing off the soil stains. If he thought she'd ask him if he'd returned to see her, he was mistaken. She'd no intention of giving him an opportunity to scoff on that score.

'Elise is worried Alex will pine for his mama as he has no brothers or sisters.' She sent that over a shoulder before standing and drying her hands on her skirt.

'Siblings can be more of a burden than a support.' Hugh joined her on the bank of the stream.

Bea glanced at his harsh, chiselled features. She was sorry that he felt that way, considering how close she was to her beloved Elise. Hugh had a sister and a brother, and she wondered to which he'd referred when making that damning comment about his kin.

Curiosity loosened her tongue. 'Are you not a close family?'

'I visit my mother regularly, but my sister only rarely now she's settled in the shires with her husband. We have no quarrel with one another.' A chuckle grazed his throat. 'Which is remarkable, considering how Sarah has tested my patience and my pocket in the past.'

'And Sir Toby?' Bea asked after a short silence.

'The less I see of him the better I like it,' Hugh replied. He jammed his fists into his pockets, turning his head to gaze out over the fields. 'He is an unpleasant character and I would advise anybody to steer clear of him. My aunt Edith couldn't abide him, so she said.'

Beatrice sensed the soft clod beneath her feet giving way and scrambled backwards. Hugh grabbed at her whirling hand, jerking her away from the water and to safety higher up the bank.

He didn't immediately relinquish her and Bea made no effort to wriggle her fingers free of his warm grip. She blushed beneath the golden gaze she sensed scorching the top of her head, finally liberating herself with murmured thanks for his assistance. She was determined not to give the impression of being susceptible to his polished charm. And he was very attractive... more so than when she'd fallen in love with him...she grudgingly acknowledged while darting him a glance.

He had the height and dark good-looks that appealed to women and made lesser-blessed fellows resentful. He also now had the wherewithal to purchase expensive tailoring to enhance his broad shoulders... Beatrice abruptly curtailed her wild appreciation. It was now nothing to her how handsome his face, or how snug his clothes! But she could understand why women everywhere—even in exotic locations—might succumb to him...

'I have been remiss in not offering you my condolences,' Beatrice uttered briskly, in order to curb her annoying preoccupation with his attractiveness. 'I had no idea that your aunt Edith had passed away till recently.' She started to walk along the bank. 'Elise told me the sad news when she came to Hertfordshire. I liked Mrs Vickers, although I spoke to her only a few times when in London.'

It had been during that particular sojourn in town three years ago that she had met Hugh Kendrick and almost disgraced herself with him.

With hindsight Beatrice was aghast at what she'd done. Why she had ever thought it a good idea to adopt the soubriquet *Lady Lonesome* when advertising for a husband in a gazette, or to arrange clandestine trysts with strangers to select her mate, she would never fathom. She'd matured in character since, with Colin's staid influence, she was sure. But the memory of what she'd risked—and forced her younger sister to risk as her reluctant accomplice—horrified her.

Bea was very fortunate that her antics had not completely sullied her future and her family's name, already tarnished by her parents' divorce. Few people had ever been aware of her stupid scheme; the man at her side had known because he'd responded to her advert. As a lure she'd pretended to possess a dowry and Hugh Kendrick had been eager to lay claim to it, if not to her…

'Ah…I do recall you first met my aunt and me at Vauxhall Gardens. You were attending a concert with your sister and the Chapman family.'

Hugh sounded as though he'd dredged up the details from the pit of his memory while strolling at her side. In fact he'd not forgotten a solitary thing about that first encounter. Neither had he forgotten that he'd replied to *Lady Lonesome's* advertisement because of Toby's refusal to loan him money to pay his rent and keep a roof over his head.

But there had also been the matter of Sophia Sweetman's expensive tastes depleting his bank balance. Sophia had been under his protection then—until he'd found he couldn't afford to keep her any longer. Now she was again his paramour, and he was able to give her all she wanted this time round; but Hugh wasn't sure he wanted Sophia—or Gwen Sharpe for that matter—no matter what delightful tricks they dreamt up to keep his interest and defeat one another. Annoyingly, he knew that the coltish blonde at his side would have no such difficulty arousing him…

Hugh cursed beneath his breath at the direction his thoughts…and his loins…were taking. 'My aunt liked you,' he said in a voice roughened by frustration. 'When you and your sister left town that year and returned to Hertfordshire she lacked your company.'

'I expect Edith missed having the details of our hasty escape explained to her.'

Beatrice had sensed his irritation. If he were already bored with her company she'd not impose on him longer. She retraced her steps towards Molly, hoping he might offer to assist her in remounting rather than watch her scramble in an ungainly fashion onto the mare's back.

'I missed you too.'

'Did you?' Beatrice jerked around. 'You had an odd way of showing it, Mr Kendrick, as I recall.'

'What does that mean?'

'I believe you were paying attention to Fiona Chapman before I had unpacked my case in Hertfordshire.'

'Were you jealous?'

Beatrice whipped a biting glance to his rugged profile but found a denial refused to trip off her tongue.

Slowly he turned his head, his hawk-like eyes trapping her, bringing her to an involuntarily halt.

'It is a shame you have become arrogant and conceited,' she whispered. 'I think I liked you better as a penniless fortune-hunter.' She marched on, but had covered very little ground when a hand clasped her wrist, jerking her back.

'And I liked you better when you were a country miss keen to please me.'

'That silly girl no longer exists.' Bea twisted her wrist in an attempt to free herself.

'I think she could be resurrected, given time...' he growled.

'And I think you might now be rich, thanks to your aunt's bequest, but the Indian sun has addled your wits.' Beatrice forced a fist between them to prise herself away from him.

Hugh grunted a laugh, dipping his head as though he would kiss her. But he skimmed his mouth past her mutinous face, letting her go. 'Quite possibly something's addled my wits,' he muttered, and walked on.

Inwardly he mocked himself for feeling like a randy youth. He'd been burning with desire for her yesterday and only the thought of an audience with her father had checked his lust. If a roomful of mourners at a wake hadn't put him off pursuing her he knew he should quickly distance himself, in case he lost control while they were alone. He should have gone home yesterday, he realised, and straight to Gwen and a long night of release.

There was nothing to be achieved by wanting her; he was tormenting himself for no reason. Alex would kill him if he seduced his sister-in-law, and Hugh was sure he wasn't ready for a wife. Inwardly, he mocked himself that if he did propose Beatrice Dewey would throw the offer back at him. But she'd accepted Burnett, and Hugh knew there'd been a suitor before the doctor…

'Did Mr Vaughan propose to you?'

Beatrice quit gazing at the mud underfoot. 'Mr Vaughan? How do you know of him?' she gasped in surprise.

'Because you told me,' Hugh replied dryly. 'Don't you remember that conversation, Beatrice?'

Bea bit her lip. No doubt when in Hugh's arms, in a blissful haze, she had confided her secrets to him. Mr Vaughan had been the first gentleman for whom she'd formed a *tendresse*. The lawyer had pursued her when she was eighteen, then repaid her shy devotion by dropping her like a stone to wed the fiancée he'd omitted to mention.

'No…he did not propose. Rather like you, he enjoyed flirting while chasing a dowry to make taking on a wife worthwhile.'

Hugh strode back towards her, caught her face in a fierce grip when she avoided looking at him. 'I told you at the time I was wrong to mislead you when I had nothing to give. If things had been different we would by now have been man and wife. Things for me are different now.'

Beatrice would have pulled back but Hugh caught the tops of her arms, keeping her against him. Oddly, he was calmly certain that whatever he thought he knew about himself, whatever secrets he'd be obliged to expose, he was on the brink of asking her to marry him.

'Things for me are different now, too,' Bea retorted, glaring into hard hazel eyes. 'Once home that year I fell in love properly, with a decent man, and soon realised that I'd felt mere infatuation for you.'

'Is that so?' Hugh asked softly. 'I wonder if I'm able to infatuate you again now your decent man has disappeared...'

This time his mouth closed with hers relentlessly, tracking every evasion until she ceded with a little gasp and allowed their lips to merge. She felt his long fingers forking into her hair, dislodging her hat and a few pins. But though she struggled Bea knew she was defeated. Since the moment he had turned up at her father's house with news of Alex's mother she had unconsciously craved this. Within a second of his caress skimming her silhouette she had melted closer.

Hugh sensed her need and immediately deepened the kiss, manoeuvring her jaw to part her mouth. His tongue teased the silk of her inner lip, sliding and circling with slow eroticism, while a determined hand stroked from her back to her buttocks, jolting her into awareness of the effect she was having on him. His hands cupped her face, forcing her back from him so he could gaze at her features. A flush had spread across a soft cheek where his stubble had grazed her and her mouth, moist and temptingly slack, was scarlet and plump from his passionate assault.

But she was not the sweet ingénue she'd been before. He could read behind the desire in her large eyes that her response was reluctant...measured...and he wondered just how much the doctor had taken before he'd gone away.

'You're easily infatuated, sweetheart,' Hugh murmured. 'I'm beginning to wish I'd bedded down at the Hall last night, after all, and got to know you again.'

His brutal comment was like a dousing with cold water for Beatrice. He couldn't have made it plainer that he thought her a wanton, desperate for his attention, just as she had been years ago when she'd promised him anything he wanted, then cried when he'd coolly told her he must stop seeing her.

A small hand, liberated from entrapment between their bodies, flew up to crack against his unshaven cheek, jerking his head sideways. 'I'm not infatuated and never will be again...not with you, at least. I'm disgusted by your lust and insolence.' She backed away, pressing quivering fingers to her pulsing lips. 'Colin might not be able to marry me under the terms of his inheritance but I'd sooner be his mistress than your wife.'

Hugh stalked her on their way back, until she realised she'd got the stream directly behind her and could go no further.

'I don't recall proposing to you...ever...not then, not now,' he gritted through his teeth, infuriated with himself as well as her.

He would have risked even worse humiliation at her

hands if he'd let those four damnable words circling his mind trip off his tongue.

'But if it's a lover you want…' Hugh continued in a deliberately lewd tone as he trailed just one torment-ing digit down a hot silky cheek. 'I'll provide a better service than the doctor…in every way. Just name it and it's yours, whatever you desire.' He grunted a callous laugh as she flinched at his crude proposition. 'So… the decent man's gone off to Miss Rawlings to keep his estates safe, has he?'

'Don't you dare mock him!' Beatrice cried. 'He didn't want to leave me! He had to for his future heirs' sake!'

'Quite the martyr, then, isn't he?' Hugh mocked. 'Yet Sir Colin, as he demands to be known, gives the impres-sion of a man content with his lot in life…whereas I have just realised I am not, because I want what he doesn't.'

Beatrice gulped down an indignant protestation. She had not seen Colin since he'd jilted her, but for her pride's sake she'd clung to a belief that he was miss-ing her as she missed him. She might tell her family… she might tell herself…that she was glad they'd parted, but in private moments she knew it wasn't wholly so. There had been tender interludes during their relation-ship, if no great passion. For this man to brutally throw her fiancé's faithlessness in her face—even if it were the truth—was galling.

'If Colin seems content it is because he is stoic and sensible enough to know he must accept what he can-not change!' Beatrice hissed. 'Whereas *you* are a dis-gusting degenerate.'

'Am I? Who told you so?' Hugh enquired with specious softness.

Beatrice pressed together her lips, as though to prevent herself repeating what she'd learned about him from Lady Groves: he was a man who preferred spending time with harlots rather than decent women, despite his popularity with debutantes. If the ladies' comments about the flirtatious Miss Rawlings were to be believed Colin's future wife seemed, with awful irony, particularly taken with Hugh Kendrick. And if that were not enough then there was the *other business* which, if she'd guessed correctly, had taken place overseas.

'Come…if you want to slander me, Beatrice, let me have some details and your source.'

'But I've not slandered you, have I?' she breathed, removing tendrils of fair hair that a stirring breeze had lashed across her vivid blue vision. 'That damning description is accurate and could be added to.'

He shrugged, cruelly amused. 'With a little more information, sweet, I'll be able to judge.'

The temptation to provoke him into admitting he had dallied with exotic women was too great, and he had invited it. 'It wouldn't matter where in the world you were, you'd sooner scandalise decent people than curb your lust.'

'Ah…I see… It worries you that I might have let my eye rove when in India. You told me you weren't jealous, Beatrice…' he goaded, glad that she didn't seem in possession of any firm facts.

'I'm not jealous…' Bea raged.

But he was ready for her fist this time and caught

the small curled digits inches from his face. 'What do you want me to tell you, sweet? All of it?'

'Get out of my way,' she choked in frustration and fury.

Her eyes continued sparking blue fire despite the burn of tears making her blink. She'd never win this verbal battle and knew she was close to breaking down so must withdraw from it. She was not jealous or upset in any way because of Hugh Kendrick, of that she was certain! Her distress came from the unpalatable news that Colin might already have eased his conscience where she was concerned. It was hard to bear, especially as he must replace her with a woman who seemed likely to stray—perhaps before they'd even wed.

As a sob raised her bosom, then grazed her throat, Hugh released her and strode away. Gathering the reins of the two horses, he brought them closer to where Beatrice still stood, holding herself rigidly, on the bank of the stream. When she refused to approach he jerked her closer and, without a word, hoisted her atop Molly with such strength that she had to cling to the mare's neck to prevent herself toppling straight off the other side.

'My offer of *carte blanche* stands,' he said with quiet gravity, gazing up at her steadily, a hand on Molly's bridle preventing her escape. 'Perhaps, in the circumstances, you should consider it.'

'And perhaps you should go to hell!' Beatrice hissed, slapping wildly at his fingers until he removed them. She set off across the meadow at a gallop, the wind drying her wet face as fast as the brine was falling.

When the Hall was in sight she realised that he had

not followed her all the way back. She clattered onto the cobbles of the stable yard and, turning her head, saw him stationed on the brow of the hill, watching her. Involuntarily Bea shivered at his dark, brooding presence outlined against a pale sky. A moment later he'd turned the stallion's head and was heading fast in the direction of London.

Chapter Ten

'You will do as your uncle wished!'

'I don't see why I must.' Stella Rawlings had been pouting at her reflection while fixing a garnet to a small earlobe. Now she swivelled on the dressing stool to give her aunt a sulky look. 'I'm becoming popular and I'd sooner have my pick of the bachelors than have a husband chosen for me.' She stood up and approached the mantelpiece to sort through invitations, selecting one. 'See…the Rutherfords want us to join them in their box at the opera.'

Idly, she waved the parchment. The Rutherfords were close to the heart of the *ton* and every chaperon wanted her ward to have their patronage.

Apart from Maggie Monk.

The woman stomped closer, snatching the card from Stella's fingers and tossing it back whence it came. 'The only reason you're in demand, my girl, is because you've drawn attention from every randy fellow in Mayfair. Bertram Rutherford is rumoured to have at least five bastards.'

Stella flounced to sit on the stool, head tilted to one side while she playfully flicked the eardrop. She'd sooner have had rubies, but at least Colin had bought her a gift to mark the announcement of their betrothal. She twisted the garnet ring on her finger. She'd sooner have had a ruby engagement ring too…but mostly she craved a magnificent diamond…from Hugh Kendrick…

Her grey eyes lifted to her reflection, assessing her features. She knew she wasn't a conventional beauty: her small snub nose was littered with freckles and her full mouth had a natural droop that made her look dissatisfied even when she wasn't. She twirled a ringlet about a finger, wishing her hair were golden-blonde rather than flame-red, but gentlemen liked her generous bosom and curvy hips; they also appreciated her brazenness, even if their wives didn't.

So, in all, Stella Rawlings was satisfied with her looks and the way things were going since she'd arrived in town. She just wished her aunt would accept that Sir Colin should be kept dangling in reserve…just in case she failed to hook a gentleman with a good deal more to offer than a minor title and a modest country estate.

'Did you hear what I said, miss?' Maggie exploded when Stella continued simpering at her reflection. 'You are making a fool of yourself, flirting with every gentleman who ogles you. Lord Whitley is over sixty and yet I thought at one point you were about to sit on his knee, so close did you get to his chair.'

'The old goat would have liked that,' Stella snorted, planting her hands on the dresser and pushing herself to her feet once more.

'Maybe…but his wife would not. You do not irk somebody as important as Lady Whitley at her own *soirée*.'

'Why ever not?' Stella piped up. 'Her husband will ensure she asks me again.'

'How do you know that?' Maggie snapped.

'Because he assured me of it.'

'I imagine Lord Whitley's assured plenty of girls of plenty of things, and none of it came to pass.'

'Oh…hush, Auntie.' Stella changed tack, embracing Maggie to sweeten her temper. 'I'm just enjoying myself and I wish you'd be happy for me.'

Maggie gave a mollified sniff. 'I'll be happy when your fiancé adds a gold band to that garnet ring. Your uncle Donald wanted you to be quickly wed to Sir Colin so your future would be secure and you'd be a titled lady. We must set the date without delay.'

'I don't want to just yet,' Stella insisted sulkily. 'There are better titles going begging than his.' She noticed her aunt's expression darkening so added, 'But if I *do* want Sir Colin I'll keep him…don't worry your head about that.'

Stella felt confident she had her fiancé wound about her little finger, and all it had taken was a sly glimpse of her shapely calves. She'd schemed to give him a taste of what she could offer but hadn't wanted Sir Colin to think her a little trollop, so had pretended to be unaware of him entering the parlour at the very moment she'd been adjusting a garter.

His fulsome apology for intruding had not been able to disguise the burst of lust in his eyes. The following day Sir Colin had presented her with the gift of garnet eardrops. Stella's lips knotted in ruefulness. She should have raised her skirts higher that afternoon…she might then have got the rubies she wanted.

Maggie shook her head in a mix of despair and appreciation, watching Stella sorting through her jewellery box. The eardrops were removed and a different set, bought by a previous admirer, tried on. She'd received that gift of oval amethysts from a besotted old coal merchant in York.

Maggie knew Stella was still a virgin, so Sir Colin had no quibble there. But the girl was adept at getting cash spent on her while preserving the goods. She could understand why Stella wanted more than Colin Burnett could give. But only he could give what Maggie Monk was determined Stella would get…so the girl was marrying him and no other.

'You must come and stay with us in London and let Hugh see that you don't care a fig for him and he'll never force you to be his mistress.'

Before joining her husband in town Elise had decided to have a final attempt at persuading Bea to fight her corner. She had packed up and left Blackthorne Hall and was en route to Mayfair via her childhood home, where she had stayed the night with her family.

'I'm sure Mr Kendrick knows he can't intimidate me.' Bea smiled, despite feeling a fraud. The dratted man's name, even an annoying phantom feeling of his body still pressing against hers, was enough to dry her mouth. But she continued with the task of folding clean linen brought in from the washing line as though undisturbed by the nature of their conversation.

'Well, even if you don't mind Hugh Kendrick bothering you, you must be worried that the gossips in town are having a field-day at your expense.'

Elise hated being so brutal but hoped that resorting to bald facts might galvanise Beatrice into preserving her pride and dignity. Elise was sure that beneath that brave face her sister was understandably deeply wounded by her run of bad luck. She didn't want Beatrice to become a recluse because of two gentlemen who'd proved they weren't worthy of her.

It saddened Elise that Hugh's upturn in fortune seemed to have turned him into a heartless Lothario. She felt a fool for having cherished a hope that Hugh might honourably pursue her sister. But now another problem had gone into the mixing pot: their father had received a lengthy missive from his sister.

Aunt Dolly had reported that tongues were wagging following publication of the doctor's engagement notice. Inquisitive people had been asking why Sir Colin Burnett favoured a bold hussy, half his age, over her niece. Dolly had made it clear she'd given short shrift to anybody suggesting Beatrice must be distraught by his defection. Dolly had further written that she strongly advised Walter to send Bea to town to scotch such damaging rumours once and for all or his elder girl would be forever pitied and avoided.

'Aunt Dolly is right, you know.' Elise pushed the letter across the table so her sister could not help but look at it. Their father had insisted they both read it and discuss if action needed to be taken. 'Are you going to quash these rumours that you're hiding away, desolate? Come to Mayfair with me and hold your head high at the best places. That will show them all!'

'You have not even discussed with your husband about inviting me to stay with you,' Bea pointed out mildly.

'Alex always loves to see you, and besides he is quite furious with that rakish—' Elise bit her tongue. In her enthusiasm to get Bea to London she had almost let slip that her husband's rage was directed at his best friend rather than Sir Colin Burnett.

Bea frowned. Her sister was now keen to escape her gaze and she could guess why that might be. 'Oh, please say you haven't told the viscount that Hugh propositioned me.' After a tiny silence Bea angrily threw onto the table a half-folded pillowcase.

'Really, Elise! She pushed to her feet. 'You promised you would not—'

'I swear I did not betray you!' Elise interrupted anxiously. 'Alex could tell I was dreadfully upset after you went home following the funeral and he kept on and on at me for a reason. He thought I might have lost the babe, and that made me even more tearful, so I admitted I was fretting about you. I swear I did not mention Hugh's name, or the nature of your problem…but Alex guessed in the end, and I confirmed it for I could not lie to him.'

Beatrice pivoted about, white fingers flying to cover her gasp. '*That's* why Alex went off to London without waiting for you to accompany him!' she breathed. 'He's gone to challenge Hugh over it.' She could tell from her sister's forlorn expression that she'd hit on the truth.

'I honestly did not ask him to, Bea; in fact I tried to make Alex see the sense in calming down before setting off.'

Bea thrust two hands into her silky hair, cupping her scalp. 'He will think that I acted like a whining child, running to my brother-in-law to complain about him.'

'Do you care what he thinks?' Elise asked pithily.

'Of course not!' Bea fumed beneath her sister's arch expression. 'Well…naturally I do not want him to think me incapable of putting pen to paper to tell him my opinion of him. Neither do I want him believing me cowed. I intended to give the impression that his offer of *carte blanche* was not worthy of any further attention.'

'Well, if you don't want Alex to stand up for you it only remains for you to tell Hugh yourself that his pursuit is most unwelcome and in vain.' Elise crossed her arms over her middle and sighed. 'It'll be sad if Alex and Hugh have fallen out. Hugh can't be an *incorrigible* rogue or Alex wouldn't have been friends with him for so long.'

Bea felt guilty that her brother-in-law might have suffered an unpleasant argument because of her, but she was also exasperated because she'd not asked Alex to champion her.

'Hugh is probably embarrassed to have overstepped the mark with you, yet won't admit it. I'll wager he's already lined up a more suitable candidate.'

'If that is supposed to make me feel better, Elise…' Bea was torn between laughter and annoyance.

'It is supposed to make you feel like damning the lot of them!' Elise fell silent as their father entered the room.

'For a lady, you cuss like a navvy.' Walter was not averse to chastising his daughters, no matter their ages or the fact that the younger outranked him.

'Sorry, Papa,' Viscountess Blackthorne said meekly.

Walter pointed to his sister's letter, a gleeful smile spreading across his face. 'So, this woman Sir Colin must marry is a cheap flirt! Hah! Just what he deserves! I've a mind to go to town and tell him so!'

'Why do you not, Papa?' Elise suggested. She had not thought her father would undertake the journey, but he seemed fired up enough to do it.

'I might…yes, I might…and while I'm at it I'll ask the skinflint where my compensation has got to.'

'Colin has not returned the money you spent on our wedding arrangements?' Beatrice sat down on the chair opposite her father, looking shocked and concerned.

'Not all of it,' Walter confirmed. 'I would remind the fellow of his promise face to face, as he has ignored my letter.'

'So she told you, then…?' Having voiced this sour response to being hit in the mouth, Hugh touched his bleeding lip. As he picked himself up off his hallway floor he sent his assailant a baleful look

'She? Are you talking about my wife?' It was an icy demand.

'I wasn't…no…I was talking about Beatrice.'

Alex Blackthorne stalked closer, flexing his sore

fingers. He halted on seeing Hugh's stance altering: his friend was balancing aggressively, preparing to defend himself. Alex might have got in one lucky punch and sent his opponent reeling, but he was certain he wouldn't manage another. The two men were evenly matched in combat skills and had sparred, fenced and shot at targets together since the age of about twelve.

'I haven't seen Beatrice since she went home after the funeral. Elise told me what you'd done. You said you'd leave my sister-in-law alone.'

'I can't…'

'You damn well will!' Alex thundered. 'If her father finds out you've propositioned her he'll crawl to town, if necessary, just to shoot you.'

Hugh used the back of his thumb to smear away the blood trickling towards his chin. 'Don't tell him, then,' he said bluntly.

'That's it, is it? Don't tell him?' Alex mimicked in disgust. He strode to and fro over the marble slabs in Hugh's palatial hallway. 'What in damnation's up with you? You've got two willing women set up in London; you've got attachments in India you're not willing to forgo. Still you're not satisfied!' Alex roared. 'How dare you treat Beatrice as though she's some cheap strumpet—?'

'I've not,' Hugh coolly interrupted. 'She can have everything she wants—including all the discretion money can buy.'

'She can have everything from you but a wedding ring?'

Hugh displayed even white teeth in a soundless laugh. 'She doesn't want one.'

That took the wind out of Alex's sails. He stopped prowling and shot Hugh a dark look. 'What do you mean by that?'

'She told me she'd sooner be Burnett's mistress than my wife.'

Alex continued glaring at Hugh but inwardly his attitude altered. If what Hugh had just said were true it put a whole different light on things. Ruining a virgin spinster was one thing; bidding against somebody else for a self-confessed paramour was another matter entirely. He'd done so himself on many occasions before he'd met Elise.

Alex thrust his fingers through his hair in exasperation, unsure now how to proceed. It was none of his business if Beatrice and the doctor had been lovers, or indeed if she'd succumbed to Hugh all those years ago when they'd been besotted with one another. His sister-in-law had made no complaint of having been ravished at any time.

Alex realised he probably owed his friend an apology, and beneath his breath he groaned at the mess of it all.

'Actually, if we're going to come to blows over grievances...' Hugh approached in a single athletic stride and knocked Alex onto his back with an efficient jab. 'It was *my* job to tell Beatrice about Rani. How much does she know about my time in India?'

Alex levered himself up onto an elbow. 'I haven't

even told my wife about that damned web of deceit!' he bawled out in his defence.

'If it wasn't you or Elise who mentioned a foreign liaison—'

'It's bound to have got out,' Alex interrupted harshly. Your brother knows, after all, and so does Lord Mornington.' Alex dragged himself upright. 'You got yourself into the confounded mess so you'll have to suffer the consequences of being so blasted noble...'

'Drink?' Hugh invited acidly. A thumb pointing over his shoulder indicated his study, situated along the corridor. He knew they were both feeling foolish for having swung first and asked questions second.

Hugh knew he was wrong for wanting Beatrice in his bed, but if necessary he'd fight his best friend to have her—because just a single memory of her silky lips slipping beneath his, and her moaning response to his ardour, was enough to send tormenting heat to his loins.

'Promise me you'll stay away from my sister-in-law and I'll take a drink with you.' Alex feared his terms and his olive branch would be rejected.

'I can't do that.' Hugh turned away from his best friend, calling over his shoulder to a footman, who'd remained stoically seated in a shadowy alcove during the fracas, 'The viscount's leaving; show him out.'

Chapter Eleven

Elise had hoped that the hostility between her husband and his friend might ease in a day or two, but she was disappointed on that score.

Raising herself up on an elbow and resting her rumpled blonde head into a cupped palm, she watched Alex pulling on his clothes. He'd welcomed her back to his side as he always did, by taking her to bed to make love to her at the earliest opportunity. As soon as his son had been settled in the nursery and his in-laws were safely occupied in unpacking and resting in their chambers Elise had been scooped into his arms and the stairs mounted two at a time.

Following their leisurely pleasure Elise had tried to question Alex about recent upsets, but he'd refused to have Hugh Kendrick's name mentioned and had stopped her words with a hungry kiss before springing out of bed.

'I'm off to see Adam in the nursery before going out. What will you and Bea get up to for the rest of the day while I pore over dusty old files with my solicitor?'

'Mischief…' Elise rolled onto her back, feeling languid, a smile tilting her mouth as she twirled a finger into the dangling golden fringe of the bed canopy.

'That I can believe…' Alex approached the enormous four-poster and leaned over his wife, planting a fist either side of her lissom body. 'And your intended victim, sweet?'

'Hugh Kend—'

A finger was placed on her lips, silencing her.

'We must speak of him, Alex,' Elise said crossly, sliding free. 'Papa likes him and is bound to ask after him. How are we to explain away your argument with him?' She sat up, using both arms to draw her knees beneath her chin. 'Also, Papa is going after Colin Burnett for the money he owes him.'

Alex sat down on the edge of the bed, sensing his wife's anxiety. 'I was unaware of any shortfall. Walter's not mentioned the debt or asked me to help in the matter.'

Elise sighed. 'He probably did not want his son-in-law to think him incapable of sorting out his own affairs. You know how independent he is.' She frowned. 'I know it wasn't long ago that my father could not abide Hugh because of the way he'd treated Beatrice. But Papa has his whims, and he thinks that Burnett is now the foe and Kendrick, as he calls him, is his knight errant.'

'If Walter knew what that gentleman had planned for Beatrice he'd call him out—and me too, for introducing Hugh to his daughters in the first place.'

'It wasn't strictly you who was responsible…it was Hugh's Aunt Edith who made the introduction.'

Alex smiled sourly. 'I don't think your father would quibble over details, sweet, he'd just reach for his choice of weapon…'

'Stay with me a while longer…please…'

Gwen Sharpe stretched out a hand to the lean contours of a naked male buttock just within reach of a fingertip caress. Her husky plea went unheeded and a pair of buff breeches sheathed the muscled flesh from her touch.

'Hugh! I want you to get back in bed!'

If Gwen had hoped an authoritative tone might work better than a seductive one she was wrong, but not surprised. She was aware that her hold on this charismatic man was slipping, and whereas once she might have blamed that doxy he kept on the other side of town now she wasn't so sure that Sophia Sweetman was to blame. Gwen flopped down onto silk sheets, pondering on the identity of the woman who'd caught her lover's eye.

She knew that a silly little debutante was flirting with him at every opportunity. She'd heard reports of Stella Rawlings even before she'd bumped into the red-headed wench in Oxford Street. Gwen had persuaded Hugh to take her shopping and had looked on, amused, as the chit negotiated several drapery counters to bring herself directly into Hugh's path. Gwen had seen genuine boredom in Hugh's face at the unexpected meeting. But he'd courteously exchanged a few words with Stella and her aunt before moving on.

It certainly wasn't Miss Rawlings stealing him away. He'd an impatient nature and no desire for novices, however willing they were to learn the sensual arts. Gwen rolled onto her stomach, watching as he shrugged his powerful shoulders into a tailcoat then straightened his shirt-cuffs.

Aware of his mistress's gaze, Hugh turned about and gave her a smile. 'Do you want to go to the opera later in the week?'

'Will you have more time to devote to me that evening?' Gwen asked ruefully.

'Perhaps…' Hugh walked back towards the bed, glad that Gwen was coming to accept, without too much recrimination, that their relationship was coming to an end. Of course ordinarily he'd have enjoyed her charms for longer than six months. Gwen was a competent mistress: shapely, skilful, passionate…the list of her attributes was almost as long as that of the reasons why he was a confounded idiot for considering forgoing them.

'I was surprised to see that your friend's wife has returned to town,' Gwen mentioned idly, sliding a long fingernail to and fro on Hugh's breeched thigh, inches from her face. Her eyes slid sideways, watching for his renewed arousal and her victory, but he seemed impervious to her teasing even when she replaced the digit with her moist lips.

'Why were you surprised? The funeral is over and the viscountess resides mainly in London.' Hugh strolled to a chair and picked up his gloves.

'The scandal concerning her poor sister is very absorbing.' Gwen clutched the sheet to her bosom, sitting up. 'It's bizarre that a fellow like Sir Colin would jilt a refined lady to marry that silly girl, don't you think?'

'Burnett's affairs are of no interest to me…' Hugh raked tidying fingers through his thick hair in front of the pier glass.

'*He* is of scant interest to anybody; it is the combatant ladies who will now be gleefully observed at all times.'

'Ladies?' Hugh selected the word that interested him, pivoting on a heel towards Gwen.

'I saw the viscountess in her landau in Hyde Park. With her were an elderly gentleman and a pretty blonde who very much looks like her, although not in the first flush of youth—older, I'd say, by a year or two. Methinks the spinster and her father have come to do battle with the minx and her aunt.' Gwen felt her breath catching in her throat at a subtle fleeting intensity in his expression. 'If the viscountess has brought her sister to town do you think sparks might fly when the rivals meet?'

'Possibly,' Hugh said, staring sightlessly at his paramour, a mirthless laugh grazing his throat. 'But not in a way anybody might expect.'

Hugh clattered down the stairs from Gwen's apartment and out into the street, unheeding of his paramour at the window, watching his dawn departure. He sprang aboard his phaeton, setting the greys to a trot. His mouth twisted in a bitter smile as he brooded that as far as he was concerned the rivals in this game were men, not women.

He was sure Gwen had correctly described seeing the Dewey family out for a drive in the park. If he were arrogant and conceited, as Bea had accused him of being he mocked himself, he'd believe she had followed him

to London to become his mistress. But it was closer to
the truth to suppose Mr Dewey had come after the doctor for compensation of some sort. Burnett was sure to
refuse ceding his birthright for Beatrice, so perhaps the
less formal role she'd stated she'd be willing to undertake might be arranged between them.

Hugh knew he could outplay the doctor at every turn
at the negotiating table and he was determined to have
Beatrice at any cost…

And damn any man who tried to stand in his way.

'The old biddies will do their best to extract from
you an account of Sir Colin's betrayal simply to be feted
as the first to pass it on. You must refrain from calling
him a swine, though he deserves it.'

Beatrice received that blunt advice from Fiona Chapman while the two of them were ascending the magnificent stairway of Lord and Lady Whitley's townhouse
on Devonshire Square. Outwardly Beatrice remained
exquisitely cool and calm. Inwardly her heart was racing, while her mouth felt arid and her palms clammy.
She moved them inconspicuously against the skirt of
her sister's blue silk gown, borrowed for the occasion.

Elise had stayed at home; her morning sickness had
lasted so long she'd finally given up hope of leaving the
house, saying she felt too queasy to socialise. Nevertheless she'd insisted Beatrice attend with Aunt Dolly
and their friends. The sisters had spent some time—in
between spells of Beatrice rubbing the expectant mother's back while Elise used a china bowl—in selecting

a perfect ensemble for Bea's first social outing since Colin jilted her.

The idea of facing down the stares and whispers had been daunting, but there was undeniable good sense in the advice to thwart the gossips and boost her pride and reputation. So, following her father's declaration that he'd like to go to London before his aching legs put him in a Bath chair, Beatrice had agreed to the trip.

Earlier that evening, during the ride over to Devonshire Square in the viscount's coach, her Aunt Dolly had bluntly stated that the wretched doctor might have dreadfully humiliated Beatrice, but it was her niece's duty not to show it bothered her in the slightest. Bea could not but agree.

Glancing over a shoulder, Bea received a bright smile and a little wave from Aunt Dolly, coming up the stairs just behind them. Despite a tilting stomach that Bea was sure made her feel as sick as her poor sister, she inched up her chin and went with Fiona towards the hum of conversation issuing from the assembly.

'It is a shame Elise is not with us,' Fiona whispered. 'She has perfected the art of batting back a snide remark.'

Bea choked a giggle and put a silk-gloved finger to her lips to hush such talk in case it was overheard.

'That's the spirit!' Fiona hissed. 'Keep smiling—it will confound them all.'

On entering the brightly lit drawing room Lady Groves and Mrs Woodley sailed immediately in their direction.

'How very nice to see you again, my dear. We heard

you had come to town and hoped you might attend this evening.' Lady Groves glanced over Bea's shoulder. 'Is the viscountess not with you?'

'My sister is indisposed, ma'am,' Bea replied.

'Ah…so I was right…' Gloria gave her companion a nod. 'The viscountess looks to be blooming because she is increasing again, Mary.'

Bea started to attention and gulped down a spontaneous denial. Only very close friends and family were aware of the good news. 'I…I beg you will not say that, madam, as it is not…um…' Bea fell short of telling an outright lie, yet neither could she hint at the truth before her sister and brother-in-law thought it the right time to make an announcement. 'Elise is in mourning for her mother-in-law…' Bea blurted, having just remembered the recent funeral.

Lady Groves patted Bea's fingers. 'Of course…I understand; that was naughty of me.'

'Ah…I see that Mr Kendrick has just arrived,' Fiona burst out, keen to change the subject lest Beatrice tried to flee after such an inauspicious start.

Though feeling compelled to do so, Bea didn't turn about. She knew her first glimpse of him would increase the weakness in her knees and make her insides again lurch painfully. She'd come here with Elise's assurances that Hugh wouldn't be interested in such tame entertainment. A meeting with the fiancé who'd abandoned her she was prepared for…but a run-in with the dangerous philanderer who wanted to sleep with her was too much…

'Gracious! Whatever has brought him here tonight?'

Gloria Groves gushed behind her fan, endorsing Elise's idea that Hugh was likely to shun the Whitleys' invitation. 'My...but doesn't he look handsome?'

'He always does, Gloria.' Mary sounded resigned to admiring him. 'Perhaps he is here to take advantage of the viscount's absence now they no longer like one another,' she suggested.

Lady Groves frowned at her companion. It was well known that the two gentlemen had fallen out, but the cause of the argument had yet to break surface. 'That was not kind, Mary. Miss Dewey is present and she is the viscount's relative.'

Mary looked suitably chastened and blinked behind her fan's ivory sticks.

'There is that little madam with her future husband.' Lady Groves had been distracted just as she'd been about to probe Miss Dewey for a hint as to why the viscount and Mr Kendrick had taken exception to one another. Elevating her hooked nose, Gloria peered down it at the new arrivals, then deliberately turned back to Beatrice. 'Don't worry, my dear. We are your friends. Disgraceful conduct. Don't know how Sir Colin has got the nerve to flaunt that hussy.'

'You are kind...' Bea rattled off, feeling light-headed with suppressed hysteria. 'Oh, I see Jago and Verity are here.' She indicated Fiona's sister and brother-in-law, some distance away. 'Shall we join them?'

As the two young women walked away Bea tried to still her racing heart, but gave an involuntary little gulp of dismay.

'You're trembling, Bea.' Fiona immediately linked

arms with her in concern. 'You must not let him un-
settle you so! I could throttle the brute,' she muttered
with asperity.

'Which one?' Bea returned on a sob of a laugh.

'Burnett, of course,' Fiona said, glancing at Bea. 'Did
you have another man in mind?'

'Shall we just take a breath of air on the terrace before joining your sister?' Bea asked, glad when Fiona
immediately complied and steered her in the direction
of the breeze.

Once on the flags, Bea approached the railings and
curled her warm fingers on cold iron, closing her eyes
and breathing deeply to still her panic.

'It is as well he *has* turned up,' Fiona said gently.
'I know it is dreadfully hard for you, my dear, especially when he has Miss Rawlings with him. But you
can show once and for all that neither of them has the
better of you.'

Bea nodded, despite her friend having got the wrong
end of the stick. She couldn't blame Fiona for misun-
derstanding the root cause of her agitation. She'd not
realised herself until a moment ago just how she'd be
affected when again in Hugh Kendrick's vicinity.

The memory of his dark silhouette against the storm-
washed sky was behind her eyelids. His final words to
her again spun in her mind: *'My offer of carte blanche
still stands...perhaps in the circumstances you should
consider it...'*

And she'd told him to go to hell...

But Fiona knew none of this and believed Hugh Kendrick was just a mutual friend of the family—as had

Bea until a short while ago, when he'd turned up out of the blue, heightening the turmoil in her life.

'Ah, there you both are!' Verity Clemence emerged through the curtains. 'I was wondering where you had disappeared to.' She approached Bea and took her hands. 'It is very brave of you, Bea, to turn out like this. But quite the right thing to do.' She added, 'Never fear, you have plenty of good friends here tonight and Colin Burnett and Miss Rawlings have very few—if any.'

'That seems rather pitiable...' Bea said, stepping away from the balustrade to link arms with her friends. 'Well, I'm ready to join the fray...are you?'

Chapter Twelve

'Ah…Jago's over there with Hugh.' Having spotted her husband in the throng, Verity set off to join him.

Instinctively Bea dug in her heels, then covered her cowardly lapse by needlessly adjusting her satin slipper. Smiling, she allowed her friends to lead her on, having bought a few seconds to boost her courage.

'I've not seen you in an age, Bea!' Jago Clemence was glancing appreciatively at his wife's friend. 'You look exceedingly well—and how is your father? Did he not fancy a game of Faro tonight?' Jago diplomatically avoided mentioning anything sensitive in his welcome.

'Papa is well, thank you, but he rarely socialises now as he is not very sprightly.' Bea felt relieved to have kept her voice level, despite the blood pounding in her ears.

'I doubt Mr Dewey would have wanted to be in the same room as that odious man!' Fiona's eyes targeted the doctor, stationed some yards away.

'We must all show Sir Colin that Bea has our support and he has our disgust.' Verity gave her verdict.

'The man is a fool!' She admired the sleek blue gown swathing Beatrice's figure, emphasising her tiny waist and creamy décolletage. 'Bea looks exceedingly young and beautiful this evening, don't you think, Hugh?'

'Indeed…she always does…' Hugh replied, far too seriously. 'And Burnett already has my opinion of him.'

Beatrice felt a tingle of heat in the profile she'd presented to him. She knew without glancing up to find out that the faint irony in his voice would be mirrored in his eyes. She bit back a spontaneous reminder that she'd no interest in his opinion of her looks and she'd sooner he didn't meddle in her affairs.

'Hugh took Burnett to task before anybody else knew of his hateful behaviour,' Fiona praised. 'He did you a service, Bea, on the evening he sent Sir Colin packing from Verity's *soirée*.'

Beatrice realised the ensuing quiet was to allow her to thank her gallant. 'I've told Mr Kendrick my thoughts on it,' she said huskily. 'I'm hoping he's heeded them…'

'I always listen to what you say, Beatrice.'

'Good…' Bea breathed. 'Because I meant every word…'

'As did I,' Hugh returned silkily. 'And will repeat it all if necessary.'

Verity cleared her throat, aware—as were the others—of a tense atmosphere developing. They were all saddened that Hugh and Alex had fallen out over some unknown matter, fearing it might result in divided loyalties. 'Shall we mingle, then play cards?' Verity slipped a hand onto Jago's elbow, urging him forward.

Fiona took Hugh's arm a fraction before a dark sleeve

appeared in Bea's line of vision. Wordlessly Hugh had offered her his escort and she raised solemn blue eyes to him, looking at him properly for the first time that evening. Lady Groves had commented on his distinguished appearance not one hour ago, yet Bea was unprepared for the full effect of his raw masculine appeal.

He turned away first, but behind his lazy glance had been an emotion that momentarily stopped her heart. If she'd harboured a tiny hope that he might signal remorse for having treated her like one of his doxies, she was to be disappointed. She feared that his veiled threat, issued moments ago, referred to his readiness to again insult her with a proposition rather than to renew his attack on Colin Burnett.

Not wanting to draw further attention to them, Bea allowed her hand to skim his fine suiting as they followed Jago and Verity through the throng.

'Isn't that Sir Toby over there, Hugh?' Fiona tapped Hugh's arm to draw his attention. 'I've not seen your brother in an age.'

'You're fortunate, then,' Hugh returned dryly, barely glancing at Toby. 'I wish I could say the same.'

'I'm sure he's not as bad as you would have us believe,' Fiona reproved, chuckling. 'I see that Toby has his fiancée with him for a change. Katherine rarely accompanies him anywhere.'

'She's a sensible girl and probably escapes him when she can.'

'Hugh! How can you be so mean? The poor thing would not agree to marry a man she dislikes.'

'Quite so...'

'Have you heard the wedding might be off?' Fiona whispered, aghast, as she flicked a glance at the couple.

'I couldn't possibly make a comment,' Hugh muttered.

He'd been told yesterday in White's that Katherine's father had had enough of his future son-in-law's ways. Toby was indiscreet with his paramours, but Hugh reckoned it was more likely to be his brother's wheedling for money that had finally made Mr Lowell reconsider the wisdom of allying his family with such a character. Hugh sympathised with the man's predicament and only wished he could just as easily make a break with his brother.

'Another failed engagement...' Fiona murmured, then glanced apologetically at Bea for her thoughtless remark.

Bea had been aware of their conversation flowing back and forth and was feeling rather ambivalent. Once upon a time she'd been able to enjoy Hugh's company, and had laughed and joked with him in the way her friend was now doing.

The fingers she'd placed on his arm curled against her palm as she realised she envied the easy intimacy the couple shared. Hugh had courted Fiona for longer than he had her, and Bea wondered if her friend had yearned for his teasingly tender kisses and caresses never to end, as she had...

'I see my aunt Dolly is beckoning me.' Bea hastily stepped away, hoping that putting distance between them would drive such maddening thoughts from her head.

She'd not lied; Dolly had been gesturing, trying to catch her eye.

'I shall keep my aunt company for a while or she will sulk.'

Weaving a path towards Dolly, Bea was aware of many pairs of eyes following her progress. On coming level with groups of people she heard the whispering fade, only to resume the moment she had passed by.

'Take no heed,' Dolly said, glaring at a woman who seemed particularly intent on gawping at her niece. 'You are doing very well indeed. Hugh Kendrick does not give his attention to many young ladies in the way he does to you.' Her eyes bolted to one side. 'See—the doctor and his fiancée are looking quite forlorn, all alone over there.' She clucked her tongue in disgust. 'Of course Lord Whitley hovers around, but we all know why that is!'

'I don't...' Bea replied, genuinely puzzled.

'The little wanton is always making eyes at him, even if he is old enough to be her grandfather and his wife is close by.'

Beatrice glanced over to see that indeed Colin and his female companions did appear to have been abandoned by all but an elderly fellow she now knew to be their host.

'Oh, *she* is the girl's aunt.' Dolly anticipated Bea's query about the middle-aged woman by Stella's side.

'Miss Rawlings is pretty,' Bea said quietly, having made a quick assessment of her child-like successor. 'Her hair is an unusual colour.'

'Nothing like as fair and glossy as yours, that's for sure,' Dolly sniffed.

Beatrice felt compelled to once more peek at those tumbling red locks…until she noticed Colin watching her. She dragged her eyes away, unexpectedly pitying him. He looked miserable, yet she'd expected him to seem proud of his new status and his young bride-to-be.

Lord Whitley had ambled away, leaving the trio quite isolated, and on impulse Bea started towards Colin, hesitantly at first but then with increasing confidence. She didn't falter even when her Aunt Dolly guessed her purpose and followed her for a few steps, hissing at her to halt. Neither did she waver on becoming aware that the hum of conversation in the room was receding.

Everybody present was watching her, Bea realised. Still she carried on, till her steady, graceful pace brought her to stand in front of the newly betrothed couple.

'Hello, Sir Colin.' It was a level greeting, if lacking in warmth. 'I hope you have been well since we last spoke.'

Colin ran a finger inside his tightening collar. 'I've been very well, Miss Dewey, thank you,' he croaked. 'And you have been well?'

Beatrice inclined her head in answer, smiling at him to put him at ease as his eyes darted hither and thither like a trapped animal. Bea turned her attention to the women, noticing that the younger appeared careless of her arrival. Bea guessed that Stella hadn't been told the whole story…or perhaps she felt secure enough of her hold over her future husband not to care that a short while ago he had professed to love and want to marry another.

'Are you not going to introduce me to your fiancée?'

'Of course… Stella, this is Miss Dewey. We were once…' Colin's words tailed away, confirming Bea's idea that Stella had been ignorant of her existence.

Bea held out a hand and Stella took it, rather lazily, with the hand that sported a garnet engagement ring. Bea wondered if Miss Rawlings had done it deliberately, to flaunt in her face that she now possessed the gem that her predecessor once had proudly worn. But Bea got the impression that the girl's attitude was prompted by boredom and a lack of breeding rather than rivalry.

'Margaret Monk is my name.' The middle-aged woman spoke before Colin had time to make an introduction, and barely touched Bea's fingers before dropping them.

'The weather is changeable today, don't you think?' The formalities over, Bea made conversation to cover the ensuing awkwardness.

They remained under observation, although a rumble of voices had now lightened the depressing silence. Enduring a few more minutes with her ex-fiancé and his future wife would achieve her purpose. The worst of the excruciating exercise was over and quiet contentment bathed Bea, because this meeting with Colin had stirred little emotion other than her sympathy for him.

She could tell from the intensity of his gaze that he would like to speak privately to her, and indeed she would like to speak to him, too. He owed her father an amount of money that he had promised to repay. Beatrice thought it mean of him to hold on to it now he had bettered himself, and at the first opportunity she would tell him so.

'We were saying it might storm,' Colin burst out, when it seemed neither of his companions was going to bother herself with chitchat. Reassured that she had not approached to make trouble, but rather the reverse, Colin gazed at Bea with eyes glowing with gratitude.

'There'll be a storm… Oh, indeed there will…' The look passing between Stella's future husband and his past love had made Maggie Monk's blood boil. Stella might not know that Miss Dewey had almost got Sir Colin to the altar, but she did. She gave Beatrice a frosty smile. 'I think a lady is trying to catch your eye, my dear.'

'Ah…my aunt…Mrs Pearson…is accompanying me this evening.' Beatrice stepped away, aware that Mrs Monk had dismissed her and that Colin had allowed it. Stella, on the other hand, seemed as uninterested in her farewell as she had in her greeting. The young woman was sliding coy peeks at her elderly admirer, observing the scene from a distance.

'Well? What did he say? What did *you* say?'

A barrage of garbled questions met Beatrice when she was once more at her aunt's side.

'I…I think our meeting went well,' Bea answered, smiling slightly on realising she'd spoken the truth. 'At least the expectancy is over for everybody. Miss Dewey and Miss Rawlings have come face to face and then civilly parted without attempting to scratch out each other's eyes.'

'Very disappointing for one and all, I'm sure,' Dolly

sniffed. 'Never mind that; what did the doctor say? He could not take his eyes from you, Beatrice...puppy dog eyes they were too.'

'I'm sure Colin was pleased I'd attempted to clear the air...once he'd got over the shock of me confronting them like that.'

'He looked more than pleased to me!' Dolly smoothed her neck with restless fingers, peering askance to ascertain whether the doctor was still watching Bea. 'He looks like a man who knows he's just lost a sovereign and found a shilling.'

She was a bold chit—Hugh had to give her that. He had been aware of Stella Rawlings behind him from the moment he'd stepped into the Whitleys' gaming room. In fact, if he'd not dismissed the notion as being unworthy of consideration, he'd have believed her dogging his footsteps. She'd shaken off Lord Whitley and her fiancé, and seemed irked that her aunt was sticking close to her as she sashayed to and fro, tossing her red curls.

Hugh despised Colin Burnett, but in his estimation the fellow at least deserved some moral support from this young woman, considering he was taking criticism on her account. Stella Rawlings was obviously thick-skinned; she'd observed him eject Colin from the Clemences' house so knew they were at loggerheads, yet it didn't seem to bother her. She was attempting to flirt with him, although Hugh had shown no interest in her that night or this.

Hugh had no intention of being hounded into a duel by her enraged fiancé should he be tempted to take up the offer in her saucy gaze. In Hugh's opinion young ladies should be taught about the dangers of coquetry along with their music and French lessons. He dearly wished his sister had had such schooling, saving him the cost of rescuing her reputation.

Hugh knew that his roving eye was being jaundiced by the memory of Beatrice. Frustratingly, he found that her honeyed taste and fragrance were always infiltrating his mind, overriding his desire for other women. His mistresses had enthusiastically welcomed him back to town when he'd returned from the dowager's funeral, yet even with Gwen's sinuous body writhing beneath his he hadn't been able to banish Beatrice's image from the backs of his eyelids. He wanted her and he wasn't about to give up after one setback…or a hundred…he reminded himself with savage humour.

Bea was likely to be a virgin, and he could no longer deny that acknowledging her inexperience made him a first-rate hypocrite. His long-held beliefs that untried spinsters weren't fair game for artful seducers like him had so far been pushed back in his mind where she was concerned.

That morning by the stream, when he'd offered her *carte blanche,* it had suited him to think her Burnett's mistress. He despised men who took advantage of chaste women…yet he was tempted to do exactly that with Beatrice. He was in danger of losing his best friend and his own self-respect, yet still a gnawing obsession to possess the only woman he had ever loved pervaded his being…

A few moments ago Hugh had been tempted to drag

Bea to his side, and then out of the house, when he'd seen her approach Burnett. Within minutes of observing the meeting he had felt admiration and respect for her salve the jealousy knifing his side. He'd realised that rather than wanting to irritate her rival, or win back the doctor, she'd hoped to put an end to the speculation that she was bitter over her fiancé's defection. The trouble was Hugh couldn't be absolutely certain that Bea wasn't acting aloof with Burnett just for her audience. If the love she'd felt for the doctor were rekindled she might succumb to an offer of informal protection before Hugh could win her for himself...

'Are you not going to join the gentlemen having a smoke on the terrace?' Fiona had seen Hugh standing quite alone, watching a game of Faro, while Miss Rawlings prowled very obviously in his vicinity.

Sensing he was about to go, Stella quickly moved so close to Hugh that he felt a movement of air on his profile caused by her fluttering fan.

'Considering she is spoken for, I don't know what game Miss Rawlings thinks she's playing.' Fiona gave the redhead a glare as she steered Hugh away. 'The shameless baggage was most definitely flirting with you and needs to be taught a lesson in propriety.'

'I didn't notice,' Hugh lied glibly. He saw no sense in stirring up trouble; he was determined to leave and visit Gwen, so she could attempt to soothe his restlessness.

'A hand of cards, Hugh?' Jago suggested, having returned from the terrace.

'I'm leaving in a moment...'

'Oh, do stay for a while yet,' Verity bubbled. 'Never

mind tedious gaming, the rug is being pulled back and soon there will be dancing.'

On a raised dais a few musicians were tuning up and, in front of it, two footmen were rolling back an Aubusson carpet to reveal the polished wood beneath.

'You're likely to frighten him off even sooner with such talk.' Fiona consolingly patted Hugh's sleeve. 'Never fear, I will protect you from being frogmarched into a quadrille.'

Fiona liked Hugh, despite the fact he'd once made an effort to woo her and been gently rebuffed. She'd known all along that he'd approached her on the rebound. He had still been in love with Beatrice and would have returned to his first choice in an instant if he had managed to raise the money to enable him to propose.

Hugh gazed again in Bea's direction, feeling a frustrated desire to stride over and take her somewhere quiet and secluded. The hope of talking privately to her had brought him here in the first place, although it wasn't fair to run the risk of embarrassing not only her but also her aunt and their mutual friends. He cursed beneath his breath, acknowledging the insanity in his behaviour; he should have avoided this genteel party and attended one of his usual haunts. There would have been a better time to approach her again... The trouble was he was too impatient to wait for it to crop up...

Having said goodbye to his friends, Hugh had nearly reached the exit when Colin Burnett appeared in front of him, blocking his path.

'I believe you owe me an apology, sir.' Colin had had ample time to brood on his dressing down by this man.

The opportunity to salve his wounded pride and subdue his bubbling resentment had presented itself this evening and he'd been unable to ignore it.

'I owe you nothing, Burnett. However, if you would like to take this up with me somewhere more appropriate do call round to Grosvenor Square tomorrow. I'll be pleased to see you.' Hugh made to pass, a curl to his lips.

'You may address me by my title if you speak to me or about me,' Colin enunciated. 'I have taken my birthright and am Sir Colin Burnett.'

Hugh's mouth slanted in a mirthless smile. 'Yes...I realise you've improved your lot.' His tawny stare slewed to Stella, now watching them from beneath her lashes. 'Or have you...?'

Colin understood the sarcastic remark. He'd noticed that his future wife had been shadowing Hugh Kendrick's movements. It was bad enough watching her flatter and tease other gentlemen with her batting lashes and soppy smiles, but to have her take such an interest in this fellow was galling. Contrarily, Colin also felt injured because Kendrick seemed to find Stella contemptible rather than alluring.

'Perhaps I *will* call on you,' he snarled beneath his breath. 'I don't like you paying such attention to my fiancée.'

Hugh grinned, genuinely amused. 'I've not a shred of interest in the girl and I find it pitiable that you do...'

Jago had observed the exchange between the two men from a distance. Seeing he might kill two birds with one stone—defuse the situation between two of

Miss Dewey's past loves and keep some interesting male company for a while longer—he strolled up.

'Lord Whitley would like you to roll dice with him, Hugh. You'll oblige the old fellow, won't you? A couple of games won't delay you by more than fifteen minutes or so.'

With a muted oath Hugh allowed himself to be once again steered towards the centre of the drawing room.

Chapter Thirteen

The sound of Mrs Monk's voice close to his ear transformed Colin's moodiness to annoyance. He had
guessed what had prompted Maggie to suggest they
leave even before he'd glanced in his fiancée's direction. He realised that in polite society it was considered
de trop for a gentleman to object to his lady's circle of
admirers so up to now he had bitten his tongue—apart
from earlier, when confronting Hugh Kendrick. But
Colin's patience with Stella's behaviour was almost expired. She had four fawning gallants dancing attendance
on her, and from her aunt's stern expression it was obvious Maggie was also at the end of her tether where
the girl was concerned.

Two of Stella's lapdogs were army officers in red-
coats—eager and fresh-faced, perhaps not yet turned
twenty-one. The other two gentlemen were older but
apparently equally ensnared.

Colin cursed beneath his breath. If only his damnable uncle hadn't meddled in his life he'd have mar-

ried the woman he wanted. He had been observing Bea since he'd arrived, and before the evening was out he hoped to have a proper conversation with her. She was everything a man could want in a genteel wife, whereas Stella…was not.

He had noticed the way Kendrick circled Bea and suspected his nemesis had come to a similar conclusion about Beatrice's charms and was about to take advantage of her availability. To his shame, Colin knew that Stella fired his blood in a way that Bea had never done. The flame-haired vixen made his hands itch to rip off her clothes. But he'd come to understand that Stella purposely teased other fellows in the same way she did him. His fiancée was making a fool of him, prompting people to snigger that he'd be a cuckold before he'd taken his vows.

Maggie Monk had been nagging at him to name the day but, having got to know the woman's niece better, Colin was no longer in a rush to do so. Why should he? He had his birthright, and as long as he wed no other but Stella he would keep it. He had a feeling that the little wanton would lie with him for a few baubles whether he walked her down the aisle or not…

So he wasn't about to leave this party early. He hadn't given up on the idea of having a talk with Beatrice and perhaps confiding his feelings on all sorts of matters… They might never be able to marry, because of his dratted uncle, but Colin was confident Bea might appreciate an invitation to come back into his life in a less formal role than that of wife…

* * *

'I'm so proud of you...'

The moment Lady Groves drew Dolly Pearson away for a chat Fiona snatched the opportunity to speak privately to Beatrice.

'Verity was worried when you approached the doctor, thinking you might be rudely rebuffed, but I knew you'd be fine. It was very brave, and quite the right thing to do,' she enthusiastically praised.

'I'm glad it is over with.' Bea gave a heartfelt sigh.

'Stella Rawlings has been flirting outrageously. Was she impolite to you?'

'Nothing unpleasant occurred,' Bea answered. 'It was just a bit awkward, that's all.' She chuckled. 'Now it is done, and I have escaped my aunt's beady eye too, by the looks of things.' She glanced at Dolly, in animated conversation with her cronies. 'I think I deserve to enjoy myself for an hour or so before going home.' She squeezed her friend's fingers. 'Shall we play cards? I have brought some money for a little flutter.'

'Jago has lost five pounds already.' Fiona grimaced a caution.

A pile of cash littered the green baize of the Faro table. Jago was seated beside his wife and looking rather glum. Verity was smiling, perhaps because she appeared to be doing rather better, judging by her stack of coins.

'I think I might try my luck.' Bea felt quite carefree now the burden of her meeting with Colin had been lifted. 'Papa says I'm good at Faro, although I suspect when he's banker he lets me win.'

'My allowance is already overspent.' Fiona glanced about. 'I wonder where Hugh is? He was throwing dice earlier with our host. I hope he has not already gone...'

Bea frowned, her eyes darting to and fro for a glimpse of him. She too hoped he hadn't left yet, which was odd considering she'd been dismayed when he'd turned up.

As a fellow threw in his hand and vacated the table Bea sat down opposite her friends.

Some time later she realised that the fellow slouched in a chair, with his chin sunk low on his chest, was Sir Toby Kendrick. Of his fiancée there was no sign. Bea had never before met Toby, but recalled Fiona pointing him out earlier. Hugh's caustic remarks about his older brother were also still in Bea's mind. She hadn't noticed the two men exchange even the briefest of greetings during the evening.

In her buoyant mood she decided that Fiona had spoken wisely when observing that Sir Toby might not be as bad as Hugh would have them all believe. Sibling rivalry was often to blame for such animosity, she decided, having unexpectedly received a smile from Hugh's brother.

'You're doing rather well, Miss Dewey.'

Beatrice smiled, flushed with pleasure and excitement. Her three shillings had won her over four pounds so far. Only a few gamesters remained at the table, the others had folded their hands on hearing the orchestra start up. Jago still toyed with a few chips, and a Hussar in splendidly brocaded uniform was staring intently at the cards in his hand.

It had been Toby Kendrick who'd congratulated Bea a moment ago. As the banker pushed her winnings her way Bea again considered that Hugh had been unfair about his brother; Sir Toby had been unfailingly pleasant. Perhaps Hugh had a tendency to deliberately rub Toby up the wrong way…just as he did her…

Despite his elevated status Sir Toby was not as charismatic or as handsome as his younger brother. Nevertheless his light brown hair and regular features were attractive, if somewhat marred by a complexion that was turning florid from the effects of the brandy he was steadily consuming.

'If I had your luck I'd be tempted to up the ante.' Toby placed his bet.

'I must not!' Bea lightly remonstrated. 'I will be jinxed if I do and might lose my winnings.'

'Superstition.' Toby made a dismissive gesture. 'Only the faint-hearted would hold back on such a run of luck—and you, Miss Dewey, are not a coward, are you?' He held Bea's gaze with a stare that mingled admiration and challenge.

'Miss Dewey can make up her own mind on the state of play,' Jago said, with an undercurrent to his voice.

Bea sensed Jago was warning her against betting heavily. She knew he was doing it kindly, to protect her, but she felt quite drunk with exhilaration, and flattered that Sir Toby had faith in her ability. Besides, if she netted a tidy amount she'd be able to reimburse her father for her wedding expenses. Not that Colin Burnett should be let off the hook; when an opportunity arose she would remind the doctor of the solemn promise he'd made to honour his debts on the day he jilted her.

It was the sense of a hand pressing on the rail of her chair that alerted Beatrice to Hugh's presence… that and a faint familiar redolence of cigar smoke and sandalwood. If she had not been in shock at what she'd done she might also have guessed at someone being directly behind from people's reactions: they were no longer pitying her with sly eyes but gawping over the top of her head.

Sir Toby Kendrick had a particularly malicious glint beneath his dropped lashes. But Beatrice was no longer surprised at his meanness. That gentleman had minutes ago transformed from kindly advisor to debt collector.

'Ah…my dear brother…come to rescue the fair lady,' Toby drawled. 'Indeed she needs *somebody's* help as she now owes me…let me see…' He made a show of counting on his fingers. 'One hundred and fifteen pounds.' He tapped a hand on baize. 'Too late to be a hero, I'm afraid.'

Beatrice felt as though a knife had stabbed at her heart, making her physically wince. 'No…it cannot be as much as that!'

She made to rise, but a cool hand on her shoulder stayed her, then withdrew slowly in a way only she might recognise as a subtle caress. She glanced up, her lovely face bloodless with strain. Following an infinitesimal wordless reassurance Hugh's eyes were once more on his brother, his jaw tense with controlled fury.

'Miss Dewey is retiring from the game and I'm taking her place,' Hugh announced quietly. 'Does anybody object?' His gaze swept the remaining players at the Faro table, lingering for a moment on Jago, making his friend squirm beneath a blaze of wrathful accusation. Jago's attempt at gesturing in explanation was ignored; Hugh's attention had gone.

'I object,' Toby purred, smugly sprawling in his chair.

'You're outvoted,' Hugh said.

'Those aren't the rules I play by,' Toby returned defiantly.

'They are now.' Hugh stared at the banker, who in turn peeked at Lord Whitley, standing amidst the audience to this spectacle.

Their host inclined his head rather reluctantly, because the old fellow enjoyed a scandal and a scuffle and he thought that both were in the offing this evening. The fact that a newly jilted spinster now had two brothers fighting over her was quite piquant, and an air of horrified excitement was electrifying the atmosphere.

With a nod the banker indicated that Hugh could join the game in Miss Dewey's stead.

'In that case I shall withdraw my person and my winnings…and my IOUs stand.' Toby knew that to act in such a callous way and prevent the young lady having a chance of cancelling a debt he'd deliberately led her into would brand him a cad. But he didn't care what people thought; he was obsessed with feeding the envy and enmity he had for his brother.

Toby had always known that Hugh wanted Beatrice Dewey. He'd known it years ago when the couple had been inseparable for weeks. His suspicions that his brother still lusted after the blonde had been confirmed when Hugh had unexpectedly strolled into the Whitleys' drawing room earlier. Miss Dewey had quite quickly distanced herself from his brother, enlightening Toby, if nobody else present, to the nature of the rift between Viscount Blackthorne and Hugh. Toby hadn't imagined an opportunity would arise this evening to torment his brother, but the moment it had he'd happily made use of it.

He surged out of his chair as steadily as his inebriated state allowed, grabbing his cash and sneering as a murmur of disapproval grew in volume. Pushing his way through the hushed spectators, Sir Toby Kendrick quit the room, then the house. He chuckled as he sauntered along the pavement. He might have lost his fiancée tonight—Mr Lowell had taken his daughter off home a moment after Toby had asked the miser for a few sovereigns to use as stake money. But luckily, he'd had some pocket change with him, and he'd cleverly turned those few coins into a tidy sum...

'Come...stand up, Beatrice...it's time to go...'

Beatrice heard the quiet baritone commanding her, felt gentle fingers touching her arm to coax her out of her seat. But she was unable to move. Tears were burning her eyes, but she managed to keep them at bay until a shrill voice heralded her aunt's approach.

'What have you done?' Dolly cried, thrusting her panic-stricken face close to the miscreant's blurry vision.

When her niece seemed incapable of explaining herself she pulled out a chair next to Bea and collapsed into it. Just minutes ago Fiona had sidled up to warn her that Bea might be in a spot of trouble, interrupting Dolly mid-flow in singing her niece's praises to her friends. *A spot of trouble* hardly did justice, in Dolly's mind, to this latest disaster threatening the Dewey family.

'My poor brother!' Dolly whimpered. 'How is he to repay the odious fellow that amount of cash? What were you thinking of, playing so freely, you stupid girl?' Dolly clapped her hands in frustration.

It was the trigger that Beatrice had been dreading. She stiffened, attempting to control her inner quaking at her aunt's fully deserved reprimand.

'What is to be done?' Dolly turned to Hugh for support as Bea dropped her forehead into a hand and used a thumb to smear away the moisture on her lashes.

'The matter can be rectified,' Hugh soothed.

He sat down on the opposite side of Bea and immediately she raised her glistening eyes to him. 'You think your brother is lying? I don't really owe him that much, do I?'

'Yes…you do…' Hugh disabused her. He'd had a muttered confirmation from the banker that the sum was correct. Sir Toby had encouraged Beatrice to engage in cocking—her whole pot of money had been risked on the turn of a card—and then, when she'd had nothing left and had panicked, his fiend of a brother had pretended to help her recoup her losses by loaning her more cash to stake.

'Papa shall not know of this,' Bea whispered.

'Indeed he must!' Dolly spluttered. 'However are

you to save yourself from ruin if your father does not settle with Sir Toby—?'

'He shall not know!' Beatrice interrupted, so forcefully that her aunt shrank back in her seat.

'You are overwrought, Beatrice, to speak so.' Dolly sounded miffed and glanced about.

Thankfully most people had had the good manners to exit the room while the crisis was debated by kith and kin. But Dolly knew that by tomorrow every breakfast table would be alive with gossip about Miss Dewey. Beatrice's good deed in being nice to Miss Rawlings would be overlooked and only the gory details of her misbehaviour picked over.

'I shall go home now.' Beatrice slowly gained her feet, but with a strengthening determination shaping her features. Drawing in a deep, inspiriting breath she elevated her chin. 'If I must run the gauntlet I'd sooner do it right away.' She felt ashamed that Hugh had witnessed her stupidity. She'd gone against him in trusting his brother when he'd made it clear Sir Toby was a bad character. 'Thank you for trying to save me by taking my place,' she whispered.

'My pleasure…' He inclined his head.

'Will you leave with us now?' Fiona had arrived with them in the viscount's coach and Beatrice realised she might like a lift home.

'Indeed I shall not!' Fiona replied with asperity. 'I'm going to stay here with Verity and Jago and defend your reputation by telling everybody what a vile monster Sir Toby is!' Fiona's cheeks were flushed with anger at what Hugh's brother had done. 'I can get a ride home with my family later.'

Verity murmured full-hearted agreement to her sister's plan. 'Jago has told me that he feared Sir Toby was playing a dastardly game with you…'

'It's a shame he didn't think to come and tell me,' Hugh pointed out, in a tone of voice that caused Verity to squirm on her spouse's behalf.

The little party exited the gaming room, Bea and Dolly escorted by Hugh, and the sisters marching right behind them.

Feeling light-headed with embarrassment, Bea involuntarily gripped tighter to the muscled flesh beneath her fingers, causing Hugh to smile encouragement at her. She snapped her head higher, her eyes steadily on the exit…until she came level with Colin and their gazes merged. His brows were drawn together, making him seem puzzled rather than disapproving. However, Bea noticed that Stella and her aunt looked to be relishing her disgrace.

'Is this evening's blasted bad luck never to end?' Dolly cried, hands jigging in distress. She peered up and down the road, seeking any sign of a coach bearing the Blackthorne coat of arms.

'It doesn't matter that the coach has disappeared,' Hugh said mildly, flicking his fingers to attract his servant's attention. Immediately a sleek vehicle stationed at the opposite kerb was steered to a halt in front of them.

'It doesn't matter? I think the viscount might dis-

agree on that!' Dolly shrilled, already tottering gratefully towards the open door of Hugh's transport.

A moment ago they had descended the stone steps
from the Whitleys' townhouse to find that Viscount
Blackthorne's carriage was nowhere to be seen. On
questioning one of the footmen stationed at the base of
the steps, Hugh had ascertained that the vehicle had left
almost as soon as it had dropped off its occupants. The
servant had guessed why that was, and so had Hugh:
the driver had had an assignation to keep and had believed he'd time to see his sweetheart before returning.
The unlucky swain had been caught out because his
passengers were departing far earlier than expected.

'You are good to us, sir, to help like this!' Dolly's
belated thanks were heartfelt and thrown over a shoulder as a groom sprang from his perch at the back of the
coach to assist her boarding.

Dolly had felt appalled at the idea of calling a Hackney, with no money to pay for it—and of course her
niece now had not a penny on her either. All in all,
Dolly deemed it a very bad ending to what had started
as an enjoyable affair.

Wordlessly, Hugh extended a palm to Beatrice. For
a moment their eyes tangled, and he could tell from her
reticence in accepting his help that she suspected he
might have an ulterior motive in offering her and her
aunt a ride home. As indeed he did.

'Do you want to walk back to Upper Brook Street?'
he suggested softly.

Beatrice nibbled her lower lip but finally placed her
fingers in his. As she settled into the luxurious seat

she kept her eyes averted from the man who'd leapt in and slammed the door then lounged opposite. She was alarmed by the thought that she was now unsure which Kendrick brother intended doing her reputation the most harm.

Chapter Fourteen

'It is a bit late to make a fuss about etiquette, miss!' Dolly snapped. 'Your reputation has been patched up too many times for that. You are now beyond the pale and fortunate Mr Kendrick is willing to put himself out for you.'

Scooting forward on the seat, she profusely thanked Hugh for his assistance in helping her alight from his coach.

Turning to her niece, Dolly poked her head into the vehicle's interior. 'Don't think your father shall remain in ignorance of this latest mischief. If you will not tell him that you have again added to his woes, then I shall.'

Beatrice had guessed her aunt had been simmering on the night's shocking events on the way home to Marylebone. The journey had passed in virtual silence and every time Bea had tried to make a little conversation her aunt had barked at her. Even Bea's quiet, stuttered apologies had been angrily flicked away by Dolly. As for the man ensconced opposite… Bea had tried to avoid looking his way, acutely conscious as she was of his powerful presence.

A few moments ago, when it had become clear from passing landmarks that Hugh had instructed his driver to head to her aunt's house first, Bea had urgently whispered to Dolly that it would be seemly if she were the first to quit their Good Samaritan's company. In response, her aunt had snappily overruled her.

'Mrs Pearson is over-anxious; she'll see things differently in the morning.'

Bea glanced at the pair of broad shoulders easing into the squabs as the coach once more set off. 'I think you are being over-optimistic, sir,' she murmured.

'Do you? Why?'

'Because in the morning things will be worse, not better, than they are now,' Bea answered unsteadily. 'And well you know it. So if you are trying to kindly make light of my folly…please do not bother. I must face the consequences of my actions. I am not a child.'

'I know you're not a child, Beatrice…far from it…'

There was an insinuation in his husky reply that put Bea on her guard as she peeked at him from beneath thick lashes. Ever since he'd helped her into his coach an idea had been circling her mind that he might try to take advantage of her predicament. He'd told her weeks ago to consider his offer of protection. Then she had been a jilted spinster, living with an ageing parent. Now her position—and her father's—was even more precarious, due to her foolhardiness.

Bea hated the idea of her father taking on the burden of her debt; neither did she want to seek help from

Viscount Blackthorne. Walter would be mortified to discover that money had been borrowed from his son-in-law to pay off his dependant daughter's gambling debts.

Queasiness in her stomach—part excitement, part dread—made Beatrice fidget on the seat. She had a feeling that she'd given Hugh Kendrick an opportunity to remind her why she should become his mistress. And many women of her age and unfortunate position might listen to such a rich and charismatic man's persuasion...

'When we last spoke you seemed determined not to come to town. What changed your mind?'

The unexpected question jolted Bea from her reflection into stuttering a reply. 'My father...well, both of us, actually...decided we would after all like to stay with Elise for a week or two.'

'Did the fact that Burnett was in London have a bearing on that decision?'

'I'm not sure it is any of your business either way,' Bea returned stiltedly, her indignation rising as a flash of white teeth in the dusk demonstrated that her tartness hadn't bothered him.

Hugh hauled his back from the upholstery to lean towards her. His eyes slanted up at her mutinous profile. 'Are you expecting the good doctor to sort out this evening's mess for you, Beatrice?' he suggested.

Bea swung an astonished face towards him. 'No, of course not. What on earth made you think he'd offer to do so?'

Hugh shrugged, brushed a speck from a dark sleeve. 'It's what a gentleman does for a woman he cares for.'

Bea moistened her lips, trying to fathom his meaning. 'Sir Colin now cares for Miss Rawlings, as you know.'

'So he does…' Hugh dulcetly concurred, straightening on the seat. 'But perhaps he cares for you too. *Does* he?' His lazy tone had turned demanding.

'If you think that just because I went out of my way to speak to him this evening that I am trying to wriggle back into Colin's life, then you are mistaken, sir.' Bea's fists were planted either side of her on the seat as though she might shoot upright at any moment.

'You're to be commended for treating the couple civilly. Burnett seemed pleased you had, and might approach you next time rather than the other way around. Will you encourage him?'

Finally understanding his hints, Bea gave him an icy glare. She had nobody to blame but herself for him thinking what he did. That particular seed had been sown in Hugh's mind when she'd declared she'd sooner be Colin's mistress than his wife. Stupidly she'd flung at Hugh intentionally wounding words, uttered thoughtlessly, and they'd returned to haunt her.

'If you believe that Sir Colin Burnett might pay your brother off for me if I sleep with him then you are utterly wrong,' she breathed. 'You should not apply your own lax morals to others. *He* is a respectful gentleman, and besides he has not yet settled his own account with my father…' Beatrice's small teeth were suddenly clamped on her lower lip. She regretted that she'd disclosed details of Colin's meanness.

'Burnett owes your father money?'

'It is none of your concern.' Beatrice turned her head, watching the darkling street scene. She wished to be quickly home, to avoid any more awkward interrogation, yet part of her craved to continue savouring the dangerous thrill of Hugh Kendrick's company.

'No matter, if you'd rather not say…' His voice was again as smooth as honey. 'I'm sure Walter will be happy to oblige me with an answer.'

'You will not speak to him about it!'

Her father might with alacrity take up any offer Hugh made to act as debt collector, especially once he discovered that his financial position had considerably worsened following her recklessness. There was already bad blood between Hugh and Colin. She had no intention of heightening their feud, and with it the damage to her reputation.

'It's likely everything is now resolved and resurrecting the matter will upset Papa.' Bea hoped her blurted argument was effective.

'I think you know it is not resolved,' Hugh countered. 'I think you intended giving your father your winnings to mitigate his losses. Am I right?'

It seemed pointless fibbing. She gave a single nod, glad the gloom concealed her chagrined blush. 'Instead I have stupidly made things much worse.'

'It was good of you to think of your father's gains rather than your own.'

'I owed it to him to try to help. My wedding expenses have left him out of pocket—' Bea knew it was silly continuing to pretend her father had been paid up.

'It's Burnett's duty to make amends, not yours,' Hugh interrupted mildly.

'I know…' Bea sighed, staring at her clasped hands. 'And he said he would.'

'Perhaps you of all people should know that his promises are not worth the paper they are written on.'

Again Bea felt her face heating beneath his soft sarcasm. But she couldn't deny that his criticism of Colin was accurate and well-deserved.

'There is a solution.'

Again Hugh closed the gap between them so their heads were mere inches apart.

Bea felt her heart cease pounding, then resume with breathtaking speed. Eyes that gleamed like black diamonds in the coach's interior had entrapped her and she steeled herself not to flinch when a long cool finger circled with seductive slowness on her burning cheek.

'I know we've had our differences. I know you don't trust me because I've let you down in the past.' Hugh took one of her hands, raising it and touching his lips to her fingertips. 'I admit I pursued you, told you I wanted to marry you, all to no end. But I didn't lie and I withdrew from your life the moment I realised I could not raise enough cash to take a wife.'

Hugh paused, angled his head to watch her averted profile.

'Throughout our friendship we were always very compatible indeed…in one way. I believe we still are, and I want to prove it to you.' His hand opened, forked on her narrow chin as he turned her towards him. 'Forget Burnett. He's not worthy of you; he never was. I can

protect you and easily deal with my brother's spite.'
Without warning his mouth covered hers, expertly parting her lips, daring her to deny his next brutally honest words. 'Where's the shame in mutual pleasure, or
in letting me care for you and your father?'

Bea couldn't deny it...or him... Her mouth softened
beneath his renewed wooing and when he lifted her
onto his lap with a groan of frustration her instinctive
resistance was easily overcome.

Hugh's hands plunged beneath her cloak, caressing
her midriff, his thumbs thrusting upwards to tease the
hardening nubs beneath her bodice. Bea continued a
token struggle and yet her back began arching so she
might have more of his rapacious touch. It was all the
permission Hugh needed to sweep his mouth down the
slender column of her throat to the undulation of her
bosom, tempting him closer with every panted inha-
lation.

'Tell me you don't want this and I'll leave you be,'
Hugh growled, his breath steaming against her milky
skin.

He raised his head from her naked throat to read her
expression but Bea moaned, tightening her fingers on
his nape, wanting more of the tantalising magic of his
cool, clever mouth soothing her fever.

Hugh smiled. 'Is that a yes to my offer of *carte
blanche*, sweetheart?' he murmured as some of his long
fingers disappeared into her cleavage, curving beneath
a warm breast so he might feast on the satiny flesh with
eyes and mouth.

Bea gasped at the exquisite delight of cold air and

hot tongue on her sensitive nipples and when he began to draw upwards the silk of her skirts her protest was lost in an instant beneath the onslaught of an erotically demanding kiss.

His stroking fingers slipped to the smooth skin of an inner thigh, just one insinuating itself beneath the lawn of her undergarments to fondle her a fraction away from the core of her femininity.

Bea writhed against him, parted her limbs in wonderment as a tingle streaked through her veins. No man had ever before touched her so intimately, and as he fractionally entered her with a fingertip a jolt of untasted pleasure made her panic and ram together her knees. Hugh groaned a chuckle, dipping his head to skilfully suckle a taut nipple, drawing her back into his web of desire.

Bea squirmed on his lap, and when his hand again slipped beneath her skirt she made no effort to stop him knuckling the sensitive dewy bud hidden in crisp curls. She bucked her hips to nudge the instrument of her delight, allowing him to reposition her so she was straddling his body, then pressing her pelvis willingly against his solid torso. The rocking motion of the coach was tormenting her, as was Hugh's long, drugging kiss. His tongue thrust little by little into her in time with the fingers he was moving between her legs. Bea's whimpering gasps became louder, her body more tense as inner friction mounted towards an unknown crescendo.

'I promise I'll never leave you,' Hugh whispered against the febrile heat of her shoulder. 'Should I marry to get an heir I swear I'll still want you in my life. I won't abandon you, Beatrice…'

It seemed to Beatrice that his vow of loyalty came from a long way off and was intended to lull her; yet it instantly stole away her bliss. When his mouth swooped again to hers she shook her head, freeing her lips, and two small fists were jammed between them, holding him at bay.

Struggling to keep her footing in the swaying coach, she slapped away hands that would have dragged her back and stumbled against the opposite seat, skimming over the hide to huddle in the furthest corner. Tugging down her clothes, she whipped aside her face, closing her stinging eyes.

'Your future wife need fear no rival in me,' she croaked, feeling desperately ashamed of what she'd let him do to her. She knew just seconds ago she had been close to crying out in rapture and was thankful she'd called a halt before losing all control. Trapped in his seductive net a moment longer she might have ended up pinned beneath him on the seat, a willing party to her thorough ruination.

'And your future husband—whoever he may be— has no rival in me,' Hugh returned quietly. 'So long as we adhere to the accepted rules, my dear, where would be the harm in carrying on enjoying each other's company?

'The harm would be in the deceit and the hurt to other people, and it is telling that you do not understand that. *If* I should marry, my husband will know he can trust me when I pledge to love and lie with only him. In return I would expect to be equally honoured.'

Hugh laughed soundlessly. 'You are holding out for a love-match, are you, and a faithful spouse?'

'Don't you dare mock me,' Bea cried. 'You might intend seeking a wife to improve your status but such mercenary plans are abhorrent to me.'

'I'm not mocking you, my dear. I'm impressed…but dubious you'll get what you want. Most married couples of my acquaintance have…other attachments…'

'Is my brother-in-law being unfaithful to Elise?' Bea whispered. She had always admired her sister's seemingly perfect relationship with Alex Blackthorne, and would be devastated to know it was a sham because he kept a mistress.

'There's always an exception to prove the rule,' Hugh replied gently. 'To my knowledge Alex is enviably content in every way with your sister.'

Bea expelled a pent-up breath.

'It would sadden you to know otherwise, wouldn't it?' Hugh murmured.

'Of course…Elise would be devastated. Alex is the love of her life.'

'And Burnett…was he the love of *your* life?' Hugh asked in a voice devoid of emotion.

'I have given up on love…' Bea prevaricated, gazing through the coach window.

'You just said you would marry for love…'

Bea choked a bitter little laugh. 'So I did, and thus will need to remain a spinster—for the likelihood of finding somebody suitable is remote.'

'Spinsters are entitled to get pleasure from life, Beatrice…discreetly, perhaps, and with no hurt caused to anybody else.'

'Apart from your wife…'

'Alas…like you, I fear I might be doomed to a single life,' he returned solemnly.

'I have said do not mock me,' Beatrice answered levelly while continuing to watch the stars. Her anger and embarrassment seemed to have drained away, leaving her calmer.

'I wasn't. I was telling the truth. Why do you feel you must deny yourself the comfort I offer?'

Hugh stretched out a hand but Bea knocked away his fingers.

'Are you going to tell me you didn't like what we just did?' he taunted.

'I'm going to tell you never to touch me again,' Bea said. 'Keep your empty promises and your payments for services rendered for your courtesans. They are sure to appreciate them, whereas I do not.' She met his gaze squarely, unflinchingly. 'You will not degrade me with your lust any more than will your brother with his malice.'

Bea glanced away from the flinty glitter in black eyes. She knew she'd angered him by thwarting him, and by comparing him to Sir Toby.

With a sigh of sheer thankfulness she glimpsed the top of Upper Brook Street and knew she was finally able to escape. One of her hands darted to the door, but she hesitated before jumping out of the coach. 'I trust in the future you will keep to your word and leave me alone as I've asked you to. I know you are entitled to visit the Blackthornes because you are the viscount's friend…'

'Not any more…' Hugh said smoothly over her words.

There had been no hint of accusation in his reply and yet still Bea felt suddenly guilty that the two men, companions since childhood, had fallen out over her.

'I did not complain to Alex that you had propositioned me and I regret that he went after you, resulting in a bad argument.' She paused before adding, 'I told Elise what had occurred in confidence and she…' Bea tailed off, not wanting to blame Elise.

'Did you think your sister would not confide in…*the love of her life*?' Hugh asked ironically.

'It's not Elise's fault. She didn't betray my trust; Alex badgered her till she hinted at what was troubling her.'

'Have I been troubling you too, Bea?'

'Not at all…you are never in my mind…' She blurted out the lie while studying the sliver of moon in the navy blue heavens. 'And I would not have you and Alex becoming worst enemies over me.'

'You're the viscount's sister-in-law and it's right he protects you; in his position I would have done the same,' Hugh admitted tonelessly. At her questioning glance, he shrugged. 'I'd risk that friendship again for your sake. Nothing has changed…I want you…' He repeated it with emphasis. '*Nothing* has changed, Beatrice.'

'Nothing has changed for me either,' Beatrice echoed in a voice that had lost a little composure. 'I have told you to stay away and hope, as a gentleman, you will accept my wishes.'

She noticed a corner of his mouth tilt upwards. 'I'll do whatever you want, sweet…' He moved towards her, his narrowed, gleaming eyes steady on her. 'How about a wager?' he suggested. 'I'll bet the money you lost to-night that within a week you come to me.'

Bea shrank back against the side of the coach, alarmed by his indolent confidence and the reason for it. Her eyes were drawn to his thin mouth…the lips that had so recently soothed and excited her and no doubt could savage equally efficiently…

'All you need stake in return is one night spent with me.' Hugh captured her chin with a masterful hand as she tried to avoid his eyes. 'Come…you're adamant you don't want me…never think of me…what's to fear? Take the wager and clear your debts in one fell swoop.'

His fingers fell away from her skin and were held out for her to shake. Beatrice stared at those outstretched digits, then impetuously she grabbed at them, before flinging away his hand as though she'd been scalded. Without a word of farewell she hurtled out of the carriage and up to the Blackthornes' house, breathless by the time she'd reached the top step.

When the butler opened the door to Bea's agitated rap she darted past and immediately dropped her face into her shaking palms, making the fellow glance at her in concern.

Chapter Fifteen

'Please accept my sincere apologies for having called so early.' The impatient visitor shoved his hat beneath an armpit as he jerked a bow. Behind him hurried a housekeeper, who'd been barged aside by the fellow so he might waste no time in securing an audience with her employer. 'I must let you know that papers requiring your urgent attention have just come to light, Sir Colin.'

In fact Percy Withers Esquire had known for over a week that a severe discrepancy had occurred. In the interim he had been frantically trying to discover how to mitigate his grave error in order to preserve his reputation as an attorney gentlemen might rely on to efficiently manage their business affairs. Having rallied his courage that morning, Mr Withers had set out without delay, praying he might deflect the barrage of criticism he was sure to face.

Colin Burnett rose to his feet, intrigued and yet also exasperated at this intrusion before he'd even dressed for the day. He tossed his napkin onto the breakfast table, tightening the belt on his dressing gown.

'Well, come in, Withers,' he invited, a touch sarcastically. He dismissed his hovering red-faced servant with a curt nod.

Colin had been renting this modest townhouse since he'd turned up in the city, and had pondered whether to invest some of his inheritance in buying the freehold. The staff would have to go, of course. He found them all—cook, housemaid and manservant—far too lax in manners and industry.

Confronted with the task of commencing his report, the lawyer seemed momentarily unable to do so. He coughed, jutting his chin twice in quick succession, his Adam's apple bobbing nervously.

'These urgent documents?' Colin prompted, feeling in no mood for bad news.

He'd risen late, having spent a restless night brooding on the events at the Whitleys'. On the journey home Stella had nestled into him in the carriage while Mrs Monk turned a blind eye to her niece's canoodling. But despite the heat in his loins caused by memories of his betrothed's teasing touches Stella had faded from his mind when his head had touched the pillow, leaving just his former fiancée dominating his thoughts.

Colin regretted many things where Beatrice was concerned. Mostly he was sorry she had got herself into a bad scrape by listening to Sir Toby Kendrick's poor advice. Previously Colin had harboured no opinion of Hugh's elder brother; now he disliked the two men equally. Again and again throughout the night Colin had cursed his damnable uncle for altering the terms of his bequest and denying him the chance of contentment with Beatrice. Instead he had to contend with being shackled to a coquette and to receiving his solicitor at an ungodly hour of the morning.

Irritably Colin cleared a useable space on the cloth by rattling crockery sideways, then indicated Withers take a chair at the table.

Percy remained where he was but did bring forth a scroll from the cavernous inside pocket of his coat. 'You might recall, Sir Colin, that shortly after your uncle's will was read, and certain unpalatable clauses were found to be contained therein, you asked me to examine the document for loopholes to allow you to have a bride of your own choosing.'

About to reseat himself, Colin instead unwound, pivoting slowly on a heel, his features a frozen mask. For a long moment he said nothing, simply staring as the fellow's complexion alternated between sickly pallor and bright pink.

'Are you about to tell me that finally you have found something…when it is too late?'

'I examined the text minutely, Sir Colin, as indeed I told you at the time,' Percy lied robustly.

'You did say as much…' Colin remained unmoving, his expression perilously quizzical. 'Yet I sense you are about to add that something vital was overlooked.' He watched his visitor shift uneasily. 'What was overlooked?' It was a deceptively dulcet enquiry.

'The authentic document.' Mr Withers raised the roll of parchment gripped in his hand. 'The other is a forgery, sir…'

Colin took a single stride towards the fellow, mouth

agape. 'A forgery?' he bellowed. 'Where in damnation did you get a forgery?'

'From you, sir,' Percy croaked, shrinking back.

Pulling out a chair from the table, Colin slumped into it. He gazed up at Withers, casting his mind back to the critical time and inwardly dissecting what had occurred just prior to his predecessor's death.

'Mrs Monk gave me the will. She had nursed Sir Donald during his last days and told me he had ordered her to hand his personal papers to me and no other.'

'Indeed…' Percy said in a commiserating tone.

'What are you implying?' Colin barked. 'Mrs Monk was Sir Donald's sister-in-law. When his brother died and Maggie was remarried to Peter Monk they remained friendly. The woman has nothing to gain from meddling.' Colin jumped to his feet, pacing to and fro. 'Donald provided her with an allowance when she was widowed for a second time. The amount did not increase or decline after my uncle expired.' He ceased prowling. 'The only person to improve their lot, if she considers marrying me to be a positive step,' Colin muttered bitterly, 'is my cousin Stella.'

He gestured away the idea. Colin believed his fiancée to be an ambitious chit but innocent of criminality. He'd noticed that at times Stella seemed careless of his presence, and she never pressed him for a date to be set for their wedding. Only Maggie did that. Stella might cosy up to him when worried she'd angered him with her flirting, but it was absurd to suppose her guilty of falsifying the will to trap him and he told Percy Withers so.

'Indeed, Sir Colin, neither do I think the girl had a hand in it. I believe we must look to her mother…'

'Her mother is dead!' Colin exclaimed testily. 'My uncle became Stella's guardian when her parents sadly died. Of course I know we are not natural cousins, and previously I had not met Stella, but she grew up calling her benefactor "uncle", and Mrs Monk has been an honorary aunt to her.'

He paused, gesturing wildly as though exasperated by his own explanation.

'Over the years information filtered down through the family that Sir Donald had formed a friendship with Stella's birth father when they served together under Nelson. So, despite being a bachelor, my uncle stepped in to help when at ten years old the girl was orphaned following a fire at her home.'

'A fiction, I believe, concocted for propriety's sake,' Withers sighed out.

'By whom?' Colin demanded, forcing his fists against his hips.

'By the child's true mother under direction from the reluctant sire, I imagine.

'How can you possibly know that?' Colin spluttered.

'I have lately attempted to trace the girls' parents—a Mr and Mrs Rawlings of Pontefract, who perished in the fire—and have found that no such people ever existed.'

Percy twisted his hat between his hands, anticipating that once his client had conquered his obvious amazement he would furiously demand to know why such diligence had not been applied sooner. Withers was unwilling to admit that he had allowed a junior clerk to peruse Sir Donald's will because business accounts for a more prestigious client had occupied him personally. Mr Kendrick paid handsomely, and on time, and never quibbled over necessary expenses as Sir Colin did. Thus the solicitor had considered the wealthy mine owner worthier of his attention.

But he was regretting his lack of vigilance now that he had finally compared the signature on the document Sir Colin had given him with the earlier version held in his office. The fraudster had made a fair effort to mimic the deceased's wandering scrawl, but it could not fool the man who had dealt with Sir Donald's papers for over two decades. And the only difference from the original document was the insertion of a clause that stated Colin Burnett must promise to wed Stella Rawlings in order to take his birthright.

Deeming it prudent to use his ace before Sir Colin had mustered his thoughts and threatened to sue, Percy confidently resumed. 'During my investigation I turned up the fact that Mrs Monk's maiden name was Rawlings. It is my belief that she has deliberately deceived you; furthermore I believe she is Stella's mother and Sir Donald fathered the girl…'

Hugh Kendrick had enjoyed no better sleep than had Colin Burnett, and for the same reason: Beatrice had been on his mind the night through. Whereas Colin had tossed and turned, rueing that a sweet, decorous woman had slipped through his fingers, Hugh's thoughts about her had been reprehensibly torrid. To Hugh, Beatrice was no poised goddess worthy of a pedestal; she was a maddeningly sensual temptress whose silky limbs had entwined perfectly with his while she'd panted sweet breath against his lips.

Till dawn light he'd lain with his hands pillowing his head, scowling at the ceiling, with the scent of her skin teasing his nostrils. So aroused had he felt following their passionate encounter in his coach that he'd almost flung off the silk sheets and got dressed. But he hadn't set off for Gwen's or Sophia's, despite being charged with sexual frustration, because he knew it would have been pointless. Neither woman had the power to heal an ache that had started years ago in his loins and then spread to enclose his heart.

Bea was the one he desired above all others; she was also the woman with whom he wanted to grow old. He wanted her in his bed and at his table; he wanted to host parties with her by his side, dressed in satins and sumptuous jewels, then watch her blush in pleasure beneath his adoring gaze. He wanted her to mother his children…

Hugh knew that he loved Beatrice and wanted to marry her, and but for his damnable pride getting in the way he would by now have told her so—although he'd have some explaining to do about his time in India. But he trusted Bea to understand; she had an empathetic and kind and loving nature… He grimaced ruefulness. Obviously she'd held back on bestowing it on him recently…and with just cause.

He could have proposed last night and vowed to protect her as his wife from his foul brother. Instead he'd come very close to losing control and taking advantage of her while she was at a low ebb. From her startled response to his increasingly intimate seduction he'd learned that the doctor hadn't bedded her. Hugh knew he'd come close to taking her virginity on the seat of the coach, and had he done so he would have deserved her loathing and disgust. He would certainly have had his own.

What point had there been in coercing her into a stupid wager? He could not remember taking more than a couple of shots of whisky at the *soirée* and yet he now believed he must have been drunk to act in such a way. Whether he won the wager or not, forcing Bea to surrender and come to him, he'd deal with Toby. He'd make certain his brother never again dared hurt Beatrice because he was too cowardly to pick a fight with *him*.

Hugh pushed away his coffee cup and stood up. He'd stop acting like a sulky youth and declare his feelings and his honourable intentions. If she refused him... He tossed back his head, frowning at the ceiling. What would he do if she refused him? Revert to trying to make her his mistress? Or would he give up gracefully? A mirthless laugh grazed his throat. He knew he couldn't give her up...

'Your brother is in the hallway, sir...'

Hugh snapped his face to the servant hovering on the threshold and his features, shaped by agonised indecision, began displaying his aversion to the imminent meeting. He had not been expecting Toby quite so soon, yet had guessed he'd be confronted by his gleeful brother, keen to rub salt into his wounds, at some point during the day.

'Bring him in.' Hugh resisted the urge to ask the footman to fetch him a brandy decanter at the same time. Instead he poured himself another cup of coffee from a silver pot.

'I thought you'd be partaking of something stronger this morning.' Toby swaggered over the threshold.

'Why is that?'

'Come…are we to pretend that you are not furious with me for putting Miss Dewey in a bad light?'

'You showed yourself up more than you did her,' Hugh responded contemptuously. 'Could you not see that, you fool?'

Toby coloured as that barb hit home. He'd never been popular, but the few friends he did have had probably now deserted him…just as his fiancée had. He'd received a note from Katherine's father that morning, advising him that he intended cancelling the marriage contract. Toby was incensed that an alternative source of income had been cut off and he must rely solely on his brother for hand-outs. He knew he had to tread carefully…yet press home his advantage.

'I'm not fretting, but I think you are. You want the chit—you always have done. I know you don't like seeing her at the gossips' mercy…or at mine.' Toby's expression became calculating. 'As you know, I'm not a callous chap. I've kept my mouth shut about your *commitments* in India, haven't I?' He sniggered as his comment strengthened Hugh's acerbic smile. 'But needs must when the devil drives, dear brother. You keep threatening to tighten your fist against me, so what am I to do but find another way to make a shilling?'

Toby sounded confident but in fact felt dubious. The amount he'd won from Miss Dewey would hardly keep him in women and cigars for a year, let alone keep a roof over his head. He pulled out the fistful of IOUs.

'Would you like these?'

'Are you giving them to me?' Hugh asked, barely glancing at Beatrice's debts.

'For a price…'

'And that is?'

'A thousand pounds.'

Hugh's answering grimace was unfathomable.

'She's worth that and more to you.' Toby slyly eyed his brother while fingering his fleshy lower lip. 'Of course I could go and see her father…or I might approach the young lady herself. How do you think she'll take knowing of your lust for exotic harlots? Perhaps she might not want you then and I might think of a way she could repay me. I reckon she'd taste sweet as honey…*does* she?'

Toby's intentional provocation received an immediate response.

Simmering with pent-up rage and frustration, Hugh delivered a single punch that sent Toby reeling to the ground.

'Fifteen hundred pounds is the price now.' Toby wiped his bloodied lips with the back of a hand, chuckling contentedly. 'I seriously underestimated just how enslaved by her you are, dear brother.' He struggled to a seated position, wrapping his arms around his knees. 'In which case you might like to throw in Gwen Sharpe for me, too. I've always fancied that vixen.'

Hugh turned his back on his brother. He understood that once it became known he'd protected Beatrice financially the purity of his motives, and her virtue, would be questioned.

'I'll think it over and let you know.' Hugh made for the door before the temptation became too great to again remove the smirk from Toby's face with his fist.

'Well, don't think about it for too long.' Toby scrambled to his feet, incensed that his brother would take himself off before an agreement had been reached.

Chapter Sixteen

'Now do you understand, you stupid girl, why I wanted you married as soon as maybe?' Maggie Monk raised a hand as though to slap some sense into her daughter.

'It is all your fault everything is lost!' Stella cried hysterically, scrubbing at her eyes with a hanky. 'You should have told me sooner all about it. Why keep it secret? I cannot be *your* offspring…I cannot.'

She sent her mother a look of utter distaste. In Stella's opinion such a drab-looking woman could not be so closely related to her; she deserved parents who were charming and glamorous. Since childhood Stella had imagined her father to be a tragic gallant who'd perished in a fire while bravely attempting to rescue his wife and baby girl from an inferno. She'd been brought up thinking she'd been safely dropped from a bedroom window into the trusty arms of a servant, then her poor parents had succumbed to the flames, lost to her for ever…

Stella had now learned that no such heroics had occurred and that she'd been brought into the world following a sordid affair between an old miser and a plain-faced adulteress.

'I cannot be *yours*.' Stella gave a pitiful sniff.

'Well, you are, my girl!' Maggie boomed. 'You're mine and Sir Donald's and you're entitled to his protection from beyond the grave.' Maggie wrathfully wrung her hands. 'The tight-fist left no provision for you in his will and he left me nothing more than I'd already got, despite me tending to him till he'd expelled his dying breath.'

Her mouth knotted in bitterness.

'So I did what I had to do to keep us comfortable. My meagre pension would never run to fine gowns for you so you might socialise with the Quality and find a good husband.' Maggie strode up to her daughter and pinched her chin in cruel fingers. 'Did you fancy a yokel touching you with his callused hands?' She gave a grim smile as Stella flinched from the idea of marrying a labourer. 'Sir Donald's name and his wealth are yours by right and I did my utmost to get them for you.' She shook Stella's shoulder in emphasis. 'You should thank me for what I did. Once vows had been taken Sir Colin would never have admitted to being hoodwinked; neither would he have wanted the scandal of a divorce.'

'But he's not bothered about abandoning his fiancée!' Stella screeched, again dabbing her watering eyes. She'd not cared much for Sir Colin, but she'd loved the life and the people to which he'd introduced her. She'd been determined to keep him hooked while she cast about for a better catch. Her circle of admirers would disperse once those fellows discovered she was a bastard and her mother a fraudster.

'You're not the first Colin's jilted; he'll be known as a fickle rogue.'

The only crumb of comfort Maggie had was that Sir Colin Burnett's reputation might suffer following his breaking off another engagement. Maggie was banking on him keeping the matter to himself as far as he was able. She'd forged Sir Donald's signature on a replica will when bubbling with rancour because the man to whom she'd devoted her life had treated her and their daughter shabbily. Maggie had cuckolded her mild-mannered first husband for almost a decade with his brother, then carried on sleeping with Donald for the duration of her second marriage. After her lover's death she'd finally realised that she, and their child, had meant little to the man she'd adored. He'd left everything to a nephew he barely knew and nothing to his own flesh and blood.

At noon that day Sir Colin Burnett had turned up, thunder-faced. Stella had still been abed and Maggie had been relieved that her daughter had missed most of the argument that had taken place. At first Maggie had denied everything. Once Sir Colin had produced the authentic will she had known the game was up and taken refuge in bluster. Their raised voices had eventually drawn Stella downstairs and Sir Colin had tarried only long enough to demand back his engagement ring before storming off.

Maggie was anxious to know how Burnett might retaliate. If she were mistaken in thinking he'd wish to smooth over the matter to protect his credibility she must prepare to flee to avoid arrest. If she were imprisoned her beloved Stella would be at the mercy of rough sorts in need of a wife but with nothing to give her but coarse manners and backbreaking work.

'Damn that solicitor and his eagle eyes,' Maggie spat resentfully.

Stella knuckled her wet eyes. 'Are we in bad trouble, Mama?'

'No…' Maggie stroked her daughter's fiery tresses, pleased to hear the girl call her Mama. 'Sir Colin will not want this all played out in court because of the risk to his reputation. It will blow over.'

'What of *my* reputation?' Stella wailed. 'Lord Whitley will never again have me in his house if he knows I'm a bastard…'

'Never mind that old man!'

'But I like him…'

Maggie sighed, eyeing her daughter shrewdly. 'I reckon Lord Whitley likes you, too, my dear.'

Once the old lecher found out her wedding was off he might proposition Stella. It was no perfect solution, but Maggie believed her daughter would be better off protected as a rich man's mistress than a poor man's wife…

'You must allow me to pay off Toby Kendrick…prior to knocking his teeth down his throat.'

'You may knock the blackguard's teeth down his throat with my blessing, but paying my daughter's debts is my responsibility.' Stubbornly Mr Dewey turned from his son-in-law to cast a censorious look in Beatrice's direction. 'Would that she had a husband to keep her in check,' he muttered darkly, 'For I am fast running out of cash and patience with her.'

'Papa! It is not wholly Bea's fault! The vile wretch tricked her into thinking he was offering sound advice during that game of Faro.' Elise attempted to soothe her father's agitation.

Beatrice's sorrowful shake of the head indicated to her sister that she deserved their father's wrath, and would bear it if it eased his mind. Approaching Walter, Bea took one of his withered hands. She hated seeing him overwrought.

Walter shook off her comfort, limping to an armchair to flop down. 'You have overstepped the mark this time, miss, with your impetuousness.'

Alex shrugged, wordlessly enquiring from his wife how else he might persuade Walter to sensibly allow him to take control of the matter.

'Papa, listen to me. It is best that the odious man is quickly paid off or he might charge interest on the debt, you know,' Elise warned briskly.

'Hah! He can try! I'll broadcast far and wide that he is a dastardly money-grabber.'

'I think most people have already come to that conclusion,' the viscount commented dryly. 'What's more, Toby Kendrick gives the impression he's too thick-skinned to care about vilification.'

'He was not liked before this blew up; now people roundly despise him,' Elise chipped in. 'Why would he go out of his way to make a target of Bea?'

Alex had his own ideas on that, but realised he'd

better not air them or his father-in-law might have apoplexy. He and Hugh had been close for decades, and Alex was sorely missing his friend's companionship. He knew Hugh almost as well as he knew himself. In Alex's opinion Hugh had never stopped loving Beatrice and desired her with a passion bordering on obsession. Alex also knew that Sir Toby Kendrick was bitterly resentful of his younger brother's success. If Toby had discovered Hugh's Achilles' Heel he would jab mercilessly at it and enjoy watching his brother squirm.

'Your sister had it from Kendrick that his brother was no good.' Walter wagged a finger at Elise. 'Beatrice told me that herself; yet she ignored the good fellow and heeded the bad character.'

Again Beatrice winced beneath her father's rebuke, clapping her hands over her ears as the debate over Sir Toby's hatefulness and her stupidity continued batting to and fro.

Two days had passed since the evening she'd gambled so heavily. Early the following morning she had told her father and sister what she'd done. Under chaotic interrogation, when questions had been fired at her from every direction, she had admitted that Hugh Kendrick had said he didn't consider his brother a trustworthy individual. Bea was glad she'd owned up straight away that a scandal was brewing, before her family learned gory details from gossip.

Aunt Dolly had arrived in high dudgeon just after luncheon, to complain to her brother that his elder daughter had learned nothing from her past mistakes and had cast a shadow over them all once more.

Beatrice hadn't ducked any criticism, and simply wished to put matters right...but how? She dared not tell her father that the gentleman he lauded had made her an indecent proposal in order to clear her debt.

The idea of carrying out the forfeit both excited and appalled Bea. At the time, the wager had seemed too good to be true. As, of course, it was. Once the anxiety fogging her mind had lifted Beatrice had realised that she had shaken hands on a deal that she could never win. In the eyes of the *ton* she'd be damned if she did go to Hugh Kendrick and damned if she did not.

There was only one reason a gentleman would pay a young lady's debts if she were unrelated to him, and everybody knew what it was. Toby Kendrick would reveal that his brother had paid off Miss Dewey's IOUs and revel in seeing her suffer the dreadful consequences.

But what right had she to feel outraged? She had already come close to becoming Hugh's paramour. The memory of the exquisite pleasure Hugh had aroused in her was preventing her focussing on finding a solution to this latest crisis. Even now she was conscious of the low throb in her belly caused by a need to see him. She felt restless enough to want to leave the house—even if it meant enduring stares and whispers—so she might meet Hugh by chance rather than by design.

'I have some insurance policies that can be sold to pay off the rogue...'

Mr Dewey's sighed declaration pierced Bea's consciousness. 'But...but those policies provide your pension, Papa,' she stammered. 'You cannot sell them and leave yourself without an income.' Bea was coming to accept there was little option but to let her brother-in-law salvage her reputation by dealing with the matter.

'So what else do you suggest I do, miss?' Walter bellowed.

'A gentleman caller, my lord,' a liveried footman announced.

Viscount Blackthorne quirked an eyebrow at his manservant.

'Sir Colin Burnett, my lord.' The footman answered his master's wordless enquiry.

'Show him to my study.'

'What in God's name can *he* want?' Walter muttered testily once the footman had withdrawn. 'Mayhap he's come to crow over our worsening misfortune. And he set the ball rolling, damn him!'

'I'm sure he has not.' Beatrice spoke up for the man who'd jilted her. Her father rarely used expletives with his daughters present so she knew how angry he was feeling. 'Colin was pleasant to me at the Whitleys'.'

'Was he, now? Well, perhaps he'll be nice enough to hand over my expenses so I can put the cash towards those other costs you have dumped at my door.'

'What do you think he wants?' Elise whispered to Bea as they sat together on the sofa.

Alex had gone to meet his visitor and the two sisters had settled down, allowing their father to brood moodily in his armchair. Every so often Walter would thump down his stick on the rug as some private thought vexed him. But he'd directed no further reprimands at Beatrice.

'I hope his purpose is to belatedly open his purse

and hand over what he owes,' Beatrice replied in an undertone. 'Papa might then calm down while we sort out the other mess I've caused.'

Elise knew Bea was feeling very guilty indeed. 'Perhaps Colin will ask to see you, if you are again friends,' she suggested, giving her sister's hand a comforting pat.

'I wouldn't go so far as to say we're *friends*.' Bea sounded rueful. 'I've nothing more to say to him. Papa is quite able to speak for himself about his expenses.' She slipped a glance at their father, glowering into space. 'He seems ready to do so, too.'

Bea cast her eyes heavenwards, acutely regretting having spoiled what might be her father's final outing to town.

'It is lovely staying with you, Elise, but I wish now I had remained in Hertfordshire. Every time I come to London I seem to bring problems with me.'

'Indeed you do not!' Elise again attempted to buck up her morose sister. 'You don't deserve the bad luck you get, Bea...'

'Sir Colin would like to speak privately to Beatrice.' Alex had re-entered the morning room and closed the door before making his announcement.

'Would he, now?' Walter used his stick to assist him to his feet. 'Well, you can tell the turncoat that *I* am the one he ought to visit, and you can also tell him that my daughter sees no gentleman privately without my permission.'

'Papa!' Beatrice sounded mildly irritated. 'I am twenty-five years old and have been alone with Colin many times before.'

'That was when you were his future wife,' Walter

retorted. He turned to his son-in-law. 'What reason did he give for asking to see Beatrice?'

'He said there had been developments, but wouldn't disclose more to me. He seemed prepared to leave if his request was denied. I've had him shown to the small salon to await his answer.'

Her father's high-handedness had made Bea feel contrary; she was also becoming increasingly curious to know what Colin wanted to talk about. She remembered Colin's bemused expression as she quit the Whitleys' house in disgrace. If he'd brought news concerning that calamity it would be best to have the gossip sooner rather than later, and she told her father so.

'Very well, you may have a few minutes with him.' Walter backed down because he was also keen to find out why Colin had called; they had all parted company under a very black cloud. Therefore he reasoned it had to be a matter of some magnitude that would bring the doctor, cap in hand, to see the woman he had jilted while she was in the bosom of her family.

Chapter Seventeen

'Would you like some refreshment, sir? I can ask for some tea to be brought to us.' Beatrice made her polite offer on entering the small salon and closing the door behind her. Her arrival had interrupted Colin pacing and, remembering him as a staid character, she found it remarkable that he appeared so restless.

'No…nothing…thank you…' Colin immediately approached, grasping her hands and then raising them as though he might kiss her fingertips.

Flustered by such an eager and inappropriate greeting, Beatrice speedily freed herself from his clasp. She didn't want him to believe they were now friends just because they had exchanged a few courtesies at the Whitleys'.

'I have made a dreadful error, Beatrice, and would beg you to hear me out,' Colin erupted. 'I know you have every right to hate me but I'm optimistic you do not. You were kind enough to come and talk to me the other evening, and you have agreed to see me today.'

He raked back from his forehead an untidy fringe of auburn hair.

'I am hoping that your natural grace and goodness will allow you to forgive me. Indeed, I pray you will, and that you'll take pity on me when you hear of the injury I have suffered.'

'The injury *you* have suffered?' Beatrice echoed, rather tartly. If her memory served her correctly she had been the wounded party.

'I have been duped, Beatrice!' Colin exclaimed, a whirling hand and furrowed brow emphasising the gravity of his situation. 'My uncle's will did not after all contain a stipulation that I must marry Stella Rawlings.'

Beatrice blinked, momentarily rendered speechless. 'You have only just thought to check on it?' Despite her astonishment Bea realised there was no immediate relief at having Colin's news. In fact, as an inkling of his reason for visiting her pricked her mind, she inwardly mustered a rebuff.

'Oh, I ordered it all to be checked thoroughly.' He tutted. 'There is no point in picking over upsetting details now, because what is done is done. I shall sue my solicitor, of course, and am confident of eventual success…but enough of that.' He gazed pleadingly at Bea. 'One vital aspect must be remedied straight away. There was never any need for our engagement to be broken, my dear.'

Once more, Colin captured her small hands in his sturdy digits.

'I cannot reveal all to you at this stage, but suffice to say that a crime has been committed and Miss Rawlings and I are no longer engaged. I am free to marry you, and would do so this very moment if I could.' Her crushed fingers were taken to his heart and held there, miming his devotion. 'We must set a date before the end of the month…next week if you like. Your father will not need to spend a farthing more than he already has, I swear.'

Delving into his pocket, Colin drew out the garnet ring he had just hours ago demanded Stella return to him. In finger and thumb he held it out to Beatrice, anticipating her joy at the sight of it.

'It gives me immense satisfaction to return this to its rightful owner. I have never stopped loving you, Bea…'

'But I have stopped loving you.' Beatrice jerked her hand back to her side as Colin would have forced the ring on her finger. 'I'm very sorry to be blunt, and to hear that you and Miss Rawlings are not to be married, but I refuse to be drawn into your problems or substitute myself for her.'

Colin smiled softly. 'You must not be indignant that I have come back to you; I wanted you as my wife all along, Beatrice. You are not second fiddle, and I have not rushed here on the rebound from her.'

Bea coughed a startled laugh. 'I do not think of myself as second fiddle, and I am not indulging in a fit of the sulks because of wounded pride.'

She stepped to a sofa, using its back as support as the magnitude of what she'd heard sank in. She knew her family—waiting patiently in another room to hear the outcome of this meeting—would be shocked to learn that there had been no reason after all for Colin to jilt her. And yet, in a way, it had been right that the wedding had been cancelled, Bea realised. She'd since come to accept that her feelings for Hugh Kendrick had never completely died, and now had rekindled to a passion that threatened to overwhelm her. Every waking moment and every restless night were disturbed by thoughts of him. When she tried to force her mind to other, pressing matters she could not concentrate on them for longer than a minute before his dark sardonic features were before her eyes.

'I'm not sure you understand all the advantages to be had from marrying me, Beatrice.'

Colin's stern words startled Bea into focussing on him. He looked taken aback at her rejection.

'I'm sure you will again admit to loving me in time.' In renewed agitation he strode to and fro before the chimneypiece. 'I'm prepared to make you my wife as soon as possible and would naturally accept the responsibility of your debts.' He grimaced. 'I know that Sir Toby Kendrick took advantage of your trust and innocence during that card game. It is being bandied about that he did so more to spite his brother than to spite you, but your reputation will be salvaged when you take my name—'

'What do you mean by that?' Beatrice interrupted. It had never occurred to her that she might be a pawn in a battle of egos between the two Kendrick brothers.

'Hugh Kendrick's interest in you had been noted even before his inappropriate intervention during that card game. The two brothers are at loggerheads, and what better way for the elder to get at the younger than through a matter of the heart?' Colin's eyes narrowed on her. 'Is it a matter of the heart for you, also, Beatrice?'

'I…I think it is none of your business, sir, and impertinent of you to ask.'

Tilting his head, Colin assessed Beatrice's flushed countenance and blazing blue eyes. 'When I say Sir Toby might attack his brother through *a matter of the heart* of course I am assuming that Hugh Kendrick is capable of finer feelings where the fairer sex is concerned. I have no liking for the arrogance of the fellow, and I've heard rumours he is a callous suitor.'

'And I have heard similar things said about you,' Beatrice spontaneously retorted.

'You champion him…' Colin swung away angrily from Beatrice. 'Kendrick might flirt with you but he will not protect you in the way your father would want. I'm optimistic his calculated flattery has not turned your head…am I to be disappointed in that, Beatrice?'

Blood prickled beneath Beatrice's cheeks. She should have guarded her tongue when Hugh's name cropped up rather than readily betray herself.

'Has he proposed? I mean marriage rather than an informal arrangement.' Colin smiled sourly at the telling reaction he got. 'I vow to be a steadfast husband to you. If you choose him you must be prepared to face disgrace and share him with his other women.' Colin barked a laugh. 'It is common knowledge that Kendrick has a mistress set up either end of town; where he might position another paramour is anybody's guess.'

'I think you should go now, sir,' Bea said icily, though burning with ire. 'There is nothing more to discuss. I'm sorry for your problems and wish them quickly resolved.' She moved towards the door and held it open in a significant way.

'I shall speak to your father before leaving and have his opinion on the matter.' Colin jerked a bow, then strode past into the hallway.

'He will be pleased to grant you an audience, sir,' Bea returned with admirable aplomb to his retreating back. 'Some time has elapsed since our aborted wedding. There will be no marriage between us, therefore it is high time my father received all the repayment he was promised.'

Colin spun about, his ruddy complexion white about the mouth. 'I imagine your father might sooner I took you off his hands than reimbursed him.' His expression was as severe as his voice as he continued. 'I came to know Mr Dewey as his physician and his future son-in-law during my time in Hertfordshire. I am certain he regrets that a child of his has acted in the manner you have. A gentleman's daughter of your age should know better, and act with some decency and decorum.'

Before Bea could conquer her indignation and summon up an appropriate response Colin had turned on his heel.

Stella had been surprised and delighted by her mother's attitude to securing her future since Colin Burnett had abandoned her. Shrewd by nature, Stella understood that she must capitalise on her youth and virginity before both were gone. She had no more liking for the idea of being tied to a middling gentleman than she had for being a farmer's wife. Socialising with the cream of society was vital to Stella, and for that she needed to inflame a rich man's desire. So, with the hurdle of her mother's objection cleared, Stella had allowed her excited thoughts free rein on the subject of being a kept woman.

Snaring Lord Whitley was no trouble. But he was old enough to be her grandfather and, though nice enough, he might pop off at any minute and leave her in the lurch. Stella also knew she did not fancy him in the way a woman should if she were to lie with a man. Again and again her mind returned to the person she'd wanted from the first moment she'd spotted him in London.

Hugh Kendrick was everything a girl might dream about: a wonderfully handsome bachelor in the prime of life who had fabulous wealth. If rumours were to be believed he was also, and most importantly, ridiculously generous to the women with whom he consorted. Stella believed that to be no exaggeration. She'd seen him with his mistress when out shopping and had immediately coveted the role of the pretty brunette decked in expensive finery and sparkling gems. The woman's air of smugness had simply heightened Stella's longing to take her place.

Maggie had told her that the woman was Gwen Sharpe, currently Hugh Kendrick's preferred paramour. Stella guessed Gwen to be a few years her senior, and was hoping that a man as jaded as Hugh Kendrick was sure to be lured away with the promise of her maidenhead. Stella knew if she kept him interested for a year it would be enough, so long as she did not fall in love with him. But the rumour that he always discarded a mistress giving her a plump pension pot was sure to mend her broken heart…

'You've got a look of mischief about you.' Maggie caught Stella's crafty eyes in the dressing mirror while hanging up the clothes her daughter had discarded on the bed. Picking up a hairbrush, Maggie began drawing it through her daughter's Titian hair. 'Come, tell Mama what you are thinking,' she teased fondly. 'Are you hoping to flatter old Lord Whitley into buying you a pretty trinket next time you meet? If he does, you'll have hooked him.'

'I wasn't thinking of him at all,' Stella answered airily. She twisted about on the stool, raising an animated face to her mother. 'I'm after more than pretty trinkets and old codgers. I want diamonds and…and a handsome man—' She broke off, giggling, without naming her quarry.

'So you're after Mr Kendrick, are you?' Maggie guessed, bringing a sulky thrust to her daughter's mouth. 'Well, that one won't be as easy to twist about your finger.' Maggie dropped the hairbrush on the bed. 'If your heart's set on him you'll need your wits about you.' Maggie's smile turned calculating. 'One thing I have learned along the way is that a gentleman loves to have what another fellow covets—especially when the two of them are at loggerheads.'

Stella perked up; she believed that Colin desired her, even if he didn't want her as his wife. She also knew he and Hugh Kendrick intensely disliked one another. 'You think that if Sir Colin shows an interest in me as his mistress Mr Kendrick might then want me too?'

'Pah!' Maggie swept away the notion with a flick of her hand. 'Hugh Kendrick would waste no energy on *him*! The one beneath his skin is that brother of his. Mark my words: he would do much to ease that particular itch...'

'Are you certain you've not too quickly turned Colin down?'

'I no longer want to marry him...I'm surprised I ever did.'

Bea had not long ago broken the news to her family that Sir Colin had reissued his proposal. Oddly, none of them had seemed as astonished as she'd imagined they would be. Her father had gone off, muttering, to speak to Colin before he left the house. Alex had tactfully withdrawn to allow his wife to speak privately to her sister, as Bea now seemed under siege on all sides.

Beatrice turned from the window, where she had been gazing over the rose gardens, and gave Elise a wry smile. 'When I was first introduced to Dr Burnett I recall you warned me that I might fall for him on the rebound. Had we gone ahead and married all those weeks ago I would have done my best to be a good wife to him, although I have discovered I still have feelings for...'

Elise had been holding her son by his tiny hands, helping Adam take a shaky step on the carpet. As her sister's voice faded away she sent Beatrice an astute glance. 'I'm guessing that the person who years ago propelled you towards Colin has now drawn you away.'

Beatrice's head swayed back on her shoulders in despair, but it was answer enough for Elise. Lifting Adam to sit on the sofa, she came quickly to her sister's side. 'I like Hugh—you know I do, Bea—but he is...different from the charming gentleman we knew all those years ago. I'm not saying his good fortune has spoiled his character...' she began diplomatically.

'Well, if you won't say it, I will,' Bea quietly replied. 'But it doesn't matter...I love him anyway. I think I knew it that first time when he came to Hertfordshire with the news about the dowager's illness.' Bea turned to face Elise. 'It frightened me that he could turn up out of the blue like that and turn my world upside down...'

'Does Hugh know how you feel about him?' Elise asked hoarsely.

Bea shook her head. 'As you say, he is very different now. I wouldn't embarrass myself, or him, with a declaration of love. Oh...he desires me—he has made that clear too—but what future is there in being taken into his harem?' Bea stifled a mournful chuckle with the back of a hand. 'Colin took pains to tell me that if I chose Hugh over him I would disgrace myself and my family and should expect to have several rivals for his time and affection.'

'You need not heed Burnett's opinion!' Elise had spoken dismissively, yet she feared the doctor was right in his forecast of her sister's prospects. Hugh was a rogue where women were concerned. 'Shall I ask Alex to visit Hugh and discover if he might be persuaded to propose marriage?' Elise asked anxiously. 'Alex is moping since he fell out with his best friend. I know he's keen to make up with Hugh, so he'd probably appreciate the opportunity to talk to him...'

'No!' Beatrice emphasised the single word with a deep frown. 'Promise me you will not mention any of our conversation, Elise, even to Alex.'

Bea didn't want Hugh to believe she'd again sent her brother-in-law to sort out personal matters because she lacked the courage to do so herself. If Hugh were ever to know she loved and wanted him, she'd sooner be the one to tell him.

'You are not seriously considering Hugh's proposition of *carte blanche*...are you?' Elise asked. She could see why her sister might be tempted by such an offer from a handsome and generous man. Bea had every right to be heartily fed up with regular romance when in the past three gentlemen pursuing her as a wife had let her down. But she could see nothing but heartache ahead for Bea if her sister drifted into a liaison with a man as jaded and cynical as Hugh.

'Of course not,' Bea said breathily, pushing back a blonde curl from her forehead. She wished she'd sounded more convincing. Objectionable as many would deem the idea, Bea had found herself wondering whether a discreet, informal arrangement with a man she truly loved and desired would be preferable to an arid marriage to suit convention. When younger she had desperately wanted to be a wife and have a family of her own, but always her dream had eluded her. Constant disappointment had eroded the yearning till she no longer knew what she wanted...other than Hugh. If she could not have a wedding ring from him, would it be so bad to accept the gift of his passion instead?

'Burnett's just gone.'

The sisters turned in unison as Alex entered the parlour. He scooped up his gurgling son from the sofa, chucking him beneath the chin. 'I think your father might like to speak to you, Beatrice.'

With a fierce look for Elise that threatened dire consequences should she tell Alex what they'd talked about, Bea quit the room.

'I don't blame you one bit, my dear, for turning Burnett down this time. Bumptious fellow!'

Walter's abrupt exclamation met Bea on entering the room. 'Sir Colin tried to bully me into persuading you to have him back, you know.' He sighed deeply. 'That fellow has changed since he inherited his money…and not for the better…'

'It seems to be the way of things…' Bea gave a hollow laugh.

'He made it plain that your gambling debt would be cleared the moment the marriage contract was signed. I made it plain that I'd like him to clear his own debts and mind his business about yours. He said he would send me a bank draft this afternoon. I'll believe it when I see it,' Walter concluded pessimistically.

'I'm sorry that I'm such a trouble to you, Papa,' Bea said softly.

'Oh…don't take any notice of my huffing and puffing, my dear,' Walter patted the delicate fingers his daughter had laid on his arm. 'I didn't mean what I said earlier about wanting you wed and out of my hair. You're a good girl, if far too rash at times. Let's forget about Burnett and that blackguard Toby Kendrick.'

'You will not sell your pension policy, Papa, will you?' Bea asked in concern.

Walter gestured wearily. 'An old man like me needs little money to live on, and one day soon a good man will come along for you and keep you in a far better manner than I can. I know your luck will change for the better.' Walter gave a final comforting pat to Bea's hand, then sank down into a chair, lying his head back against the upholstery. 'Don't let's speak of money any longer…I'm sick of hearing about debts and bills.' He sighed. 'It will be nice to go home. I feel tired out by all this frantic business in London. Shall we pack up tomorrow, ready to leave at the weekend?'

Bea nodded, watching her father's eyes flutter shut. She felt a pang of deep affection and regret that they would not be leaving town unburdened but with problems of her making hanging over them. 'Yes…let's go home, Papa,' she murmured, settling a cushion beneath her snoozing father's drooping head.

She stepped back, gazing at him as he settled into sleep. A fierce determination rose in Bea to cure the ills she'd caused. She would make sure her father enjoyed his twilight years, and the independence that was so important to him, buffered by his modest pension income. He would not sell the policy and live in penury to get Toby Kendrick off their backs! She could not allow it…

Chapter Eighteen

Maggie Monk nipped behind a large shrub protruding from a railing. Then, from her vantage point, she watched her quarry hurtling down the steps of Viscount Blackthorne's mansion. Having noted Sir Colin's rigid bearing and black expression, she felt her spirits lift.

Earlier that afternoon she'd been on her way to the bakery when she'd spotted her daughter's former fiancé. Ever conscious of their dwindling fortunes, Maggie had been hoping to haggle over a stale pie to share with Stella for their dinner. Burnett might have bought her daughter little gifts but he'd kept his fist tightly closed when it came to helping out with their household bills. Maggie had come to town with a little pot of savings gleaned from her small pension from Sir Donald. However, with Stella wanting every pretty frippery her eyes landed on in shop windows, the money was almost run through.

On spotting Burnett all thought of food had fled. Sir Colin had been striding purposefully along on the other side of the street. His air of urgency had prompted Maggie to follow him, curious to know where he was heading. When she'd seen him charging up the steps of a house on Upper Brook Street she'd easily guessed why Burnett might pay a call there. Boiling with resentment, Maggie had waited for him to reappear. She was glad she had tarried, for she now felt cheered up. If she'd been correct in thinking he'd just proposed again to Beatrice, his demeanour proclaimed him as having been roundly rejected.

It seemed that Miss Dewey now had bigger fish to fry than Sir Colin. Gossip was rife that the spinster must be under Hugh Kendrick's protection since he'd championed her at the Whitleys'. It stuck in Maggie's craw that the two eligible bachelors who should have been competing for Stella's favours were instead under an older woman's spell.

Before emerging from her hiding place Maggie watched Colin stride across the road and turn the corner. She sent a grim scowl at the house he had quit. Miss Dewey was beautiful but past her prime, and couldn't match Stella for youthful freshness in Maggie's opinion. If Stella were hungry for Hugh Kendrick's protection, Maggie would do her utmost to bring about her wish.

Since Stella's birth Maggie had had to idolise her daughter from afar, in case suspicions were aroused about their true relationship. Now there was no secret to keep and the floodgates of her maternal affection were wide open. If Stella couldn't have Hugh, then neither should Beatrice get him.

But all was not yet lost; she still had a hand to play,

and had noticed when they'd passed Sir Toby Kendrick on Regent Street that he readily responded to Stella's coy glance with an eager grin. Hugh and Toby Kendrick loathed one another, and Maggie knew there was always a profit to be had when love or hate skewed the odds. As far as she was concerned there remained a chance to win the game.

'I'm intrigued, madam, to know what vital news you have that could not have been conveyed in the note that summoned me here.'

As he looked Maggie Monk over an expression of disdain shaped Toby Kendrick's features. He had pitied Colin Burnett, having a future shackled to a shameless hussy like Stella Rawlings. Though of course, in common with other red-blooded fellows, he'd jump at a chance to take up the offer in those impish eyes of hers. It was that hope that had drawn Toby here to meet Mrs Monk by Marble Arch at the appointed hour.

Maggie licked her lips. She'd heard rumours that Sir Toby was a profligate on his own account but a tight-fist where others were concerned. She had no real desire for him to take up with Stella for, baronet or no, she feared he'd turn her daughter into a skivvy to get his money's worth out of her. But so far Hugh Kendrick had ignored Stella. Maggie was praying she could change that by enabling him to spite his older brother by snatching her daughter away from Toby.

'Come, woman…what is it?' Toby demanded testily. 'I've not all afternoon to tarry with such as you.'

'Your brother has been showing an undue interest

in my sweet Stella,' Maggie rattled off. 'I thought you should know of his pursuit.'

Toby shouted a laugh. 'What do you expect me to do about it? The chit plays up to every man she meets.'

Maggie resented his scoffing criticism. What he'd said might be true, but she didn't want her nose rubbed in it.

'She's a vivacious beauty, I'll give you that,' Maggie said, struggling for levity. 'But she has her...*preferences* in gentlemen, and appreciates a fellow's breeding. Now that rogue Sir Colin has done the dirty and left my dear girl to her fate she is keen to meet a fellow of similar status...such as your good self.'

'Got cold feet, has he?' Toby purred. It was news to him that the engagement was off, and suddenly the carrot the woman was dangling was looking exceedingly tasty. He guessed that for all the girl's sauce she was still intact, and taking maidenheads was a sport Toby enjoyed above all else. 'If you think I'll wed the chit now she's been cast off—'

'Mayhap you will, sir, given time,' Maggie hastily interrupted. 'But that brother of yours might come up to scratch for my Stella first. Mr Kendrick is smitten, and will naturally want to have children for that fortune of his...'

'He might get her increasing but he won't marry her,' Toby chortled. 'He's produced a boy already and left it abroad.'

Toby suddenly realised how very stupid and indiscreet he'd been. His lust for Stella had overridden his sense and he'd risked losing his valuable hold over

Hugh. If his brother found out he'd broadcast his secret he'd cut off his money…maybe knock him senseless into the bargain. He groaned inwardly on noticing the gleam in Maggie Monk's eyes as she digested this confidential information.

'A bastard, has he?' Maggie grunted a coarse laugh, turning away satisfied. She'd got far more than she'd bargained for and might no longer need to manipulate Toby after all. She left him gawping after her and hurried away, muttering gleefully, 'Well, well…I wonder if the spinster knows about *that*…'

Bea could not risk being spotted in a clandestine tryst with Hugh. She had reasoned that a rendezvous in the open, as though they had bumped into one another by chance, would be the only option if she were to avoid heaping more embarrassment on her family.

Following her talk with her father earlier, Bea had acted before her courage fled, despatching a note to request that Hugh meet her at Oxford Street in the environs of Meredew's haberdashery. Far too impetuous, her father had called her, just a few hours ago, and indeed she was, she realised, frowning at her pale reflection in a shop window. She feigned an interest in a feathered hat behind the glass, not wanting to appear to be aimlessly dawdling.

Glancing at the clock inside the premises, Bea noticed that the appointed hour was nearly upon her. She took a deep calming breath as her heartbeat accelerated, sending blood to pound deafeningly in her ears. Of course her note might have gone unheeded: Hugh might either be out of town or otherwise engaged and unable to respond to her summons.

Unsure whether that possibility gave greater relief than disappointment, she reminded herself that she didn't want it all to be a squandered effort.

The street scene behind her was reflected in the pane and she began scouring the crowds. She longed to see Hugh approaching, yet confusingly also dreaded a first sight of his powerful presence. What would she say? What would *he* say? Would he laugh in that infuriating way of his that mingled lust and mockery? She feared he might unwittingly shrivel her determination to bare her soul and admit that she wanted him in the same way he desired her. If he were unable to say he loved her but promised instead his affection and respect it would surely be enough…

'Bea!'

A familiar voice startled Bea from her tortured thoughts. At any other time she would have been delighted to see Fiona Chapman flying towards her on Oxford Street, but a rather strained smile was all she could manage as her friend closed the gap between them.

'Is Elise out shopping with you today?' Fiona came to a gasping halt by Bea's side.

Bea shook her head. 'Are you on your own too?'

'I am now…' Fiona answered flatly. 'I was with Verity and her mother-in-law. Mrs Clemence is driving my poor sister mad, going on about arrangements for a christening before the babe is yet born.' Fiona pulled a face. 'I've escaped with the excuse that I must go home because of a headache. Now I've run into you

I won't have a completely spoiled afternoon.' With a cheeky grin, Fiona linked arms with Bea, urging her to stroll on. 'I'll come window-shopping with you; you deserve to be cheered up after that hateful episode at the Whitleys'.'

Bea's faint smile disappeared at that reminder.

'You must not worry that people blame you!' Fiona reassured her. 'Everybody is saying what a weasel Toby Kendrick is to have manipulated you in the way he did…'

Suddenly she began waving frantically.

'Now, over there is a Kendrick I *do* like—very much!'

The driver of a sleek curricle appeared unaware of Fiona's enthusiastic welcome as he steered towards the kerb.

'What a lucky coincidence to run into Hugh,' Fiona announced, glancing at Bea. Having taken a closer look at her friend's rosy complexion, she murmured conspiratorially, 'Ah… I see…' Fiona's lips curved. 'Not such a coincidence after all, is it?' She tugged on Bea's arm. 'I've always thought the pair of you were a perfect match. This is no time to turn shy. Let's go over and say hello now he's arrived.' She chuckled. 'He's looking for you already and seems rather stern; perhaps he thinks you've stood him up.'

Bea watched as Hugh vaulted from his seat and immediately frowned at the vacant spot by Meredew's shop window. He did seem severe, she realised with a sense of womanly satisfaction, that she hadn't been where he expected her to be, meekly awaiting his arrival.

'Well…it's a lovely day for a drive,' Fiona piped up, causing Hugh to turn around. 'Are you going to be kind and offer to take us for a spin around the park, Hugh?' When he seemed more interested in gazing at Beatrice than answering, Fiona prodded his arm. 'Oh, say you will. I can act as chaperon.'

Hugh's narrowed gaze slid from Bea's beautifully bashful expression to settle on Fiona. 'You are extremely forward, not to mention bossy at times, Miss Chapman.'

'Yes, I know, but there's no point in waiting for you two to dither over how to escape prying eyes so you might talk privately.'

Fiona's warning was called for; she moved a gloved hand, acknowledging Lady Groves and her friend, who had seen them.

'We must all go off together for propriety's sake,' she whispered. 'Then you may lose me along the way.'

'I imagine you're prepared to take a drive with me, Miss Dewey, as you've brought suitable company?'

Hugh's smooth confidence heightened Bea's blush.

'Of course she is, or she wouldn't be here at all, would she?' Fiona declared, thrusting a hand at Hugh so he could help her aboard his curricle.

With a despairing look and a tiny head-shake Bea hoped to convey that she'd not sought her friend's moral support because she was afraid to be alone with him. Hugh's expression remained darkly quizzical and, conscious of Lady Groves bearing down on them, Bea accepted Hugh's assistance in alighting.

'Thank you,' she murmured, settling back next to

Fiona and withdrawing her hand from long fingers that seemed reluctant to release her.

Bea slid a glance at her companions, wondering why she'd ever felt jealous of Fiona's relationship with Hugh. The way they sniped so good-naturedly made them more suited to being brother and sister than lovers. But there were other faceless women who stirred that new and unpleasant emotion in her. Ever since Colin had taunted her about Hugh's mistresses Bea had felt curious: were they blonde or brunette, younger or older than she was? His Indian lover…lovers—how many were there?—would be dusky-limbed with jet-black hair. Of course all her rivals were bound to be exceptionally pretty…

The horses were set to a brisk trot and Bea tipped back her head, relaxing a little beneath the cooling air on her flushed face. The respite was short lived. Hugh suddenly captured her eyes with a stare of such intensity that she was jolted back to the night he'd taken her home in his coach. The memory of what they'd done in the dark, while the vehicle swayed through the deserted streets, grazing together their bodies, sent fiery heat rippling through her. The piquant excitement she'd experienced had been unforgettable, as had the sensation of his artful hands tormenting her bare flesh.

Involuntarily Bea's eyes travelled to his dark fingers, tangled in leather as they capably mastered the sinuous greys to a pace he liked.

'Goodness! I have a migraine.' Fiona put the back of her hand to her head in a theatrical pose, drawing glances from both her companions.

'I'll take you home,' Hugh said easily, and turned right at the next crossroads.

Beatrice was sure Fiona gave her a wink…or perhaps a genuine headache was making her squint…

'I should return home too.' The words tumbled out of Bea.

Colin Burnett's criticism of her had suddenly refused to cease thudding at the forefront of her mind. A gentleman's daughter should indeed, at her age, act with some decency and decorum. What was she thinking of, running after a notorious womaniser to tell him she'd chosen to lose the wager they'd made and become one of his mistresses? Being in thrall to unrequited love was no excuse for acting like a dullard or a doxy…

Fiona's elbow dug Bea's side and her friend gave her a fiercely encouraging look. A moment later Hugh handed Fiona down from the carriage and she set off towards her front door with a cheery wave.

In an easy leap Hugh was again aboard, taking the reins. In quick succession Beatrice darted several anxious glances at his shady concave cheek, hoping he'd sense she wanted him to talk to her. Any chitchat would do, she thought wistfully. But he remained uncommunicative as he wove in and out of traffic, then gave the horses their head on a clear stretch of road.

'Are you feeling pleased with yourself?' Bea burst out, unable to stand the silence any longer.

'Should I be?' There was no hint of either lust or mockery roughening his tone.

'You've won our wager, as you said you would.' A tremor had crept into her voice.

'Forget about that stupid game.'

Hugh's words were so quiet that Bea had to strain to hear them. 'It was a game to you?' she demanded in a suffocated voice.

He ejected a low expletive that was more unsettling to Bea than hearing him acknowledge his victory. But he said no more and set the greys to a faster pace.

'Will you take me home, please?' Bea's hand flew to her bonnet as the breeze lifted it from her shimmering fair hair to droop at her nape.

'Eventually.'

It was difficult for Beatrice to discern his mood from his abrupt conversation. 'What does that mean?' She strove for composure while removing the bonnet and laying it on her lap.

'It means I'm not yet ready to do so.'

Hugh turned in through the park gates and within a few moments had brought the curricle to a halt beneath a canopy of undulating tree branches. He rested back into the seat, easing a muscular leg out in front of him.

Bea again forced her eyes to meet his, moistening her mouth. She saw he was watching from under long black lashes as her tongue trailed to and fro, so sank small teeth on her lower lip to still its quiver.

'I sent that note to you on the spur of the moment,' she blurted.

'Do you regret doing so?'

'I'm not sure,' she answered honestly. 'I've been told time and again that I am far too impetuous, and I admit it's true.'

'It sounds as though your sister has been dispensing pearls of wisdom.'

'It wasn't Elise…although she always does try to set me straight on such things.'

'I recall she tried to talk sense into you years ago, when we first met. She told you not to waste your time on me, didn't she?'

'Indeed she did…' Bea's mouth slanted wryly. 'And after all this time it has still not sunk in.'

Hugh barked a short laugh, frowning into the distance. 'I'll admit I'm glad of that, sweetheart, even if you are not.'

'My papa called me impetuous today.' Beatrice avoided his eyes.

'And did he warn you to stay away from me too?' Hugh asked quietly.

Bea noticed his thick dark brows drawing together in a wordless demand for some details. But she wasn't prepared to be distracted into telling him about Colin Burnett's visit. There were far more pressing matters to deal with.

'Any number of people, concerned for my reputation, might advise me to avoid a notorious rake—as well you know.'

'Notorious rakes can reform,' Hugh pointed out with dulcet mockery. 'Your sister could vouch for that…'

'Alex told Elise that he grew up when he fell in love with her,' Bea remarked, sounding wistfully reflective.

'Are you hinting I'm immature?' Vague amusement modulated his voice to a velvety huskiness.

'If the cap fits…' Bea started sourly, before biting

back the rest of the phrase. But there was never likely to be a better moment to condemn his philandering. And he had asked for it! 'Actually…I do think that in certain ways your behaviour is immature,' she said.

'In what ways?'

'I think you can guess at them.' Hungry as Bea was to know more about his other women, she backed away from letting him glimpse her jealousy.

'If my memory serves…you've called me disgusting and a degenerate in the past, and now you've added being immature to the list of my faults… Yet still you wanted to meet me today. Why was that?'

'I had little choice but to contact you,' Bea retorted. 'If I've been drawn into a feud between you and your brother and suffered for it then I think you owe me an apology and your assistance.'

'I gave you assistance when I made plain my opinion of my brother, yet still you trusted him, gambled with him and accepted his loan.'

Bea felt her cheeks burn. The comment had been idly made, yet she recognised the reprimand and the truth in it.

'Why did you do that, Beatrice? To annoy me?'

'Perhaps.' Her mouth slanted mutinously

'And your reason for wanting to annoy me…?'

'Do I need a reason other than that you constantly annoy me and insult me and…?' She gestured impatiently.

'Such an explanation makes *you* sound immature,' he said, straight-faced.

'Oh…this was a mistake!' Beatrice fumed. 'I might have known we would do nothing but bicker.'

'We could go somewhere private and do something far more pleasant.' Hugh's suggestion was coupled with a sultry look before he turned his head, watching the paths becoming more populated as the fashionable hour approached, bringing strollers and carriages into Hyde Park.

'As you seem to want to make light of it all,' Beatrice hissed, blushing furiously, 'I'm sorry I wasted my time and asked you to meet me. Would you take me home?'

'I wasn't making light of it, sweetheart,' Hugh said quietly. 'I was being very serious.' His eyes swept over her, burning like coal embers.

'In that case,' Bea whispered, 'you have your answer on why I think you immature; simply reflect on what you have just said and your obsession with—'

'Please carry on,' Hugh invited with studied gravity.

'Your obsession with womanising…' Bea rattled off.

'There's only one woman I'm obsessed with, Beatrice.' He paused. 'If wanting you, thinking about you day and night, makes me immature, then I admit to the fault.'

Bea blinked, then her large luminous eyes began searching his face for signs of irony. But she could see none. He returned her stare quite openly and calmly.

'When have I insulted you?'

'What?' Beatrice breathed.

'You said a moment ago that I had insulted you.'

'I think you know very well the answer to that.'

'You think that offering you anything your heart desires is an insult?'

'My heart desires more than I think you are able to give, sir,' Bea murmured poignantly.

'Ah…you are still pining for the good doctor, are you?'

'No! I am not! And I have today impressed the fact on him too.' Bea had spoken hotly, without due consideration for the interrogation that was sure to follow such a declaration.

'Have you seen Burnett?'

There was no reason not to recount that Sir Colin had called on her and reissued his proposal but Bea twisted together her fingers in her lap in indecision. Such information would beg the question of why she had rebuffed a man she had recently been sure she loved and wanted as her husband.

'He paid us a visit earlier.'

'And his reason for that…?'

'He came to tell me that he had been tricked into believing he must marry Miss Rawlings to get his inheritance. He said he'd broken their engagement and wanted to marry me instead.'

Bea watched the surprise in Hugh's eyes being overtaken by another darker emotion.

'As you're here with me, I am guessing that you turned him down?'

'I did…'

'Why?'

'My reason is none of your concern.'

'You know that's not true.' Hugh unfolded an arm

along the back of the seat. 'I thought Burnett was the love of your life.'

'So did I…' Bea stifled a mournful giggle.

'What has changed your mind?'

'Sir Colin aired some unpleasant views and now my father and I have seen him in a different light.'

'What did he say?' There was an abrupt hardening in Hugh's tone.

'He told me that a gentleman's daughter of my age should act with some decency and decorum.' The admission trickled out of Bea as she gazed at the leaves fluttering overhead. In her opinion her former fiancé was a hypocrite to voice his disapproval when—whether in error or not—he'd abandoned her to better himself.

'Was he criticising your behaviour with my brother?'

'No…he was criticising my behaviour with you…'

Chapter Nineteen

'As I've been named in Burnett's slander I think I should be told more about it.'

Bea hesitated before blurting, 'In short, Colin told me to avoid your company or suffer the consequences.'

Hugh laughed soundlessly. 'It sounds as though you championed me, Miss Dewey. Did you?'

Bea fidgeted beneath his warm, humorous regard. 'I didn't find his lecture necessary. Neither did I like being told who I might choose as a friend.'

'Am I your friend?'

'I'm not sure any more,' Bea said with bittersweet honesty. 'Despite our squabbling, I'd like to think we were friends at least…if only for Elise and Alex's sake. I know they'd like everybody to be harmonious.'

'As I would, too,' Hugh said. 'But I'm aiming higher than harmony between us, Bea.'

Bea turned doubtful blue eyes his way, remaining still as he raised a hand, smoothing the backs of his fingers over the silky dip beneath her cheekbone.

His wooing touch was gone too soon; Hugh's clenched fist dropped to his lap as a carriage rattled closer at quite a pace, its female occupants gawping inquisitively at them.

'It's getting too crowded,' Hugh muttered. 'I should have taken you somewhere else…just to talk, that's all, I swear.' He grimaced in self-mockery. 'I know you think me a lecherous reprobate, and perhaps I have been. But I do understand it's vital to sort out certain matters between us.'

Bea gave him a small grateful smile and for the first time felt hopeful that things could come right between them.

'I'm determined to kiss you…if nothing more…' he groaned.

I want you to… The unspoken response keened in Bea's mind, making her dusky lashes droop over her soulful sapphire eyes.

'I will before the day's out,' Hugh vowed, as though sensing her need. He stared moodily after the disappearing carriage, then suddenly jumped from the curricle and came round to open the door. 'We'll arouse less interest if we walk for a while.'

Bea allowed him to hand her down, glad to stretch her legs but conscious of time passing. 'I must go back soon. I said I wouldn't be out shopping for long. I don't want my papa to fret over my absence.'

'How is your father?'

'Tired and depressed…and it's my fault,' Bea admitted through a lump forming in her throat. 'He wants to go home to Hertfordshire.'

Hugh drew Bea's hand through his arm as they strolled, his large palm warming her delicate fingers. 'He'll cheer up soon and perhaps choose to stay…'

'No…he wants to go, and so do I.'

'When are you planning to leave?' he asked distantly.

'In a few days' time.' She sensed his stare heating the top of her head.

'In that case we've not much time.'

'I know…' Bea murmured, lowering her eyes and marshalling her thoughts. 'I don't want my papa to live out his days in straitened circumstances,' she confided quietly. 'Alex, being the good fellow he is, has naturally offered to set everything straight, but my father is too proud to let him. He is intending to sell his pension policy to settle my debts rather than accept help.' She sighed. 'You said you would deal with your brother, so I wrote that note to you. I can't bear that Papa must suffer the consequences of my folly.'

Having expressed her private heartache, Bea glanced at Hugh for a comment, but he remained worryingly quiet while escorting her to a bench. While she perched on the edge he remained standing, one foot raised and braced against the planks, his expression inscrutable.

'And you? Can you bear to suffer the consequences of your folly?' he asked solemnly, his eyes drifting away as though he were more interested in the verdant scenery than in having her answer.

Very conscious of the breeched thigh close to her cheek, Bea darted her eyes from its muscular contours to his saturnine profile. She wanted him to look at her now they'd finally reached the purpose of this meeting:

the wager she'd lost… But he remained aloof, giving no encouragement or comfort.

It was only pride, she told herself as she tried to force words past the ache in her throat. Why could she not tell him that she craved his kisses and caresses? Why make it seem that he had her backed into a corner and she would acquiesce only reluctantly to his lovemaking?

Hugh plunged a hand into a pocket and pulled forth some crumpled papers. He let them fall, one at a time, onto the seat.

Bea glanced at her IOUs, then raised wide blue eyes to his preying gaze. 'You have already paid Toby?' she whispered. 'You were very certain of your victory, then.'

'I bought those days ago—long before I received your note.'

Bea imagined that with such animosity between them Sir Toby would have extracted the best possible price for her markers.

'How much did you pay him?' she breathed.

'It doesn't matter. Take them.' He swooped on the notes, held them out, smiling sardonically when her fingers clasped together in her lap.

'Are we not friends, then, Beatrice?' Hugh gently taunted.

Bea knew if she accepted the notes she would have tacitly agreed to their becoming lovers. When she'd left the house earlier she'd persuaded herself that having his promise of respect and affection was enough for her. Yet now…now the scene was real—not in an imaginary theatre in which she played the part of a tragic heroine.

With those IOUs in her possession she must lie naked with a man...*this* man...for the first time, and allow him licence to do whatever he wanted...whatever she wanted... So he'd promised her weeks ago, when coarsely propositioning her.

A sweet shiver raced through Bea but she flicked aside her face, forcing her mind to examine the dark side to her ruinous pleasure. Her ostracism from society was a mere breath away; so was her father's despair. Discreet as she and Hugh might endeavour to be when they rendezvoused to make love, gossip would eventually reach Walter's ears and break his heart.

But there was more firing her indecision than the effects of her disgrace: she couldn't bear to toss and turn jealously, wondering whose bed Hugh shared when he was absent from hers. He might say she was the woman with whom he was obsessed, but what about when the chase was done and he'd had his novice mistress? Would he grow restless and desire a new hunt? Or again visit paramours well versed in ways of pleasing him?

Suddenly, and very bleakly, Bea realised that crumbs of his affection would never be enough when she was greedy for so much more. She wanted him to tell her that, like his friend before him, he too had given up carousing because he'd finally found a woman he could cherish and adore—the only one with whom he wanted to live his life and rear his children...

'Nothing...' Hugh said gruffly, having watched raw emotion flitting over Bea's profile.

His single word penetrated her mind and Bea raised

an expression of wonderment to his face. 'Toby gave up my IOUs for *nothing*?'

'No… Toby wanted to be paid…' Hugh removed his boot from the wooden bench and strode off a few paces. 'Whereas I don't. I'm not expecting a thing from you.'

'Why is that?' Bea finally touched a finger to the IOUs, shifting them to and fro on the timber.

'It's what a gentleman does for a woman he cares about.'

She'd heard that from him before, spoken with the same caustic inflection.

Hugh glanced sideways at her, ramming his hands into his pockets. 'Don't look so scared, Beatrice,' he said. 'Stupid game, maybe, but you've won…hands down.' He gazed across the park towards the water glistening in the afternoon sun. 'I was going to have a servant deliver them to you tomorrow. I'd have brought them myself, but I know Alex might not want me darkening his doorstep.'

'He is pining for your company. Elise said so.' Bea collected the papers and put them in her pocket, then rose from the bench, joyous optimism unfurling in her breast. She had just glimpsed the gentleman Hugh had once been, before his good fortune turned him into a sophisticate.

'Why would a rogue act with such chivalry and kindness?' she asked with a hint of teasing.

'I've been asking myself the same question,' Hugh muttered, a cynical slant to his thin lips. But he avoided her eyes as she glided closer to him. 'I owe it to you and your father. I let you down before, years ago, leading you into thinking I was in a position to propose.' He gestured roughly. 'I was a fool to ever want what I couldn't afford.'

'And now?' The question sighed unbidden out of Beatrice.

'And now I can afford whatever I damn well like...' He turned ferocious golden eyes on her. 'But some things can't be bought, can they...?'

'No...they can't...'

'Did Burnett offer to pay off your debts?'

'He did...'

'So why did you come to me?'

'Colin said I must marry him. That was the deal he offered.'

A mirthless sound scratched Hugh's throat. 'Trumps mine, I think,' he muttered sourly.

'Ask me why I could not accept him.' Boldly Bea touched his abrasive chin with a finger to make him look at her when he would have turned away.

'Are you again about to tell me that you'd sooner be Burnett's mistress than my wife?'

'Of course not! I regret that I ever made such a daft and dishonest statement.' With dawning enlightenment she choked out, 'Did you really believe I meant what I said?'

Hugh stared at her, then stepped forward purposefully, as though intending to take her in his arms. Instead he gripped her wrist, tugging her behind a stout tree trunk. Before they were completely out of sight his mouth swooped on hers, brutally passionate, soothingly wooing. His fingers cradled her skull, protecting it from the rough bark as the pressure of his mouth forced back her head. The texture of timber was at her back, and his hard muscular body moulded about her softly curving silhouette, keeping her trapped to him. Inside her cloak, a hand stroked her hip…and Bea could sense the tremor in his caress…

Hugh suddenly spun away from her and Bea, sensually dazed, clutched behind her at the bole of the tree to steady herself. The second time a cultured baritone boomed Hugh's name Bea heard it through the blood pounding in her ears. Hastily she stepped into view, her heart in her mouth.

Cursing beneath his breath, Hugh began to prowl casually over the grass, his raging frustration masked by an indolent expression.

The approaching barouche slowed to a halt and Lord Whitley affably doffed his hat. The two women seated in the vehicle made no attempt to inject sincerity into their smiles.

Maggie Monk resented Lord Whitley for having alerted the couple to their having been spotted. Another moment and she reckoned that refined Miss Dewey might have allowed the gentleman to sully her virtue beyond repair. Of course once the spinster knew about Hugh Kendrick's brat she might no longer want to be taken down the aisle—or to bed—by him. Maggie was still determined her daughter would get the diamond magnate, but Whitley was first reserve so she was keen to keep him sweet.

'Mr Kendrick…and Miss Dewey too! What a surprise to see you…*together* like that…' Maggie slyly exchanged a knowing look with her daughter. Despite his mild manner Maggie could tell Hugh was enraged, and his conquest was rosy with embarrassment.

'Fancy a nip of brandy, Kendrick?' Lord Whitley held out his silver flask, hoping to lighten the heavy atmosphere. 'Getting chilly now at this time of the day...'

A lazy hand-flick was Hugh's response. Unconcerned that his hospitality had been rejected, Lord Whitley took a swallow himself. Ordinarily he might have been on better behaviour in mixed company; but recently he'd had confirmed his idea that his female passengers were no ladies. And his suspicions about Miss Dewey's character were growing.

Yesterday Maggie Monk had accosted him as he emerged from his club. Whitley had not been surprised at her audacity, nor to learn that Burnett had jumped ship on marrying Miss Rawlings. It was plain that the girl was fashioned in looks and character to be a wench rather than a wife. Whitley was still mulling over Mrs Monk's list of requirements. Before getting down to serious negotiation with the bawd he had brought the chit out to test her enthusiasm for it all.

It seemed he'd interrupted Hugh Kendrick auditioning Beatrice Dewey for a similar role. Whitley was surprised such a proficient philanderer hadn't headed to a more secluded spot for the seduction.

Not long ago people had speculated about the reason for the animosity between Hugh Kendrick and Alex Blackthorne, but they no longer did so. All had become clear when Kendrick had rescued the viscount's sister-in-law in that card game.

Little wonder that Blackthorne was livid with his best chum for sullying Beatrice before she had a husband's name to shield her reputation. It was the girl's father that Whitley felt sorry for. The poor old fellow would be distraught if he heard that the wanton had been spotted kissing Kendrick behind a tree in Hyde Park.

'Would you help me down, sir?' Stella imperiously extended a hand to Hugh, eyes flashing challengingly at Beatrice. 'I should like to rest on that pretty bench.' Angry colour lit her cheeks when he appeared not to have heard her demand, and continued strolling to and fro, frowning into the distance.

Having regained composure, Bea stepped forward, a wavering smile curving lips that still pulsed from being kissed. 'I'm sure Mr Kendrick will escort you.' She hoped Hugh would conquer his exasperation and play his part in smoothing over the situation. 'You are quite right, Lord Whitley, the weather is cooler now.' Bea rubbed together her gloved palms.

Hugh had complied with her signal to help Stella onto the grass, but Bea knew she was in grave trouble if this excruciating episode wasn't properly defused. She couldn't be sure what the trio had witnessed, but was praying they'd seen no more than a couple standing close together in the shade of a tree.

Stella dimpled up at Hugh. She'd yearned to bump into him by chance but had not wanted to see him embracing another woman. Her mother had made an attempt yesterday to waylay him and hint at her willingness to be his mistress. Stella had peeked from behind the window blind of a Hackney, but Hugh had barely stopped to talk to Maggie before striding impatiently on towards his house. Her mother had been grumpy on her return, insisting they waste no time in transferring their efforts to Lord Whitley as their little kitty was almost run through. Then today her mother had bucked up and, intriguingly, said she might have found a way to hook Hugh. But Maggie would give no more details of her plan to snare the gentleman Stella wanted above all others.

'I'll stretch my legs too, I think.' Lord Whitley alighted in quite a sprightly hop, then offered to help Mrs Monk down.

'I was saying to Mr Kendrick that I should love a drive in his racing curricle.' Stella turned excitedly to her mother.

'I'm sure the charming gentleman will oblige you with your wish, my dear.' Maggie's lips knotted in satisfaction. Her daughter was playing her part well, with no rehearsal.

'Unfortunately I have no time,' Hugh began coldly, removing Stella's clutch from his elbow. 'We were just leaving as Miss Dewey is expected home shortly.'

'Oh…I can run that errand for you, Kendrick. Why not take Miss Rawlings for a spin? Do you object, my dear, to me taking you home?' Lord Whitley turned gleaming eyes on Beatrice, confident she'd snatch at his proposal to avoid further embarrassment. Beatrice might be older than Stella, but she had a rare classic beauty and a figure that Whitley would pay handsomely to see naked. If Kendrick tired of her, Whitley would, with alacrity, take his cast-off.

'It would be kind of you to drop me off, my lord.'

Bea ignored her sinking heart; she and Hugh had no option but to appear nonchalant on parting but there was so much left to say to him, she thought wistfully as she allowed her elderly escort to help her climb aboard the barouche. With a wave they set off, and she noticed that neither Hugh nor Stella glanced at the departing vehicle.

But Mrs Monk did, and it seemed to Beatrice that there was something vilely triumphant in her smile.

Chapter Twenty

'I told you Kendrick was a good fellow.' Walter beamed at his daughter, picking over the IOUs spread on his lap. 'It's my lucky day…I received Burnett's bank draft while you were out.'

Bea smiled on hearing that Colin had eventually paid her father. 'You don't mind that a gentleman has settled my gambling debts, Papa?'

On reaching home, Bea had immediately gone to see her father to ease his worries—and hers. She wanted his reassurance that he had not yet brokered his pension but had kept it safe.

'Kendrick isn't *any* gentleman—is he, my dear? He's the scoundrel's brother, so his family's honour is at stake. I shouldn't like kin of mine to act in such a despicable way. I'll wager he gave Sir Toby a cracking facer before parting with his cash.' Walter chortled, neatening the notes into a stack. 'Of course Kendrick should have dealt with me when handing them over… but that's a minor peccadillo compared to all those that have gone before.'

That bald fact brought a remorseful blush to his daughter's wan cheeks so he gave her a smile.

'I shall write and thank him, but not too enthusiastically.' Walter rifled in a desk drawer for a parchment and dipped his quill in ink.

Beatrice rose from her kneeling position by Walter's armchair, her relief at his attitude slightly dampened by twinges of guilt. Her father was unaware there was yet another misdeed, committed that afternoon, and she hoped he would remain in blissful ignorance of it.

It was early evening, and Elise was still out at an afternoon salon with her friends. Alex was no doubt ensconced at one of his clubs. The house seemed unusually quiet, and the family would not dine for over an hour, but Bea didn't have any appetite for company or food. She felt exhausted from the day's events, and from constantly reflecting on what might have passed between them if she and Hugh had not been interrupted in the park. For one bittersweet moment earlier that afternoon she'd sensed that her wounded heart was finally healing...

'I'm going to rest in my room for a while, Papa.'

Walter raised a hand to his daughter while continuing to scratch on parchment.

Bea was sure she'd never settle into a snooze with her mind so muddled, but she drifted off almost immediately. When she woke over an hour later the brightness at the window had dimmed and just a hint of strawberry sunset streaked the ceiling.

Rubbing her eyes, she swung her toes to the floor, then pattered to the sash to peer at the sky. The vividly painted horizon was a wonderful sight and, sighing, Bea rested her warm forehead against the cool glass as fraught memories of the day caught up with her.

Glancing down into the street, Bea blinked, her eyes bolting back to a familiar figure huddled on the opposite pavement. Mrs Monk stared back at her, then nodded slowly in such a significant way that Bea's lips parted in surprise. A moment later the woman repeated the signal.

Frowning, Bea let the curtain drop into place. Daft as it was to suppose that Mrs Monk had been awaiting an opportunity to accost her, Bea could see no other reason for Mrs Monk's loitering outside. If the woman desired an audience it seemed odd she'd not knocked at the door…unless her news was too sensitive to be conveyed other than very privately…

Bea twitched the curtain an inch and peeped down; she was still there, chin lowered into her collar as she fidgeted around a lamppost, glancing, at intervals, at her window. With a sense of foreboding Bea wondered whether Mrs Monk's presence had something to do with their meeting that afternoon in Hyde Park. Bea realised it was highly probable she *had* been observed kissing Hugh in broad daylight.

With a tingle of alarm hurrying her, Bea straightened her clothes, grabbed her cloak, then went downstairs.

'Have you something to say to me, Mrs Monk?' Bea kept her voice level despite the butterflies in her stomach.

'Indeed I have, my dear.'

The woman's friendly tone increased rather than lessened Bea's uneasiness.

Maggie gestured at the street corner. 'Shall we take a walk?

'If you wish…'

'No point in beating about the bush,' Maggie announced abruptly as they set off. 'I saw you disgrace yourself with Mr Kendrick, and I know Lord Whitley's eyes aren't blind either.'

Beatrice's complexion grew hot but she gave no other outward sign that the woman's accusation disturbed her. If Mrs Monk had come to blackmail her in some way let her voice her threat rather than hide behind innuendo.

'Don't fret. I'm not about to gossip and cause trouble for you…unless I have to.' Maggie's piercing dark eyes assessed Beatrice. 'I reckon a lady of quality like yourself will choose to be sensible. If such a tale got out it would put you beyond the pale, and your poor papa with you. Quite a risk you took, letting Mr Kendrick do that to you out in the open—but then he's an irresistible charmer, isn't he? My Stella could vouch for that.'

'Is there a point to this?' Beatrice demanded coldly, although she'd already guessed the gist of it. Now that Colin had dropped Stella like a stone Maggie Monk had turned her sights on Hugh, but she was concerned about her charge having an interfering rival.

And indeed the woman was right to be worried!

Bea wasn't about to be intimidated by other females' jealousies and ambitions. Had they not been driven apart earlier that day, she believed that Hugh would have told her his feelings for her ran deeper than mere lust.

'I know what you're thinking, my dear,' Maggie purred. 'You're thinking he wants you, not Stella. Hugh

Kendrick is a fellow who wants lots of girls. The one he wants in particular, though, is my Stella. Do you know why that is?'

Instead of telling the woman she was talking rot, Beatrice heard herself murmur, 'No...tell me...'

'Sir Toby's after Stella too. When warring brothers clash heads the victor takes all the spoils, even those he might once have overlooked.' She grinned at Bea's involuntary intake of breath. 'My Stella wants Hugh and he wants her—that's plain to see.'

'I don't believe you,' Bea whispered, abruptly turning for home.

'So you thought you were the only one worth kissing, did you, Miss High and Mighty?' Maggie chuckled coarsely, hurrying after Bea. 'You'll never match up to my girl and get a Kendrick diamond on your finger; you're too old, my dear, and sullied by scandal. Why not take Sir Colin after all?'

'What do you know about Sir Colin and me?' Bea demanded on swinging around.

'I know he abandoned you for Stella and she broke his heart because she wanted more than he could offer. Burnett came back to you with his tail between his legs, didn't he? Hugh Kendrick told us all about it. We had a fine time once you'd gone. Of course I had to leave the lovebirds alone for a while,' Maggie lied slickly, without a hint of conscience.

Bea took a backward pace, her heart drumming in consternation. Nobody knew about Colin recently reissuing his proposal to her other than her close family... and Hugh. The idea that he might have discussed her private business with this vulgar woman was making her feel nauseated.

'You think about what I've said,' Maggie warned, grim-faced. 'Stella's like a honeypot where those brothers are concerned. You keep away, I'm warning you, or you'll get stung.'

'You're lying!' Bea said in a shaky exhalation of breath.

'Am I, now? I'm giving you a friendly warning, but if you upset me I'll have a chat with Stella in Oxford Street about what Miss Dewey was up to with Mr Kendrick behind a tree. If society ladies eavesdrop on our conversation you'll suffer the consequences, my dear— not us or him.'

'Say what you like about me. I'll never bow to blackmail!' Bea gritted through her teeth with a confidence she was far from feeling.

'Perhaps you'll think differently about your lover when he tells you *his* secrets.' Maggie was ready to use her trump card, because Miss Dewey was made of tougher metal than she'd anticipated.

'Mr Kendrick makes no secret of his affairs…'

'You didn't deny that you're lovers!' Maggie pounced.

'Good day to you, madam,' Bea said icily, turning away.

'Has Mr Kendrick told you about his bastard son in India?'

Bea felt frozen to the spot, then pivoted about very slowly. The smirk on Maggie's face was gleefully triumphant and Bea needed no further proof that the woman was speaking the truth. The memory of Lady Groves implying there was an overseas scandal in Hugh's background sprang to Bea's mind. She had assumed Lady Groves's hint concerned an Indian mistress, but would never have guessed a child might also be involved.

Despite a thickening in her throat Bea whispered in desperation, 'You're lying again…'

'Ask him, if you dare.'

Maggie swung away. She'd hoped to keep that ace up her sleeve in case she got a chance to play it another day. She knew Stella would have to settle for Whitley's protection after all. Hugh would never soften towards her daughter once Miss Dewey threw her knowledge of his son in his face and revealed her source. But Maggie was confident there'd be no happy ending for the diamond magnate and Miss Dewey either, and she realised that consolation would have to suffice…

Bea didn't run back the way she'd come, though she was tempted to when she heard Maggie let rip a raucous chuckle. Tilting her chin, she straightened her shoulders, glad her tormentor couldn't see her blinking back the tears scorching her eyes.

Halfway up the steps to her door, Bea clutched double-handed at the iron railing to support her shaky legs. She knew Mrs Monk hadn't followed her because she'd looked back over a shoulder, just once, and seen the older woman disappearing in the opposite direction. Bea sank down to sit on a step, aware of curious glances from passers-by. She couldn't make herself go inside the house because she knew she'd fidget and fret; neither could she share this latest appalling news with her family. She had burdened them far too much already with her woes.

There was only one person capable of soothing her torment. Only he could tell her whether he'd fathered a child and then abandoned the boy overseas. Whatever Hugh admitted to, his carousing in India might excite a furore but it would eventually die down. Wealthy men and their bastards were nothing new, even if the woman seduced was a foreigner.

Of course being spotted kissing a gentleman behind a tree in Hyde Park would secure lifelong ostracism for a genteel spinster. And if she were discovered visiting Hugh at home it would simply add to her infamy. But what did it matter if she committed one final, vital sin and went to his house to demand an explanation?

She was right to have been worried, Bea realised as a regal-looking butler stood, appalled, at the sight of her.

A few minutes ago Beatrice had paid the Hackney cab driver and gazed up at the dauntingly imposing façade of Hugh's townhouse on Grosvenor Square. The sunset had faded to twilight and she'd quickly ascended a flight of stone steps before her courage evaporated and she turned tail. As she tilted her chin up to squarely meet the butler's eyes she cocooned herself in her anger and jealousy, though realised she had little to gain from either.

Hugh had not professed to love her or to want to marry her. He had not offered to remain faithful to her. He had promised her nothing that might make her entitled to have his past exposed to her scrutiny or forgiveness. Yet deep within Bea felt she deserved every possible explanation and apology from him...

Having conquered his outrage, the butler politely asked for her name and her business.

'My name is Miss Dewey and I should like to speak to your master, if you please,' Bea said firmly.

As she stepped unsteadily over the threshold into a vast cool hallway Bea noticed the manservant's eyes dart to the street, as though checking whether her lone arrival at a bachelor's house was under observation.

Having led her to a huge hallway chair, the fellow disappeared. Bea sat rigid-backed, unaware she had been holding her breath until the sound of her sighing exhalation echoed eerily in the silence of her opulent surroundings. A moment later she spotted the butler marching back towards her. He threw her a flustered frown before diverting to the stairs and scooting up them.

When two housemaids appeared and gawped at her from behind a marble pillar Bea's awkwardness increased to such a degree that she was tempted to leap up and leave. She clasped her hands, then untangled her fingers as minutes passed and other servants crept up to congregate and whisper about her.

Bea could stand it no longer. She was on the point of announcing that she would return another time when the butler flew down the stairs. This time he ignored her, glaring instead at his inferiors, who melted away into the shadowy corridors.

'Mr Kendrick will be here directly. He has invited

you to wait in the blue salon.' He held out a gloved hand, his demeanour once more phlegmatic as he led the way.

They had got no further than the first set of ornate doorways when Bea heard a familiar baritone voice.

'You may leave us.'

Hugh had addressed his manservant from the top of the wide curving treads. Now he approached, hands plunged in pockets, a towel draped negligently about his shoulders.

Following a stiff bow the butler backed away, then turned towards the vestibule.

Bea raised her eyes, overwhelmed with embarrassment as Hugh came closer to her. No wonder his staff had acted as though she were a nuisance and a spectacle to behold. Nobody, let alone an unaccompanied young woman, should interrupt a gentleman in the middle of bathing. Why had he not just sent her away? she wailed inwardly as another wave of heat deepened her blush.

Hugh raised the cloth to his slick dark hair, drying it, and the more casually he took her intrusion the more acutely awkward Beatrice felt. He appeared to have dressed in a hurry, and his ruffled linen shirt was damp and clinging to his broad torso, exposing an expanse of tanned skin at his throat.

'I'm so sorry...' Bea croaked, finally forcing words past strangling embarrassment. 'I shouldn't have come. I'll go...and leave you to finish your...umm...' She turned to bolt towards the door.

Hugh had caught hold of her before she'd made it more than a yard or so.

'No, you don't,' he said softly, turning her about.

'You've found the courage to come here to see me so it must be on an urgent matter. I want to know what it is.'

'It *is* an urgent matter...' Bea blurted, finally forcing her gaze to his face.

His lashes were still heavy with water, fringing caramel-coloured eyes, and slick ribbons of jet hair adorned his temples. If he still hadn't got a penny to his name Bea knew he could enslave her with his breathtaking good looks as easily as he had three years ago.

Then he hadn't been able to afford even one residence to call his own. Now Hugh Kendrick, diamond magnate, had the wherewithal to support households and dependants at home and overseas. Bea knew there was so much more to discover than whether he'd revealed Colin's renewed marriage proposal to Mrs Monk and Stella. But with startling clarity she realised that answer was more important to her than any other. If it transpired that he had done so then those other questions crowding her mind about his life in India would no longer be important. Love him maybe she would, till the day she died, but she could never see him again after tonight if he'd betrayed her trust to the vile Mrs Monk.

'Come with me...' Hugh extended a hand to her. 'Let's find somewhere comfortable to talk.

'There's no need for me to tarry.' Bea ignored his beckoning fingers, pleased that her composure was strengthening and the wobble had gone from her voice. 'It's very wrong of me to be here, and I apologise for coming, but...but I have an important question to ask.'

'Go ahead...' Hugh's mouth skewed as he sensed he was about to be accused of something. He could haz-

ard a guess at what it was. But how Beatrice had found
out that Mrs Monk had tried to solicit his protection for
Stella Rawlings he could only guess. The woman was
a mischief-maker and the girl was made in her image.

The vision he wanted to keep lodged in his mind was
that of a tantalising temptress sharing his bath, her golden
tresses floating on soapy water, her limbs entwined with
his… A dry chuckle rasped in Hugh's throat as his phantom lover brusquely interrupted his fantasy.

'Did you tell Mrs Monk that Colin had again proposed to me?'

'No.'

Bea moistened her mouth. She hadn't anticipated
such a concise response, nor that he would follow the
single word with a steady, low-lashed stare. She waited
for him to elaborate, but he didn't.

'I see…' she blurted. 'And did you kiss Stella this
afternoon?'

'No.'

Again Beatrice shifted beneath his ruthless regard
as the silence lengthened.

'Are you accusing me of such behaviour?'

Bea hesitated just a moment too long before shaking
her head so vigorously that her bonnet loosened on its
ribbons, hanging at her nape on flaxen waves. Before
she could carry on her interrogation masterful fingers
manacled her wrist. Hugh forced her with him towards
the nearest doorway, propelling her inside when she
seemed unwilling to step over the threshold.

'Sit down,' he growled, standing with his back against
the door.

'Please don't order me about,' Bea returned haughtily. Nevertheless she perched obediently on the edge of a fireside chair in what appeared to be a small reading room. Newspapers were on a table and ceiling-high bookshelves flanked one wall.

'Now I have some questions to ask,' Hugh dulcetly drawled as he strolled to ram a foot against the fender. 'Did you have a *tête-à-tête* with Mrs Monk or Stella after you left me?'

'Not by choice!' Bea answered hotly, shooting to her feet. She could tell from his attitude that he thought she'd been secretly checking up on him. 'I've no wish for anything to do with either woman.'

'No more have I.'

'That's not what Mrs Monk says!' Bea retorted frostily.

'So…tell me what Mrs Monk says…' Hugh quit the fireplace, stationing himself in front of her. 'Come, I answered you a moment ago—I'd like the courtesy returned, Beatrice,' he needled her, his expression impenetrable. 'If I'm to be charged with something at least provide your evidence.'

'Mrs Monk loitered outside the viscount's house till I went out to speak to her.'

Bea nibbled her lower lip, sensing that behind Hugh's cool exterior lay a simmering fury…directed at *her*. Of the two of them, Bea judged she had more right to feel angry and ill-used. Fearing she was within a hair's breadth of shouting that opinion at him, she took a deep, calming breath.

'Mrs Monk said you'd told her that Colin had returned to me with his tail between his legs after Stella jilted him.' She glanced up to find a pair of tawny eyes preying on her face. 'The woman warned me to stay away from you because you and your brother were competing for Stella's favours and Stella had chosen you. She said if I didn't heed her she'd broadcast that I'd been caught kissing you in broad daylight.'

'That's it?' Hugh asked with an amount of ennui.

'No…indeed it is not!' Bea exploded. She'd not expected a fulsome denial, but had anticipated more of a reaction than she'd just got. 'Mrs Monk added that you'd all had a fine time this afternoon and hinted that you and Stella had flirted and kissed.'

'Was anything else mentioned about my lecherous intentions towards that damned minx?'

'What more might have been said?' Bea stormed, dreading to hear the answer, yet desperate to have it too.

'The meddlesome witch might have told you that I took them home immediately and declined an invitation to take refreshment; she might have told you that I refused the girl's services as a paramour when they were offered to me…for the second time,' Hugh clipped out.

'What?' Bea asked faintly. She'd imagined that Mrs Monk was after a husband for Stella.

'So have you anything else to say to me?' Hugh asked, taking her chin in strong fingers and tilting her face up to his so she couldn't avoid his black-eyed stare.

Bea felt the words jumbling in her mind before clogging her throat. During the journey to his house she had rehearsed how she'd demand to know if he'd fathered a child with an Indian woman and then left them both behind when he'd returned to England. Now, when she needed them most, she realised her impetuous nature and quick tongue seemed to have deserted her.

'Perhaps you might like to apologise and admit you were wrong to accuse me of having designs on that chit's virtue.'

Bea bristled beneath his arrogant drawl. It spurred her on, firing her indignation. 'I accused you of nothing. I merely asked questions. Even had I assumed you guilty it would have been an easy mistake to make.' She stepped back from him, her blue gaze adopting a glacial hardness. 'When trying to warn me about your womanising, Colin said you had a mistress at either end of town and wondered where you might position another.' Bea tilted her head to a challenging angle, forcing her eyes to meet his squarely. 'If only I had known then what I know now I might have been able to tell him. India is the answer, is it not?'

Chapter Twenty-One

She watched carefully, and, yes, there was an unmistakable flicker of cynical acceptance that something hidden had been unearthed.

'Mrs Monk told you about that too?'

'She did…' Beatrice croaked, gripping at a chair-rail to steady herself. 'And I'm sorry that she was mean enough to do so. I'm certain you'd not reveal anything so personal to her, and don't know how she found out about your Indian mistress and the little boy.'

'Toby probably told her; from what you've said it sounds as though they've been in touch,' Hugh said tonelessly.

'I'm sorry if your brother has betrayed you…it is a very personal matter,' Bea repeated in a voice roughened by emotion. 'It was none of that woman's business…just as it is none of mine…' She gulped in a shaky breath. 'I must go now, but first will again apologise for intruding like this.'

She'd reached the door and half opened it before he spoke.

'Don't you want to know more about the affair?'

Bea twisted about, eyes blazing. 'What possible interest would I have in your family abroad?'

'I have no family abroad...'

'You are a very callous man to say so,' Bea whispered. 'What else are the mother of your child and a son...even a bastard son...but members of your family?'

Bea's fists clenched at her sides in rage and frustration. She had been wrong about him all along; despite his arrogance and philandering she had harboured a hope—a hope that had soared this afternoon—that he was an inherently decent man. He'd not denied the little boy's birth, yet had easily dismissed him.

'Have you finished?'

'Utterly finished... I've no wish to say or hear more on the subject. Good evening...' Bea had her fingers on the door, pulling it fully open, when his dark fist hit the panel overhead, slamming it again shut.

'I don't think you mean that, do you, Beatrice?' he said quietly. 'I think you're keen for every detail about Rani and Shay.'

Bea spun about, her back pressed into the door. She gazed up at him with glittering eyes, hating him for understanding her turmoil and for making real people of the ghosts in her mind.

'You're wrong!' she spat. 'I've had enough proof that your lechery causes hurt to innocent people. You will never hurt me in that way.' Tears trickled down her cheeks. 'How can you abandon your own flesh and blood in a distant land?'

'Shay isn't my flesh and blood...'

'What?' Bea whispered. 'Are you now going to lie—?'

'It's not a lie,' Hugh interrupted harshly. 'He's not my flesh and blood and, much as I want the best for him, I'm content to let Rani care for his welfare.'

Hugh pressed thumb and forefinger to the bridge of his nose, as though to ease strain.

'I want to tell you, Beatrice…let me tell you… And then, if you want nothing more to do with me, I'll try and accept your wishes and stay away.'

His hoarse words held a note of authority, and Bea realised he'd force her to listen whether she chose to or not.

'Sit down…please…' Hugh abruptly strode away from her, thrusting hands that ached to touch her in his pockets. One was withdrawn to gesture at the chair she'd previously used.

Slowly Bea approached the seat, perching again on its very edge, as though she might flee if the details of his foreign affair were too unbearable.

'Rani became my mistress shortly after I arrived in Hyderabad,' Hugh started without preamble. 'She'd had an arranged marriage when little more than a girl. Her husband was much older and they had no offspring. She craved a child to love…'

Bea's slender fingers gripped the chair-arm as though she would use its support to rise.

'Let me finish, Bea!' Hugh ordered with a note of pleading. He quickly resumed. 'There were many English families in the area connected to the East Indies trade. I became friendly with one fellow, Keith Wheeler, who had his wife and only daughter with him. They'd planned to return to England so the girl could make her come-out. Then they found out Louise was pregnant by a married Indian potentate.'

Hugh's mouth hardened at the memory.

'Once the seduction was done the fellow distanced himself, and there would have been a diplomatic incident and a scandal if he'd been pursued over the matter.'

Bea relaxed her tight grip on the chair, returned her fingers to her lap. She gazed at Hugh's profile, her mind racing ahead. But she remained quiet, breathlessly waiting for him to continue.

'Louise's parents were understandably distraught and keen to keep the matter concealed. When Rani discovered that a baby was to be born in secret and then given away she wanted it. She pleaded with me to make the necessary arrangements. I refused, so behind my back she spoke to the expectant mother and the parents…offered to pay them for the child. The Wheelers wanted nothing other than that the whole affair be dealt with as discreetly as possible.'

Hugh paused, threw his head back to sightlessly stare at the ceiling.

'The Wheelers begged me to put it right for them if I could. I resisted, and tried to dissuade Rani too, but her obsession with being a mother overrode all else and eventually I agreed to help them all obtain the longed-for outcome.' He gestured briefly. 'My liaison with Rani was in the open, and accepted by the locals as a practical arrangement. Rani's elderly husband didn't object to his wife sleeping with me. They were not peasants, but neither were they wealthy people, and the family welcomed my friendship and financial assistance.'

Hugh shifted position, lowering his moody features to the empty fire grate.

'Louise concealed her weight gain; Rani padded out her clothes and begged me to claim the child as mine. She didn't want to be vilified as a trollop, unable to name her baby's father, and a fair-skinned sire would be required as the baby was sure to look of mixed race. As indeed he does…'

A softening about Hugh's mouth caused Beatrice a pang of joy rather than jealousy. Despite everything, the little boy held a place in his heart. 'You love him, don't you?'

'I grew to adore the little chap…'

'And you named him Shay?' she asked, in a voice so quiet it was almost inaudible.

'Rani chose the name. Shay means gift…and that's how she saw the boy… Whereas I…'

'Whereas you…?' Bea prompted in a whisper.

'Whereas I knew word of Shay's existence would leak out, and I could see the problems and inconvenience that lay ahead in my becoming embroiled in such deceit.'

'But you did it anyway,' Bea said, her voice soft with wonder. She knew she believed what he'd said… Every single word was true—outlandishly dramatic tale though it was. A spontaneous sob of admiration and love for him welled in her chest. 'You must have loved her very much to sacrifice what you believed to be right so she might have her dream of becoming a mother.'

'No…' He grimaced wryly. 'I was fond of Rani, but we both knew I didn't love her—and neither did she love me. It was an exchange of basic needs that suited us both at the time.'

'It was good and selfless of you, nevertheless…'

'In the end I did it for Louise. My sister was compromised when young and it nearly ruined her future. I could understand why Louise's parents were fretting over what lay ahead for their daughter.'

'How did Toby find out?' Bea asked, puzzled.

'He came to India, uninvited, to try and wangle himself an interest in my mining company. He got nothing from me but of course he's used the knowledge of Shay's birth to his advantage. My brother has hinted at spreading what he knows…but up to now he's shrewdly kept quiet, fearing my revenge. I expect he's already worried that he'll not be able to extract another penny from me.'

'He's been blackmailing you?' Bea sounded outraged.

'In a subtle way… But it seems he's now burned his bridges, and in a way I'm glad. The gossip will spread like wildfire; Mrs Monk will make sure of that now she knows I've no interest in her daughter.'

'It will die down…' Bea reassured him.

Hugh shrugged carelessness. 'A few other people already know of Shay's existence. Of course Alex has had the full story; he's the only person, apart from you, to hear it from my lips. He said he's never had reason to mention it to Elise.' Hugh prowled to and fro in front of the chimneypiece. 'Lord Mornington was in India at the same time as me, attending to his investments. I expect he's told his close circle that I fathered a child abroad. I've noticed his sister looking at me oddly at times. But Lady Groves is obviously not a gossip or word would have already got round.'

Hugh gave another lazy shrug.

'It no longer matters who knows, and thankfully Toby never discovered the truth behind the boy's birth. Had he done so he'd have held the means to destroy many people's happiness.'

'What of Louise and her parents?'

'They returned to England and Louise was quietly married in Kent to a nice young fellow… I was invited to the ceremony…'

'A happy ending all round…' Bea gave him a tiny smile.

'Is it?' Hugh plunged his hands in his pockets, his eyes darkening. 'Why did you assume I was a deceitful villain before allowing me to explain?'

'I told Mrs Monk she was lying about you from the start. I was sceptical about your interest in her daughter even when she said you'd take Stella just to ensure Toby couldn't have her…' Beatrice rattled off, wishing she had a more robust defence to present to Hugh.

She had recklessly flown here in a fury, believing the worst of him. She'd called him names and quizzed him over being a liar…but now that her jealousy and indignation were no longer colouring her reason her earlier opinion of him had changed drastically. In fact he had moments ago provided her with yet more cause to adore him, she realised. He might be self-indulgent where women and pleasure were concerned, but he was not weak or mean. His kindness towards Rani didn't irk Beatrice; such consideration reassured her that, however nasty and corrupt his older brother might be, Hugh had escaped being infected with a similar nature. Hugh Kendrick was an honourable man, and she loved him.

Blinking back the heat in her eyes, she gazed at him, wanting him to say something, but he remained stubbornly quiet.

'I'm conscious that you have great trust in me to have disclosed your secret… I swear I will never betray it.' Still he said nothing, and Bea slowly turned away. 'I must go now, and hope that nobody knows I've been here other than your servants.'

'You took a great risk for a man you don't trust.'

'I *do* trust you…' Beatrice keened, swinging back to gaze at him beseechingly.

Hugh suddenly cradled her face in his hand. '*Do* you, Beatrice?' he demanded throatily. 'Prove it to me, then…'

Chapter Twenty-Two

'How can I? What do you want me to do?' Beatrice whispered. She glimpsed the smoky desire burning at the backs of his eyes and a piquant thrill rippled through her. 'I shouldn't have doubted you, but Mrs Monk is adept at stirring the pot...' She began a diffident mitigation.

'If you're curious about my past ask me about it and I'll tell you everything you want to know.' Hugh dipped his head to tantalise a corner of her lips with his own. 'Or perhaps you'll think me lying to cover up my sins... will you?'

'No! I won't! I trust you...' Bea's eyelids fell as the kiss continued.

'Good. But I'm after more than just your trust, sweet, you know that. I always have been.' His fingers smoothed over a warm satiny cheek, a thumb brushing lightly on her lower lip. 'I want us to finish what we started in Hyde Park this afternoon, before we were interrupted by those infernal people.'

He held her back from him a little, tilting his head to watch her bashful expression.

'Come…don't be shy; we both know it didn't begin today but years ago, and we've waited far too long to satisfy this need for one another. It's time now to surrender, Beatrice.'

'You want me to kiss you to say sorry?' Beatrice murmured, glancing at him from under her curly dark lashes.

'That would be a nice start…' Hugh sounded huskily amused as he moved his mouth to a position fractionally above hers, daring her to take the initiative and close the space between their lips.

Raising herself onto tiptoe, Bea kissed him with innocent sensuality. A scent of tangy sandalwood soap enveloped her as their bodies merged and she slipped her arms onto his shoulders, entwining her fingers in his tousled hair.

'You feel damp…' she teased, trying to temper the sizzling atmosphere between them. 'I'm sorry I interrupted your bathing…'

'There's time yet to finish that too before the night's out,' Hugh growled against her mouth. 'Will you wash my back?'

Bea stumbled back a pace from him, her smile uncertain. 'I hope you're joking…'

Hugh tracked her evasive paces until her spine was touching the library table. Indolently he placed a hand either side of her, trapping her between his muscular arms. 'No joke… I want you with me everywhere, Beatrice…even in my bath.'

Confused by an overwhelming mix of excitement and embarrassment, she clasped the solid forearm closest to her with two small hands. Sinew flexed beneath her palms as he resisted her attempt to move him. Bea's eyes roved features that displayed an uncompromising raw carnality. Slowly she exhaled a pent-up breath. Why fight him? She yearned for his loving as ardently as he would bestow it. She couldn't deny it. Neither could she deny that the idea of his sleek skin slipping beneath her wet palms as she soaped him was making her feel restless.

This afternoon she had been ready to take his terms and become his mistress. What matter if she yielded and agreed to go to his bed or his bath now? Hours ago it would have seemed a shocking notion: she'd always assumed Hugh would arrange for them to make love at a secret location so as not to cause outrage.

But the damage was already done: she'd shocked his servants, who no doubt imagined she was a harlot. Besides, Mrs Monk would be bent on revenge and would besmirch Bea for the sin of a single kiss. In Bea's rueful estimation she might as well get hung for a sheep as a lamb and stay awhile with the man she loved.

It *was* time for her to surrender and prove her love and trust to Hugh. When word got out about her visit to Mr Kendrick's Mayfair mansion she would be home in Hertfordshire. In time a new scandal would erupt to entertain the *ton* and gossip about her would fade.

Bea's reflections were interrupted by the touch of gentle fingers at her throat, untying her bonnet strings. Hugh tossed the hat to the table, his eyes capturing her vivid blue gaze as his fingers threaded into her silken hair.

'This afternoon when I came to meet you in Oxford Street I brought something with me to give to you.'

'I know…and my papa was as grateful as I to have those IOUs,' she said with trembling sincerity. 'I own I thought he might be livid that a gentleman had paid my debts, but he claims you did the right thing, protecting your family's honour and thwarting your odious brother's spite. You are still my papa's good friend.'

Hugh's mouth tilted wryly. 'And will he think me his friend after tonight?'

'I doubt he will if he finds out what we've done,' Bea admitted with a catch to her voice.

'And what will he think of you if he finds out what we've done?'

Bea averted her face as her eyes prickled, but she attempted a steady reply. 'He will be very upset, of course, but I think he will allow me to stay with him in Hertfordshire—although many would deem me unfit to again darken his doorstep.'

'Are you prepared to risk so much for me, Beatrice?' Hugh asked gently.

'Yes…' she murmured.

'Why?'

She knew she should tell him now that she loved and wanted him, and no other man would do. She should say she'd far sooner have an uncertain future with him than settle for respectability and the prospect of an arid marriage of convenience when her aged papa died and was no longer her companion. But an obstinate pride remained, blocking the confession in her throat. He might not love her, or want to marry her, but the least she required of him was that he allowed her some dignity, offering up some affectionate words first.

'Shall I tell you why I think you'd do all that for me, sweetheart?'

Beatrice nodded, the painful throb in her throat preventing her from voicing a need to have his fullest explanation.

'I think you would risk everything you hold dear because you love me as greatly as I love you. I also think you're hoping I'm not the immoral lecher others say I am, and will protect you with my name as well as my heart.' Hugh soothed her quiet sob by stroking his cool lips against her brow. 'I've loved and desired you for years, Beatrice. I've tried to force you from my memory by carousing, but you stubbornly resisted being put aside and curbed the worst of my excesses.'

His mouth slanted on hers, sliding with silky sweetness, his tongue teasing her with tiny persuasive touches.

'The worst of your excesses?' Bea echoed against his shoulder, although a quiet joy was burgeoning within. 'You keep *two* mistresses close by, sir. Did you restrict yourself then?'

Hugh bent his head, laughing soundlessly against her crown of golden hair. 'Perhaps in my immaturity I might have liked more, but now I have seen the error of my ways I have no desire for even one mistress, or any woman other than my future wife.'

Bea raised glowing eyes to his face, uncertain still,

yet daring to hope. 'You are to take a vow of celibacy then, Mr Kendrick…?'

'I suppose I must for the short duration of my betrothal…unless my adorable fiancée will take pity on me and let me love her.' Hugh gathered Beatrice in his arms, rocking her against his chest. 'Do you know how many times I've railed at myself for letting you slip through my fingers? From the moment I walked away from you three years ago I've bitterly regretted my decision to act the martyr, leaving you to enjoy your life with a worthier man who could give you what I could not.' He paused. 'When I found out you'd attracted another suitor so quickly I was sure you'd easily forgotten me.'

'Elise warned me I had fallen for Dr Burnett on the rebound. I remember feeling hurt and humiliated by your rejection and wanting somebody to boost my pride,' Bea admitted.

'I'm sorry, sweetheart, that I hurt you. At the time I thought I was the only one suffering. Your friend Fiona knew, of course, what a mess I was in, and kindly tolerated my pathetic courtship without taking offence. She told me bluntly to come back to you…but I'd heard Burnett was already courting you. I was a damnable fool! We might have started off as man and wife living in a garret, but we would have been together now for three years…'

'No…it would not have worked, Hugh,' Beatrice interjected on a sigh. 'We might have quickly grown bitter towards one another, constantly fretting over bills and hating feeling beholden to Alex, who would have offered loans of money,' Beatrice pointed out.

Hugh gave her a grateful smile for understanding so completely how humiliating such a situation would have been for him. His greatest fear had been losing Bea's respect.

Suddenly Hugh urged her towards a chair and made her perch on its edge. Then, dropping to a knee, he pulled out a grand-looking box from his inside pocket. 'Will you marry me, Beatrice, and keep me from slipping back into wicked ways?'

His teasing tone earned him a prim look from Beatrice. But soon her mock reproof was overcome by an expression of wonderment. Hugh had opened the casket to reveal a scintillating diamond ring nestling on a luxurious bed of satin.

'Is this the gift you brought with you this afternoon?' she asked, struck by its opulence.

'No…I wanted to give you your betrothal ring somewhere more appropriate than Oxford Street.' Again his hand disappeared into a pocket, to withdraw a smaller, plainer jewellery box. 'I brought this with me to show to you. I wanted to convince you that I was not toying with your affections when we first met. It was always my intention to propose to you, even if the best I could afford was a betrothal ring of very little value.'

'You have kept it all this time…?' Bea breathed softly. 'Show it to me…please…' she coaxed hoarsely when he hesitated in opening the lid of the little box. Reaching out a single digit, Bea stroked the tiny cluster of sapphires embedded in a thin golden shank.

'I bought it because the blue stones match your eyes.

I hoped you might be swayed to accept it with such a sweet thought attached to it. Then my pride took over...'

Bea raised her eyes to his face, seeing for the first time a bashfulness shaping his features, making him look appealingly boyish. 'Indeed, there was no need for you to have felt ashamed of your gift,' she reassured him. 'In fact, if you were to allow me to choose between the two...'

She reached out a hand and removed the small golden band from its resting place. Handing it to him, she extended her left hand towards him.

'I will marry you, Mr Kendrick, even though you have made me wait far too long to hear you ask me to be your wife.'

After he'd slipped the sapphires onto her finger she curled the digit, securing it in place.

Springing to his feet, Hugh whipped her up into his arms, making her gasp as he spun them both about. 'You've made me the happiest man, even though you don't like your flawless Golkonda diamond.'

'Oh, I do, Hugh!' Beatrice cupped his abrasive chin between her palms. 'Of course I do. But this is my betrothal ring...the one I always wanted...the one I would so proudly have worn three years ago.' She extended her finger, admiring the small blue gems. 'That other, finer gift you may give to me another time...perhaps on the birth of our first child...' she murmured, blushing.

Hugh let her feet drop to the floor in a way that sensually slid together their bodies. 'Well, I want to see you wearing that diamond, sweet, so we'd better start on making our family very soon.'

With a confidence that stopped her heart he covered her mouth with his in a kiss that was simultaneously demanding yet reverential. Keeping their faces fused together with a hand cupping her scalp, Hugh manoeuvred them slowly towards the armchair. He sat with Bea on his lap, deepening the kiss as he repositioned her to sit facing him, straddling his thighs.

Swift fingers worked open the buttons on her bodice and the ribbons of her chemise. With teasing leisure he lowered his mouth to the breasts he'd exposed, feasting on the plump milky flesh like a ravenous man. One of his hands swept up her skirt, his fingers caressing the soft inner skin of her thighs with long strokes that stopped a hair's breadth from their apex.

'Hugh…' Bea groaned, throwing back her head and squirming against the tormenting pulse rocking her body. 'Should we not go upstairs? I don't care—honestly I do not—if you make love to me properly before I go home. But I must return because they will all worry where I am…'

She gasped in a shuddering breath as his hot mouth and tongue tantalised a rigid nipple. Bea gave herself up to the tension building within, parting her thighs to his artfully sliding fingers. Her panting grew shallow as her back arched, then an explosion of pleasure made her buck wildly against him.

Hugh drew her face forward, soothing her bruised lips with a courteous kiss. 'Did you like that?' he asked gently as she collapsed like a rag doll against his shoulder.

Bea nodded slowly, feeling too enervated to speak. A moment later, when her heartbeat had steadied, she glanced up at his shady jaw. 'Do you want me to take off my clothes so you might also like it?' she asked shyly.

Hugh buried his lips in her hair. 'I'd like that more than anything, sweet, but not now…it's not right…'

'I want to please you. I don't care what you do…' Bea started, but a gentle finger laid on her pulsating lips silenced her.

'But *I* care, sweetheart,' Hugh said. 'I'll not take your virginity like this. I want to savour every second of our first proper time together. I want us to share a feather bed covered in silk sheets. I want to enjoy your beautiful body for hours and hours—not snatch a few minutes' release on an armchair with the servants listening at the keyhole.'

Bea started in his arms, darting a horrified glance at the door. 'Do you honestly think they are?' she wailed in a whisper.

Hugh chuckled. 'No… They wouldn't dare, if they value their employment with me.'

'Mrs Monk will do her best to smear my name.'

'Your name will soon be my name, and after that nobody will give a damn for a word she says. And neither should you…' Hugh terminated his concise reassurance with a light kiss on her brow. 'Besides, I'm conscious of the fact that I've been a rank hypocrite where you're concerned. I've protected my sister and Louise from ruined futures, yet would have made you my mistress and put your reputation in jeopardy.' He dropped forward his head, quite bashfully. 'I'm sorry… I can't help wanting you, so I'd do anything to have you and keep you always with me…'

'You don't have to do anything but love me…that's enough, Hugh,' Bea said softly.

As she snuggled, satisfied, into his shoulder Hugh neatened her clothes, doing up buttons and laces with an expertise that might have worried Bea had she not been still pleasantly dazed with sensuality.

'I'll get a special licence and we can be married before the end of the week. Just a quiet affair—if you're happy with that?'

Bea nodded dreamily, feeling utterly content. 'There is just one thing I would ask for…'

'You can ask me for anything, sweet, and I'll grant you your wish,' Hugh said.

'I should like us to honeymoon in India… I should like to meet Shay.'

Hugh's eyes whipped to hers. 'I was going to offer to cut my ties with them if you wanted me to. I never thought I would ever do so for anyone. I'm very fond of my…of Shay,' he corrected himself. 'But I realise you might find the situation hard to accept.'

'I understand why you keep in touch with Shay and his mother,' Bea said softly. 'I expect you support them financially, don't you?' She tilted her head, watching his expression. 'I really don't mind…in fact I think it is very worthy of you to do so.' She kissed his stubbly cheek. 'I'm not jealous of Shay or of Rani. I believe you, you see, when you say your future wife is the only woman you want.' She urged huskily, 'Take me to India, please; I should love to meet your adopted son, and you said you would grant me anything I wished for…'

Hugh turned to her, a new depth of adoration for

her burnishing his golden eyes. 'Of course I shall take you to see my boy,' he said huskily. 'And when we have our first child, and he or she is old enough, we shall go again, if you would like to, so the children can get to know one another.'

'That sounds perfect...' Bea cuddled into him.

Hugh suddenly buried his face into the warm curve of her shoulder. 'It is time to go and see your father and tell him our wonderful news.'

'You will certainly be his good friend now.' Beatrice choked a little laugh, tangling her fingers in his glossy hair. 'I know I have driven him to despair on occasion with my recklessness; he will be pleased to be rid of me, I'm sure.'

'He has my sympathy.'

Hugh lifted his face. His lashes, wet earlier from his bath, were again clumped with moisture.

'You are a wild and wanton young woman,' Hugh scolded on a sniff. He took her mouth in a kiss that bordered on bittersweet pain before transforming into a tender salute. 'But I think I know a way of taming you, Beatrice, that we'll both like very much...'

* * * * *

MILLS & BOON

MODERN

Power and Passion

Prepare to be swept off your feet by sophisticated, sexy and seductive heroes, in some of the world's most glamourous and romantic locations, where power and passion collide.

Julia James
Heiress's
PREGNANCY
SCANDAL
MILLS & BOON

Jennie Lucas
Chosen as the
SHEIKH'S ROYAL
BRIDE
MILLS & BOON

Kim Lawrence
A WEDDING
at the
ITALIAN'S DEMAND

Sharon Kendrick
The
SHEIKH'S
SECRET BABY
MILLS & BOON

MILLS & BOON
Desire

Indulge in secrets and scandal, intense
drama and plenty of sizzling hot action
with powerful and passionate heroes who
have it all: wealth, status, good looks…
everything but the right woman.